make me

BETH KERY

Berkley Sensation   *New York*

BERKLEY
An imprint of Penguin Random House LLC
375 Hudson Street, New York, New York 10014

Copyright © 2016 by Beth Kery
Excerpt from *Behind the Curtain* © 2017 by Beth Kery

Library of Congress Cataloging-in-Publication Data

Names: Kery, Beth, author.
Title: Make me / Beth Kery.
Description: Berkley trade edition. | New York: Berkley, 2017.
Identifiers: LCCN 2016036488 (print) | LCCN 2016042086 (ebook) | ISBN
9780399584664 (paperback) | ISBN 9780399584671 (eBook)
Subjects: | BISAC: FICTION / Romance / Contemporary. | FICTION / Contemporary
Women. | FICTION / Romance / General. | GSAFD: Romantic suspense
fiction. | Erotic fiction.
Classification: LCC PS3611.E79 M35 2017 (print) | LCC PS3611.E79 (ebook) |
DDC 813/.6—dc23
LC record available at https://lccn.loc.gov/2016036488

PUBLISHING HISTORY
InterMix eBook edition / April-May 2016
Berkley Sensation trade edition / February 2017

Printed in the United States of America
1 3 5 7 9 10 8 6 4 2

Cover photos: abstract jewelry background © passion artist/Shutterstock;
woman © Inara Prusakova/Shutterstock
Cover design by Sarah Oberrender
Book design by Kelly Lipovich

make me

1

make me
FORGET

one

There was something about the Tahoe air that made everything clear and luminous. Not just physical things, either, Harper McFadden thought as she jogged down a stretch of beach, the cerulean lake glittering to the left of her. Her perception felt sharper in her new home. She felt a little lighter. The brilliant sun and pure air seemed to penetrate even the murkiest, saddest places of her spirit.

Alive.

That was it. She felt more alive here than she had since her parents' tragic death last year. Hopefully she was slowly—finally—leaving the shadows of grief behind.

She tensed and pulled up short in her run when a large, dark red dog with white markings began to charge her. She staggered back, dreading the imminent crash. The slashing teeth. *"Stay calm around them. Keep your fear boxed up tight. It'll only make them more aggressive if they sense it."*

The big dog pulled up at the last minute. He started to spin in excited, dopey circles in front of her.

She gave a startled laugh.

"You're not so scary, are you?" she murmured, reaching down cautiously to pet behind floppy ears. The dog immediately stopped dancing around and lifted his head, eyelids drooping and tongue lolling. Harper laughed and rubbed harder. "No, you're just a big pushover, aren't you?"

The dog whimpered blissfully.

Clearly, this particular dog was a cuddly pup with the appearance of a bear. Even so, her limbs still felt a little tingly from anxiety. This was one of the few things she *wasn't* so fond of in her new town. People adored their dogs here, to the point where they brought them inside the local stores and even the post office, and no one complained. She'd also noticed Tahoe Shores canines tended to be of the enormous variety. Unlike her former home in the Nob Hill neighborhood of San Francisco, leash laws were largely ignored here.

A figure cast a shadow over her and the dog.

"Sorry about that. He's like a two-year-old kid with the body of an ox. He doesn't know his own weight."

Harper didn't glance up immediately when the man approached. The thought struck her fleetingly that while his dog was a hyper, quivering beast, his owner's voice sounded mellow and smooth. Unhurried.

She dropped her hand from the enraptured dog and straightened. His head and shoulders rose above the background of the Sierra Nevada mountains and the setting sun. His dark shadow was cast in a reddish-gold corona. She held up her hand to shield her eyes and squinted. He came into focus. Her hand fell heedlessly to her side.

He was wearing a pair of dark blue swim trunks and nothing else. He'd just come out of the water. The way the trunks molded his body shredded her thoughts. Water gleamed on a lean, powerful torso, gilding him even more than the sun and his bronzed tan already did. His short, wet hair was slicked back from a narrow, handsome face. Like her, he squinted as he examined her, even though he was turned away from the sun.

"It was a little intimidating, to be honest," she managed, gathering herself. He was gorgeous, sure, but she was still a little irritated that he let his gigantic dog roam free. Not everyone thought it was fun to be run down by a hundred-and-fifty-pound animal. People around here really needed to watch over their dogs better. "He was coming at me like a locomotive," she added.

"This is a private beach. It belongs to a friend of mine."

Harper blinked at the sudden coolness. It wasn't just his clipped tone, either. His narrow-eyed gaze was somehow . . . *cutting* as it moved over her face. It was like being scanned by a laser beam. The thought struck her that whoever this guy was, he regularly left people feeling tongue-tied and about six inches tall.

"I'm sorry," she said stiffly, standing tall to diminish the shrinking effect of his stare. "I was told by my Realtor that a Tahoe Shores resident could walk or run along the entire lakeshore within the town's city limits." She started to walk away from him.

"You misunderstood me."

"What?" She halted, looking over her shoulder.

Something crossed over his features, there and then gone. Was it frustration?

"You're right, technically speaking. The beach directly next to the lake is the town's property, even if we *are* on my friend's property at the moment," he said dryly, nodding at the distance between where they stood and the lake forty or so feet away.

"I'll get closer to the water, then."

"No, that's not what I meant. I wasn't calling you out for crossing my friend's beach. He'd be fine with it. You're welcome anytime."

"Oh." She gave a small shrug of bewilderment. She glanced uneasily at the lovely, sprawling, ultramodern mansion to the left of her, the one that must belong to his friend.

"I was just giving you fair warning. You might have another run-in with Charger, or some other dog. Here, Charger." He calmly held out a large, outspread hand and the dog bounded over to him. She spun fully to face him, unable to hide her smile at the vision of the rambunctious dog hopping up to reach his master's touch.

"I guess you knew him pretty well when you named him," she said.

"Yeah. I imagine he even charged out of the womb."

Charger frisked around a pair of long, strong-looking legs. He was a tall one. Six foot three or four? Her gaze stuck on his crotch.

The wet trunks were revealing. *Very.* Heat flared in her cheeks.

"He interrupted your pace," he said.

She jerked her gaze guiltily up to his face. He waved at her jogging attire.

"Oh. It's okay. I never go that fast, anyway. And I'd just gotten started," she assured, her breathlessness at odds with her reply. "What breed is he?" Harper asked, nodding at the dog, hoping to distract him from her face. With her coloring, her blushes were annoyingly obvious.

"A Lab-pointer mix. I *think*, anyway. He didn't come with any papers. I got him from the local shelter."

"The Tahoe Shores Animal Shelter is close to the offices of my new job. It's huge. I heard it was the largest in Nevada." *Maybe that's why everyone is so dog-crazy around here.*

"You work at the *Sierra Tahoe Gazette*?" he asked. He noticed her surprised glance. He gave a small shrug. Harper experienced a stirring deep inside her, and realized it came from that small, sexy . . . yet somehow shy smile. But that couldn't be right. How could a man as cold and imperious as he'd seemed just seconds ago come off as *shy*?

"This is a small town. The *Gazette*'s office is the only building close to the shelter . . . besides the North Shore Fire Department." His gaze dropped over her slowly, and that flickering of her body swelled to a steady, pleasurable flame. "Although you *are* in good shape. Are you a firefighter?"

She laughed. No, he *definitely* wasn't shy. "You were right the first time." She stuck out her hand. "Harper McFadden. I started last week as the news editor at the *Gazette*."

He stepped closer. His hand felt damp and warm. It enfolded hers completely. She tried to make out the color of his narrowed eyes and saw shards of green, brown, and amber. Her heart gave a little jump.

Agate eyes.

"You left your job at the *San Francisco Chronicle* as a reporter."

Her mouth dropped open. "What?" she asked hollowly, almost certain she'd misheard him. Did his godlike attributes go beyond his phenomenal looks and aloofness? Was he omniscient as well?

She pulled on her hand, discombobulated, and he slowly released it from his grasp.

"I've read your articles in the *Chronicle*. I have offices in San Francisco. That piece you did on San Francisco's homeless children was top-notch."

"Thank you," she managed, still knocked a little off balance.

He nodded and took a step back, as if he'd realized his unsettling effect on her. He did unsteady her, just not in the way he probably thought.

"You don't plan to write anymore?" Her spine stiffened a little. Force of habit. She'd been hearing that question a lot lately, usually accompanied by disappointment or bewilderment. Had she heard a hint of disapproval in this man's tone, or was it her own lack of confidence in her recent career change tainting her interpretation? *The latter, of course.* Why would a stranger care enough to be condemning?

"I wouldn't say that. I just wanted to experience a different side of the newspaper business," she replied neutrally.

"I love Tahoe Shores as much as the next resident, but . . . aren't we a far cry from San Francisco?" He reached down to distractedly scratch Charger, but his gaze on her remained sharp.

The easy richness of his voice beguiled her, but it was his calmness, his absolute, easy confidence that truly nudged her to let down her guard. There was a grace to him that one didn't usually see in such a masculine, virile man. It was that intangible quality that had called a walking god to mind.

She kept her gaze on his face, but it was just as distracting. He wore a thin, well-trimmed goatee that highlighted a sensual mouth. The hair on his face, chest, and head was wet at the moment, but appeared to be brown. Harper couldn't stop staring at his firm, well-shaped lips. She forced her gaze away and found herself watching his long fingers rubbing the dog's neck instead. It didn't help matters any.

"Sorry," he said after a short pause. "That's none of my business, is it?"

"No, it's not that. I just needed to get away from the grind." She tossed up her hands and glanced out at the aquamarine alpine lake, clear blue skies, and surrounding pine-covered mountains. "I wanted to try editing, and there was an opportunity here."

"Might be a shortage of actual *news* for a news editor, though," he said with a half smile. She saw the sharp gleam of curiosity in his hazel eyes.

"Maybe. But I could use the slow pace. The peace." His eyebrows arched. "For a little while, anyway," she added.

He nodded, and she had the fleeting, illogical thought that he understood. Maybe he really did. He had said he'd read her articles. Harper threw herself into her stories wholesale. Each one consumed her. Every one took a bit of her with it.

"Where are you staying?" he asked, looking down at Charger and gently squeezing a floppy ear. The dog quivered in pleasure. Harper shifted her feet restlessly as another frisson of sensual awareness passed through her.

She really needed to snap out of it.

"I just moved in last Monday. Back there. Sierra Shores." She waved behind her to the beachside complex of townhomes. He nodded, his face striking her again as solemn and beautiful. His gaze flickered distractedly out toward the sparkling lake. He was losing interest in their conversation.

"You're from the south," she said impulsively.

His shadowed gaze zipped to her face. Why did he look so stiff? "Your accent," she said by way of explanation. "I didn't notice it at first, but it's definitely there." *Like a hint of rich, smooth dark chocolate.*

"Yeah. Most people don't catch that. South Carolina, born and bred," he said after a pause.

"I grew up in DC—Georgetown, actually. DC is a melting pot—so I have some experience with teasing out accents."

A silence descended, punctuated only by the hushed, rhythmic sound of the soft surf caressing the beach. He ran his hand distractedly across his damp, taut abdomen, the action scattering her thoughts. "Well . . . ," he said after a pause, waving vaguely in the direction behind her. "We should let you get on with your jog. Sorry again for the interruption."

"I'm sorry for trespassing. I did it unknowingly."

"Like I said. You're welcome here."

She wondered what his friend thought of him handing out free passes to his property, but then dismissed the thought as quickly as she'd had it. He seemed the type of man to have friends who wouldn't argue with his proclamations.

"I hope you find what you're looking for here. The peace, I mean," he said.

Her heart fluttered. There it was again: a glimpse of unexpected sweetness, something that tugged at her and was in direct opposition to his potent masculinity and epic, effortless confidence.

Her strange musings evaporated in almost an instant when without another word he sauntered away from her, calling to Charger with that deep, mellow voice. After a moment, he lifted his arms to a casual boxer stance and broke into an easy jog. Charger bounded into a gallop to follow him, barking ebulliently up at his master. Harper blinked, realizing she was entranced watching the rippling muscles of his gleaming back, hard, rounded biceps . . . and an incredible ass.

It took her a dazed half minute of resuming her jog in the opposite direction to realize he'd never told her his name.

It was all for the best, anyway. Harper was a little wary of men as good-looking as he'd been. She was *way* too prone to getting herself mixed up with self-involved narcissists. At age thirty-two, she'd finally learned the difficult lesson that what she wanted sexually—a powerful, confident male—was highly at odds with what she wanted emotionally—a smart, stimulating companion whom she respected, someone who really cared, a guy who *occasionally* thought enough of her to sacrifice his own needs in order to fulfill hers. Not all the time, of course. She wasn't needy and cherished her independence. But damn . . . *once* in a while? Was that really too much for a woman to ask?

Apparently so.

At any rate, she'd resolved to break her dysfunctional pattern. Each and every one of her past lovers had shone brilliantly in the beginning, and then proved himself to be gold-painted crap by the time she broke things off.

Don't kid yourself. None of your old boyfriends shone like he *had just now.*

Dangerous, a voice in her head insisted.

That was another habit Harper was trying to break: the fact that when it came to her heart, she found potentially risky, powerful men fascinating, and yet . . . she feared them, as well. It seemed her head and her sexual appetites did constant battle.

Not that it mattered, she discounted, inhaling the pristine air to cleanse herself of thoughts of the man and the strangely charged moment. She settled into a comfortable jog. She had way more important things to consider than men and sex. Like her new life here, for instance. Her new job. A whole new future.

And it's not like he'd seemed remotely interested, anyway.

It was time for her to face up to the fact that she was alone in the world. Maybe she should consider getting a dog . . .

She imagined her parents' incredulous expressions if she ever told them she had a dog. She resisted an urge to laugh, but then almost immediately, that familiar hole opened up in her chest.

It'd never happen again, that she'd tell them about some new, exciting addition to her life.

As a teenager, Harper had suffered from debilitating anxiety. Her father had been a psychiatrist. Philip McFadden had spent a great deal of time and effort years ago to cure his daughter of several phobias and associated panic attacks. One of her phobias had been for dogs. Her mom and dad might have been stunned if they'd known she was considering a dog as a pet, but they would have been proud, too.

She'd come a long way from being that anxious, sad little girl. She'd never really thanked her parents for that.

Sheldon Sangar, the *Gazette*'s editor in chief, waved Harper in from across the newsroom. Or at least he beckoned her as best he could while clutching several bottles of water and a carton holding what looked like two strawberry smoothies from Lettie's Place, the local coffeehouse a couple of blocks away. In Harper's previous jobs, the typical fuel of the newsroom was adrenaline, caffeine, and junk food. At the *Sierra Tahoe Gazette*, the employees preferred salads, bottled water, and jogs on their lunch hour. Sheldon Sangar was no exception to this easygoing, health-conscious company attitude. It was strange to have an editor in chief who could have passed as a hippie if it weren't for his neat, short gray hair and newsroom badge.

"Do you have something for me?" Harper asked Sangar eagerly as she approached.

"Do you want a smoothie? I got one for Denise, but she had to take off early to bring her daughter to the doctor for an infected spider bite," Sangar said, holding out the carton.

Harper briefly tried to picture her former bulldog-like editor-in-chief, Frazier Sorrenson, letting his assistant, Roberta, leave early because of a sick child. She failed in her imaginings. Roberta was lucky to get out of the newsroom every day by eight p.m. Harper doubted Frazier would let her go home early if her baby came down with typhoid.

"No, I mean . . . do you have a story for me? Things are pretty slow. I've already finished my edits and layouts." *By ten o'clock this morning.*

Sangar gave her a knowing glance over the frame of his glasses. "Sorry, no page-burners at the moment. I told you things could be pretty slow at the end of August. A lot of vacationers have cleared out now that school is starting, crime is at a standstill, and we haven't even got much to say about the Tahoe Shores football team yet. You *did* tell me you wanted an easy pace."

"I know. I'm not complaining," Harper assured.

And she wasn't, really. It was just hard to adjust her brain and body to the snail-like pace of a small town. It'd take some practice.

Sangar blinked as if he'd just thought of something and glanced down at the bottles of water he clutched. "I *do* have something for you. Almost forgot. Denise told me to give it to you when I walked in. Came special delivery." He extended his thumb and forefinger, and Harper realized for the first time he held a white linen envelope. She took it, curious. Her name and the office address for the *Gazette* were written in elegant cursive on the front.

"Looks fancy. Like a wedding invitation or something," Sangar said, readjusting the bottles of water against his body. He turned and loped in the direction of his office.

"Yeah, except I don't know anybody around here who would ask me to . . ."

She trailed off when she realized Sangar was out of earshot. She started toward her office, tearing open the envelope. The stationery was a plain white linen card with the exception of some bold dark blue and gold lettering at the top: *Jacob R. Latimer, 935-939 Lakeview Boulevard, Tahoe Shores, NV, 89717.*

"Jacob Latimer?" she mumbled, her feet slowing. The name sounded familiar, but she couldn't pin down why exactly.

"What about Latimer?" a woman asked sharply.

Harper glanced up and saw that Ruth Dannen, their features, society, and entertainment editor, had halted in front of her. She was in her midfifties and had been pleasant enough to Harper since starting her new job, if a little gruff. Ruth was a polished, thin woman who gave off an air of hard-nosed sophistication and always being in the know about Tahoe people and events.

"It's an invitation," Harper said, puzzled. She reread the handwritten message inside out loud. "'Mr. Jacob Latimer requests the honor of your presence at a cocktail party tonight at his home. Please bring your invitation and present it to the security guard at the entry gate at 935 Lakeview Boulevard. Our apologies for the inconvenience in advance, but for security reasons, identification will be required and there will be a brief search of your car and person. No additional guests, please.'"

The note was signed by an Elizabeth Shields.

She glanced up when Ruth gave a low whistle.

"Well how do you rate?" Ruth wondered, giving Harper a sharp, incredulous once-over.

"What do you mean? Who's Latimer?"

"Only the richest of all the rich bastards who congregate around this lake. You've never heard of Latimer? The software mogul? Came out of nowhere when he was still practically a kid, making his first millions in the Clint Jefferies insider trading pharmaceutical scandal? No one could ever pin anything on him, of course. Jefferies was actually the focus of the Securities and Exchange Commission's investigation, which was eventually dropped for lack of evidence. They always go after the one with the money, not the small potatoes, like Latimer was at the time. If there *was* insider trading going on, both Latimer and Jefferies got away with it. By the time the scandal faded, Latimer was serving in army intelligence. He's a brilliant programmer. The military snapped him up in a New York minute from MIT to create anti-hacker software. I hear they gave him huge bonuses every time he managed to get into the government's high-security files, and then gave him even more money to utilize the knowledge for creating programs that kept criminals from doing the exact same thing he'd just done. He parlayed all he learned from serving in army intelligence—and all the money he made in the Jefferies pharmaceutical windfall—into—"

"Lattice," Harper finished, realization hitting her. Lattice was a well-known software giant. Of course. That's why she'd heard the name Jacob Latimer. Harper didn't know much about big business or technology movers and shakers, but she'd heard of Lattice. Even though Latimer's company had begun based on an antivirus security program for the military, it'd quickly moved on to public sector applications for human resources, and most recently to antivirus software for personal computers and devices.

"What does the owner of Lattice want with me?" Harper wondered.

Ruth just arched her plucked, dark blond eyebrows and dropped her gaze over Harper speculatively. "Maybe hair the color of copper and a girlish figure has more mileage than I'd thought these days. Latimer loves women. Rumor is, he has some unusual tastes in that arena."

Harper opened her mouth to tell the older woman that was ridiculous. And Harper's looks weren't *unusual*, thank you very much. She'd been referred to as the girl next door more than once in her life, much to her irritation.

"I don't see how he'd know anything about my existence, let alone my hair color. Seriously, what do you think this is about?"

Ruth held out her hand. Harper gave her the invitation. Ruth examined the contents, frowning slightly.

"It's genuine. I recognize Elizabeth's handwriting. She's his primary personal assistant. I think he has several, but she's his main one for the Tahoe compound. You have *no* idea why you're getting this? You don't know Latimer or any of his staff? His acquaintances? Never met him while you were in San Francisco?"

"No. I didn't even recognize his name at first."

"Well," Ruth said, giving the card back with a flick of her thin wrist, "that's an invite that almost everyone in the country would kill for, including me. Latimer keeps to himself in that lakeside compound of his. He's paranoid. Some people say it's because he's got plenty to hide. Lots of rumors have flown around about him over the years. Is he still involved with the U.S. military? Does he pull strings to move players on the chessboard of international relations? Is he a spy? He's definitely a big philanthropist—probably to gloss over the gaping holes in his respectability as far as his rise to power. Who knows, really? That's the question when it comes to Latimer, and I suspect the answer is: only Latimer himself. And possibly Clint Jefferies."

"Who's Clint Jefferies?"

"The pharmaceutical and real estate tycoon? Owns Markham Pharmaceuticals? Worth billions. Nice-looking, but a bit of a douche if you ask me," Ruth replied with a sniff.

Harper definitely recognized the company name Markham. It was one of the top six pharmaceutical companies worldwide. "Right," Harper mused. "So how are Jefferies and Latimer related again?"

"Nowadays, they *aren't*, because that's the way Latimer wants it.

Jefferies was his mentor a long time ago. But Latimer has held him at arm's length ever since the Markham insider trading scandal. That whole affair has been shrouded in mystery for years, just like Latimer himself. He's a reporter's dream and nightmare at once. *Someone* has done a good job of brushing the trail of his history clean," Ruth said with a pointed glance. "My bet is that the main trail sweeper is Latimer himself, with a little help from his buddies in military intelligence. I've been invited to a few charity events Latimer has sponsored at a local hotel. He only attends once in a while, and when he does, he's like a ghost. No one ever gets a good look at him, let alone talks to him. Rumor has it, he even has his women imported from other parts of the world. His deliberate avoidance of the women around here only adds to his mystique and allure. *And* to local females' frustration. You *have* to tell me every detail about the cocktail party."

"You mean you think I should go?"

Ruth looked scandalized. "Aren't you listening to what I'm saying? That's a golden ticket you're holding right there. His staff guards him like Fort Knox, both here and in San Francisco. Even if Latimer does his ghost act at this cocktail party, though, just getting behind those gates is a major coup. I've never been invited to the compound."

"But—"

"You *will* go," Ruth said with a glare. Harper gave her a dry *don't even think you can push me around* look. Ruth seemed to realize her harshness and laughed. "Jesus, how to explain to a peasant that you don't turn down an invitation from the king?" Harper opened her mouth to defend herself. "Oh, calm down," Ruth said, cutting her off with a wave of her hand and the air of someone who had more important things to consider than soothing a frayed ego. She took Harper by the arm and urged her toward her office. "I'm not being difficult, Harper. Honestly. It's just you don't *get* Tahoe Shores yet. Sure, we're a little Podunk town, but at the same time, we host some of the biggest movers and shakers in the world on that lakeshore. The Silicon Valley elite flock to the Nevada Tahoe shores for the tax breaks and the incredible views, and Jacob Latimer is one of the biggest of them all." Ruth stepped back in front of Harper's desk, letting go of her arm. "Now. Are you a newswoman, or not?"

Harper stilled at the challenge, eyes narrowing. "Of course."

"Then you're going to that damn party because this is the best bit of news this pitiful newspaper has had in ages. Who knows, maybe you'll get some dirt on Latimer in that close of proximity."

"I'm an editor now, not a reporter. Let alone an undercover one."

"I don't care if you're Ben freaking Bradlee, you're *going.*" Ruth pointed at Harper's chair. "Now sit down, and I'll try to prepare you for what you're about to get into. As best I can, anyway, since I only have my imagination to go on as far as what happens behind those gates."

Harper gave a bark of disbelieving laughter, but started around her desk, nevertheless. Some people might have been offended by Ruth's manner, but plainspoken bossiness was familiar to her. Ruth was the closest thing to a savvy newspaperwoman Harper had run into at the *Gazette.* The truth was, she wouldn't let Ruth boss her around if she wasn't curious herself about the invitation.

"You make a cocktail party sound like it's life altering," Harper said, plopping into her chair.

"You never know," Ruth replied drolly. "We're talking Jacob Latimer here. He's made it a business to alter lives. Maybe his own, most of all. He made a giant of himself out of nothing but shadows and whispers, after all. *That's* the potential story, if you ask me."

two

What the hell are you doing here?

She'd asked herself that question too many times to count before she pulled her Toyota Camry up next to a security station at 935 Lakeview Boulevard that evening. It'd been less than a half mile from her condo. Harper felt a little stupid driving the short distance on such a gorgeous evening. She'd rather walk. From the sound of the invitation, however, she got the definite impression she wasn't expected to stroll casually up to Jacob Latimer's gated compound.

The guard seemed amiable enough as he approached, but something about his muscular, fit body and sharp eyes as he examined her face, the invitation, and then her face again suggested he was something more than just easygoing part-time help stuck out at the front gate. The word *ex-military* popped into her brain. Well, Ruth had said that Latimer had done a stint in army intelligence. Maybe he'd hired some buddies from his army days to do his security.

"You're all set, Ms. McFadden," the guard finally said, handing back her invitation and identification. "Just keep heading straight down the road and you'll dead-end at the big house."

"You're not going to search me or my car?" she asked, referring to the mention in the invitation about security measures.

"No, ma'am," he replied, deadpan. "You've been pre-cleared for entry."

This just keeps getting weirder and weirder. What did Ruth get me into?

It wasn't Ruth's fault, though. Not really. Harper's reporter instinct had been nudged by the unexpected invitation and Ruth's gossip about

Latimer. She had no interest in doing a big-business exposé. But she *was* known for having a nose for a good story. Harper usually gravitated toward human interest pieces, though . . . to big stories seen through the eyes of seemingly small, everyday people. She couldn't imagine what a good human interest story might be in regard to Jacob Latimer. By all reports, the man more resembled a machine or ghost than a flesh-and-blood man.

At least it won't be boring, Harper thought wryly as she progressed down a stunning drive canopied by soaring pine trees, landscaped grounds, and several outbuildings. Suddenly the sprawling main house came into view. The mansion blended features of the old Tahoe style with a clean, minimalist, almost Japanese aesthetic: Western log lodge meets Frank Lloyd Wright. The result was stunning.

A woman in her thirties wearing a black cocktail dress briskly stepped down the stairs when Harper pulled up at the porte cochere. A young man followed and came around to open Harper's door.

"Just leave your keys," the woman said. "Jim will park your car for you. Welcome! I'm Elizabeth Shields," the woman said when Harper alighted. She peered at Harper through a pair of tortoiseshell-rimmed glasses. Harper sensed she was pleasant, but guarded . . . and *curious,* as well.

"Harper McFadden. It's a pleasure to meet you," Harper said, extending her hand.

Elizabeth was an attractive brunette in her midthirties. Something about the way she wore the expensive-looking but simply cut cocktail dress called to mind a uniform instead of party attire. As Jacob Latimer's assistant, Elizabeth must have to dress up for work a lot.

"Follow me," Elizabeth said, nodding her head in the direction of the stairs. "I'm sorry about all the security measures. The software industry is ridiculously competitive these days; it's a necessary precaution, I'm afraid," Elizabeth explained as she led Harper through a pair of enormous carved pine doors with wrought iron handles. Harper didn't have time to tell Elizabeth the security check had been surprisingly brief. She was too busy goggling as they entered a high-domed entry hall and then a great room featuring lodgepole-pine-beamed thirty-foot ceilings, two soaring river rock fireplaces, and a long stretch of floor-to-ceiling windows revealing a jaw-dropping panoramic view of Lake Tahoe and the surrounding mountains. Despite the open, old Tahoe design of the structure, the furniture and finishes were contemporary, utilitarian, and elegant. It was the most stunning room Harper had ever seen, whether in photos or real life.

Elizabeth turned as they walked, and saw her gawking. "It's pretty, isn't it?" she asked, smiling.

"That's a bit of an understatement."

Elizabeth laughed and opened a glass-paned door for her. "I find myself thinking that a lot. Mr. Latimer has a way of making regular speech seem inadequate."

"I can imagine," Harper muttered, following Elizabeth out the door and onto an enormous terrace.

The scene was breathtaking, something straight out of a movie set. The section of the terrace closest to the house was under a protective roof, so that one could use it even in inclement weather. Given the two outdoor stone fireplaces on the upper deck, a person could sit out there comfortably, enjoying the scenery even as the surrounding mountains became white with snow. Even in late August, the nights could turn pleasantly chilly in the alpine setting. Cozy flames flickered in the fireplaces, beckoning a person to curl up on one of the many couches or chairs near them.

Elizabeth led her down some stairs, and they arrived at the second terrace level. This and the next deck down were places to bask in the sun. Again, there were multiple seating areas, landscaped flora, trickling fountains, and stone paths. Harper's eyes caught on one of several circular-shaped, deep wicker divans with a sunscreen attached to the top of it. The opaque sunscreen on one had been lowered to block what was happening in the deep couch. Six bare feet stuck out of the bottom of the obscured divan. Harper heard muffled male and female laughter.

Steam rose from a large sauna to the far right. Down on the next level of the terrace was a pool. From there, another set of wide stairs led down to the beach. Towering Jeffrey and ponderosa pines framed the view. Two long docks stretched out onto the sapphire blue lake, three Jet Skis tied up to one of them. In the distance, a yacht was moored alongside one of the beautiful, handcrafted wooden motorboats that were favored in Tahoe.

Elizabeth led her toward a square-shaped stone pedestal that contained a fire pit. Twenty or so people had gathered around the open fire. They stood or lounged in cushioned sofas and chairs. Most of them wore sunglasses to protect their eyes from the brilliant setting sun. A waiter was moving among them, serving hors d'oeuvres and drinks. In the distance, a jazz quartet was playing a lazy, sensual tune. Several of the well-heeled partygoers glanced over at Harper and Elizabeth as they approached.

A quick surveillance told her that more than half of the people were women. Not just any women, either. Stunning ones. Exotic ones. Were these some of Latimer's *imports*, as Ruth had mentioned? Some of the women's stares on her were rapier sharp and speculative . . . like they were eyeing the competition? Annoyance flickered through her at the idea of being considered a candidate for Latimer's harem. Maybe now that she'd seen the haloed interior of Latimer's compound, she had enough information to satisfy Ruth's curiosity and could sneak out of here ASAP. She didn't relish spending the evening in a den of clawing cats.

Elizabeth turned to her and murmured quietly as their pace slowed. "I'll introduce you to him right away. He's very anxious to meet you."

Harper's bewilderment soared. An urge to laugh struck her. That was the final straw. *Clearly* there had been some kind of mistake. They thought she was someone else. She'd been granted entry into this forbidden paradise because of a colossal error.

Latimer's assistant stopped next to a man with short, spiky, bleached white hair. He wore a fitted, trendy European-cut dark blue suit, a pink plaid tie, and a pair of old-fashioned Ray-Ban sunglasses.

He immediately gave off an air of being dapper, quirky, and sharp as a whip all at once. So *this* was Latimer? He hardly seemed mysterious. She couldn't imagine this man's flamboyance being called ghostlike. He was about as obvious as a slap to the face. He peered over the top of his glasses at Harper pointedly.

"Is this her?" he demanded of Elizabeth in a clipped British accent. Without waiting for Elizabeth to reply, he addressed Harper. "Are you Harper McFadden?"

"Uh . . . yes."

His gaze dropped over her in an assessing fashion. "Well aren't you gorgeous. I *love* that dress," he declared, reaching to take her hand.

Elizabeth laughed. "Harper McFadden, meet Cyril Atwater. He's been looking forward to meeting you."

"Really?" Harper strained to remain polite, but realized she sounded incredulous, anyway.

"Of course. This film is going to be spectacular. I think it'll be a shoo-in to win at Sundance, and it might even be a dark horse for some commercial success Stateside."

"What film is that?" Harper wondered.

"The one based on your story, of course," Cyril said, looking vaguely put out by her ignorance. "Didn't you tell her?" he asked Elizabeth sharply.

"I don't know anything about it. I just follow orders," Elizabeth said. Again, Harper caught Elizabeth's curiosity as she regarded her.

"Excuse me, I don't mean to seem rude," Harper said at last. "But I don't know what you're talking about. And I have no idea why I've been invited here tonight."

"I'm Cyril Atwater," the man repeated. "The *director*?" he added with a trace of annoyance when Harper gave him an apologetic look for her ignorance. She suspected he rolled his eyes behind his Ray-Bans. "I realize you Yanks have been spoon-fed tedious car chases and shoot-'em-ups since the cradle, but surely a woman of your obvious intelligence and compassion occasionally watches a documentary or film of actual *substance*."

Despite his acerbic tongue, a smile twitched at Harper's mouth when he'd seamlessly switched from his clipped English accent to say *shoot-'em-ups* with a perfect cowboy drawl.

"Can I get you something to drink, miss?" a waiter asked her over her right shoulder.

"Yes, I'll have a glass of chardonnay, thank you," Harper said. She turned back to Cyril. "I'm sorry, I don't watch many movies, either of the documentary or shoot-'em-up variety."

"But you must realize that the story you did on Ellie, that homeless teenager in San Francisco, would make a brilliant film."

"And this is why I've been asked here tonight?" Harper asked dazedly. Well, *this* certainly was an odd turn of events.

"It must be," Elizabeth said. "I asked you because Mr. Latimer requested it, but I wasn't sure about the details." Elizabeth glanced over at a still-bristling Cyril. "Mr. Atwater has won several major film awards, including the Academy Award last year for his documentary *Bitter Secrets.*"

"I'm not a child, Elizabeth. You don't have to soothe any feathers," Atwater said peevishly. Elizabeth's upraised brows and amused glance at Harper seemed to say she felt differently. "So what do you think, Harper? Is it all right if I call you Harper?" Cyril asked.

"Of course."

"Well? What do you think of letting me do the film?"

Harper shrugged dubiously. "I don't think that'd work, to be honest."

"Why not?" Cyril demanded.

"Because it's not just me you'd have to get agreement from, but Ellie."

"That's done easily enough."

"But she doesn't live on the streets anymore," Harper explained. "She's a waitress and attends junior college part-time."

"Thanks to your story, I'm sure that's all true. I'm not planning on doing an actual documentary for this. It'd be done with actors and actresses, but based on the feature you did."

Harper glanced over at Elizabeth and gave a short laugh. "This *isn't* what I expected in coming here tonight."

"What *did* you expect?" Elizabeth asked.

"I didn't know what to expect. I was surprised when I got the invitation. I was under the impression Mr. Latimer was responsible for it, which confused me even more. I see now that it was you"—she glanced at Cyril—"who was behind it all."

"Oh, Jacob *was* responsible for it. He suggested the whole thing to me at lunch a few days ago. I thought his idea was brilliant. But of course, everything Jacob suggests *is*," Cyril said as though stating the obvious.

The waiter arrived with an empty wine goblet and a bottle on a tray.

"Is he here?" Harper asked, smiling in thanks as she took the glass. She noticed the label as the waiter poured the chardonnay: It was Latimer's own.

"Mr. Latimer, you mean?"

Harper nodded at Elizabeth and took a sip. She blinked in pleasure at the subtle, oaky taste of the wine. *Nothing but the best for Latimer.*

"No, he got caught up in an emergency work situation, unfortunately," Elizabeth said smoothly. Harper had the impression this was Elizabeth's standard reply for queries in regard to Latimer's presence . . . or absence, as the case likely usually was.

"Jacob hardly ever attends these things. I tell him this place is his cave"—Cyril waved his crystal highball glass at the magnificent mansion—"and he's the hermit who inhabits it. If I didn't come over and push my way in a few times a week, I'd never catch sight of him. He'd be just as much a legend to me as Sasquatch and our local Tahoe Tessie. I live just a house down," he explained to Harper, pointing behind her. "I suppose if I harp too much, the hermit will toss me out on my bony butt, so I try to—" Cyril paused, his brow furrowing.

Harper instinctively turned to where he was staring. Other partygoers looked around in the direction of the house, as well. Conversation faded off until a breathless hush prevailed.

It was like a charge had ignited the evening air and an electrical current passed through them all. Or at least that's how it felt to Harper as she watched the man from the beach saunter toward the party with easy grace, eyes trained directly on her.

"To what do we owe this honor?" Cyril boomed incredulously as the man approached their small grouping. As if on cue, the other partygoers turned back to their conversations, and the quartet began another number. Even though everyone resumed the cocktail party routine, Harper noticed several sideways, surreptitious glances in their direction. It wasn't just women looking, either. It was clear that Latimer's presence at the party was not only unexpected, but also exciting.

"I looked out my window and saw Harper's hair."

There was a burning in Harper's chest cavity. She realized it was because she hadn't drawn air as she watched him approach. And . . . had he *really* just said that about her hair?

"Jacob Latimer," he said, extending his hand. "I don't think I ever got the chance to actually introduce myself the other day on the beach."

"No, you didn't," she said, grasping his hand. She stared up into a pair of long-lashed golden-green-brown eyes. He wore a suit, including a vest and tie, but somehow he managed to make the suit seem as casual and easy as the swim trunks she'd seen him in yesterday. Just as sexy, that much was certain. Here was a man who was supremely confident in his own skin. *And why shouldn't he be?*

"It's the color of the sunset," he said quietly, and again, there was that small smile, almost as if he was a little embarrassed by his poetic turn of phrase, but had said it anyway. He released her hand slowly and pointed at her hair when she just stared at him stupidly. She managed to return his smile despite her discomposure, all too aware of Elizabeth and Cyril's fascinated gazes on them.

"A sunset is one of the kinder things it's been compared to. Ask any redhead how much they liked their hair color as a kid," she laughed.

"So it's real?" Cyril asked. "I don't believe I've ever seen that particular shade naturally. It's absolutely brilliant, to say the least. You're quite right about the sunset, Jacob."

Harper knew her cheeks had turned the color of her hair. She couldn't believe the iconic Latimer and the man on the beach were one and the same. He was way too young to be so accomplished, wasn't he? Too young to already have acquired such an aura of mystery and fascination?

"Has Cyril been talking to you about his film idea?" Jacob asked her, politely changing the topic. He'd probably noticed her discomfort on the topic of her hair.

"Actually, he mentioned it was *your* idea," she said.

"I brought up the subject of you and your article. Cyril thought of the movie, and I agreed it would be brilliant," he said, gracefully avoiding her pointed statement. "So he has mentioned it?" he asked, glancing inquiringly at Cyril, Harper, and Elizabeth.

"He'd just brought it up when you arrived," Harper told him. *Of course.* He'd mentioned that particular story on the beach. Cyril had just said his home neighbored Latimer's. It must have been Cyril's beach they were on when Charger raced toward her. Then he'd mentioned their brief meeting to Cyril, the director . . . and here she was. Understanding the chain of events that had gotten her to this unusual situation steadied her a bit from a whirlwind of confusion.

Got it. I'm good. I can handle this.

"I was telling him that I didn't think it would work," Harper told Latimer frankly.

"She's concerned that the young woman, Ellie, won't consent to having her story told," Cyril told Jacob. "But we can use another name, after all. Perhaps you can broach the topic with her? If she's hesitant, I'm sure I can convince her."

"Cyril is very convincing," Elizabeth said, although she wasn't looking at Cyril, but Latimer. Latimer, in turn, was steadily regarding Harper. Harper was highly aware of his stare on her cheek.

"Ellie aside, *you* don't like the idea," Latimer said. "Why not?"

She blinked at his astute observation. She hadn't even been aware it was true until he said it. "I felt like writing Ellie's story was worthwhile. Still . . . part of me felt a little guilty—*still* feels a little guilty—for exposing her entire life for public consumption."

Latimer nodded once solemnly. "How did Ellie feel about it? Do you think she'll worry about having her history become even more exposed?"

"She never complained. In fact, she was thankful. She was glad to have her story, and the experience of many of her friends and acquaintances, told."

"It's a story that *should* be told," Cyril stated unequivocally. "We call ourselves civilized in the Western world, and yet innocent children are living in the most appalling circumstances right in the midst of our cities. You wanted to expose that story, and you did, Harper. Why wouldn't you want it to reach an even wider audience?"

"I . . . I'm not saying I'm against it," she replied, flustered. A cool lake breeze swirled around them, cutting through the silk of her cocktail dress. The temperature had dipped as sunset approached. A shiver rippled through her. This wasn't a conversation she'd prepared herself for. "And like I said, it's not primarily up to me."

"As I said, I'm sure we can convince—"

"Give it a rest for the moment, Cyril," Jacob interrupted, his voice quiet, but steely. He slipped a hand beneath Harper's bent elbow. "Ms. McFadden is feeling a bit ambushed, I think. Elizabeth, could you have one of the waiters bring Harper and me a hot drink? We're going to sit up by the fire."

No one contradicted him. Harper had the impression no one would dare. She followed him up the stairs, highly aware of two things: the stares on her exposed back, and Jacob Latimer's hand on the sensitive skin on the underside of her elbow.

"There. Is that better?" he asked a moment later when he led her to a deep sofa situated before one of the stone fireplaces. She nodded and set down her wineglass on a coffee table before she sat. Realizing she still clutched her purse, she quickly tucked it in the corner of the sofa. He came down on the cushion next to her. His long, strong thigh was only an inch away from hers. His stark masculinity—his potent attractiveness—crowded her brain and rushed her body.

"It got chilly so fast. It was really warm when I left my town-home," she said, her voice steady despite her ruffled state. Her halter dress left her arms and a good portion of her back exposed. The warmth from the fire felt good on her chilled skin.

"Tahoe is a place of extremes. The temperatures at night can plunge thirty, even forty degrees from the daytime highs. It's alpine desert, but it's still the desert. In the winter, I can ski on a foot of new powder and come down the mountains to the lake and broil a bit in the sun."

She smiled. "That sounds nice. Thank you," she murmured to the waiter when he approached and placed two steaming cups on the table in front of them. Latimer leaned forward, elbows on his thighs, and grabbed the drinks. She accepted the mug gratefully, cradling the drink with both hands.

"Cider," he said, inhaling the steam from his cup.

Harper took a drink. "And . . . whiskey?" she added, stifling a gasp. The beverage was tasty and warming, but strong.

He smiled and set down his cup. "Blended bourbon, actually. Would you prefer something else?"

She shook her head and took another sip. "It's delicious. I just wasn't expecting the up-front punch."

"Just like you weren't expecting all that talk about the film."

"I wasn't expecting you," she said frankly, turning toward him.

His expression sobered.

She hadn't meant to say her impulsive thought out loud. She cleared her throat and clutched the intoxicating beverage tighter in her hand. "I mean . . . I hadn't put Jacob Latimer the icon and you together, when we met down there on the beach."

"Icon," he repeated slowly, that X-ray stare narrowing on her. "An icon is representative of something. What do you think I symbolize?"

She laughed but squirmed a little in her seat. "I don't know. The

American Dream, rags to riches, glamour and wealth, mystery and speculation, and—"

"Ill-gotten gains?" he murmured, his silky tone at odds with the sudden glacial quality of his eyes.

Jesus. The rumors about him being paranoid are true.

"I wasn't going to say that," she replied.

"I'm not a symbol of anything."

He closed his eyes briefly, as if to calm a sudden rough chop of emotion. When he opened his eyelids, he once again seemed completely under control, if a little weary.

"I'm sorry if I seem suspicious," he said slowly. "It's a constant battle to keep my private life private. Cyril is interested in your story for the film, and I want to help him if I can. But I don't usually allow the press into my home. The invitation was for you. Harper McFadden. Not a member of the press. I want to make that clear from the outset. From what I've learned about you, I assume you'd have the decency to tell me right now if you planned to print anything you learned here tonight."

"I didn't come here for that," she said stiffly. "And you're right. I'd tell you if I was planning on publishing anything about tonight. Or about you."

He merely regarded her steadily for a moment by way of response, and then transferred his gaze to the fire. Her brief flash of annoyance in reaction to his suspicion seemed to drain away under the influence of the flames, the strong drink . . . and her heightened awareness of him. For a few moments, neither of them spoke.

"I can only imagine how hard it must be for you to live your life away from prying eyes, rumors, and misunderstandings," she said at length. "But I'll remind you that you were the one to ask me here tonight. I didn't come with any underhanded motivations."

"So you definitely didn't come because of interest in doing a story on Jacob Latimer or Lattice?" he murmured.

"For the newspaper?"

His small shrug caused his jacket to brush lightly against her bare arm. A shiver of awareness passed through her. She glanced sideways at him. She hadn't been able to discern it on the beach when he was wet, but his hair was somewhere between a dark ash blond and light ash brown. It blended ideally with his arresting eyes—all those colored shards of amber and brown, the green only adding another layer of complexity. He was almost alarmingly handsome.

"No," she replied. "I always tell people when they say something along those lines: it's like if you invited a food critic to your house for a dinner party, or a psychotherapist, or . . . *anything*, really. They aren't going to publically critique your meal or waste time developing a personality assessment. I exist beyond my job, you know."

"So why *did* you come?" he asked.

"I was interested. Who wouldn't be curious? About this place. About you. I may not be planning on writing it, but I love a good story as much as anyone."

His brows slanted. "What are you so curious about, exactly?"

"You're awfully young," she stated with blunt honesty.

"Age is relative, isn't it? You're young, too, to have found so much success in your chosen field, to have been given so many awards in journalism."

A wave of warmth and relaxation went through her as she watched his mouth move. Her limbs tingled. The pleasant sensation somehow twined with his mellow, seductive voice. *What was in this drink*, she wondered, idly taking another sip. *Liquid Xanax?*

"Any success I've had is comprehensible," she said after a short pause. "It followed a logical path. Your success is astronomical for someone so young and who, from what I understand, wasn't born into wealth." Despite her entrancement at his closeness, Ruth's earlier references to his shrouded, possibly illegal rise to riches and power came to mind.

"So you've decided my success in the business world is illogical?"

"No," she defended. "It's just a glaring thing, isn't it? You can't be more than what . . . thirty-five?" she guesstimated. "And"—she waved around at the spectacular surroundings. "Anyone would be curious about how you got here. And I'm more curious than most, by nature. It's an annoying, but unchangeable characteristic."

"It's what got you where you are today."

"As the news editor at a paper with a circulation of all of thirty-five thousand?" she countered wryly.

He blinked. "I wouldn't have thought the *Gazette* had *that* many."

She laughed. He smiled full-out for the first time, white teeth flashing in his tanned face. Something hitched in her chest. There it was again. That crack in his armor. He really did shine bright, when he wasn't so busy being paranoid.

"We all feel the need to hide away at times in our life. To forget the past. Surely you can understand that," she said softly as their amusement faded.

Her heart thumped very loud in her ears for a suspended moment when he didn't immediately reply. She was so sure she'd made another misstep, saying something so personal to such an aloof, private man.

"Where's Charger?" she asked, referring to his energetic dog in a desperate attempt to change the subject when he continued not to speak.

"In the house."

"Oh."

He glanced away distractedly. An awkward silence ensued. Like she had on the beach, she had the impression he'd discounted her or lost interest. She started to set down her cider, assuming their conversation was coming to an end.

"Do you want to go see him and some of my other dogs?" he asked suddenly.

"You have several?"

He nodded, his expression completely sober.

"Uh . . . sure," she said, taken off guard. But again, she was curious. Fascinated, in truth.

He nodded and stood smoothly, putting out a hand to help her stand. He headed toward the glass doors. She followed his tall form, feeling a little dazed. She understood how people could find him intimidating. He could be glacial. Impenetrable. Then she'd catch a glimpse of his warmth. His humanity. Raw sexuality twined with something she could only call a sweetness, impossible as that descriptor seemed given the rest of the package. It was the mystery of that paradox that had her tantalized. But she'd have to be careful.

A person could get dizzy and disoriented—maybe even lost—trying to figure out the puzzle of Jacob Latimer.

three

e led her through the empty great room back in the direction from which she'd entered the house. When he opened one of the large pine doors, she saw darkness had fallen in the opposite direction from the lake and setting sun.

"How many dogs to you have?" she asked in a hushed tone as she followed his silent, graceful shadow down the front steps. The winding sidewalk ahead was illuminated by lanterns, but the black night sky, towering pines, and landscaped greenery surrounding them seemed to suck up their meager light.

"Sixteen," he replied.

"*What?*"

"I know," he said, and much to her amazement, he sounded a little sheepish. "It seems like a lot, but I like dogs."

"Apparently," she said under her breath, smiling. *Well, the extremely rich do have their quirks, don't they?*

"Clarence," she heard Latimer say quietly.

"Mr. Latimer. Nice night, isn't it?"

Harper let out a stupid little cry at the disembodied, gruff voice that came out of the dark woods to the right of her. She stumbled in her heels. Two hands grasped her shoulders, steadying her.

"Whoa. You okay?" It was Latimer's mellow voice.

"Yeah, but—" She glanced over to where the unexpected voice had come from. A bulky man in his forties with a crew cut stepped out of the trees and into the dim light.

"It's just Clarence. He works here," Latimer explained.

Harper looked around, startled. Latimer had sounded close. She realized the tips of her breasts were pressed against the lapels of his jacket. He towered over her. His face was shadowed, but she made out his gaze fixed on her upturned face. She could feel the metal of his belt buckle against her belly. And the fullness beneath it.

It happened in the amount of time it takes electricity to travel. Her blood became the current, turning into the equivalent of jet fuel. It seemed to roar through her veins, sparking her flesh to life. She felt his cock stir against her. His nostrils flared slightly as he stared down at her.

"Sorry for startling you, miss."

Harper blinked at the sound of Clarence's rough voice behind her. She stepped back, breaking contact with Latimer. The electrical connection didn't seem to cut off entirely, though. Her skin still tingled. Her sex felt warm, heavy, and tight, like a pleasant ache.

She glanced over to Clarence, trying to steady herself.

"It's okay," she replied shakily.

The man's sharp gaze ran over her briefly. *He's part of Latimer's security staff,* Harper immediately knew. Apparently, Clarence found nothing alarming about her appearance. He was likely used to seeing Latimer around the property in the presence of a female.

"Off to the doghouse, sir?" Clarence asked pleasantly.

"Yeah," Latimer replied. Harper jumped slightly when his hand enclosed hers. She gave a disgusted, frustrated sigh at her show of nerves. "Night, Clarence."

"Good night, sir. Miss."

"Night," Harper managed despite her breathlessness. Latimer tugged slightly on her hand and she moved up next to him. As they continued down the dimly lit path, now side by side, she saw that he peered over at her.

"Are you okay?"

She blinked. A feeling of uneasiness went through her that she couldn't comprehend, a feeling like déjà vu . . . or dreaming of another person's life.

"Believe it or not, most people aren't used to having men hiding in the shadows next to where they're walking," she said, injecting some humor into her voice to minimize her sense of the surreal and her embarrassment.

"No. I suppose you're right."

A building was suddenly in front of them. Latimer released her hand and placed his forefinger on a lit keypad to the right of the door. It appeared to be a fingerprint scanner.

"Where are we?" she wondered when she heard the *snick* of a lock releasing.

"The doghouse."

He took her hand again and drew her over the threshold. Harper was aware of a scurrying sound and some barks. Latimer flipped on a light.

"Oh, *shit.*"

A dozen or more canines were in various stages of racing to the door to greet them. Flopping ears, bounding paws, gleaming coats of various colors, and wagging tails abounded. She recognized Charger at the forefront of the onslaught, galloping toward them with a fury. Harper's heart lunged in a prequel to panic. She was sure she was going to be knocked over by Charger's weight, but Latimer put out his hand, palm down, and not only Charger, but the rest of the dogs, pulled up short, jumping and prancing around them, yelping and barking. Not one of them touched her or Latimer. Her heart still pounded in surprised alarm, but then she noticed something that distracted her.

"Oh no," she said.

A black puppy had stumbled amidst the stampede and struggled to get up. She waded through the canine sea, forgetting her momentary fear. She knelt, righting the puppy on his feet. Not four feet.

Three.

"What happened to him?" Despite the lack of one paw, the puppy seemed healthy enough, turning his head to lick at her hand shyly. Reacting instinctively, she lifted the pup to her mouth and kissed his smooth head before setting him back on the floor again.

"His foot was amputated," Latimer said from behind and above her.

"Was he sick, or injured?" Harper wondered, petting the wiggling puppy.

"No. He was tortured."

Harper turned her head and gaped up at Latimer, horror slinking into her awareness. "You mean . . . someone cut off his foot just to . . . *do* it?"

"That's right. He and his brothers and sisters were found locked in a stifling hot barn just south of Genoa. They'd all been tortured. Two of them were dead when they were found, and the other three—including Milo there—were brought in to the shelter. Two of the puppies died in the vet's office from the effects of open wounds and extreme dehydration. Milo was the sole survivor of all his siblings."

Sobered and chilled, Harper turned back to the puppy. She scooped him into her arms and stood, caressing Milo all the while. For the first time, she actually looked around the large, comfortable room. Several dogs hadn't joined Charger's rambunctious run to greet them at the door. They lay on cushy-looking dog beds and regarded them with sharp interest and perked-up ears. Given some of the white around their maws, Harper thought they were the older dogs.

"Oh. Not a *doghouse*. You meant a *house* for the dogs," she said, comprehension dawning. Because that's what this was. The building was a small home. Her gaze traveled over a pair of glass doors, one of which included an opening with a flap that presumably led outside. There was a well-appointed kitchen in the distance.

"I guess so," Latimer said. "There's a vet's office down the hall for doctor's visits, and they have a caretaker-trainer during the day. But they're on their own most of the time. They have a nice patch of woods out back, where they can roam."

She turned to him slowly, her fingers caressing the smooth head of the puppy.

"You sponsor that animal shelter in town, don't you?" she asked him, but somehow she already knew the answer. It just made sense to her, which was odd. She barely knew him.

He was turned in profile to her.

"Jacob?"

"That's not public knowledge."

"I understand. I wouldn't say anything to anyone. But you do, don't you?"

He continued to keep his face averted as he petted Charger and a big, brown dog. "Yes," he finally replied.

"Have you always liked animals so much?"

A pit bull nuzzled his hand. He just nodded silently. The idea struck her that he looked perfectly natural surrounded by animals while wearing an impeccable suit. She also thought at that moment that while he seemed completely open and warm with the animals, he'd grown wary toward her questions. Shut off.

Shy? No, it *couldn't* be. That characteristic just didn't fit with the rest of the man. But neither did this house for abused and forgotten dogs. Something inexplicable quivered within her, elusive and fleeting. He was such a strange, compelling man. And he seemed so alone in that moment, standing there and carefully petting the dogs that vied for his attention. No wonder rumors and speculation clung to him like metal filings to a magnet. Harper herself experienced his haunting, powerful pull. She needed to be very careful.

He straightened and faced her.

"What about you? Do you like dogs?" he asked.

"Sure. I mean . . . as much as the next person." She glanced down at the adorable puppy in her arms and kissed Milo's smooth head again. "I think I like them a little bit more this size than say . . . that one," she admitted, nodding toward the brown pit bull. She realized her vague anxiety must be on display, because his gaze on her was sharp. She tried to laugh it off. "I just get a little nervous when big or aggressive dogs come at me."

He nodded. "Most people do. Especially if they've had a bad experience in the past. I should have warned you."

"I haven't had a bad experience with dogs." Had she said that too sharply? She suspected she had, given his knitted brow.

She gave the black puppy another fond caress and set him down on the floor. She smiled as she watched his surprisingly smooth three-legged trot toward the pack of bigger dogs. It horrified her, to think of an innocent, powerless thing being tortured in that way. Who would do such a thing? It would require a degree of depravity—of evil—that her brain shied away from considering.

"It's nice that you do it. Give shelter to the animals. Medical care. And for these, a home."

He shrugged off her praise. An awkward silence descended. Harper was wondering if she should take her leave, but he spoke first.

"Won't you consider asking Ellie about the film?"

She exhaled on a bark of laughter. "Why are you so dead set on doing it?" she asked incredulously.

"I told you on the beach. I've admired of your work in the past, but I was particularly drawn to that story. I'd like to see it reach a wider audience."

She threw up her hands helplessly. "I suppose it wouldn't hurt to ask Ellie about it. She's kind of a Hollywood fanatic. She might be thrilled at the idea. I'll call her."

"Good," he said, stepping toward her. The dogs had scattered, several of them returning to their beds and a few ducking out the flapped opening to the backyard.

"Cyril will offer you and Ellie payment for rights to the story, of course, so there are details to work out there. I think he might ask you to help him write the screenplay, as well."

"Really?"

"I take it from your reaction you've never written a screenplay before?" he asked, a small—very distracting—smile molding his lips.

"No, never."

"Would you be interested?"

"Maybe," she replied dubiously. It actually sounded pretty exciting . . . like the exact kind of opportunity she needed to shake up her life even more than her recent move and job change had.

Precisely the kind of thing that would help me avoid that black hole of grief.

"You're a good writer. You'd get the hang of it, if it's something you decide to do. But most importantly . . . if Ellie agrees, *you* won't stand in the way?"

"I don't see why I would, as long as it's agreed upon that the story is told in a tasteful, compassionate way."

"Cyril wouldn't consider handling a story like this with anything but the respect it deserves. As his producer, I'd demand it."

"You're his money man, then?"

"He's a good investment. Usually," he added with a half smile.

Harper nodded. "I'm sure my father would want me to have a lawyer look over everything if the project ever progresses that far . . . I mean . . . He *would* have wanted it—"

She broke off abruptly, stunned at her stupidity.

"Harper?"

"Hmmm?"

"What's wrong?" he asked, stepping closer.

"Nothing."

He reached out and grasped her upper arm. "Did something happen? To your father?"

She gave a brittle smile. "He passed last year. It just happens sometimes, that I find myself talking like he's still alive. It happened so suddenly, it's like part of me can't get used to the fact, like my heart hasn't caught up to my brain. Like it doesn't *want* to." She swallowed through a suddenly tight throat, fighting off a rush of emotion. When would it stop—damn it—the grief crashing into her unexpectedly? On this occasion, it hadn't seemed random, however. She suspected it had something to do with Jacob Latimer's gaze. It seemed disconcertingly all-seeing, at times. It acted like a mirror to her confused inner world. She shook her head.

"Sorry. We were very close," she said, shrugging.

"You miss him a lot," he said slowly, studying her face. His thumb moved, caressing the bare skin of her arm. It was a simple gesture. It should have *felt* casual, too. It didn't. Pleasure rippled through her, and she felt his stroking thumb somewhere deep inside her being. "Were you two alike?" he asked quietly.

"My father? In some ways. Everyone says I was more like my mother, though," she said, avoiding his stare. "She started out in journalism, like me, and eventually went on to write over a dozen books on international relations, national politics, and a few biographies."

"Jane McFadden?"

She nodded, still unable to meet his stare, almost every ounce of her awareness focused on maintaining her self-control . . . and on his firm, warm hold and the pad of his thumb sliding against her skin.

"I read her essays on Afghanistan and her biography of Winston Churchill. It's no wonder you're such a good writer, with her as your teacher. She had the ability to humanize even the most complicated of people and situations. You got that from her. Your compassion. Was your father a writer, too?"

She fought back the knot in her throat. "He was, after a fashion. He was a psychiatrist, but he regularly published case studies in academic journals—"

Emotion pressed on her chest from the inside out. It was humiliating. She felt very exposed.

"I really should be going," she said, drawing in a ragged breath and starting to move past him. "I have a press conference first thing in the morning,"

"Wait." He grasped both of her shoulders, stilling her. "I didn't mean to upset you." She was caught in his stare. "Is this what you wanted to forget, in coming to Tahoe Shores?" She could smell him, as close as he was standing: sandalwood and spice and clean skin. The ache in her throat expanded to her chest.

"Maybe. Yes," she said, almost defiantly. She was irritated at him for pressing the topic. Although in truth, she could have just further sidestepped the issue. That's what she usually did when people probed her about her loss. She hadn't been able to lightly gloss over the issue with Latimer, though. "Not to forget them. Just to forget . . . you know? The pain."

"*Them?*"

"My mother, too. It was an accident. You heard about that train derailment in Spain last year?"

He nodded.

"They were on it. It'd been my mom's fantasy to do a European rail vacation. She was so excited." She shook her head irritably. "So pointless. All of it."

"Jesus. I'm sorry, I didn't know."

"Why *would* you?"

"I try to keep apprised of the news. I told you, I read some of your mom's stuff. She's a well-known author. I never heard their names connected with that train derailment, though."

She just nodded, her throat too tight to speak for a few seconds. Finally, she inhaled with a hitching breath, and forced a smile.

"It probably sounds stupid, that I'm still grieving them so much, a thirty-two-year-old woman. It's just . . . I was an only child. And we were close, even though we lived on opposite coasts." She swallowed thickly. Why was she telling him all this? It was inappropriate. Her thoughts couldn't stop her from continuing. "I could have been with them, at the end."

"What do you mean?"

"I had a ticket," she said hoarsely. "That was part of Mom's dream, for it to be a family vacation. But another reporter had to go in for surgery, and I had to take over his beat. I was forced to cancel the trip."

"Thank God."

"You don't understand. I mean . . . I wouldn't have *chosen* to die with them. It's not that. I just regret . . ."

"That you couldn't have spent those last days and hours with them. No one can put a price on that."

Her gaze jumped to his. *He had* understood. He stood so close. She found herself sinking into his eyes.

"Even though I lived so far away from them, I never realized until after they were gone—"

"What?" he asked when she broke off.

"That I'd never felt alone before, even though I'd lived on my own since I finished college. They were always there, somehow, with me in some intangible way that I'd never bothered to consider before."

He leaned forward, his lips brushing against her temple. "Until they weren't anymore," she finished shakily, her head tilting back.

Suddenly, he was kissing her.

A shock of pleasure went through her at the contact. His mouth was as firm as it looked, but surprisingly warm and gentle. He plucked at her lower lip seductively, sandwiching her flesh to his, until a shaky moan vibrated her throat. The kiss was a little cautious at first, as though he was testing the waters . . .

No, more like he was coaxing her to be with him, asking her to connect with him.

But as the spark ignited in her—in both of them, apparently—his kiss turned dark and demanding. He gripped her upper arms tighter, bringing her closer to him, and penetrated her mouth with his tongue.

It was as if he drugged her. A haze of lust overcame her brain. His scent and taste pervaded her. He felt big and hard, so solid next to her. So fantastically male. His tongue pierced and stroked her mouth, discovering her with patient yet total possession. She could feel the contours of his body, the sensation of his hardening cock deepening her trance of harsh, unexpected need.

His hands swept over the bare skin of her back. Her nerves leapt at his touch. She pressed her breasts tighter against his torso, instinctively using his hardness to ease the ache at the crests. She felt his cock swell higher against her. His fingers raked into her hair. He gently fisted a bunch of it and tugged. Her neck stretched back, and suddenly his mouth was on her pulse, hot and greedy. He inhaled and gave a low growl, the feral sound thrilling her. She whimpered as he kissed her neck and shivers of pleasure rippled through her. He found her mouth again unerringly.

She felt herself go wet . . . ready for him so quickly. So completely.

He lifted his mouth from hers. Her eyes drifted closed at the heady sensation of his warm, firm lips caressing the corner of her mouth.

The realization that he avidly kissed the small scar there jolted through her. She flinched. Her eyes sprang open. She'd caught herself, just as she was about to spin out of control. It was akin to not realizing how strong an alcoholic drink was until you tried to stand, and couldn't.

She stepped back, breaking his hold. She clamped her teeth hard at the abrupt deprivation, but forced herself to put three feet between them. He didn't move. He appeared strained, as if he'd been chained into place. His eyes seemed to burn in an otherwise frozen face. Was that anger that tightened his features? Was he pissed off that she'd stopped him?

"I'm going," she said simply.

She thought he remained in place. She couldn't know for certain, though, because she didn't look back as she rushed out the door.

The valet was just returning with a couple's car when she reached the front entrance. Harper waited impatiently as he alighted, glancing back toward the path through the woods. But Latimer hadn't followed her. Perhaps he'd taken another path back toward the main house. He probably wouldn't think twice about her, once she'd refused him.

Don't be such a bitch, she scolded herself. *For the most part, he was nothing but kind toward you all night.*

Although, why *he was so attentive remains a mystery.*

I acted like a sixteen-year-old, running away just because he kissed me.

At the same time, something told her that her hasty decision to avoid Latimer came from the wisdom of a full-grown woman, one with enough experience to know when she was swimming in choppy waters way over her head.

She'd dated quite a bit in San Francisco. She'd put plenty of hard stops on sexual overtures before, and she'd let a few of them unfold naturally when she was interested. It wasn't because Jacob Latimer had dared to kiss her that she felt the need to run. It was *how* that kiss had affected her, how it had left her spinning.

That, and the fact that his kiss was so hot and drugging it felt like she'd just participated in something excitingly illicit. When it came to Latimer, she had a feeling that was just the tip of the iceberg.

She mumbled a cursory thanks to the valet when he arrived with her car. It wasn't until after she'd left the locked-down Lattice compound and was driving down Lakeview Boulevard toward her townhome that she realized she hadn't tipped the valet.

A jolt of unease went through her and she glanced over at the passenger seat. She *couldn't* have tipped him, even if she'd wanted to. She'd left her purse on Latimer's terrace.

four

A few hours later, Latimer stood alone on the pier, watching the moonlight shimmer in the black water.

Harper McFadden was in Tahoe Shores. She'd just been in his home. Her lips had just been beneath his own, her body molded against him.

Harper.

Here.

Or she *had* been, anyway. Until he'd given in to an urge that had first germinated and swelled in him as a scrawny, malnourished thirteen-year-old boy. Who knew that an eighty-three-pound kid could have felt so much lust? So much longing? So much need?

Just so much. Period.

He hadn't known much of anything when it came to feelings twenty years ago. He'd known hunger and fear. And perhaps worry: a chronic, painful anxiety for the other helpless creatures that were forced to depend on a very undependable, violent man. If it weren't for a few of the dogs and Grandma Rose, he would have run away from his Uncle Emmitt in an instant. They were the only things that kept him tethered to that grimy, threadbare existence. In the case of Grandma Rose, Emmitt would surely have let his mother die from neglect if it weren't for Jake's reminders and cautious, subtle urging for visits, food, and money for medical care.

But he had left them all behind that summer of his thirteenth year. He'd abandoned the animals, a few of which had been his only friends. He'd forsaken Grandma Rose. He'd offered his life.

All of it, he'd risked for her.

It'd all come to nothing. She hadn't kept one of her promises. She hadn't written, even when he'd written dozens of letters and left various forwarding addresses. Of course, her solemn pledge to convince her parents to allow him to visit her in DC, her insistence that she'd find a way for them to be together again, had never played out. He hadn't been surprised about the visits. He'd been a hell of a lot more familiar with the cruel realities of life as a kid than Harper had ever been. The suspiciousness and fear he'd witnessed in her parents' eyes when they'd looked at him as Harper and he clung together on that cot in the tiny Barterton police station had driven that harsh truth home.

Those stupid, humiliating letters. A good majority of them he'd gotten back marked *return to sender*. Why hadn't he burned the damn things a long time ago?

So she didn't even remember him. Well, thank God for that.

But what if she did? What if her lack of recognition had been a performance?

Not a chance, he discounted abruptly. He doubted anyone could fake that blank expression in her eyes when she'd first looked up at him on the beach.

Of course that handful of days and nights hadn't meant to her what it had to him. She had been a cherished, prized child, adored and protected by her parents. Their time in the West Virginia wilderness together, their desperate flight for their lives, had faded into a dim, distant nightmare once she'd been returned to the haven of her parents' arms.

He'd faded from her life. Why did that fact hurt, when he wanted so much for it to be true? When he was so relieved that it *was* true.

He'd last seen her in the courthouse on the day of Emmitt's sentencing. She'd walked away within the anxious circle of her parents' arms, Harper looking over her shoulder while her parents urged her forward. Away from the nightmare . . .

She'd walked away tonight, too, despite the dazed fascination in her eyes, the yielding he'd felt in her body, the heat in her kiss. It was for the best.

It *definitely* was for the best. Why did he have to keep repeating that fact to himself?

He knew why.

Because *damn,* she'd grown up beautiful. Stunning. It didn't surprise him. She'd been beautiful, even at twelve years old. Her fresh luminosity had undoubtedly been what had first snagged Emmitt Tharp's dangerous attention. Even though she'd been a year younger than Jacob when they'd first met, she'd begun to develop. She'd looked older than him. To skinny little Jake Tharp, she'd been the ideal of perfection. Of cleanliness. Of a beauty so rare, it must by its very nature elude his grimy grasp.

He'd been ridiculously naïve. It was laughable in retrospect.

Still . . . Jacob didn't even smile as he stared out at the shimmering water. Somehow, seeing Harper McFadden was one of the most sobering things that had happened to him in a long, long time.

Her hair was a shade darker now, but the copper color was just as singular as it had been back then. He recalled how he'd stared at it with slack-jawed wonder when he first saw it as a boy. On the beach yesterday, when he'd had his first jolting encounter with her after two decades, she'd worn it in a high ponytail. Tonight, her hair had fallen in loose, sexy waves down her bare back. As he'd passed a window in his office, he'd caught a glimpse of it out on the terrace. The vision of her from the back had stopped him in his tracks. For a few seconds, everything had gone still and silent as he stared out the window, and his past and present had collided.

She wore a stunning aquamarine silk cocktail dress, the color echoing the alpine lake. He didn't need to see her up close to know it also matched her eyes. She was fair, like most redheads. The palette of her copper hair, flawless skin, and the sumptuous fabric of her dress created a feast for the eyes. Even from that distance, he'd had a graphic, potent fantasy of burying his nose in her hair, sliding his lips against her flawless, soft skin . . . gently biting the flesh of her fragrant shoulder.

When he'd noticed the thin, inch-long scar at the corner of her pretty mouth the other day on the beach, something had sunk like lead inside him. The small imperfection only highlighted the overall harmony and beauty of her face. Someone who carried that scar shouldn't have such an open, expressive countenance. They should be guarded and wary. It was a wonder to him that Harper wasn't.

He'd seen more beautiful women. He'd had them. Many of them. But he'd never seen a woman more desirable than Harper McFadden. *Still.*

He'd thought himself completely severed from Jake Tharp. He resented Harper, for making it so clear that boy was still alive inside him, still making him do things he'd regret . . . like suggesting to Cyril that he make a movie based on her story and offering to finance it. Like invite her here tonight, because he'd proved too weak to resist.

Like submit to the temptation of her pink, sexy mouth, fragrant hair, and soft skin.

His body hardened of its own accord at the piercing memory, making him frown. He'd wanted her so badly when he was a kid. He'd been so naïve, he hadn't even understood *how* he'd wanted her. How was it possible, that the unfulfilled desire of a thirteen-year-old boy could have such an effect on him now? It was as if Harper had reanimated that hungry child inside him. It was unbearable. Unacceptable. And yet . . . that hunger continued, gnawing at him like a dull ache.

"Jacob?"

The surprised call tore him out of his brooding. Elizabeth walked down the stone path that led to the dock.

"I assumed you were up in your suite," she said, sounding startled. He turned back to face the lake, distractedly listening to her footsteps approach. "I was just making sure that everything was cleared. All of the guests are gone. That is if . . . Did Harper McFadden go?"

"She's gone."

He sensed her hesitation, and realized belatedly he'd been sharp. He knew Elizabeth had seen him leave the terrace with Harper. She'd assumed Harper had accompanied him upstairs. Another spike of irritation went through him. Despite his self-lecture about how Harper's departure was for the best, he was still annoyed that she'd rejected him.

How contrary could he be?

"Well, I thought the night went well, anyway," Elizabeth said briskly, determined to ignore his brusqueness: just one of her many good qualities. "It was nice that you were able to attend for a bit. Stewart Overton called earlier. He wanted to confirm your meeting. He's taking a chopper in from Travis," she said, referring to Travis Air Force Base.

"Any news from Alex on ResourceSoft?"

"Everything is going smoothly with that, apparently. Fingers crossed, anyway. Regina Morrow just called, as well."

His head swung around. "Did she sound all right?"

"I think so. I mean . . . better than she has on other occasions, anyway."

Jacob nodded slowly, aware of Elizabeth's delicacy on the subject of Regina Morrow. Elizabeth and Regina had formed a friendship of sorts over the years. He told Elizabeth almost everything. As his primary assistant, Elizabeth saw to many details in regard to Regina's upkeep and care. But there were a few cards he held close to his chest, like the one relating to the nature of his and Regina's complicated relationship.

"It's late. I'll call her in the morning," Jacob said.

"I put a few faxes on your desk that came from Jenny, if you'd like to take a look at them before bed," she said. Jenny Caravallo was his secretary in San Francisco. Elizabeth knew he often took work to bed.

"It'll wait until morning. I'm taking a swim," he said, turning abruptly.

"Oh." She sounded surprised, and Jacob understood why. He didn't make a habit of taking midnight swims. "Do you need anything?"

"Nothing that some cold water and exercise won't cure. Make sure you don't activate the terrace security system. I'll do it when I go inside. Tell Tim to go. I'll call at the guard station when I go in for the night," he said, referring to Tim Stanton, a security employee who usually took nighttime watch at the rear of the property. He paused next to Elizabeth and met her stare. "I want complete privacy."

She blinked at his quiet adamancy.

"Of course. Whatever you need, Jacob."

"I'm sorry for being so brusque earlier. I have a lot on my mind. Thanks for staying late tonight. Why don't you take tomorrow off?"

"I have too much to do, you know that," she said with a smile.

"Then don't come in until noon. Relax a little."

"That's not necessary—"

"I insist. You work way too hard. Good night, Elizabeth," he said before he walked off the dock.

Harper was feeling restless.

Or maybe *reckless* was the right term.

After tossing and turning for an hour plus, obsessively reliving Latimer's kiss, and growing hotter and pricklier by the minute, she finally got out of bed. She hurried into yoga pants, tennis shoes, and a long-sleeved shirt. She twisted her hair into a sloppy bun. Not allowing herself to think of any motive past a soothing midnight walk to calm her nerves, she headed toward the lake.

In addition to a three-quarter full moon, the ground lights of several restaurants and private homes lit the beach. After several minutes of brisk walking, a distressing thought occurred to her. Her press pass was in the purse she'd left behind at Latimer's, along with her driver's license and credit cards. She needed the press pass, at the very least, for the mayor's press conference in South Lake Tahoe in the morning.

Maybe she could contact Elizabeth in the early morning, in order to retrieve it? But no, Elizabeth had never actually supplied her with any contact information.

She recognized the modern mansion to the right of her. It was Cyril Atwater's home. That meant the next property down the beach was . . .

Latimer's.

A moment later, she slowed as she neared the perimeter of the

Latimer compound. The huge, multileveled terrace of the mansion was sparsely lit and largely occluded from the shore by several tall pines.

Her purse would likely still be up there. She'd left it tucked in the corner of the couch, and it wasn't large. There was a good chance no one had noticed it during the post-party cleanup, especially since Latimer and she had been the only ones utilizing the upper level of the terrace. It was only yards away from her reach.

Couldn't she just pop up the stairs and get it?

That was her logic for tentatively approaching the first set of stone steps that led from the beach and dock to the pool level. Her rationalization was the sole thing on which she'd let herself focus. Her return had nothing to do with her regret for walking away from Latimer . . . with her irrational lust for a man she'd just met.

No. It was all about her press pass.

Her heart began to thump in her ears as she rose up the steps. She suspected an alarm might go off at any moment. A dozen guards might rush her. As much emphasis as Latimer put on security, surely there were motion detectors out here at the very least, if not video surveillance. She wasn't scared, though. Not precisely. She was tingling with something that felt like anticipation.

A splashing, trickling sound entered her awareness. She paused on the stone terrace, her breath stuck in her lungs.

The pale blue pool glimmered to the left of her, dimly illuminated by several perimeter lights. There was enough light for her to see that the trickling sound wasn't coming from the pool, however. The surface of the water was as smooth as blue glass.

A low, harsh groan cut through the hushed night. Harper jumped, air hissing out of her lungs. The sound had come from behind a cedar enclosure just to the left of her. The wall of the enclosure didn't reach all the way to the stone terrace. Beneath it, she could make out a gray mist and water splashing around a pair of muscular calves. As she watched, the solitary man parted his legs several inches, planting his feet. Another tense groan vibrated the still air.

She didn't tell herself to move. She was drawn irrevocably. Irrationally. Her heart now drumming furiously in her ears, she rounded the wall. It was a shower enclosure, a place to remove the sand after being on the beach.

Latimer was turned in profile to her, completely unaware of her presence. Steam from the running shower curled around long, muscular legs. Moonlight gleamed on the stretch of his wet, naked back and round buttocks. Water streamed down his shoulders and ridged abdomen. His muscles were pulled so tight, she had the random impression he was about to break from the strain. He stood with one hand bracing himself on the cedar wall, his head bowed forward, eyes clamped tight, his body coiled as tight as a spring.

His other hand fisted his cock.

He was furiously erect, his sex as long, hard, and intimidating-looking as the rest of him. He jacked himself with a forcefulness that both shocked and aroused her. Whatever rode him in those tense seconds, whatever desire commanded him, it was a savage, ruthless thing . . . and it pained him.

The realization must have made her make a sound of distress, because his head jerked around. His pumping arm froze. In a split second, his entire focus was yanked entirely from his single-minded search for release, and fastened onto her.

For a lung-burning few seconds, neither of them spoke. Harper wondered numbly if the air itself could catch flame.

"I'm so sorry. I forgot my purse."

Her lame words had no substance. They seemed to be incinerated to mist in an instant in the silent storm that hovered between them.

Slowly, he released his erection and removed his hand from the wall. He straightened and turned toward her. He stood tall. The moon, stars, and the pool lights dimly illuminated a good portion of his body. She could easily make out his cock springing out from between hard, strong-looking thighs.

"You forget a lot of things. Or maybe you just want to forget."

"What's that supposed to mean? Do you mean I forgot my purse on purpose?"

"No."

He took a step toward her. She became aware that her body was vibrating subtly, as if dual forces were doing battle inside her.

What the hell are you doing? Move. *Get the hell out of here.*

But his virility, his power, and his sheer beauty choked her. It chained her to the spot.

"I mean just what I said." He tilted his head slightly, and she saw the moonlight glint in his eyes. "I mean that you want to forget so many things. I can help you forget, Harper. You can help me forget some things, too. Maybe *that's* why you came back."

He held out his hand, beckoning her to him.

five

nstead of dipping into the pool after he left Elizabeth on the dock, Jacob walked out onto the beach, naked. He needed something to help him exorcise his brain of Harper, and a tepid pool wouldn't do the trick. The alpine lake was frigid, as usual. The round rocks interspersed with sand hurt his feet as he waded into the water. He was glad. It kept his focus from settling on anything but his discomfort.

He swam out far past the dock, his brain gratifyingly shocked into numbness by the cold water. By the time he surfaced beneath a midnight dome of stars, he'd warmed from the exercise, however.

He was once again subject to the unruliness of his mind and body.

He treaded water as the memory of Harper's body pressed against him, of her sweet, responsive mouth, swamped his consciousness. Again, he experienced that wild need to possess her . . . sink into her scent, drive into her body fast and furious. Just the thought of penetrating her—of even taking her in a simple missionary position—of her mouth beneath his, of his cock high and hard inside her . . .

It made him uncontrollably aroused. He stiffened with the vigor of a teenage boy.

It surprised him, because the simple fact was, he hardly ever bothered with simple, traditional sex anymore. Maybe he was depraved. He'd never really thought about it before, because his partners were in total agreement with his desire. He required a healthy dose of kink to stimulate him, nowadays. It was one of the downfalls of wealth. Women were willing to give him almost anything he wanted sexually.

At that moment, treading water beneath a spectacular midnight sky, he longed for something different, though. He wished he could again touch a woman like it was the first time, with the wondrous lust of a teenage boy.

He wished it wasn't just Harper McFadden that inspired that longing in him.

Besides . . . it wasn't as if he wouldn't enjoy the hell out of doing some grittier things to her as well: tying her up, pleasuring her. . . maybe taking her places she'd never been before, watching her as ecstasy tightened her beautiful face and she surrendered to him.

He couldn't do those things to Harper, though, as much as the idea tore through him and left stinging hunger in its wake. Not with his past, he couldn't. Not with Harper's. If others considered his sexual preferences sick, he could tolerate that. He never hurt a woman, and had enough experience to know that his partners were very well satisfied.

But exposing his sexual bent to Harper would also expose his vulnerability. With others, his preference for sexual domination had no history. No basis. It just *was*: an in-the-moment heat, a consensual hunger with no roots.

It'd be different with Harper. It'd be messy. It wouldn't be just a release of sexual tension, pleasure, and good-bye.

Would it?

The recalled sensation of how her breasts had felt crushed against him, the nipples defined and hard, rushed into his consciousness and tugged at his cock. She was larger than she had been when she was a girl, of course. To him, her breasts were perfect: large enough to make a man want to lose himself in them for hours, yet high and firm enough to accentuate her elegant, slender figure.

He plunged face-first into the cold water. Maybe it wouldn't be easy or simple to have her. But God, it'd be so fucking good. Besides, why was he so worried about his effect on her, his demands on her sexually? What had she done to deserve so much consideration on his part? She'd left him.

More importantly, she'd *forgotten* him.

A few minutes later, he gave up the fight. He submitted to his hunger, even if only in the safety of his mind. He stood beneath the hot spray of the poolside shower, his cock in his hand, his eyes clamped shut.

In his fantasy, they were in the forest, not another human being for tens of miles in any direction. There was no one to interfere, no one that had the power to stop them, to threaten their lives.

To separate them.

There was only Harper and him, and their need.

She looked up at him from where she lay on her back on a blanket, her blue-green eyes wide with anxiety, but also heat. And trust.

She was bound with rope, the black silk, twined strands a jolting erotic contrast to her pale, naked skin. He'd restrained her like he wanted her, so that her beauty was fully exposed to him. Nothing hidden. Nothing denied. Her feet were raised off the blanket, her knees bent in the direction of her chest, her legs spread wide. He'd restrained her so that her calves pressed tight against the back of her thighs. Her wrists had been bound to the outside of her thighs, displaying his strong, elegant rope work. He'd opened her to him completely.

The hair covering her sex was a dark copper, a few of the curls dampened from her arousal. The color of it was such a striking, erotic contrast to her white thighs. The vision of it drove him mad. He knelt and dipped his thumb into her cleft, rubbing her clit in a tight circle. She was wet and warm. He heard her whimpering in pleasure, but couldn't pull his gaze off the sight of her pussy.

Enthralled, he drew closer and fisted his heavy erection. He rubbed the swollen crown between her sex lips, wetting himself with her. This time, her groan made him look up at her face. She slicked the tip of her tongue along the seam of lips that were as lush and pink as her glossy, fully exposed sex.

"Please," she whispered. "Fill me up."

Unbearably aroused, his fantasy flashed forward to driving into the soft, tight clasp of her body and staring down at her as her cheeks flushed red and her lips formed his name.

"Is it enough for you?" he snarled. He was on fire, enraptured by the jolt of her firm breasts as he thrust into her furiously, entranced by her eyes. "Is my cock enough for your little pussy?"

"Yes. It's more than enough . . . it's so good," she managed, because in the fantasy, he took her harder. Faster, and her bound body rocked beneath him. She was his.

His for the taking. His to liberate . . . when he was ready.

In reality, his body flexed and strained as he jacked his cock with savage abandon. God, he needed this after seeing her tonight. Smelling her. Tasting her. As always, she was so close, and yet so far from him.

But not in his fantasy.

"You're mine. Mine to do with as I please."

"Yes," she moaned feverishly.

"I'm going to come. I can't stop it." He grimaced, deep in the grip of the graphic fantasy. "I'm going to come on your beautiful pussy and then rub myself on you until you're shaking right along with me." Because of course, in his fantasy, there was no condom to separate them. Not even that thin barrier was allowed between Harper and him in the fires of his mind. "Would you like that, Harper?"

"*Yes*," she moaned. But instead of sounding crazed and on the verge of climax, her acquiescence came out like a distressed whimper.

It stopped him dead in his tracks, ripping him out of his lurid fantasy.

His head jerked to the side. He saw the unmistakable, real-life form of Harper McFadden standing there, her body rimmed with moonlight. It'd been *her* whimper. *Shit.* He was held so fast in the grip of arousal that, for a moment, he wondered if his lust had somehow bidden her to him. The thought faded completely when he made out how pale and tense her face looked in the dim light . . . how stiff her posture was. Her gaze flickered downward over his body, and he became hyperaware of his throbbing cock squeezed tightly in his hand.

"I'm so sorry. I forgot my purse."

He hardly registered her words. Instead, he heard the tremor in her voice. He knew what it meant. It was Harper, after all. They'd always been connected. Perhaps his out-of-control lust hadn't called her here, but it did affect her now. Slowly, he released his erection and removed his hand from the wall. He turned away from the warmth of the shower toward her.

"You forget a lot of things. Or maybe you just want to forget."

"What's that supposed to mean? Do you mean I forgot my purse on purpose?" she asked, sounding a little offended. She also sounded breathless. And she wasn't avoiding looking at him. All of him. He could feel her stare on his cock.

"No."

Fuck logic. It was as if in that moment, there was only one possible direction to take when it came to Harper, and it had nothing to do with rationality. He took a step toward her. He sensed her unease as he took another step, but her feet remained planted.

"I mean just what I said. I mean that you want to forget so many things. I can help you forget, Harper. You can help me forget some things, too. Maybe *that's* why you came back."

He honestly wasn't sure if it was just bold, wishful thinking on his part, or an accurate guess at Harper's intent. He didn't have his true answer until he held out his hand, and she slowly walked toward him as if in a trance.

She was out of her mind. She knew it, but it didn't stop her from walking toward the naked, moonlit form of Jacob Latimer. Nor did it halt her from lifting her hand to meet his.

His fingers felt long and warm and wet enfolding her. The shower water must have been hot. She had the electrifying thought that he grasped her with the same hand that had pumped his cock so furiously a moment ago. A tremor of mixed arousal, anxiety, and amazement went through her. She touched his damp face, moved by something she sensed in him.

"Why are you so . . ."

"What?"

She blinked at his tense query. *Sad. Intense. Lonely?* She thought those things, but she didn't say them. How could she, when he was practically a stranger to her? Those weren't things someone thought about a stranger, let alone said.

He doesn't seem *like a stranger. Mysterious, exciting, forbidden . . . yes. But* not *a stranger.* She shook her head, bewildered.

"Shhh," he murmured, obviously feeling her shudder. He pulled her against him, his arms surrounding her. His heavy cockhead bumped against her belly, but he pulled her closer still. It slid up further against her stomach, the rigid column of the shaft sandwiched between them. His flesh steamed into her. He was so hard. So large. Everywhere. She pressed her lips against a damp, dense pectoral muscle. Without telling herself to do so, she slicked her tongue against his warm skin, gathering water droplets. He grunted softly and clasped the back of her head, his fingers burrowing into her upswept hair.

"That's right. Put your mouth on me," he whispered darkly from above her.

She encircled his waist with her arms and licked him again.

"Come here," he said, and he sounded almost angry, he was so tense. So primed. His hands cupped her chin from below, and he was lifting her for his consumption. His mouth covered hers, and she felt that rush of heat she'd felt earlier from his kiss. He must have felt that spike of electrical excitement, too, because his cock jumped between them.

He held her in place while his tongue pierced and stroked and discovered her. He drank from her with a fierce focus. Harper moaned shakily as she reciprocated, overwhelmed with flooding lust. She shivered and pressed closer to his heat. How could a man possibly taste so good?

"God, you taste good," he muttered against her upturned mouth a moment later, and she wondered dazedly if he'd read her mind. He plucked at her lips. "I'm going to taste you everywhere." Another shiver tore through her at his grim promise. One of his hands coasted down her spine, amplifying her quaking. "But right now, you're cold. We should warm you up."

"I'm not cold," she insisted, craning her neck to pluck at his firm mouth with her lips. How could she possibly be cold, standing next to him?

"Yes, you are," he growled, because she'd just gently scraped at his succulent lower lip with her teeth. He accepted her challenge, dipping his head and piercing her mouth again with his tongue. His kiss was firm. Forceful. Addictive. Their tongues tangled, and another shudder of purest arousal went through her. He broke their kiss and began to lift her shirt.

"I'm getting you wet. It's chilly out. Let's get under the shower. It's nice and hot."

He drew her long-sleeved cotton shirt over her head and tossed it to a dry part of the stone terrace.

"But will anyone see—"

"No," he cut her off. She looked up at his absolute answer. His face was shadowed as he looked down at her. His hands were at her back. Her bra snapped open. He stepped away from her slightly. His erection continued to jut forward, only the mushroom-shaped, fat cockhead pressing into her belly. With her shirt off, she could feel him more intimately, sense the soft skin stretched so tightly against the stony flesh beneath. His cockhead was the size of a small, firm plum. The place on her skin where it rested seemed to burn.

"No one is going to see you but me," he said as he drew the bra off her shoulders. He threw it in the direction of her shirt. "*No one* is going to interfere."

No one would dare.

He didn't say it, but she heard those words, anyway. His authority was absolute. His focus on her was total. His gaze never left her face. She stared up at him, enraptured as his big, warm hands cupped her breasts from below. His thumbs whisked over her nipples, tightening them. She bit her lip to keep from crying out as pleasure snaked through her. "Such a beautiful shape. So soft. I wish I could see you better."

His voice hypnotized her as he continued to play with her sensitive breasts, molding her flesh to his, rubbing and lightly pinching her nipples. "But feeling you is enough for now. It'll have to be, since I don't have the time or patience to take you to bed. Take off your shoes." Harper blinked. His tone had been clipped. A little harsh. Instead of being offended, her arousal mounted. She liked seeing the evidence of his need displayed large.

Kneeling, she untied her tennis shoes, removed them, and then stripped off her bootie socks. She stood and began to peel her yoga pants off, but Latimer came closer. He stepped between her feet, wedging her thighs apart with his leg, and jerked down on her pants. For some reason, the dominant stance he took, the way he parted her legs with his and pressed her mons against his thigh, sent a rush of warm wetness through her. He lowered both her underwear and pants below her ass. Then his hands were back, cupping her buttocks, molding them to his palms. She moaned shakily, because he was pressing her pussy against his hard thigh while he fondled her. It felt so good, she couldn't stop herself from circling her hips, getting friction on her clit. His response was to squeeze her flesh more forcefully.

"God you're gorgeous," he growled, and again, he sounded tense. Angry? Harper realized he *was* a little angry at that moment. Not at her, any more than she was at him. Angry that he couldn't control himself.

Any more than she could.

He grasped her buttocks, grinding her sex against his thigh for a thrilling moment. Then he muttered a curse, and bent, yanking down her pants all the way. She'd barely acknowledged him throwing the garments aside, then he was lifting her in his arms. Harper gasped in surprise at his abrupt move. He held her beneath her ass. Her clutching hands coasted up rock-hard, bulging biceps. Her arms instinctively circled his neck, her legs tightening around his waist.

He took several steps, and hot water was coursing down her back.

She *had* been cold, and just didn't realize it while under the spell of Latimer's hands and mouth. Her skin roughened at the contrast of the hot water against her chilled skin. Her throat vibrated in pleasure. Latimer caught her open mouth with his, capturing her cry. And again, she was drowning in him.

A moment later, he set her feet on the ground.

"I can't think straight when you kiss me," she mumbled distractedly, because he was still doing it, his mouth moving hungrily along her neck.

"I can't think straight when I kiss you, either."

"Why did you really ask me here tonight?" Her fingers delved into his damp, thick hair in a clawing gesture when he planted a hot kiss on her shoulder.

"I didn't ask you," he mumbled. "You came, like some kind of dream."

"No, I mean to the party."

"I don't know," he said against her skin. He gently bit at her shoulder muscle. She gasped and moved closer to him, pressing her breasts against his ribs. Water coursed around their bodies. His cockhead prodded her hip bone. He opened one hand at her back and stroked the length of her spine at the same moment he cradled a breast. His thumb found her nipple. She shivered. He rubbed her with the lubrication of the hot water. "Because of this," he said gruffly. He swept his open hand from neck to upper thigh, pausing to cup her ass. "This," he breathed against her upturned mouth.

She moved back slightly and found his cock with her hand. She closed around the rigid shaft. "This," she agreed, stroking his length. He didn't reply, but she'd felt the tension that leapt into his body at her touch. His face was shadowed as she stared up at him. Her lungs burned as her hand moved up and down on his wet cock. He felt wonderful in her hand, so hard. So vital. Maybe he was right. *Here* was a comprehensible truth, an amazing one: stark desire pulsing right in her hand. She slid down his rigid shaft and cupped his firm, shaved balls. She whimpered softly. *Jesus.* His masculinity was flagrant, even while the man himself was a shrouded enigma.

"Who *are* you?" she whispered dazedly, stroking his shaft to the succulent cockhead again, squeezing him firmly.

"Jacob Latimer. And that's all you need to know," he growled, and then was grabbing her wrist, pulling her hand off his cock. His demanding mouth silenced her sound of protest. He pushed his hand against her tailbone and kissed her deep, leaning over her so that her back bowed to accommodate his tall frame. He slid his hand over her ass, swooshing rivulets of water from her skin. He molded a cheek to his palm. Long fingers delved between her thighs. She started and moaned into his mouth when he surely found her slit and penetrated her with his forefinger. His rough groan twined with hers as he plunged in and out of her body. All the while, his kiss was deep, his taste delicious and dark.

Like she had earlier that evening when he kissed her, Harper recognized she was spinning. Slipping. Now . . .

. . . Free-falling.

This time, she was too far gone to save herself.

He hated to be out of control of himself. Despised it, in fact. But as he sunk his tongue into the taste of Harper McFadden and his finger into her warm, creamy clasp, he acknowledged that he *was*. Possessing her meant more than remaining safe.

His mind went blank with lust. His need rode him, goaded him, lashing at him. He'd almost come with her hand pumping and squeezing him. It was embarrassing. Humiliating.

It was like he was a stupid, fumbling teenage boy all over again.

He growled at the thought, angrily breaking the addictive kiss. He shifted his hand between their wet bodies, his fingers finding her cleft and her clit unerringly. She was gratifyingly creamy. At least he aroused her, even if she couldn't possibly be as worked up as he was. She cried out shakily, and he felt her muscles tense. His hand pressed; his fingertips circled and tapped out a demand into her flesh.

"You're going to have to come for me," he said.

"I . . . what? Why do you say it like that?"

"Because I'm about to come," he said, grim and bitter in his acceptance of the truth. She made a choking sound, and he knew that he'd confused her. But what else could he do, when he was as bewildered as she was? Despite it all, her hips gyrated firmly against his hand and she gasped in pleasure. There was so much to discover about her, so many things to relish. Yet here he was, bulldozing her into climax. As much as he hated the idea, he tensed with excitement at the prospect of feeling her shaking against him.

He lowered his head and brushed his mouth against her parted lips. Her soft moan enraptured him. Enraged him.

"You're as wet and warm and sweet as I imagined you'd be while I was jacking off a minute ago."

Her body trembled against him. Her hard, wet nipples poking against his ribs were a cruel reminder of all he was missing.

"You're not going to try to convince me you thought of me," she insisted shakily. He continued to agitate her clit while he plunged his middle finger into her pussy. She cried out sharply. He grasped a taut ass cheek and used it to apply a firm pressure for a counterstroke against his finger. "Oh God. Oh God, that feels good," she moaned, sounding incredulous.

He snarled in triumph when he felt the tension in her break. Warmth rushed around his finger. She tightened around him, shuddering against him. It was too much. He released her ass and clutched at his cock, stepping back to give himself room.

Everything went black as he pumped himself. Pleasure ripped through him, trumping everything else for a blessed moment: Logic. Mastery.

Shame.

When he came back to himself, it was to the sound of the water beating on the stone terrace and her soft gasps. One of his hands was buried between her thighs, his finger still high inside her. His other squeezed his cock furiously.

Moonlight and distant outdoor lighting allowed him to see her upturned face and her dawning expression of disbelief. Wonder? He jerked viciously at his cock one more time. More semen streamed onto her smooth, glistening belly.

This is what it all had come to. Jacob Latimer was back to the beginning, once again no better than that helpless boy, bewildered and laid bare with a need he couldn't comprehend, but which owned him, nevertheless.

He'd been dragged back against his will, back to those days and nights in the West Virginia wilderness, of moments of innocence and sweetness, of camaraderie and abiding trust, of the first knowledge of sexual hunger and jarring betrayal . . .

Of Emmitt Tharp. Of casual cruelty, and blinding fear.

Now he was going to have to make sure Harper continued to forget, even while he remembered with painful clarity.

2

make me TREMBLE

Harper stood there naked, panting, and completely undone. Her nerves still zinged following an intense climax wrought by Jacob Latimer's magical hand. But that wasn't what had her so overwhelmed and shockingly rearoused.

What had her so awestruck was witnessing his savage abandon as he'd found his own pleasure.

It'd really happened. All of it. Tension still seemed to roll off his body in waves. He'd jerked off, even as he'd nursed her through a powerful orgasm. Her stomach was wet with his semen. His cock was still clutched in his hand. She looked from his glistening sex to his shadowed face, stunned by how powerful the moment had been for her.

"I'm sorry," he muttered between uneven breaths.

"Why?" she asked, her voice hollow with amazement.

"For the rush."

"Oh," she managed, bewildered. Her impression of him from earlier that evening was that he was typically in consummate control. Unhurried. She didn't know him well enough to tell him that she'd found his raw, unchecked need arousing. *You don't know him at all, and yet you're wet with his come and his hand is pressed against your pussy and his finger is inside you.* The thought made her tighten around him. His head jerked up. He moved his hand subtly. Much to her horror, she moaned in reanimated pleasure.

She clearly *had* lost her mind.

"I guess it was all kind of . . . unexpected," she said, reconsidering the strange turn of events of the past half hour. Of the whole evening, for that matter.

68   Beth Kery

"You showing up here might have been unexpected. This wasn't," he said, again circling his hand on her sex for emphasis. She shivered.

"It wasn't?" she whispered.

"No. I thought I made it clear I wanted you," he replied quietly. "It *was* you I was thinking about, when you walked up. I had a head start on you."

Harper suppressed an urge to laugh. He sounded so calm, talking about something as intimate as being caught masturbating.

He released his cock. The crown brushed across her belly. Then he was turning her in his arms to face the showerhead. Harper started to question him, but then he stepped closer and reached around her. He used his hands to rinse his semen from her skin. It was a surprisingly gentle gesture, especially when she considered how raw and forceful he'd been as he'd brought himself to orgasm. It distracted her, the feeling of his hands and the flowing hot water, the sensation of his still-formidable cock pressing against her lower back, his balls next to the base of her spine. His last words repeated in her head.

"I'm the one who should be apologizing to you," she said, watching his dark hands glide across her stomach and ribs.

"Hmm?" He'd lowered his head. A shiver coursed through her at the low, rough rumble of his voice near her ear.

"I didn't even do anything."

"You exist. That's enough, trust me." Her cheeks heated at the warm amusement she heard in his tone. It'd been a potent compliment, genuine or not.

"I really did come to get my purse."

"If you say so." He reached around her and turned the tap, shutting off the shower.

"I couldn't have known I'd find you out here," she defended, turning because she'd sensed he'd moved away from her. Her mouth fell open at the moonlit vision of his gleaming, muscular back, powerful, long legs, and a mouthwatering ass. God, he was beautiful. Was it any wonder she'd been so uncharacteristically impulsive? He opened a cupboard, his actions once again unhurried and controlled. He turned toward her and she saw he held two towels in his hand.

"You could have come back in the morning," he said, handing her a towel.

"My press pass is in my purse. I have a conference in the morning. I needed it first thing," she replied, covering her body. He, on the other hand, didn't bother to hide his nakedness. He used the towel to briskly dry himself with one hand.

"What would you like to do now?" he asked after a moment, dropping the hand that held the bunched-up towel to his side.

"Do?" she repeated. To hide her confusion, she busied herself with fastening the towel above her breasts.

"Do you want to go? Or do you want to stay the night?"

She looked up slowly.

"Surely you'll give me another chance at this," he said when she didn't reply immediately. "You're not going to let *that* stand as my record." He waved vaguely in the direction of the shower.

This time she couldn't stop herself from laughing. He really was something. So cool and intimidating one moment and yet so self-deprecating the next. She warmed even more when his low chuckle twined with her own.

"You don't have anything to prove. I'm . . . quite satisfied," she said after a pause, a smile lingering on her lips. *Very* satisfied, in fact. *Very curious about what other secrets you hold, what other mysteries you might unlock in my body with the ease of a master thief.* She pushed the incendiary thought aside. A cool breeze rippled over her damp skin. The rush of humor and warmth had suddenly abandoned her.

"But . . . I really should be going. It's an early morning for me."

He nodded and quickly wrapped the towel around his lean hips. "I'll just go and get your purse, then."

Disappointment flooded her when he didn't persist in his invitation to stay. In his absence, she scurried to find her clothing. By the time he'd returned, she'd donned her socks, underwear, and pants, and was fastening her bra. It was as if with every garment she put on, the unreality of what'd just happened grew greater. She glanced up self-consciously when he returned, her clutch purse looking tiny in his big hand. She was glad for the cloak of semidarkness. He bent down and retrieved her shirt.

"Thanks," she murmured when he handed it to her. She shoved it over her head.

"I meant what I said. Before."

"What?" she asked, jerking her shirt down over her abdomen. He stepped closer, and she froze.

"I can make you forget some of your sorrows," he said. "For a little while, anyway. If you let me. What's the harm in that?"

Her mouth fell open.

"What?" he asked, obviously sensing her unease.

"This is weird," she replied in a rush.

She saw his brow furrow. "That I want you? That you want me?"

"No, not that," she said, flustered. She jammed her foot into one of her shoes. "I mean . . . I was told by someone that you usually don't . . . date local women," she explained, flushing at the word *date*. She hid her eye roll by looking down while she put on her other shoe. He didn't want to take her to dinner and a movie, for Christ's sake. He wanted her for the purpose of exchanging single-minded pleasure. Which sounded pretty damn exciting at the moment. The thought of his rigid face and bulging arms as he'd made both of them come a moment ago flashed into her mind's eye, stealing her breath.

"I don't." She looked up sharply. He'd stepped closer. "I don't like complications."

"And you don't think I'll give you any?" she wondered in amazement.

"I think in your case, the complications are unavoidable," he replied, his voice deep and rich and weighty in the still night air.

She realized he'd calmly extended his arm, handing her the clutch. She swallowed thickly and reached for it.

"What do you say, Harper?"

"I'll think about it," she muttered, head bowed.

His voice just now had sounded beguiling. Close. She didn't want him to kiss her again. She didn't want to give in to a powerful urge to kiss *him*. This whole situation was already murky and confusing enough without adding more of the intoxication of his mouth and touch into a serious decision. "Good night, Jacob."

She moved past him.

"Let me see you home, at least—"

"*No*," she said, biting her bottom lip when she realized how abrupt she'd sounded. She glanced back at him. His face looked shadowed from this angle. Had she offended him? "The beach is well lit all the way to my place. Good night," she repeated, feeling foolish. He didn't reply.

She flew down the stairs to the moonlit beach, highly aware of his stare on her back. Maybe it was her imagination—because she refused to look back to confirm it—but she had the distinct impression he watched her for her entire trip home.

The complications are unavoidable.

The thought kept reoccurring in his head as he lay in his bed later, moonlight spilling into his suite and onto his naked body. He'd already masturbated again, a fact that didn't surprise him at all.

He'd screwed up out there. That was a simple, unavoidable reality. The wise choice would be to avoid Harper altogether. If he couldn't see fit to be wise and restrain himself—which apparently, he couldn't— then his other choice would be to possess her completely . . . to get her out of his system once and for all.

Instead, he'd acted like an impulsive, clumsy teenager, getting so turned on by the feeling of her wet, supple body and the taste of her sweet mouth beneath his, he'd jerked off on her.

He grimaced at the exciting, embarrassing memory.

He'd given her the wrong impression of him.

Or had he?

Was that yearning, desperate kid really still alive in him?

Jacob didn't think so. But still . . . even though Jake Tharp was dead to him, he was having an effect on Jacob's present reality. Somehow . . .

It wasn't the first time in his life that he'd thought Harper McFadden was worth the complication. It probably wouldn't be the last. In the case of himself—Jacob—the complication was risking his exposure. His shame. His weakness.

For Jake Tharp, the stakes of getting involved with Harper had been even greater. In helping that girl so many years ago, Jake had risked nothing less than his own life.

seven

J ake woke up to the sound of the dogs barking furiously. His uncle, Emmitt Tharp, ran one of the largest dogfighting and gambling operations in the Appalachians. Emmitt's run-down house, barns, dog cages, and fighting rings were well hidden in the mountains and forest from the police.

There was no fight scheduled tonight, though; no dozens or hundreds of loud, drunk men arriving in their pickups or with the boat service Emmitt provided, which dropped off gamblers at nearby Shaker's Landing. The dogs had been alerted to something—or someone—on the property, though. Jake sat up on the thin mattress when he heard Jarvis, one of their more aggressive dogs, bawl extra loud.

Maybe the mountain lion that had prowled around the dog pens last summer had returned? If so, it'd be best to leave dealing with it up to Emmitt. Jake hated his uncle, and feared him more than anything he could imagine, but one thing was certain: Emmitt could handle a mountain lion. Emmitt Tharp was as lean, mean, and strong as the bred killers bawling right now out in the pens.

Word had it that Jake's father, Emmitt's older brother, Marcus, had been even taller and stronger than Emmitt, a rumor that fascinated Jake. He still doubted it, though. Emmitt was brutal, but he was still the most physically intimidating, fastest, and most fearless man Jake had ever known. His uncle was probably already shaking off his nightly whiskey drunk and reaching for his shotgun at this very moment.

But Jake heard no sounds emanating from the direction of the living

room, where Emmitt usually passed out every night in front of the television. His uncle must have really overdone it this time. Jake usually
made himself scarce once the bottle left the cabinet at around four
o'clock every afternoon. Hell, he made himself as invisible as possible
from Emmitt *all* the time.

Earlier that afternoon, Jake had tried to make an escape to the cave
to avoid his yelling and his heavy hand for a few blessed hours. Emmitt
had been unusually aware today, however, grabbing Jake by the too-
long hair at his nape when he'd tried to slink silently out the back door.

"You're not sneaking off anywhere to play whatever games you
play all alone. I'm starting to think you're a little faggot. Probably
dolls you're playing with out in them woods," his uncle had said
around a wet, sagging cigar.

This was a new bullying theme Emmitt had taken a liking to since
Jake turned thirteen: insinuating he was gay because he was five foot
two and skinny as a rail.

Using his hold on Jake's hair, Emmitt shoved all eighty-three
pounds of him. Jake flew across the worn wood floor of the living
room, landing with a thud against the wall. He scrambled to his feet
quickly, ignoring his pain, so that Emmitt wouldn't find him in that
vulnerable position. Jake prayed daily for a bigger, stronger body so
that he could start to defend himself against his uncle . . . but was
starting to worry it'd never happen. He'd be weak and helpless forever.

"You get on back to your room and don't come out until tomorrow. If you do, I'll make you sorry. You know I will."

"But I gotta see to Mrs. Roundabout."

"You don't need to worry about that born cold bitch. She's done
for. Only use she has is to train the other dogs on her."

Terror had shot through Jake's veins at that. Mrs. Roundabout had
suffered multiple puncture wounds, severe bruising, and a shattered
thighbone in a recent fight. A pit bull's jaws were lethal, horrible
weapons. Dogfights were brutal, and not primarily because of the
dogs' savagery. In Jake's unvoiced opinion, the true offenders were the
men who got off on the violence.

He'd been terrified when Emmitt had declared two weeks ago that Mrs. Roundabout would go in the ring. It'd been nearly two years since the frisky brown and white puppy had been unfortunate enough to be brought onto Emmitt's property. Jake had hid his bond with the dog as best he could but his efforts were useless—just like most things were when it came to caring about something in the vicinity of Emmitt Tharp.

After the fight, Emmitt had left Mrs. Roundabout to heal, suffer, or die. Each was the same to him. But Jake had silently set up a bed of sorts for her in one of the barns and was tending her as best as he could with limited supplies. At the edge of his awareness loomed the idea that he was just prolonging the dog's agony, but he refused to give up hope. Emmitt hadn't interfered with Jake's doctoring of Mrs. Roundabout until now, mostly because the situation had been beneath his notice. But he'd just called Mrs. Roundabout *cold*, which meant Emmitt believed she was born not to fight. Emmitt had no use for a cold dog . . . except to use her as a patsy for the other dogs to sic on, to nurture their killer instinct for the ring.

"She's not cold," Jake insisted, knowing the only way he could try and save Mrs. Roundabout's life was to defend her as a worthy contestant for the ring. "You saw her fight—"

"I saw her cower and whimper, just like you. No wonder you like that bitch so much. Two of a kind," Emmitt had bellowed, shoving Jake toward the hall. "Get back in your room and stay *put*. Don't you come out, even for food, until I say so. Hear?"

Jake had known better than to argue. Sometimes Emmitt got like this when he was planning some kind of dirty deal—a drug or a weapons exchange. Emmitt's illegal endeavors spread far beyond dogfighting. Or more correctly, dogfighting, by its very nature, drew in a variety of ugliness and crime.

His room had been sweltering hot. He'd drowned in his own sweat, lying on his bare cot. He'd found a book abandoned at a campsite three miles through the woods—*Dune*. He'd reread it thirty-one times now, and guarded it like a religious icon. Usually, he reserved all his reading for the public library in Poplar Gorge. If Emmitt saw a book in his room, Jake cringed to think of the shit he'd get.

But it was too hot to focus on reading tonight. Luckily, he'd brought a glass of water into his room last night, or he might have dehydrated. With nothing to do in the nearly empty room, he'd eventually fallen asleep.

Only to awaken hours later to the sound of the dogs barking in excitement . . .

He heard the scuffling sound of footsteps near his window and flew out of bed. Cautiously, he peered around the wooden frame of the curtainless, dirty window. It was a clear night with plenty of star shine. He saw the unmistakable outline of Emmitt's tall, powerful form walking toward one of the barns. There was a pack or bag of some kind thrown over his shoulder. As Jake watched, a slender, pale forearm fell from the bag. The hand hung limply in the empty air, the fingers unmoving. A sick feeling rose in his stomach.

Oh no. Not again.

Anxiety shot through him at the recollection of finding another girl once, two summers ago. Afterward, he'd prayed it'd only happen that one time. He'd hoped Emmitt would never venture into this particular scheme for profit again. Wasn't it bad enough that he abused and took advantage of animals the way he did? Now he was going to subject innocent human beings to his, and other men's, sick appetites?

But fear shot through Jake's veins for yet another reason. Emmitt had gone batshit crazy when he'd found out Jake had seen and spoken to that other girl two years ago. He'd promised to kill Jake, and Jake believed wholeheartedly he'd do it. Emmitt had held him down on the barn floor and nicked his tongue with his huge buck knife, ranting about how he'd cut his tongue out completely before he killed him if he ever uttered a word to anyone about seeing that first girl.

And now, here was another one.

What if she was dead?

No, Emmitt had as much use for a dead female as he did a cold dog.

An icy sweat broke out over his body despite the fact that it was probably ninety degrees in his tiny, unventilated room. He may not get the exact specifics, but he understood now more than he had when he'd been eleven years old and discovered that first girl. He knew what rape was from the sly, ugly innuendo of not only the adult men who were drawn to Emmitt's place, but his experience at Poplar Gorge Junior High. Boys could be graphic, even if most of his idiotic classmates didn't understand a tenth of what they were talking about.

Whatever his uncle had in store for that female was the stuff of nightmares. He knew about sex and breeding, not only from living with dogs and in the middle of the woods surrounded by nature, but from his uncle and other men who attended the fights. Prostitutes were often brought in on fight nights—rough-spoken, hard, usually drug-addicted women that Jake regarded with mixed distrust, pity, and disgust. He'd heard the disturbing exchanges between those women and men in the woods or out on the landing in the darkness of night. Whatever his uncle had in mind for that female with the slender hand, it somehow involved turning her into one of those pitiful women.

Where'd Emmitt nabbed her from? Surely his uncle couldn't have been so bold as to snatch her from nearby Poplar Gorge, the town where Jake sporadically attended school. He hadn't known at first where Emmitt had gotten that first girl. Later, after doing some research at one of his favorite sanctuaries, the Poplar Gorge Public Library, he'd found out. There'd been several newspaper articles on the kidnapping in the *Charleston Gazette*. She'd been taken from a campground ten miles down the river.

She'd never been found by the police, that Jake knew.

Could he possibly scout out a couple of the campgrounds in the morning? If there was news of this new missing girl, maybe he could somehow leave a hint as to where she was before Emmitt transferred her elsewhere?

Don't think about it. Block it from your mind. There's nothing you can do.

Jake couldn't help that girl any more than he could save the other one two summers ago. And he couldn't save Mrs. Roundabout from what was going to be an agonizing, painful death from her injuries no matter how much he tried to doctor her. Emmitt reminded him several times a day of how useless he was. He couldn't save *himself* from Emmitt. How could he possibly save anyone else?

Nevertheless, he didn't go back to bed that night. The memory of that small, motionless hand haunted him. For some reason, he needed to see the face of its owner.

He waited until he saw Emmitt leave the south barn and lock the doors with a heavy chain and padlock. He pretended to sleep as he listened to Emmitt's heavy tread approach the house.

Eventually, even the dogs his uncle had put into the south barn to guard the girl quieted their bloodthirsty barking. Jake waited until the sky over the trees turned a pale gold.

Dawn was for the clean of spirit. That's what his Grandma Rose liked to say. Jake knew from experience it was the period when Emmitt slept the deepest. He also knew dogs that had been given an excessive amount of blood and meat often slipped into a deep sleep afterward. Jake suspected Emmitt had given the guard dogs just that, not only to gain their cooperation and temporarily silence their bloodlust, but to amplify their murderous hunger upon awakening . . .

Moving with the silence of an experienced eluder, Jake snuck into the kitchen and opened a cabinet, searching for food. He slipped out the back door and across the grounds to the south barn. He could pick the lock his uncle had put on the door. Being a prisoner of sorts himself, Jake had learned long ago how to open every lock Emmitt owned on the property. But he hesitated. The clanking sound of the chain sliding through the clasp was a risk. It might awaken the dogs. Or Emmitt.

But he knew of other openings and secret places. He was small enough and agile enough to slip through them.

As he climbed to the highest branches of the old maple at the back of the barn, the sun's rays shone through the top of the tree line and pierced the thick foliage. Ignoring the forty-foot drop below him, he shimmied out onto a narrow limb. There were *some* advantages to being skinny . . . although this trusty branch was bending more and more with his weight each passing summer.

Clinging to the limb like a leech, he reached his goal: a window in the hayloft used for ventilation. It was too small for even him to crawl through. The tiny glass pane was intact. It was open as far as the hinge would allow.

He peered inside the window. The maple tree was now ablaze with first morning light, and it was hard to adjust his eyes to the darkness of the interior barn. Suddenly, there was a flash of brilliant copper in his eyes, and a face appeared in the window. He started back in surprise. He and the girl were only inches apart. Her skin was pale, but reddened. She'd been crying. The next thing he became aware of was her eyes. They were huge and the color of the sea—or at least that's what he imagined, never having seen an ocean or sea. He recognized what he saw in her eyes from firsthand experience, on the other hand.

Pure fear.

She opened her mouth, but he put his finger to his mouth in an urgent hushing gesture.

"The dogs," he mouthed, barely a whisper leaving his lips.

"He said they'd kill me," she whispered, and he saw the wildness in her eyes. Jake knew the layout of the barn. Emmitt had put the girl in the loft and stationed some of their more vicious dogs at the bottom of it. Emmitt hadn't been boasting. Those pit bulls would tear her to pieces if she tried to escape.

"The dogs won't kill you," he whispered, straining to sound confident when he wasn't. Instinctively he understood that she verged on panic. If she started screaming, it'd waken the dogs, and his uncle in turn. "Stay calm around them. Keep your fear boxed up tight. It'll only make them more aggressive if they sense it."

"Who are you?" she whispered after a tense pause, in which Jake realized he'd been gawking at her hair. The sunlight was setting it ablaze, and it was so pretty.

"Jake," he mouthed.

"Get me out of here, Jake. I want to go back to my parents." Her soft whimper and trembling, pink mouth sliced through him.

"I can't," he whispered. Her desperation was so palpable, it felt like a weight on his chest.

"You have to," she insisted, those blue-green eyes going fierce.

"I *can't*. He'll kill me," Jake whispered. Wild to do something, he clawed in his jeans pocket. "Here. I brought you some Pop-Tarts," he said, holding up the package triumphantly. "They were from my grandma Rose's groceries, but I don't think she'll notice if a few are missing. They aren't good for her heart anyway, but she loves them so much, I talk Emmitt into getting her some once in a while . . ."

She stared at him like he'd gone mad. He realized how lame his offering was, given the direness of her situation. It struck home again just how lame *he* was. How inadequate.

"He tied my hands behind my back so I wouldn't try to get down the ladder," she whispered. She blinked the tears welling in her eyes. He felt himself dying a little inside.

"Oh."

"But I am hungry. And weak," she added.

"I'll feed it to you," he whispered. He ripped open the paper package. "Come closer," he directed. She came nearer, and the sunlight fully illuminated her face. There was a sprinkle of light freckles on her nose. He saw the mottled bruise on the left side of her forehead. It stood in such contrast to her pretty face and pale, smooth skin. He paused in the action of extending his hand.

Anger pierced his helplessness. He recognized Emmitt's handiwork. She was staring hungrily at his hand, which held the Pop-Tart. She parted her lips, and he got ahold of himself.

He shimmied out farther. The limb dipped alarmingly. Her eyes went wide.

"'S okay. It'll hold," he assured. He held out his hand and it crossed the pane of the window. She craned her neck and took a large bite out of the Pop-Tart and, without chewing, bit off another. She *was* hungry. When had Emmitt taken her? Had it been before she'd had her evening meal? Or were fear, adrenaline, and her injury responsible for her sharp hunger? He wanted to ask her, but her mouth was full as she demolished the Pop-Tart. Then, when she slowed down a little, something else preoccupied him.

Her even, small white teeth and pink mouth.

The Pop-Tart almost gone, he extended his thumb and forefinger with the last bite. Her lips brushed against his skin as she nabbed it. Pleasure tingled through him. Her gaze darted to his face and she abruptly ceased chewing. Had she felt it, too?

"You have to get me out of here," she whispered after she'd swallowed the last of the Pop-Tart with effort.

"What's your name?" he asked.

"Harper. Harper McFadden. He hit me when I was in the showers at the campground."

"Which one? Which campground?" he added when she just stared at him blankly.

"I don't know the name. It's on the river. My parents are Philip and Jane McFadden. Go to the police and tell them I'm here!" she hissed, the idea seemingly enflaming her.

"I can't do that," he whispered, thinking intently. "Town is too far away. He might have moved you by the time I got there."

"You have to do *something*," she insisted. A tear spilled down her cheek. She clenched her eyelids shut. He sensed her misery. "He . . . he took off my clothes. I'm . . ."

Her face collapsed. She couldn't bring herself to say it. Her mortification at her nakedness and vulnerability, the stark evidence that she'd been robbed of her basic dignity, made something new and unexpected happen inside Jake. His anger at her mistreatment at the hands of his uncle made him go cold . . .

Cold and hard.

He *did* have to do something.

She'd lost herself to distress. Her eyelids remained clamped but a few tears escaped down her cheeks. She was holding her breath. He recognized that she was trying to contain her fear and admired her for it. He sensed her terror, and it was huge, but she was fighting it like crazy.

"Breathe, Harper," he prompted firmly. Her eyelids remained squeezed shut. He stretched his arm and touched her damp cheek. He felt a tremor go through her. Her shimmering eyes locked on him.

"Okay. I'm going to get you out of here," he said. "But you're going to have to wait here for a few hours. There are some things I'm going to have to do to make this work. When I do come to get you, you're going to have to do *exactly* what I tell you to."

"I don't want to stay here alone. Get me out of here *now*," she pleaded in a shaky whisper.

He steeled himself. "You *have* to. I'm sorry. If I don't put a plan in place, Emmitt will catch us in about two hours flat after he wakes up, probably less. The only way we're going to get you back to your mom and dad is if you stay strong and *stay put*. You're safe, for now."

"What are you going to do?" she whispered as he started to inch back on the limb.

"Lay a false trail. Then sedate the animals. All of 'em. Including my uncle," he replied before he shimmied backward on the branch.

Present Day

Jacob jerked on his bed at the still-vivid memory, his hand thumping on the luxurious, cool bedding.

So different, Jake Tharp from him.

He wasn't sure what drove him to do it, but he switched on a lamp and rose from the bed. He entered his large closet. Behind stacks and stacks of glossy shoe boxes, he found what he was looking for. He pulled down the ragged, faded Converse All Star box and walked with it back to the bed. He tossed off the lid and picked up a folded piece of notebook paper, a feeling of mixed sadness, pity, and irritation going through him at seeing the scrawl.

Harper,

How's it going? Do you like the seventh grade? I hope math isn't as bad as you were worried it'd be. It's been so hot here, they might as well have just extended our summer vacation. Kids' brains don't work in this kind of weather. Billy Crider got sent home because he kept falling asleep in science, and about six detentions and threats of more wouldn't wake him up any. You probably have air-conditioning in your school at Georgetown, right? The heat sure hasn't been good for Grandma Rose, either. She's been pretty weak, and she hasn't hardly eaten anything but half of a Pop-Tart once in a while. I know I should give her something healthier, but it's the only thing she'll eat except for some crackers once in a while. It'll be okay, though. Weather forecast says it'll get cooler next week.

    I started reading The Hobbit, *since you said it came before* Lord of the Rings. *I feel like I already read* LOTR, *though, because you told me every detail of it. Remember? That night in the cave?*

    Hope I'll get a letter from you soon. Thought I'd have one by now, but the mail service to Grandma Rose's isn't that great. I'm looking for an after-school job. If I get one, maybe I'll get a P.O. box so I'll be sure to get all your letters.

    I guess you must know how much I miss you.

Jake

A sharp pain of longing went through him. Longing for what, he couldn't say. He refolded the piece of notebook paper and shoved it back in the Converse box. He sprawled back on the bed.

She'd never written. Not even one letter.

Despite his bitterness at that, Jacob knew Harper would always be special to him. That was a given, even if there hadn't been a flicker of recognition in her eyes when she looked at him today.

He hadn't realized it as a kid, but Jacob recognized it now twenty years later in spades. The moment Jake had made the decision to free Harper McFadden had been the precise moment he'd saved his own life.

eight

Harper plunged into work the next day, glad for the mayoral press conference and the tangible bit of news that came from it. It helped, having something to focus on beyond the bewildering, mind-blowing memory of what had happened on Jacob Latimer's moonlit terrace last night. Being in South Lake also helped her avoid the newsroom, Ruth Dannen, and her prying questions. It did until two o'clock that afternoon, that is.

"Well? What's the news from the king's palace?"

Harper looked up from her layouts. Ruth leaned inside the doorway of Harper's office.

"Nothing really," Harper said levelly, glancing back to her layouts. For some reason, she felt a need to protect Jacob Latimer. Or maybe she just felt the need to hide her outlandish behavior on his terrace last night.

"Did you figure out why they asked you?" Ruth persisted, stepping into Harper's office.

Harper exhaled in mild frustration. Ruth wasn't going to be easily shaken. Might as well spoon out a small measure of the truth. "I did, in fact. As it turns out, Latimer was a fan of a feature I did at the *Chronicle*—the one about Ellie and the homeless children of San Francisco? He'd mentioned it to Cyril Atwater—"

"The director?"

Harper shrugged sheepishly and nodded. "I'd never heard of Atwater until last night."

"I'll bet Cyril loved *that*," Ruth said, smirking. "That man has an ego the size of Texas."

"You know him?"

"Sure, Cyril is another one of our local celebrities. He gives me an interview once a year about his latest film project. Go on."

"Well, apparently Latimer mentioned my story to Atwater in regard to making it into a film, and Atwater loved the idea," she said, hoping to bring the conversation to an end. "I'm going to call Ellie about it. It's completely up to her whether or not she'd want her life put on film."

"That's it?" Ruth asked when she shifted her attention back to her layouts. "Who else was at the party?"

"I really only met Atwater. And Elizabeth, of course."

"What about Latimer? Did he make an appearance?"

"He did, in fact," Harper said nonchalantly as she did a markup. "A brief one."

"*Well?*" Ruth demanded. "Give me details, the dirtier the better."

"I haven't got much to tell," Harper eluded. "The chardonnay was excellent. I caught a glimpse of the bottle. Apparently, Latimer has his own label."

"He owns a small winery in Napa."

"The terrace was fantastic, and so was the house. There was a jazz band." Ruth looked like she wanted to bite her head off for giving such boring details. Harper hid a smile. Thankfully, her phone started to ring. She reached for it, but Ruth put her hand on the receiver, halting her.

"Did you speak to him? If not, to whom did Latimer talk? How long did he stay? What was his mood like? What was he wearing?"

"What was he *wearing*? Seriously?"

"The juice is squeezed from every detail, no matter how small."

"There isn't any *juice*. I told you, he only showed up briefly." She shooed the other woman's hand from her phone, scowling pointedly at her as she picked up the receiver.

"*Sierra Tahoe Gazette*, Harper McFadden speaking."

"Hi."

A shock went through her. She blinked, her gaze darting to Ruth. Ruth's expression segued slowly from irritation to dawning curiosity.

"Hi," Harper managed after a pause.

"I hope you don't mind me calling you at the office. I'm often told I'm not a patient man," Latimer said.

She picked up her cup, taking a sip of cold coffee in an attempt to look normal. "What is it you're so impatient about?" she prevaricated.

"Your answer."

"Oh. Yes, that. I haven't spoken to Ellie yet."

From the corner of her vision, she saw Ruth place her hands on Harper's desk and lean in.

"That isn't the answer I was referring to."

She felt a flickering sensation in her lower belly at the sound of his low, compelling voice. She glanced up at Ruth, who was watching her like a hawk.

"It's more complicated than you're assuming," she said, her manner brisk and professional.

"Is there someone there?"

"Absolutely."

"Okay, I'll make this brief. I'm picking you up at your place for dinner tonight. Six thirty? Does that simplify things for you?"

"I wouldn't say that," Harper said, squinting at her layout and making a nonsensical change.

"Yes. Well, like I said last night, some complications are unavoidable. Say yes."

"Yes?" she muttered, confused momentarily as to what he meant.

"Perfect. I'll see you at six thirty. Dress casual."

"But—"

The line went dead.

"Who was—"

"Not now, Ruth," Harper said more sharply than she'd intended, slamming down the receiver. She gathered up several papers from her desk in a random fashion. "Excuse me. I have to see Sangar."

She glided past a furious-looking Ruth.

. . .

As the clock inched toward six thirty that evening, Harper grew increasingly anxious. Latimer had said to dress casual, but what did that mean, exactly? Casual as in taking a lakeside stroll, or casual as in going to a classy, but easygoing restaurant. Plus . . . her townhome was in a gated community. He had to call to be buzzed in, and he didn't have her cell phone number or her residence number. Of course, she still had no way to reach *him*, so she was stuck.

She shouldn't have let him bulldoze her into making a decision.

It's just dinner, she thought as she stared at herself in the mirror. *You don't have to make any huge decisions—like about whether or not you want to have a physical affair with a gorgeous, mysterious, complicated male—until you're good and ready.*

She'd finally decided that a silvery gray, button-down maxi-dress along with a soft, cropped pink sweater in deference to the recent cool evenings, could be interpreted as casual. She wasn't showing much skin, which was good. Although did the sweater accentuate her breasts in a manner that perhaps Latimer would think was intentionally provocative?

Was she being provocative?

Her uncertainty on that topic loomed large.

Her doorbell rang as she began to unbutton the pink sweater in preparation to change it. Flustered, she refastened it and hurried to find her purse.

By the time she jogged downstairs and got to the front door, she was breathless. The sight of Latimer waiting patiently on her front porch made it even harder to get air into her lungs. Did one ever get used to looking at him?

His short hair was sexily mussed. There was an evening scruff on his lean jaw. He wore a cobalt blue shirt with the sleeves rolled back, a pair of worn jeans that fit his long legs and narrow hips with a casual, sexy perfection, and a pair of deck shoes. His hands were in his pockets. Harper's gaze stuck on the vision of his bare, strong-looking, hair-dusted forearms.

She realized uncomfortably that he hadn't spoken, either. He'd been checking her out like she'd been checking him out, his sharp, hazel eyes moving slowly down the length of her. Did his stare linger on her breasts? He seemed so solemn, despite the male heat in his eyes. Latimer's brand of appreciation was unlike any other she'd experienced before. By the time he met her stare, only a few breathless seconds had passed, but he'd managed to make her breasts feel conspicuous and tingly, and a warm, pleasant ache to expand in her core. She recalled vividly what it'd been like to have him touch her, and found herself craving the feeling of his skin against hers.

She cleared her throat. "How did you get in?" she asked, forcing a smile.

His eyebrows arched. "I'm not 'in' yet," he replied, deadpan, nodding at the threshold and then at her, his eyebrows quirked slightly.

She laughed and stepped back, waving him into her townhome. He moved past her and she shut the door behind him. "No, I meant how did you get past the gate?"

"I came from the lake, not the road," he said, glancing around her foyer and peering into her distant living room. He looked especially tall and striking in the familiar setting. And he smelled *good*.

"This is nice," he said.

"Thanks. Do you want to look around a little?"

He nodded and she led him into the great room, which was a large, airy space that included her kitchen, dining area, and living room. "It came fully furnished, so I don't know how much it actually represents me yet."

"Yet? Does that mean you plan to redecorate? Plant roots in Tahoe Shores?"

"I'm not sure," she admitted. "This whole thing with me taking this job has been a sort of . . ."

"An unexpected detour off the main road?" he finished for her when she trailed off.

"Yeah, I guess you could say that." She met his stare and found herself lost there for a moment. He had the longest lashes. The dark ring around the outside of his iris highlighted the complex, fascinating color of his eyes. His gaze had an almost hypnotic quality on her. No . . . it wasn't that. It evoked the opposite of the hazy, dreamy quality of hypnosis. She knew that from experience. Instead, Latimer's stare was almost alarmingly alert. It seemed to slice down to the heart of her.

Also: His mouth was indecently sexy. When she looked at it, she couldn't help but think of him doing *things* with it.

"I'm not usually so impulsive," she found herself saying. "Any detours I take are usually well thought-out and planned." His lips twitched slightly.

"Then it's not much of an adventure, is it?"

She laughed and tore her gaze off his face. "I suppose that's what you think I should consider you as well?" she asked, trying to make light of things. "An adventure?"

"Would that help?" His low, mellow voice seemed to caress the side of her cheek and neck.

"I'm not very good at adventures."

His hand enclosed hers. She glanced up at him in surprise.

"That's okay. I am." His eyebrows arched. He gave her that small, heart-knocking smile that always struck her as sweet and mind-bogglingly sexy at once. "I'll keep you safe, Harper."

For a few seconds, she just stared at him, a sense of strong familiarity going through her again. She gave an anxious laugh.

The confusing thing was, she had the strangest feeling that he hadn't been teasing her at all. That in fact, he'd just uttered a solemn promise.

He really *had* arrived by water. He led her to her townhome association's pier and a huge moored black-and-white boat. She recognized it as one of the two boats that had been tied to buoys last night at his home.

"I hope you don't mind dinner on the water," he said, leaping gracefully onto the boat and turning to extend his hand to her.

"No, that'd be great," Harper assured, her feet landing on a polished wood deck. She looked around the boat while he unfastened the moorings with quick precision. He was obviously very comfortable on the water. She enjoyed boating, but had never been on a craft this large. Strangely, although it was enormous compared to a typical motorboat, its sleekness and aerodynamic design made her think of speed. "Is this a yacht?" she asked him when he approached her again.

"A small one. But it's unique because it's deft and fast, as well. It was specially made for me by a man I know. I liked the design so much, I decided to go into business with him," Jacob said, his tone making it seem like it was a common, everyday practice for him to start a new company.

Which maybe it was, Harper mused.

He reached for her hand. Harper liked not only that he did it, but that he made the gesture seem so natural. Not only on his part. On hers. It felt nice, feeling his hand enclosing hers. Comfortable, and yet thrilling at once.

He led her up some stairs. Harper counted four separate levels on the small yacht. She noticed another flight of steps going downward from the main deck. She caught sight of a salon of sorts with indoor and outdoor seating, then on the next level—miraculously—a small outdoor pool and cabana. Jacob took her all the way to the top level, where he guided her over to an open-air bridge. He settled behind the controls. Harper sat in the leather chair next to him.

They didn't talk as he maneuvered the craft away from the pier and then slowly took it out of the small harbor. The bridge had a lot of high-tech and sonar equipment that Harper couldn't make heads or tails of, but it was clear Jacob was completely at home. She settled in her chair, surprisingly okay with the silence between them.

They left the harbor behind and soared into a gorgeous Tahoe evening. The lake sparkled and flashed in her eyes, the brilliant azure color a striking contrast to the dark green, pine-covered mountains, the pure blue sky and the white wispy clouds. She liked watching him handle the craft even more than admiring the stunning scenery. She kept stealing glances at his solemn profile and his agile, comfortable movements as he navigated the craft. Her gaze kept sticking on his strong-looking hands. She thought of what he'd done to her with those hands on the terrace last night—what he'd done to himself.

She turned her hot cheeks into the fresh breeze, cooling her flash of embarrassment and lust.

"I thought we could anchor at Emerald Bay for our dinner," he said, speaking loudly over the sound of the engine and water rushing against the boat.

"That'd be nice," she said, gathering her windblown hair at her nape. He did a double take, and she realized she was smiling broadly.

"You like the water," he stated more than asked.

"I do, very much. So do you, obviously. How long have you liked boating?"

"I was around water and fishing boats my whole life, but when I was about fifteen, I moved to a place that was on a lake," he said, keeping his profile turned to her as he steered. "I met a man there—a neighbor—who kind of took me under his wing and taught me how to drive his boats. He had a whole collection of motorboats, sailboats, and Jet Skis. I started working for him after school and in the summers. When I got a little older, he'd let me and my friends take his boats for water-skiing and camping trips."

"Nice neighbor."

He shrugged, his mouth going hard. Did he look bitter at that moment? "He got more than his share of work out of me in return." He glanced over at her. "I should have warned you so that you could have brought something for your hair. Do you want to go below until we anchor?"

"No," she said steadfastly. "It's too nice up here."

He returned her smile. She ducked her head, finding her purse on the deck next to her. "Besides, I have a hair tie in here," she mumbled, very aware of the continued heat in her cheeks. They'd flamed up again at his smile.

She told herself it was the speed of the sleek craft and idyllic evening that had her giddy as they flew across the cerulean blue lake, but she wasn't convinced. She knew the reason for her intoxication was one hundred percent him.

"It must be so incredible," Harper murmured dreamily.

It was an hour and a half later and she cradled a nearly empty glass of chardonnay while gazing out at the dramatic scenery of the tall, rugged mountains cupping the jewel-like Emerald Bay. They'd just finished a delicious dinner at a table set for two on the foredeck of the yacht. Jacob had admitted—a little sheepishly—that he wasn't much of a chef, and that their meals had been prepared by his cook, Lisa. Harper had laughed off his apology. The food had been sublime, the scenery breathtaking, and the company thrilling. He had nothing to be sorry for. He'd been an excellent dinner companion, asking her questions about herself and appearing genuinely interested in her answers. Although his somber watchfulness was his trademark characteristic, he laughed often enough. Every time he did, her heart squeezed a little. There was an elusive quality to him, something she couldn't quite put her finger on, something beyond his obvious handsomeness and his aura of quiet yet undeniable power and confidence.

She couldn't help but recall her unrealistic fantasy about finding a guy who was not only confident, smart, and powerful, but who actually listened to her once in a while. Jacob was a focused listener. He couldn't possibly be very interested in the boring things she told him about her life as a reporter at the *Chronicle* or her favorite places in San Francisco or Washington, DC, but he seemed to pay attention to every detail. No, to *absorb* it. It was probably a short-lived act to get her into bed.

But if it was an illusion, it was a nice one, she acknowledged. As the sun began to set over the mountains, Harper found herself wanting to believe in it very much. She realized she'd hardly dwelled on her parents' loss or experienced that swallowing emptiness all night.

"What's that?" Jacob asked.

For a moment, she didn't recall what had inspired his question. He held up a bottle of wine in a silent query and she nodded once eagerly. For a moment, she didn't answer and just watched as he tipped the bottle and golden liquid trickled into her glass. The moment struck her as sensual somehow . . . rich with possibilities. He set down the bottle and lifted his brows slightly, waiting for her reply. She recalled her former statement.

"Oh, I was just thinking it must be incredible. To be you," she said, smiling and waving at the fantastic scenery and the lovely table that had been set exclusively for them with lavish detail. "Does it all seem passé to you at this point? The mansions, the yachts, being constantly surrounded by beauty and luxury?" she wondered. She'd asked him earlier if he lived in Tahoe full-time, and he'd admitted he also had homes in the Sea Cliff area of San Francisco as well as in Napa Valley, where he also owned Lattice Vineyards.

He took a moment to reply, lifting his wineglass and taking a sip. "I'd like to be able to tell you that it never becomes background noise. I'd like to be able to say that the ability to appreciate the finer things and the rare opportunities directly relates to just how low and dirty of a place you had to crawl from to get there."

"But you can't?" she asked softly.

"Sometimes, I forget. Sometimes, it's easier just to imagine that this world is the one I was destined for, even though deep down, I know it's a lie I tell myself. Because the truth is, every day, every hour, I have to scramble to keep it. Sometimes, I wish I didn't have to work so hard and worry so much. Sometimes, I resent all this," he mused, waving back at the yacht. "Because I hate that tomorrow I'll have to be smarter and better and maybe even more ruthless in order to keep it. And yet . . . I *want* to keep it," he said, meeting her stare dead-on. "I want *more*."

His eyes had taken on a simmering quality. Harper realized she was holding her breath.

"Why?" she whispered.

He shrugged. "The more you have, the safer you are from losing it all." He met her gaze and smiled slightly. "Pretty pitiful, isn't it?"

"I wouldn't say that," she said thoughtfully. "I can see how that mind-set would arise. And it's not just the *things* you would worry about losing. It's all the work you've done, too, and all that it meant to you. The struggles. The failures and the victories. All the effort you've put into creating what you've become. You wouldn't want it all to be for nothing."

For a moment, a full silence prevailed as they regarded each other.

"You're wondering if I have the ability to appreciate you, aren't you? If I'll take you for granted as much as I might any of the other luxurious playthings that are scattered around me?"

She started slightly. She hadn't expected him to say that. The realization also struck her that by "playthings" he might have been making a veiled reference to his other lovers. She laughed and set down her glass of wine.

"You don't pull any punches, do you?"

"Would you like me to go easier on you?"

"No," she said, shaking her head. Her smile faded. "Of course I'm wondering about it. I don't really know how the mind of a brilliant, billionaire software magnate works."

"Neither do I. Is there a handbook?"

"I'm just trying to figure you out, Jacob. Is that so terrible? You *have* asked me to sleep with you."

He picked up his wineglass and took a sip, seemingly unaffected by her wryness. His gaze became hooded as he stared out at the sparkling water.

"What's wrong?" she wondered, sensing his withdrawal. Had he changed his mind about what he'd offered last night? That he would help her forget her loss . . . for a little while, anyway. Now, as she wondered if he'd changed his mind, she suddenly was confident about her own decision.

He was rare. Different. Maybe she was acting out or behaving impulsively in the past year. Maybe she was just running away from the sense of meaninglessness and loss that had filled her life. But she experienced the opposite of loneliness and frustrated anger when she was with him.

She felt excitement and connection.

He was worth the risk.

"Nothing's wrong," he said, setting down his wineglass. "Have you decided, Harper?"

"I think so," she said. She held his stare and nodded once firmly. A muscle twitched in his cheek.

"I think you should tell me more precisely exactly what it is you're afraid of," he said.

She hesitated, but then thought, *What the hell. He asked, didn't he?*

"I have a history of getting involved with men like you, and regretting it."

He leaned back in his chair.

"Men like me?"

"Powerful. Accomplished. Full of themselves."

His brows went up. "That's what you think of me?"

"No. Which has me a little confused, to be honest. I mean . . . you're obviously powerful and accomplished."

"It's just the *full of himself* part that you're unsure about?" She was glad to see his small smile. He hadn't been offended by her admission.

"You're confident. But that's not the same thing, is it?"

"Why do you suppose that is?"

"What? Why are you confident?" she asked, confused.

"No. Why do you suppose you're drawn to powerful men?" He put air quotes around the word *powerful*.

"I don't know," she admitted quietly. "I wish I wasn't, to be honest. I was trying to reform my ways. And . . . then you walked up to me on that beach . . ."

He stood and reached for her hand, taking her off guard. She stood alongside him, her breath locked in her lungs.

"It's a sexual thing. Your preference in men."

She inhaled shakily at his typical conciseness. "I guess. Yes But it's *only* a sexual thing. I don't want to be run roughshod over or patronized or discounted outside the bedroom."

"No one should be running roughshod over you or discounting

you *in* the bedroom, either," he said, his mouth going hard. "That's not what your preference signifies."

She could only stare up at him, mute. She wasn't so sure she understood what he meant, but she was curious . . . no, *hungry* to know.

"And about what you said earlier: I don't think it's unusual that you want to know me," he said, reaching up to cradle her jaw with both hands. He leaned down and brushed his mouth over hers. She inhaled his scent. Her body flickered in excitement. He'd held her that way last night, too, both hands cupping her face. It made her feel special, somehow. Cherished. *Hot.* "It's just that I have a feeling you *will* know me," he continued, his voice a deep, rich seduction. "Whether I like it or not. And I'm not so sure what I think about that, Harper. And as for the other? I *can* appreciate you. I do. And I *will.*"

"Sexually," she clarified bluntly, struggling against the allure of his quiet voice, his possessive touch and his magnetic gaze.

"Yes," he agreed without an ounce of apology. He kissed her lips again, plucking at her with firm, focused caresses.

Harper found herself responding wholesale. It was like sinking into a pool of warm, deep water. Letting go . . . but knowing that she could inhale a lungful of fresh air anytime she chose.

A breathless moment later, he lifted his head and peered down at her upturned face with a narrowed gaze. A small smile tilted his mouth at whatever he saw there.

"It's a nice night. How about we go poolside?" he asked.

"Okay," she whispered.

This is it. You've crossed the line now. Or perhaps she truly had last night, when she'd reached for his extended hand.

He turned away. Still holding her hand, he led her inside. Harper trailed him, listening to the drumbeat in her ears grow steadily louder.

nine

They walked up a flight of stairs to the pool deck. He led her over to a double chaise lounge that included a canopy. He felt customarily unsure . . . uncertain of what he planned to do. He wanted her. Like crazy. But he couldn't take her in the ways to which he was accustomed. Not yet. He needed to seduce her.

He *certainly* needed to prove he was capable of something beyond that rush of heated lust he'd subjected her to last night. Just the recollection embarrassed him. It also aroused him. At the same time, how he usually proceeded with a woman, his matter-of-fact, bold dominance wasn't any more appropriate than his out-of-control need had been.

He paused at the foot of the lounger, turned, and again cradled her jaw in his hands. She looked up at him, her gaze similar to that anxious yet aroused one he'd fantasized about while he masturbated twice last night . . . and again this morning.

Too similar.

She felt very delicate to him. She deserved to be cherished. Surely he could manage that, for Harper's sake?

He kissed her mouth gently, coaxing her to open for him. When she did, her taste flooded him. It made him ache so quickly, when he'd thought himself calm. Recognizing what was happening, he forced himself to be patient as he penetrated her mouth, savoring her. She made him lose control, so he would learn her. He would learn how to master this need.

He wasn't Jake Tharp anymore.

"Let's get you out of these," he murmured a moment later, forcing himself to break their increasingly fevered kiss. He began to unbutton her sweater, but instead paused to cup one full, firm breast.

"I've been wanting to do that all night," he admitted gruffly, watching the progress of his stroking hand. "I kept thinking how soft your breasts would feel beneath this sweater . . . how good. It was driving me crazy."

"Really?"

He glanced up to her face at the hint of surprise in her tone. "*You* were driving me crazy in it," he corrected. He reached up and cradled both breasts in his hands, holding her stare. "I was wrong. You feel even better than I expected," he murmured. He was being honest. The material was feathery soft and fit her breasts snugly. The sensation of her firm, feminine flesh beneath struck him as intensely erotic. He found the beading crests and rubbed them through her bra.

Her lips fell open. He liked when she looked that way. Dazed. Flushed. Entranced. He liked seeing the evidence of her arousal, especially when he himself had gone stone hard at the feeling of her in his hand.

"I hated not being able to see you last night," he said, continuing to massage her sweater-covered breasts.

"I know. Me, too. I mean . . . about you," she said shakily.

"We have plenty of light now," he said, referring to the brilliant summer evening. Holding her stare, he slowly unbuttoned the soft sweater, his anticipation shockingly sharp.

"Why are you smiling?" she asked as he unfastened the sweater to just above her waist. Instead of unfastening it all the way, he turned his attention to unbuttoning the dress beneath it.

He shook his head. "I was thinking I'm probably going to acquire some kind of fetish for fuzzy pink sweaters, thanks to you."

She laughed. He glanced up at her face, even as his fingers continued to work the buttons, this time of her dress, descending between the swells of her breasts. She looked radiant. She was made to bathe in the rosy, warm hues of the setting sun.

"You're lovely."

Her smile faded. She shook her head slightly, as if at a loss for words. "Thank you. I feel the same about you," she whispered.

He parted the fabric of her dress, revealing an ivory bra that hugged her breasts snugly. He ran his fingers over the firm, plump globes, fully intent on his task. He'd always loved every part of a woman's body, but he was known for having a thing for breasts in particular. It dawned on him in that moment that *this* female had perhaps been the very one to inspire that particular sexual preference so many years ago.

The realization stunned him. It amplified his lust, because *here* she was: the source of so many adolescent fantasies in the flesh.

The skin of her chest was flushed. He saw the spellbinding, quick throb of her pulse at her throat. It was a sweet tease, what he was doing, but suddenly he couldn't take it anymore. He hooked his fingers inside the cups of fabric and peeled them back firmly over her nipples, plumping the flesh up over her bra and clothing. For a few seconds, he just stared, feeling his blood roaring in his veins and pulsing in his cock.

"Jesus," he muttered in awe, touching both nipples at once with his fingertips. The crests were fairly large, but delicate. So pretty. They were a unique coral pink color. As he touched them, they puckered tight, the color deepening. The contrast of the color to her pale breasts was mouthwatering.

He wanted to eat her alive.

"Lie back on the chaise lounge," he said, and he realized his tone had gone hard. Lust-bitten.

"You . . . you don't want the rest of my clothes off?"

His gaze jerked to her face. "Of course I do," he assured more evenly. "But *I'll* take them off in a moment. Right now, just lie back."

She sat on the edge of the lounge and scooted back, her heart thumping in her ears. She couldn't get over the effect he had on her, his absolute focus. It was like she was the center of the universe in those lung-burning moments when he'd been touching her. Jacob Latimer was enough to make any woman go light-headed, just on his own, but combined with his intensity and the raw hunger in his eyes when he touched her . . . well, Harper was grateful he'd asked her to lie down. Her knees had gone weak.

When her feet were hanging over the ledge, he bent and removed her sandals. The skin of her ankles and feet still prickling from his light touch, she scooted back onto the many scattered pillows at the end of the lounger. Even before her head came to rest, he was coming down over her reclining form. He blocked out that sun itself, but the brilliant light shone around his dark form like a corona. Planting his left hip near her thigh, he slipped one arm beneath the small of her back. He cupped one of her breasts in his hand, holding it up for his inspection. She felt his narrow-eyed stare all the way to her sex. And then, with no further ado, he calmly leaned down and sucked her nipple into his mouth.

The contact sent a jolt of excitement through her. He sucked firmly. His tongue laved the captive nipple, as though he was determined to feel every tiny bump of the puckered flesh. Harper grasped at his head, sinking her fingers into his thick hair. Her sex went liquid and warm. She squirmed slightly against the cushion, instinctively trying to get pressure to alleviate the sharp ache at her core. His mouth moved rhythmically, drawing on her hungrily, pulling at some magical string that seemed to join her breast to her sex.

"Jacob," she moaned.

He lifted his head, but only to resituate himself over her. He swung a long leg over her body and came up into a partial kneeling position over her. She watched, her mouth falling open. He looked so solemn staring down at her, holding both of her breasts in his hands. So beautiful. His thumb feathered a wet, erect nipple, drawing a whimper from her throat.

He glanced up at the sound. How could she express what she was feeling? Impossibly, he was making her feel like the only woman in existence.

She reached for him. He captured her outstretched wrists and pressed her hands on one of the pillows behind her. She cried out shakily at his gesture, surprised.

"I'm not going to hurt you," he murmured, obviously mistaking her sound of startled arousal as fear.

"I'm not afraid of that." And she wasn't. She'd had lovers press her hands above her head in the heat of the moment before. For the most part, she'd liked it, the roughness of it, the spontaneity, although it had usually been done with some degree of hasty lust. But that wasn't what Jacob was doing. He was restraining her firmly, but his hands were gentle. It was the *deliberation* of everything he did, the focused confidence and mastery of his touch, that made her so hot.

He lowered over her again, using his free hand to hold a breast. He sucked her other nipple into his mouth, treating it to the same firm suction and gentle thrashing he'd given the first. His hunger was a palpable thing. It created a sharp pain of need in a place deep inside her. After a moment, he lifted his head, kissing and nudging the swell of her breasts, running those shapely lips she'd lusted after repeatedly over her beading nipple, before he fastened on the other crest.

Harper lay there, panting and increasingly desperate, while he feasted on her like she was his first and last meal. His focused hunger and his patient, intent consumption of her made her wild. She writhed more strenuously on the cushion, calling his name, needing his mouth on hers, the feeling of his naked skin against her own and his cock filling her . . .

Just *needing*, so much.

He lifted his head from a glistening, swollen nipple and regarded her with a heavy-lidded stare. "Am I hurting you?"

"No. It feels so good," she replied honestly.

He nodded and removed the hand that restrained her wrists. When she immediately began to move in order to touch him, his hand was back.

"Don't move. Stay like that. You have no idea how exciting this is for me. You're so beautiful. I want to play with you a little more. Okay?"

A gasp of surprise popped out of her throat. She nodded. What else could she do but agree? She felt his hand slide beneath her opened dress to her back, and her bra snapped open. His fingers slipped along her shoulder blades, dragging the straps of the bra down. He pushed the cups downward, completely freeing her breasts. Using both of his large hands, he grasped both the edges of her sweater and her breasts, plumping the mounds beneath the opening.

He glanced up at her, the small, devilish smile ghosting his lips freezing the air in her lungs.

"See, I told you. Pink sweater fetish in the making," he said with dark amusement. She started to smile along with him, but then he lowered his head and sucked a nipple into his mouth, drawing on her more tautly than before. She moaned. His hands plumped and molded her breasts while he sucked on first one crest, then the other. He held them up for his consumption, pushing the shiny, reddened nipples together for his feasting mouth. It was relatively innocent, as far as ways of lovemaking went, but his intensity made it outrageously exciting.

Now past the point of desperation, Harper lifted her hips off the cushion, needy of pressure on her sex. He'd been kneeling over her. His thighs bracketed her lower hips, but he'd kept his crotch several inches off her body. She made contact, pulsing her pelvis against the mind-blowing tease of his erection. He slipped his lips off her nipple. Harper gave a frustrated cry, partially because of the loss of his hot mouth, partially because of the feeling of how heavy and warm his cock felt through his jeans.

"Are you doing this to make up for last night, or are you just intent on driving me crazy?" she asked, panting.

A slow smile started across his handsome mouth. "Can't it be a little of both?"

"Huh?" she asked, discombobulated. She jerked her gaze off the vision of his erect cock pressing against the front of his jeans. She watched him as he once again swung his leg over her and came down next to her on the lounge, reclining on his hip.

"Maybe you're right," he said, as if to himself. He unfastened the remaining buttons on her pink sweater and began working on her dress. "I could play with your breasts forever. They're uncommonly pretty." She gasped when he reached up and pinched a hard, swollen crest gently, his fingertips sliding with the wetness he'd left from his mouth. At the sound she made, he glanced up at her face. "Your cheeks are bright pink."

"I can't help it," she managed, because his quick, adept hand was now moving down her belly as he unfastened her dress, and it was highly distracting. "It's my coloring."

She sensed his pleasure more than saw it displayed in any obvious way on his face.

"I like that. It means you can't hide anything," he said. Her breath stuck on an inhale when his long fingers paused at the last button of her dress, just an inch above her mons. He opened his hand over her bare stomach and caressed her.

"Breathe, Harper."

Her eyelids popped open at his quietly uttered words. That eerie sense of familiarity came over her yet again. She forced her eyes to focus on him. Then he slipped two fingers beneath the elastic band of her panties and buried them between her labia, and the strange feeling was washed away by a flood of lust.

No. She'd never experienced *anything* like Jacob Latimer before.

She made a disbelieving sound. Her elbows pressed into the pillows and her back arched as he rubbed her clit. She burned.

"No, you definitely can't hide that. You're so wet. Are you this wet just from having me suck on your pretty breasts?" she heard him say. She realized she'd clamped her eyelids closed when he pushed his fingers into the cleft of her labia.

"Does that surprise you?" she asked through a choked voice. He really worked some magic with those long, knowing fingers.

"A little, yeah. It's not often a woman gets this wet, this fast, without anything but a little breast play."

Her eyes sprang open. His face hovered over hers. He'd been watching her reaction to his touch closely.

"Are you complaining?" she whispered.

"A man doesn't complain over a blessing," he said, his gaze narrowing on her mouth. A moan trickled past her lips. She was so hot, and his fingers felt so good. Her clit simmered. She was going to come soon. Was that the pressure of his cock against her hip, the heat of his arousal penetrating his jeans? She wanted to touch him. She wanted to hold him while she trembled in climax.

"Let me put down my arms," she said.

"No, honey. You keep them right there," he said, the quick, gruff quality of his reply and the slant of his mouth telling her he meant exactly what he said. A ripple of excitement went through her, igniting her. She twisted her head on the pillow, pushing up on her pelvis. The friction was optimal.

"I'm going to come."

"Of course you are." He rubbed harder. Faster. Her lips parted, and he caught her cry with his mouth.

He kissed her forcefully while wave after wave of pleasure shuddered through her. It struck her in a dazed fashion while she was coming that he seemed to be drinking in her pleasure . . . making it his own. While she was still in the last clutches of her climax, his mouth blazed down her neck and chest. He drew on a sensitized nipple yet again, and she bucked against him as another sharp shudder of pleasure seized her. He caught her to him, holding her fast against him as his tongue laved her, and her climax waned to delicious tremors.

Somewhere in the midst of her pleasure, she found herself moving without thought, her fingers delving into his thick, short hair, her fingertips scraping his scalp. She came back to herself at the realization that his eyes were open, and that he was watching her face while he drew gently on her breast. Her sex tickled with rearousal at the vision of him as his cheeks hollowed out slightly as he sucked. He seemed calm, but she sensed an eruption brewing just below the surface. His hand moved between her thighs, and she shivered.

"How do you do that?" she whispered hoarsely, amazed that he could light a spark in her flesh when she'd just had an orgasm.

He slipped his lips off her nipple with an erotic tug. The crest looked rosy and wet, swollen and very hard from his attentions. Even the air seemed to stimulate the sensitive nerves. He shifted, and she brought his head down to her own. Their mouths brushed together and clung.

"Do what?" he asked, plucking at her lips.

"Turn me on so easily. Is it just practice?"

"No," he replied, sitting up slightly. She became aware that he was shoving her unfastened bra, dress, and sweater down one of her arms. She sat up slightly, assisting him. When he'd gotten the sleeves off her arms, he pushed the fabric of her dress down to her waist. She lifted her hips and he flung the garment past her pelvis and down her legs. He did it all with methodical precision.

Then his hand opened on her outer thigh, and she once again sensed his focus. He caressed her warmly from hip to waist to rib. He met her stare again. Although he didn't speak, she thought he wanted to say something else.

"What?" she asked, smiling, collapsing back on the pillows. She felt flushed and surprisingly comfortable following her climax. Happy, like she'd just made some kind of unexpected, amazing discovery. Her fingers trailed down his neck. She slid her fingertips beneath his collar, feeling the ripple of pleasure that went through him at her touch.

Suddenly, his eyes seemed to blaze. He caught her stroking hand with his and pressed it tautly back on the pillows. With it in place, he reached for her other wrist. Placing them next to each other, he pinned both her arms in place with one hand. Unlike before, he'd trapped her hands higher on the pillows. The position stretched her skin over her ribs and thrust her breasts forward.

"It's you," he said. She blinked in surprise. His gaze moved down over her slowly, creating a trail of prickly awareness along her skin. She saw her body every day of her life, but it suddenly looked and felt completely different to her, seeing it through his eyes. She was mostly naked, save some ivory-colored bikini briefs. Her body was cast in the pink hues of the setting sun. He opened his hand on her belly and stroked her ribs and then along her sides, holding her wrists tightly over her head the whole time. She shivered in pleasure, her back arching off the cushion, as if she instinctively craved more of his touch. He felt her response and glanced up at her.

"I find you exceptionally beautiful," he said.

She gave a small bark of dazed laughter. He found her to be the *exception*, among all the world-class beauties he constantly had at his disposal? His expression darkened. Her eyes widened when he brought his face closer to hers, and she sensed his fierceness.

"You don't believe me?" he breathed out, sounding a little ominous.

"It stretches the imagination, that's all. I'm okay-looking. Pretty, even—I'll give you that. But *exceptionally beautiful*?" she asked skeptically, smiling. "I saw those women at your party last night."

"I didn't."

She blinked at his succinct reply.

"I'll just have to show you, won't I?" he asked.

"You don't have to—"

He cut off her protest by covering her mouth with his, and this time, there was very little gentleness in his kiss. It was almost like he'd taken offense to her doubting his sincerity. She made a muffled sound of mixed arousal and surprise as he made an onslaught on her senses. He caressed her naked body while he kissed her. It drove her crazy, the way her hip fit so ideally in his large, curving hand, the way he coaxed goose bumps onto her skin by stroking his fingertips across her ribs like he was playing an instrument, the way he brushed the tender, sensitive skin just below her the top of her panties with teasing fingers. And all the while, he owned her with his deep, drugging kiss. He caught a breast in his hand and molded her to his palm possessively.

It became too much. She felt trapped. Delightfully so. She writhed on the cushion, struggling against his restraint of her wrists. She wanted to hold him. She made a wild, desperate sound into his mouth.

He broke their kiss roughly and tightened his hold on her wrists.

"Do you want me to release you?"

"Yes. *No*," she muttered emphatically, bewildered by her response.

"Good, because I'm not going to. Not until I do this."

He shoved his hand beneath her panties. "Spread your thighs," he demanded grimly. "Wider." Even as she opened further for him, he thrust his middle finger high into her. She *was* extremely wet. She could tell by how easily he penetrated her. Once he was lodged high in her, he used his thumb tip and the ridge of his forefinger to apply a steady friction on her clit.

She strained against his hold on her wrists, her face going tight in pleasure. Then he pressed down and began to circle his hand subtly, stirring her into a frothing bliss. Every muscle in her body flexed tight.

"Oh, Jesus," she moaned. "Not again."

"Yes. Again."

He nipped at her lower lip, and she felt his hunger. His heat. He pressed his groin tightly against her hip. "Do you feel that?" he asked, his nostrils flaring slightly. He circled his hip, grinding against her. His cock felt hard and heavy. Delicious. God, she wanted to feel him throbbing in her hand like she had last night, to have him stretch her lips wide and slide onto her tongue. She wanted him to lose control, just like he had last night, but this time, using her to find his bliss.

"Harper?"

"*Yes*," she managed through clenched teeth, pulling herself from the graphic fantasy she was having about him while he rubbed her clit.

He moved his mouth next to her ear. "I'm going to make you come right now. Hard," he emphasized grimly. More heat rushed into her cheeks at his erotic threat. She whimpered, because his hand was ruthless. She had no choice save to do exactly what he said. He came down over her face again, and she saw his white teeth flash in the darkening shadows. "And then I'm going to fuck your sweet little pussy, and I'm going to love it so much. I'm going to make you believe me about how much I want you. Now, come for me," he rasped before his mouth fastened on hers.

She fell over the edge, crying into his kiss as she exploded in climax. After her first few shudders of pleasure, he lifted his head and watched her come. He finger-fucked her for several hard, deep strokes, his palm slapping lightly at her outer sex when he penetrated her. She yelped in surprised pleasure at the taut, forceful movement. Then he plunged deep and used his entire hand to vibrate and agitate her sex.

She was at his mercy. Her body tensed in pleasure again and again. He kept manipulating her just so, demanding another tremor from her. She gave it to him, until she finally lay gasping against the cushions.

ten

He felt himself turning rabid as he watched her climax. Her pussy was a man's dream come true. The hair between her thighs was curly and soft and sweet with her juices. Her channel was warm and so snug that he could feel her shudder as she came. It suddenly became his sole mandate to feel her tremble around him while he was buried deep inside her.

She whimpered softly when he withdrew his finger. He reached into his back pocket, searching for a condom. A hasty moment later, he shoved his pants and boxer briefs down his legs and off his feet. He willfully kept his eyes averted from the splendor of her lying there, naked and flushed from orgasm. She was luminous in the light of the setting sun. It didn't do him any good to look away, though. The image of her was burned into his brain. He saw it vividly: the full, pert breasts and erect, coral pink nipples; the red-gold curls between her pale, spread thighs; her arms above her head; the arch of her spine. In his imagination, her wrists were bound together with black rope.

But no. That was for another time. He'd seen the confusion on her face when they'd talked earlier about her preference for powerful men. He suspected she was a sexual submissive, but that might have just been wishful thinking on his part.

He rolled on the condom with fingers that were still coated with her juices. Her aroma perfumed the air, the scent amplifying his hunger. He glanced up to her face and paused, his sheathed erection fisted in his hand.

She looked dazed. Lovely. She'd been watching him put on the condom and was slowly lowering her arms, her intent to touch him obvious.

"No, honey," he rasped. "Keep them above your head. That's right," he murmured when she acquiesced. He scooted closer to her and put his hand on her closest hip, urging her to roll on her side. "Roll onto your side," he instructed. "Your eyes are killing me. I can't look at them right now. I'm about to lose it. Part your thighs," he ordered.

He was panting now, the vision of the enticing curve of her hip and her round ass not making things any easier on him. Sweat sheened his abdomen, a product of restraining himself against pounding desire. He saw that her long hair had fallen into her face when he'd turned her onto her side, and he brushed it away from her pink cheeks. He grasped her wrists and pushed them into the pillow again. With his other hand, he fisted his cock. He hurt like hell for her. Leaning down, he kissed her soft shoulder and spoke near her ear. He saw her rib cage heaving in and out, and sensed her taut anticipation.

"If you don't want me to hold your arms, tell me so, and I'll let go. Either way, I'm going to have to fuck you hard. You're so pretty, Harper."

He heard her soft gasp. He waited, his teeth clenched together hard.

"Don't let go."

Arousal clawed at him at the three quietly uttered words.

All his self-lectures in regard to patience incinerated, he resituated himself to enter her. Without him telling her to, she twisted and lifted her pelvis slightly. When she reached the prime angle, he flexed his hips.

"That's it. Right there," he mumbled tensely, grasping her hip with his free hand. Just the tip of his cock was pressed against her opening. He could feel her through the condom: Her heat. The narrowness of her channel.

God, he'd love to fuck her raw, nothing between them. Nothing separating them.

He turned his chin and wiped the sweat that had gathered on his upper lip onto his shirt. The edges of his vision had taken on a red cast that had nothing to do with the dying sun. He pressed with his hips, grimacing in pleasure at the sensation of her body squeezing the entire head of his cock. Nevertheless, he heard her soft moan, and it wasn't one of pleasure.

He clutched at her naked hip, stopping himself with great effort. Sliding his hand down her thigh, he bent her knee further into her body, applying a pressure with his pelvis the whole time.

"There," he exhaled, hearing her soft whimper as he pierced her slowly. She was so sweet, but her flesh resisted him subtly. He pulsed his hips, even more determined now that he felt the glory of her. He stared blindly at the corner post that held the canopy as he flexed back and forth, sinking further into her. Her gasps and soft moans fell on his ears, but this time he recognized her arousal. The sounds goaded him on, intertwining with the throb of his heartbeat and the exquisite sensation of penetrating her. A full, wild feeling swelled in him.

His pelvis bumped against the curve of her ass. He pulled her back against him while he flexed, pressing his balls against her damp, tender outer sex.

He felt so raw. So exposed. A shudder went through him.

Her sharp, desperate cry pierced his haze.

"Harper," he bit out. Her reply was a deep moan. "Are you okay?"

"Yes. God, yes," he heard her mumble.

"Good. Because I can't take this anymore."

He drew out of her, a snarl twisting his lips as pleasure tore through him.

He finally abandoned himself to it, driving into her again and again, their flesh slapping together in a taut, erotic rhythm, glorying in the perfect friction that both satisfied and prodded him onward at once. All the while, he was aware of her sleek body moving in tandem with him and of her sharp cries of excitement. But the madness of need was what ruled him primarily in those tense minutes of decadent pleasure.

At first, he wouldn't let himself look at her. His resources were strained to the limit as it was. He fucked her hard, drowning in her, while staring with fixed determination at the bedpost, the cabana bar . . . *anywhere* but at Harper. But as his strokes grew faster and Harper's cries grew sharper, he found himself moving without thought of consequence. He drew out of her, his cock like a single slick, quivering, raw nerve, and reached for a pillow. He dragged it under Harper's hip and gently pushed her onto it, so that she was facedown.

"That's it," he praised, because when he'd released her wrists, she'd scooted her body into the precise position he'd wanted in his greedy possession of her. She arched her back slightly and edged her knees up on the chaise mattress, sending her ass up several inches off the pillow. He grabbed another pillow and shoved it under her. And there she was, full in his vision: her gorgeous copper-colored hair tossed on the pillows and across her elegant back, her lovely profile turned to him, her cheek flushed red, her lips parted as she panted, her round, pale ass poking into the air. He pushed back a plump buttock and glimpsed her glossy, pink sex.

A groan ripped at his throat. Harper McFadden. *His* for the taking.

Planting his hands on the mattress near her shoulders, he plunged into her. It was a full-fledged orgy of need. His feet clawed for a hold, and he found one on the wooden frame of the lounger. Anchored in place, his knees came off the mattress. Using his flexing legs to power him, he drove the full length of his cock into her repeatedly, heedless of anything but seeking his ultimate goal. It was selfish on his part. But that's not what Jacob would have called those euphoric, desperate moments. To him, it was a clawing compulsion to finally burn deep inside her.

He felt her tighten around him, and her sharp, wild cries finally penetrated his awareness. Her arms were outstretched over her head. She clawed mindlessly at the mattress while she climaxed around him, her ass flexing tight. He felt himself cresting at the vision. He took her with short, ruthless strokes intended to ignite.

It felt like he gave all of himself . . . sacrificed everything, just like he had twenty years ago.

As harsh shudders of orgasm began to wane, the sobering reality of that frantic realization slowly penetrated his awareness. It cleared his haze of rabid lust faster than anything else possibly could have.

He'd taken her by storm, and in the aftermath, Harper knew only one thing: She wanted to do it again. She wanted *him* again, even now as she lay there panting from her climax with Jacob Latimer still high and hard inside her. He'd said he'd show her how much he desired her, and he'd proven it in spades.

She heard his ragged breath behind her cease abruptly. Air hissed past her teeth when he withdrew from her. Her tissues stung slightly— he hadn't been joking about taking her hard. She'd never been taken that forcefully or in such a wholesale fashion in her life. But it wasn't the sting of her sex that made her gasp in discomfort. It was the loss of him filling her.

She rolled over on the pillows, swiping her hair out of her face. He pushed with his arms in a powerful gesture and came off both her and the chaise lounge in one fluid movement. She watched him as he quickly and casually removed the condom. Her breath caught. He still wore the cobalt blue button-down shirt. His glistening, long cock protruded from beneath the hemline of his shirt as he walked past the lounge toward a door behind the bar.

A flicker of unease went through her when he didn't look her way or say anything before he disappeared behind the bathroom door. She sat up partially on the chaise lounge, suddenly very aware of her nakedness . . .

Of being alone.

Her thighs were splayed on the cushion. She shut her legs. The sun had completely set now. The pool lights and a light behind the bar illuminated the deck. It had cooled off, and her body was covered in a light sheen of sweat. A breeze swirled around her. She shivered.

She heard him come out of the bathroom and instinctively reached for one of the pillows they'd tossed about while having sex. He walked toward her, looking down as he reached for the buttons on his shirt. She glimpsed his muscular chest and golden brown, flat abdomen. It didn't seem fair somehow, that she found him so starkly appealing, when she was increasingly confused by his manner. Shock popped through her when she realized he was buttoning his shirt *up*, not down. He glanced up, his gaze snagging on the pillow she'd placed in front of her belly and breasts.

Something crossed his handsome face and then . . . froze. She couldn't think of how else to describe his expression. He suddenly seemed as cold and aloof as he'd been on the beach during their first meeting.

"Are you all right?" he asked quietly, sitting on the edge of the mattress and turning in her direction. His face looked shadowed, but she could make out the glint of the gold in his eyes beneath his lowered brow.

"Yes," she replied with a fake laugh. She felt cast out to sea. The way he'd made love to her, the way he'd touched her with such a single-minded focus earlier, had seemed almost alarmingly intimate and exciting. Now he was back to being polite? "Are *you* all right?" she countered uneasily.

She couldn't read his expression. Her discomfort grew when he didn't reply for a moment. Then he turned away from her.

"I'm fine. Why wouldn't I be?"

She made a sound of disbelief at his sharp tone. He heard her, and his head whipped around.

"I just meant—" he began, then just as abruptly cut himself off. His mouth pressed into a rigid line. "I just meant," he repeated, this time more evenly. "I was very hard on you. I'm sorry."

"You are?" she asked shakily.

"I meant to show you I could be patient."

"Were you even *there*?"

"What?" he asked, his brows slanting dangerously.

"I enjoyed it. All of it," she snapped, highly aware of her understatement. She'd *loved* it. The first thought she'd had when her brain was once again capable of logic was that she wanted to do it again. Now he was treating her like a stranger.

Which—*face it, Harper*—was what they were to each other, for the most part.

Then why had he felt like the opposite of that earlier? She'd allowed her imagination and her lust to mislead her yet again.

He didn't respond. He just stared at her, his jaw tight, his face like a shadowed, hard mask.

"Jacob?" she whispered, searching his face for some hint of their former, charged . . . *amazing* connection.

"I'm sorry. I'm not very good at this," he said.

It stung more than she either expected or liked, that he could be so aloof after what had just happened. Annoyed at herself for making more of their sexual encounter than she should have, she shoved her feet off the lounger in the opposite direction from him and tossed the pillow aside. She grabbed her discarded dress and stood. Pointedly avoiding looking at him, she stepped into the opening of the garment and slipped it up over her arms.

Why didn't he say anything? What was he, some kind of a robot, to make love to her with such pointed tenderness and heat, and then to act so coldly?

What was *she*? An idiot, to have been so taken in by him?

"I didn't mean to offend you."

She looked up from buttoning her dress.

"Then why are you acting so distant all of sudden?" she demanded, fury making her voice tremble slightly. She felt very vulnerable. "I mean, granted, we agreed this was just sex, but *really*? Talk about running hot and cold, with nothing in between." She bent to grab her discarded sweater, the garment making the memory of his touching it and her breasts at once, of his wry teasing about a sweater fetish, rush into her consciousness.

"You don't understand," he said. His terse tone struck her as condescending, like she was a stupid child.

"No," she agreed hotly, shoving her hands into the armholes of her sweater. "I *don't* understand you. So why don't you just take me home?" She bent and snagged her underwear and walked to the front of the chaise lounge, where she snapped up her sandals. "I'll be downstairs."

"Harper—" he said sharply, and yes. There it was. There was barely restrained fury in his tone. What did *he* have to be mad about? She turned around, completely confused, but half-hopeful he'd say something to apply a bandage to their quickly unraveling date. She couldn't figure out how things had gotten so volatile.

"Don't walk away from me."

"Why?" she demanded after a pause. "What is it you want to say? Jacob?"

His mouth remained hard, his posture stiff. She waited. Apparently, he didn't want to say anything. He just didn't like it when people walked away from him. Undoubtedly he was the one used to doing the walking.

"Never mind. Just take me back," she said, straining to keep her tone even. He didn't deserve to see how upset he was making her. She was dizzy with confusion. The only thing she knew for sure was that this had been a mistake. "Please. *Now*," she grated out before she turned and around and took the steps to the lower deck two at a time.

3

make me
SAY IT

eleven

Jacob glanced up when Elizabeth tapped on his office door and entered carrying some files. He made eye contact with her and could tell by her arched brows she had something to tell him.

"I don't want to argue with you anymore about it," he said quietly to the woman on the screen. "We agreed before you moved into the coach house that you would have to meet my requirements."

"Your requirements are even more strict than my shrink's," Regina Morrow said. "But at least I can count on seeing Dr. Fielding regularly. When will I see *you* next?"

"Hard to say. I'm working on a few deals that are taking up a lot of my time. I can't get away at the moment. My presence shouldn't be a requirement for you to do what we agreed upon."

Regina made a predictable sound of dissatisfaction, a pout marring her otherwise stunning features.

"You just need to focus on one thing: taking care of yourself," he said. "I'll call tomorrow and you can tell me what the new therapy group is like."

"You'll call to check up on me, you mean? You're a pain in the ass, Jacob. I don't know why I love you so much." His mouth went hard at the grudging quality to her tone of voice. Regina had a habit of imagining herself victimized . . . and acting out accordingly. He hoped her fit of pique wouldn't be an excuse for sabotaging her current treatment.

"Your feelings for me—or for anyone—shouldn't affect how you take care of yourself. Regina?"

"I know, I know. Don't lecture me."

"I'll talk to you tomorrow . . . and I'll try not to lecture," he added dryly.

"Promises, promises," she teased, bringing a smile to his mouth before he said good-bye and disconnected their conversation.

Without looking up from his computer, he spoke to Elizabeth. "Please call Dr. Fielding and tell him that he should administer a drug test at her visit this afternoon. If she doesn't show for her outpatient group therapy appointment, have him call me."

"Of course," Elizabeth replied. She'd been given the same or similar instructions too many prior times to question him. His history with Regina had been a roller-coaster ride.

"Cyril is here. He wants to know if you'd like lunch at his place," Elizabeth said.

Jacob closed his eyes as regret and annoyance flickered through him. He knew Cyril would want to talk about the film. About Harper. He'd rather avoid the subject at all costs. But as much of a pain in the ass as Cyril could be, and as different as he and Cyril were, he was also one of the few people on the earth Jacob considered a friend.

He might as well just get this over with.

"We'll give him lunch here, if he'll have it," he said as his fingers flew across the keyboard. He looked up after a moment. "Out on the balcony?"

"I'll let Lisa know," Elizabeth said briskly, setting the files on his desk and turning to go.

Ten minutes later he sat across from Cyril Atwater at a table set for two. His office balcony overlooked the lake, and made a good location for working meals as well as a refreshing escape where he could clear his head.

He'd shared a workday lunch with Cyril too many times in the past to count. They'd known each other for about seven years, ever since they'd become neighbors in Tahoe Shores. One of Cyril's hallmark characteristics was his single-minded, bullheaded determination to see a project through, a quality that was both admirable and annoying, depending on which side of Cyril you were on. Cyril tended to wheedle, flatter, or bulldoze his way to get what he wanted, and Jacob had definitely erected a barrier to one of Cyril's targets the other night.

He knew that Cyril had been a small, sensitive, and sickly child growing up, which had led to a long history of bullying—both by other kids and an overbearing, coarse, heavy-handed father. Cyril's artistic brilliance had been a foreign language to his father, and Jarvis Atwater was not a man to tolerate anything foreign. What had infuriated Jarvis was not only his son's open homosexuality, but a stubborn streak that ran a mile wide. Cyril refused to bend or alter, no matter the amount of threats and physical abuse.

Predictably, Cyril brought up the topic of the film before Lisa, his cook, had even served the soup.

"I might have complicated things for you in regard to that," Jacob told his friend.

"What do you mean?" Cyril demanded, peering at him through a pair of antique Edwardian pince-nez glasses that Cyril was particularly proud of.

"I might have . . . insulted Ms. McFadden."

"*Insulted* her." A flabbergasted expression slowly broke over his thin face. "Good Lord, you don't mean insulted in the antiquated sense of the word, do you?"

Jacob gave him a bland look.

"You *slept* with her?" Cyril nearly shouted.

"Quiet," Jacob insisted as Lisa stepped out on the balcony with a tray in her hand. Cyril snapped his mouth shut into a frown as Lisa served them.

"I'm shocked. And I disapprove," Cyril said when Lisa had left.

"I didn't ask for your approval," Jacob replied, his mild tone disguising his irritation.

"That girl isn't your type, is she? I mean . . . she's stunning, of course. But she's a bit on the sweet side for someone of your tastes, isn't she?"

"And so we get to the portion of the story where I insulted her," Jacob said stoically, picking up his spoon.

Cyril shook his head, clearly bewildered. "She lives here in Tahoe Shores. What about your policy on avoiding local complications?"

"You make it sound like I have it printed out in a company policy regulation manual. It's just a preference, not a hard-and-fast rule."

"You've followed that policy like you were a devout Catholic and it was strict dogma. I've seen you walk away from considerable temptation when it comes to local women. Why is Harper McFadden worth the exception?"

"I *did* make an exception. Let's just leave it at that. And now I'm facing the unpleasant consequence," he grated out. "Not just from Harper. From you, too, apparently."

He took a bite of Lisa's usually delicious-tasting tomato bisque and frowned. Discussing his mistake could make ambrosia taste bitter on his tongue. He had gotten where he had in life by making smart, often risky choices accompanied by strict, unwavering self-discipline. His complete lack of self-control in regard to Harper had been plaguing him every waking second since she'd jumped off his boat last night like she was leaping from the mouth of hell to safe ground. She'd walked away on the dock without looking back, a fact that still infuriated and agitated him as he recalled it presently.

He *hated* when Harper walked away.

"It can't be all that bad," Cyril decided. "You'll just have to apologize to her for whatever you did." He paused in the action of bringing his spoon to his mouth. "What *did* you do?"

"I was distant in the aftermath, apparently."

"You really shouldn't have seduced a woman like that. She's not the type to be satisfied with your limitations in regard to relationships." Cyril set down his spoon abruptly. "I can't imagine what you were thinking, although I suppose I shouldn't be completely shocked. I saw the way you were looking at her the other night."

Jacob stiffened.

"Everyone was talking about it," Cyril said, shrugging. "It's not every day you see Jacob Latimer panting to go and greet a girl."

"I wasn't *panting*."

Cyril's gaze on him was annoyingly sharp. "You think she's special. That's why you brought up the topic of her story and the film. *Why?*" Cyril asked, his irritation seemingly replaced by fascination.

"If you want the second course, mind your own business."

Cyril was chastened only briefly.

"I think you should apologize. What's more, I think *you* think you should apologize. She makes you feel vulnerable." He shook his head, a smile breaking free. "Will wonders never cease? I've never seen you worked up over a girl, except for Regina upon occasion, of course, but that's entirely—"

Cyril put up his hands in a surrender gesture when he finally took in Jacob's furious expression.

"Don't kill the messenger for stating the truth. It's just common sense, to apologize to her," Cyril insisted. "Embarrassment isn't good cause to insult a person. Neither is liking them more than you think you should."

Jacob refused to rise to the bait, taking another sip of his soup. Inside, he was boiling.

"She's smart. Compassionate. Very pretty—even if not your typical taste," Cyril mused maddeningly.

"How do you know what my taste is?"

Cyril gave him a disgusted glance. "I see it regularly, why wouldn't I know? Long legs, a stunning face, a heart as cold and conniving as your own can be. The women you sleep with are lionesses, while the women you save are sad. Vulnerable."

Jacob looked up sharply at that, an unpleasant, freezing sensation shooting through his veins.

"What are you talking about? *Saving* people?"

Cyril shrugged, as if he couldn't believe Jacob was asking for clarification on such an obvious topic.

"Let's see," Cyril began, ticking off his fingers. "There's Regina, then that housekeeper of yours at Sea Cliff. Marianne, isn't it? There's Elizabeth, of course, whom you rescued from that battered women's shelter and turned into a titan of business. And that's not even mentioning all the unknown people and animals you save through your charities. You can keep most of your philanthropy from being commonly known, Jacob, but you aren't fooling me on that score."

"You're babbling," Jacob said coldly.

"But Harper McFadden . . . she's not a classic victim *or* a heartless lioness. And yet, against all odds . . . you like her. Ah—I've got it! The *scar*," Cyril said, pointing to the corner of his mouth, indicating the location of Harper's scar. "She's the gorgeous, brave reporter with a soul sensitive enough to write stories like Ellie's. She's the *vulnerable* lioness."

Jacob hissed a curse, his spoon plinking loudly against his bowl. Cyril's observations struck too close to home about many things, one of them being that he encapsulated his internal conflict about sexually dominating Harper with shocking precision.

"She's a *reporter*," Jacob bit out, as if that explained everything. "I should be avoiding her like the plague. And I don't *like* her. What is this, the fifth grade?"

Cyril twirled his iced tea glass. "You like the way she makes you feel, then. Anyone could have seen that the other night."

"You don't know what you're talking about."

Cyril just arched his brows in a sardonic challenge.

"Because in point of fact, I *don't* like the way Harper McFadden makes me feel," Jacob declared loudly. He snapped his mouth closed when he heard the glass door slide open behind him.

He blinked. He couldn't believe he'd let Cyril get a rise out of him. It hardly ever happened. Lisa appeared with their second course. He stewed in his irritation while she served. What he'd told Cyril was true. Harper McFadden made him feel torn and restless. She made him feel like *this*: uncomfortably bewildered and prickly. She made him feel like he wasn't himself . . . like he was Jake instead of Jacob.

So why couldn't he stop thinking about her, then? He couldn't seem to rid himself of this craving to possess her sexually, yet . . . he felt remorse over that. His guilt wasn't dampening the need, though. There was a charge to his lust that was undeniable.

It was because it was *Harper*. He was like a stupid kid all over again, unable to control either mind or body . . .

And what if Cyril was right, and she *was* vulnerable in addition to being strong?

It doesn't change the fact that you want to tie her up and have her until you can't see straight, with absolutely nothing to stand in your way.

So you don't like her," Cyril agreed when Lisa left the balcony. He'd said it just to keep the peace, but in typical Cyril fashion, couldn't resist sounding sarcastic as hell. "You'll still apologize to her for my sake, won't you?" He popped a cherry tomato into his mouth. "For the film's sake?"

"You just want that damn film made because your new actor boyfriend is so perfect for the part of Ellie's homeless friend."

"Of course I do. I like Miguel, and I want him to be happy," Cyril said simply, taking a sip of iced tea. "But I want it for me, as well. And for Harper. It's an amazing story. You think so, too. You'll call her?"

"You don't know what you're asking. You don't know what you're *talking* about," Jacob repeated before he began mechanically eating his salad.

"No," Cyril said with a sigh that set Jacob's teeth on edge. "I think it's *you* who doesn't know, Jacob."

Maybe Cyril was right, Jacob thought later that evening as he looked out over the shimmering cerulean lake.

He'd managed to get through the rest of lunch without allowing his friend to get a rise out of him again . . . or without making any promises he'd regret in regard to Harper McFadden. He'd successfully pushed out any thoughts of what had happened on the yacht last night while he methodically worked on the ResourceSoft acquisition this afternoon.

But then Elizabeth had left early for the night, and his phone had stopped its steady, rhythmic buzzing, and the sun had started to set. Thoughts of her began to intrude once again.

It both gratified him and rankled at once, that he was so completely different now that there was never even a hint of recognition on her face. He'd gratifyingly imagined for years that Jake Tharp was effectively dead. But seeing the evidence of that truth broadcast large on Harper's face was firsthand proof. It seemed so strange that she could have forgotten so completely when he remembered so well.

Even though he wished like hell that he didn't.

twelve

His hand shook as he portioned out the powdered animal sedative into the carafe of water. For a few seconds, he was frozen
with fear. He knew from helping out Emmitt on several occasions with new or overly aggressive animals what the appropriate portion was for both a pup and an adult dog. He had no idea what might
work for humans. But Jake was good at math. The only thing he could
do was figure an appropriate ratio based on a pit bull's weight versus
his uncle's.

He wasn't sure what he was more terrified of: that he'd kill his
uncle with a lethal dose, or that the amount wouldn't knock him out
at all, and Emmitt would discover that he'd already sedated the animals in the barn and was intent on betraying him.

You decide: What's worse? Uncle Emmitt dying? Or you?

The thought steadied him. *He* couldn't die. He had to help Harper.
Determinedly, he added more of the powder into the coffee carafe and
then shoved the bottle into his jeans pocket.

One of Jake's duties every day was to make Emmitt's morning coffee. His uncle was *always* a caveman, in Jake's opinion, but before his
morning coffee, he was totally subhuman. He usually couldn't even
form words until he'd swallowed his first cup. The coffeepot was always his second destination after awakening from his whiskey stupor,
the bathroom being his first.

But had his uncle actually drunk any alcohol last night, or had he
skipped it in order to carry out his ugly mission of kidnapping Harper?

What if he didn't reach for his coffee cup at all after he stumbled out of the bathroom this morning? What if he went and checked on his prisoner straightaway, and found his guard dogs heavily sedated?

Jake had known the dogs would be hungry for their morning feeding. Even though he was familiar with every dog on the property and on friendly terms with most, a check of the pens had told him that Emmitt had chosen three of his meanest, most successful dogs from the ring to guard Harper. The unusual situation of being put in the barn to guard a helpless human would make them more unpredictable and aggressive than usual, even toward Jake, with whom they were familiar.

Jake suspected that Emmitt had let the dogs catch the scent from Harper's clothes. They'd been stirred up by the smell of Harper's blood and her fear. It had activated their killer instincts. As a consequence, Jake had been careful earlier about picking the padlock and silently removing the chain, link by link, from the hasp.

He'd thawed out several of Emmitt's prized steaks from the freezer and added them to a large pan filled with the dogs' normal food. He'd been liberal with the sedative.

The dogs had indeed run at him aggressively when he opened the barn door, teeth bared and growling dangerously. Jake had dropped the pan, meat slopping over the side, and hastily shut the door. He could hear the animals snarling and snapping at each other and the sounds of them greedily gobbling up the food.

For the hundredth time in the past forty-five minutes, Jake silently sent up a prayer that each dog had gotten a sufficient amount of food to sedate it. If even one of the killers remained alert, Harper and he were screwed.

He heard a noise from the hallway and dropped the coffee can, causing it to clatter on the kitchen counter before he caught it.

"What are you doing?" Emmitt shouted a second later.

"Making your coffee," Jake said as evenly as possible. "It'll be ready in a second." He risked looking at his uncle from beneath his lowered brow. Emmitt's face looked mottled and his eyes were bloodshot. He looked good and hungover. If he hadn't drunk until he returned home last night, it appeared that he'd made up for it and then some before falling asleep. Now he was still half-drunk, sleep deprived and—Jake suspected—meaner than a sack full of rattlesnakes.

"I thought I told you to stay in your room until I let you out."

Jake braced himself to dodge an oncoming fist when Emmitt stepped closer.

"I thought you meant last night. I never came out. But I thought you'd want your morning coffee."

Emmitt's glares could melt a person's insides to mush. "Did you leave this house this morning?"

"No, sir. I just got up a few minutes before you did. Do you want some toast with your coffee?"

He dodged the cuff to the side of his head, but Emmitt made contact anyway. Jake staggered back, his ear ringing and throbbing with pain. It was yet another skill Jake had learned—how to move sufficiently to lessen a blow, but still grant Emmitt the satisfaction of serving it. It'd only piss off his uncle more if Jake escaped him altogether. He clutched at his ear, grimacing.

"You worthless little mongrel. Get back to your room, like I told you!" Emmitt bellowed, spraying spit. Jake turned, wiping the spittle off his cheek, his heartbeat pounding in his throbbing ear. What was he going to do, holed up in his room, blinded as to what his uncle was doing? That little room would be his coffin.

For a few seconds, his fear strangled him. Emmitt was going to find out what he'd done. He'd kill him. How could he have thought he could trick him? As he headed toward his room, everything turned hazy and weird in his vision, like he was underwater. What would it be like, dying?

"Wait!" Emmitt yelled. Jake turned slowly, unable to hide any of it anymore: His secret plan. His hatred. His fear. He was sure his uncle would see it written large on his face.

"Get me my coffee first," Emmitt said dismissively, wiping his nose on his sleeve and walking over to the sink.

"Yes, sir."

He went over to the cabinet and found the largest mug on the shelf.

An hour later, he placed one of the two backpacks he carried on the dirt near the barn door. He cautiously removed the chain and opened the door. A bar of sunlight penetrated the gloom. He looked up. Her pale face appeared over the edge of the loft, the light turning her hair into a red-gold halo around her head.

"Jake?" she whispered.

He picked up the backpack and quickly and silently moved past the drugged dogs. One of them—Wilhelm—stirred slightly, and Jake's heart flew into his throat. Harper gave a little groan from above him. She'd seen the dog move, too.

"It's okay," he assured himself as much as her as he flew up the ladder. "Wilhelm twitches in his sleep all the time."

"Stop," she said in a quivering voice.

He halted and glanced up in surprise. He was only three feet from the edge of the loft. She peered down anxiously, her long hair draping her face.

"I don't have any clothes on," she reminded him desperately. She was on her knees, looking down at him. He could see the tops of her bare shoulders, and was reminded that her hands were bound behind her back.

"I have clothes for you in my backpack," he explained. He remained still, rapidly working through some potential scenarios as to how to minimize her embarrassment and just as quickly dismissing each one as soon as he had it. "I'm sorry, but I have to come up there in order to untie your hands . . ." He faded off when he saw her distress. He couldn't even tell her to cover herself, because she couldn't with her hands bound behind her. Harper realized that, too, of course.

She nodded once stiffly.

He scurried up the ladder, hearing her scoot back into the shadows as he did so. She didn't say anything, but he sensed how wild she was to remain invisible. He kept his eyes averted as he removed some old jeans, a large T-shirt, and some socks from his backpack. He had to look up to locate her in the loft, though. Her pale skin shone, even in the shadows. He gritted his teeth in resolve and walked toward her. Moving as quickly as he could to minimize her humiliation and his own discomfort, he knelt behind her and went directly to work with his pocketknife multi-tool on the twisted rope that bound her wrists. After a moment, she whimpered softly.

His mouth twisted in fury. Damn Emmitt. He'd used the roughest hemp rope he possibly could have to tightly bind her. Her wrists were abraded, both her skin and the hemp smeared with blood. "I know, I'm sorry," he mumbled, because in his efforts to free her, he couldn't help twisting the rope into her surface cuts.

"It's okay. Just get it off me," she said in a choked voice.

A torturous moment later, the length of rope fell to the loft floor. She cried out in pain when her arms fell forward. They'd been bound behind her for so long that lowering them hurt.

"It's okay. I've got you," he said, springing up and coming around to the front of her. He reached down, grasping her upper arms.

"No," she whispered, wincing in pain. "Put the shirt on me first."

"But—"

She looked up, a beam of sunlight illuminating her upper face, allowing him to see not just her despair, but her determination.

He immediately bent to the floor of the loft and lifted his old Mountaineers T-shirt. He shoved it over her head gracelessly. She tried to lift her hands to get them in the armholes. Her moan of pain pierced him.

"Help me," she whispered, grimacing. Her arms weren't functional yet, after being bound behind her for so long.

He grabbed one of her fisted hands. "I'm sorry," he apologized, cringing at the pained expression on her face as he lifted her hand and poked it through the armhole. She sighed in relief when she could lower her arm.

"They're prickling," she muttered, referring to her arms. "It hurts so bad."

"The nerves are waking up. It'll get better soon," Jake said in a hushed tone, scrambling to free her trapped hair from the shirt. He glanced down and froze. Having one arm in the T-shirt had pulled the cloth in a diagonal direction across her chest. One small, perfectly shaped breast was left exposed while the other was covered.

"Jake?" she whispered, and he saw she was trying to lift her other hand, but her nerves still weren't cooperating. He realized he'd been gawking at her stupidly and rushed to help her. Once the T-shirt was pulled down over her hips, she seemed fortified. Her misery had been replaced with determination by the time he helped her to stand.

"What do we now?" she whispered. "Where are we going?"

"I'm going to get you out of here."

"Where's that man? Your uncle?" she frowned when she said *uncle*. Jake had never been more ashamed of his kinship to Emmitt Tharp.

"I hope he's dead," Jake said, holding up the jeans for her to put on. "But I think he's just asleep, like the dogs."

"He'll come after us, won't he?" she asked as she scuttled into the jeans. He noticed that she had to pull hard to close the fly. Her hips were rounder than his . . . fuller. His little-boy jeans almost didn't fit her.

"He'll come," Jake replied grimly, jerking his gaze off the vision of her uncooperative fingers clumsily moving over the fly. That was one task he didn't dare help her with.

"Where will we go?" she whispered, grabbing a sock when he offered it to her.

"There's no time to explain." She reached out for him instinctively when she tried to lift her foot to put on the sock. Jake braced her by grabbing her upper arm.

"But—"

"We have to get out of here and into the woods, or you may never see your parents again. Do you understand?"

She stared up at him, her jaw going slack, her eyes wide. He'd been sharp.

"You said you'd do what I say. We have to go. Now. I don't know how the dog tranquilizers work on a man. Emmitt might wake up at any minute. And there might be other men arriving at any second to take you. Emmitt wouldn't wait long for payment."

Her face went blank with shock.

"I can keep you safe, Harper. But you have to hurry."

She shoved her other foot hastily into a sock. Maybe his entire meaning hadn't sunk in. But the hint of the foulness of Emmitt Tharp's plans for her had penetrated.

"No shoes, I guess?" she whispered.

"I've got shoes for you. They're in your pack. You can put them on, but later. Emmitt's a good tracker. One of the best in these mountains." He knew she didn't understand him from her blank expression, but there wasn't time to explain.

"Time to go." He put out a hand, and she took it, stepping toward him. For a second, they looked at each other somberly. They were almost exactly the same height.

"Why are you doing this?" she whispered.

"I don't know," he replied honestly. "But I can get you back to your parents."

There was a chance he could, anyway. Jake was good at math, and he instinctively understood odds. Their chances of coming out of this unscathed were maybe fifty-fifty. They had the element of surprise on their side. And Emmitt didn't know about Jake's secret cave. Plus, he'd learned a lot about living, tracking, and evading in the woods in the past few years. Emmitt was a better hunter though, and what's more, he could move in the forest faster than Harper and him due to nearly inhuman strength and stamina.

But Jake had worked with animals his whole life. He understood that mastering his fear and showing Harper confidence would go a long way in gaining her cooperation. If they had any chance of getting through this, he couldn't have her panicking at every turn.

"Trust me," he said, holding her stare.

"I do."

He was a little stunned by her lack of hesitation, but took pains to hide it. For some reason, her unquestioned trust allowed him to make a decision he'd been dreading.

"Here. This pack is yours," he said, handing her a worn army surplus backpack. She slung it over one shoulder, wincing.

"Okay?" he asked.

She nodded.

"There's one more important thing I have to do before we get off Emmitt's property."

He headed toward the ladder, determined that Harper not be a witness to his grief over that final task.

Present Day

Harper lounged on her terrace. The hot August day was quickly morphing into a pleasant, cool evening. She'd thought that the brisk, invigorating air would help her to focus on some edits. It wasn't working, though.

Summer had always been a magical time for her growing up. Her father loved cooking out and her mother doted on her garden. How many comfortable, delicious meals had she shared with her mom and dad over the years on their terrace? They hadn't seemed like anything special at the time. Memory gave those family dinners a golden quality, though, a sweet, elusive flavor. She ached, knowing she'd never share that feeling of easy companionship or unquestioned love again.

Her terrace looked so barren and empty by contrast.

Don't move. Stay like that. You have no idea how exciting this is for me. You're so beautiful. I want to play with you a little more. Okay?

The memory of Jacob giving her those steamy directions lanced through her momentary sadness, dissolving it.

Her mind kept wandering to those moments on that yacht last night. She frowned, recalling how cool and aloof he'd been just seconds after making her burn. She stared into space, her cheeks heating as she remembered how she shook in pleasure beneath his knowing hand . . . and later, how he took possession of her so completely.

It was hard to push him out now. It was like he'd taken up residence in her brain.

Damn him.

But isn't it better than sitting here, feeling sorry for yourself because you're alone?

All day, her sex had felt tingly and slightly tender. That, in combination with her uncontrollable thoughts about what he'd done to her on that double chaise lounge, made her feel constantly on the sharp edge of arousal and annoyance. Unfortunately, not even her recollection of his coldness could dampen her body's reaction.

Admitting defeat, she tossed the story and her edits onto a patio table. Without telling herself to do it, she pressed her pelvis down against the wrought iron seat, getting pressure on her sensitive sex. When she realized she was trying to figure out just how private her deck was from her neighbors, she stood abruptly.

Great. The guy acts like a complete jerk, and yet you were considering masturbating outside while you fantasize about him. You are such a loser.

She gathered up the story and headed inside, now highly aware of the tension at her sex and the fact that her cheeks were hot. Once she was inside, she drew the blinds. Her heartbeat began to throb in her ears in anticipation. Okay, so she wasn't going to do it in potential view of a nosy neighbor. But she *was* going to do it.

To make matters worse, it wasn't the first time she'd masturbated today, either.

She lay down on the couch and lifted her skirt to her waist. When her fingers slipped beneath the waistband of her panties, she thought of his fingers doing the same last night, how he'd caressed the sensitive skin above her mons and then slid those long, masterful fingers between her labia. It'd felt so good. How did he do it, touch her more knowingly than she even touched herself?

And later, how he'd asked her permission to hold her wrists while he fucked her . . . how she'd granted it. It'd excited her, knowing that he held her at his mercy, that she had to take him.

And he'd been a hell of a lot to take.

God, yes. No matter what a jerk he'd been, this was better than dwelling on the loneliness.

She recalled watching him put the condom on his rigid erection, the shape and the color of the flaring, smooth cockhead. He was so beautiful. She craved him, even now. Before he'd behaved so coldly in the aftermath, she had a vague fantasy about him binding her with cuffs or some kind of ties. Even so, it wasn't really the idea of restraints themselves that excited her. It was his intense focus on her, how he became aroused when she was helpless to resist him. Not that he'd needed to be concerned about her resisting him. She'd been a goner in that department, hands restrained or not.

He'd warned her that he was going to screw her hard. And he had, locking his feet on the frame of the lounge and taking her without mercy. It'd been so good. So hot. She'd come without expecting to, without the usual rise of tension and the slow burn. She'd combusted because that was the only thing you could do around Jacob's pounding cock.

She moaned, her hand moving faster between her thighs. She'd be coming again soon. Her excitement at the vivid memories and the buildup of tension over the past several hours was too much.

A gasp popped out of her throat. She yanked her hand from her underwear, sitting partially up, shocked by a brisk knock on her patio door. Shit. Who the hell was it? She considered just not answering, but realized it might be a neighbor. Maybe one of them really *had* seen her on the patio just now and had come over to greet her. She was still the new girl on the block, and had met only a few of her neighbors so far.

Flustered, she stood and smoothed down her skirt. "Just a second," she called, hurrying to her kitchen where she hastily washed her hands. A moment later, she lifted a blind and peered out. She let it shut with a snap.

Jacob stood on her terrace.

She remained unmoving for a second, her breath stuck in her lungs. Finally, she drew up the blinds with a jerking motion and opened the door.

For a few strained seconds, they just stared at each other.

"What are you doing here?" she managed eventually.

His gaze flickered across her face. She clenched her teeth. Was she flushed? Her cheeks certainly *felt* warm.

"I was out for a walk," he said slowly. "Is this a bad time?"

"No. I was just doing the dinner dishes."

"I didn't see anyone in the kitchen. I thought maybe you weren't here." He noticed her stunned, questioning glance. He pointed in the direction of the kitchen. "I wasn't eavesdropping. It's just that you walk past the kitchen window coming from the beach, and there weren't any lights on in there."

Heat redoubled in her cheeks at being caught in a lie.

"What do you want?" she repeated.

"I wanted to talk to you. About last night."

She glanced aside, shielding her discomfort. He looked good tonight. *As usual.* The voice in her head sounded bitter. She resented the way he evoked this attraction in her with so little apparent effort on his part. He was dressed casually in cargo shorts, running shoes, and a heather gray sports shirt. His clothing seemed to emphasize all the things she was trying to forget, yet had just been remembering with such clarity on the couch seconds ago: his fascinating eyes, his lean torso, his muscular shoulders and chest . . . those long, strong legs that had powered his cock inside her with such eye-crossing results . . .

"I don't think that's a good idea," she replied, her voice sounding hoarse. She cleared her throat. "Maybe we ought to just let things lie."

"I can't do that."

Her gaze jumped to his face.

"Not until I apologize. I honestly didn't mean to offend you last night. It's just that—"

He broke off abruptly and glanced aside. There it was: one of those rare cracks in his armor. He was either genuinely uncomfortable, or he was a terrific actor.

"What?" she asked, opening the patio door a few inches more without being aware of what she was doing.

"You remind me of someone I knew once."

Dusk was falling. A warbling robin penetrated the billowing silence.

"I was—" His mouth went hard and he glanced away again. He shut his eyelids tight for a second.

"I was . . . I was embarrassed," he said gruffly.

Her heartbeat began to drum in her ears. His admission struck her as poignant and rare. She had the definite impression this man didn't open up often, if ever.

"Why?" she asked softly. She felt for him in that moment. She really did, despite her reservations. Still, she wasn't going to let him off easy. A muscle flickered in his lean cheek.

"For losing control."

"I didn't think you lost control, Jacob."

He regarded her silently, his face a solemn mask . . . his eyes windows to a turmoil she couldn't understand.

"But I hear you saying you think you did," she continued quietly. "So . . . I reminded you of this person from your past, and you think it made things extra . . . intense for you?" She took a deep breath for courage. "And so you closed off in the aftermath, because it felt like too much, considering how briefly we've known each other?"

"Something like that, yeah."

She nodded, trying her best to absorb what he was saying. She inhaled choppily when the full impact of his meaning penetrated, and hurt settled.

"So, you are only attracted to me because I look like someone else?"

"No."

She blinked at his harshness.

"It's not like that," he assured, a hint of frustration in his tone. "Look, do you want to walk a little bit? I'd like to talk to you."

She glanced back into her condo uncertainly. He'd just told her that the reason he'd shown interest in her was because she looked like another woman. Undoubtedly, his admission was also the reason he'd been so amazingly focused on her during lovemaking.

"I don't think so," she replied slowly. "I've told you that I was at a crossroads in my life . . . that I'm feeling pretty vulnerable lately. I thought I could do this with you. But this is different. I'm not too crazy about the idea of you looking at me and seeing someone else."

"Harper." Her gaze snapped to his face at the authority she heard in his tone. "You reminded me of someone else at first. But that . . . *she* happened a long, long time ago. What I realized today is that's all a memory. It's the past. She doesn't exist anymore. Who I was when I knew her doesn't exist anymore. The memory drew me to you."

"But—"

"It's *you* I see standing right in front of me right now. It's you I want," he said bluntly, cutting her off. His quiet, utter confidence left her speechless.

"Uh . . . let me get some shoes," she murmured after a charged pause, pointing lamely behind her.

She didn't know what to make of him. Her uncertainty remained. She was likely making a gargantuan mistake. He was the type of man who could disarm so elementally with his intensity, good looks, and brilliance. But Jacob Latimer's unsettling confession and demonstration of vulnerability . . .

Well, it'd taken her breath away.

thirteen

They talked more as they strolled down the beach together, the sky above them turning a darker and darker blue, until finally they walked beneath a midnight dome sprayed with countless stars.

"But don't you think it's a little unlikely, that you can actually separate out your past from your present?" she asked him hesitantly after a while. "I mean isn't it a little . . ."

"What?"

"Well . . . creepy, that I look like someone you used to care about?"

"I don't know," he admitted. "Maybe. But doesn't history come into play to some degree in every case of attraction we experience our whole life?"

"What do you mean?"

She stared at his stark profile as they walked. For several moments, he didn't reply.

"You don't find that there are certain things about me, for instance, that remind you of something from *your* past?"

She gave a small laugh. "*No.*"

"You're sure?" he asked quietly.

"You're not like anyone I've ever met. But I get your point," she mused after a moment. "We're all a product of our histories. I just want to make it clear that even if I look a little like this other woman, I'm not her."

"You actually don't look all that much like her. It's just you remind me of her."

"How do I remind you of her?"

Only the soft surf penetrated the thick silence for a moment.

"I don't know. In some kind of . . . deeper sense. Not that I'm very spiritual. And not to shortchange the physical aspect of things, by any means," he added dryly under his breath. "It's a feeling of connection." He shrugged uneasily. "Who knows where something like that comes from? Maybe you don't feel it, but—"

"I feel it."

His stark, startling honesty had yanked the bewildering truth right out of her throat. "Still . . . I want to be appreciated for who I am. Even if—"

She cut herself off abruptly.

"What?" he asked.

"Even if this is only a sexual thing. That's not too unfair to ask, is it?"

He stopped and reached for her hand. She halted, looking up at the star-filled sky behind the blackness of his outline. Why was it that he always seemed so mysterious to her, so cloaked? And yet, at other times, he seemed achingly familiar. The paradox of him pulled at her. It was making her do things she shouldn't.

"Of course it's not unfair. It's a given. You're a unique, beautiful woman. You deserve to be more than appreciated. You should expect it."

"Thanks," she said breathlessly.

"Let me take you home so I can appreciate you more."

A laugh popped out of her throat. He'd said it deadpan. Her smile widened when she heard his warm, low chuckle above the surf, twining with hers.

"Seriously. I want to talk to you about something else. Something important." He touched her cheek. "Let's do it back at my place. I want to be able to see your face."

Her amusement faded. She stepped closer to his body, drawn irrevocably despite her doubts.

"I understand you saying you want a no-strings-attached relationship, and I *think* I can do that," she murmured. She *hoped* she could, anyway. "But it makes things complicated, what you just told me. What I just admitted. I'm not going to be okay with it, if you go into silent stealth mode about it again."

"I told you," he said, cradling her jaw with one hand. He stepped closer, his groin brushing against her belly, the tips of her breasts coming into contact with his rib cage. Arousal flickered through her like heat lightning fluttering across the night sky . . . the promise of a coming storm. "It's in the past," he breathed.

"I'm not saying you have to talk about this other person or your history with her ad nauseam," she said, highly aware that his head had lowered over her uplifted face. Their mouths were only inches apart. She could smell his clean, spicy man-scent. Arousal curled in her lower belly and tingled her sex. "I'm saying that if I think you're going aloof and cold because you're thinking of this other woman, I reserve the right to call you out on it. And I don't want to be shut out if I do."

There was a tense pause where he didn't move and she didn't draw breath. Again, she was highly aware of the fact that he wasn't used to women making demands of him. She wondered if he'd refuse.

"All right. As long as you hear what I'm saying right now. It's *not* going to happen again. I've thought about it. I wouldn't have shown up at your house if I hadn't come to a solid decision. If there's one thing I've learned about life, it's that dwelling on the past is like carrying around a ten-ton load because you're too stupid to drop the damn thing and move on. Every day is new," he said, sliding his firm lips against hers. Her lungs hitched. "I remake myself every day," he said quietly, his warm breath brushing against her mouth.

She craned for him, her lips caressing his when she smiled.

"Do you really believe that?" she asked, her whisper barely heard above the sound of the soft surf.

"No. I *know* it," he said, plucking at her lips teasingly one more time before he covered her mouth in a hot, melting kiss.

By the time he lifted his head a heart-thumping moment later, her brain was hazy and her sex had gone warm and achy. When he took her hand in his and led her in the direction of his beachside mansion,

Harper followed without question. After that kiss, it seemed like the most natural—the most inevitable—thing to do.

They approached the terrace doors, Jacob still holding her hand in his while he touched his forefinger to a pad on a security monitor near the door.

"Good evening, sir," a male's voice resounded into the dark night. Harper started.

"Ms. McFadden is here with me, Tony," Jacob responded calmly, giving Harper the impression it was common business for him to communicate with discarnate voices coming not only from dark woods, but as in this case, from the very air itself.

"Thank you, sir. Have a good night."

The lock on the door clicked and Jacob opened it, drawing Harper over the threshold. She followed him through the shadow-draped great room toward a magnificent, sweeping staircase made entirely of lodgepole pine, the hushed sense of anticipation building in her. He drew her down a high-ceilinged hallway to a large carved door. He glanced back at her as he turned the knob. Harper swallowed a knot of anticipation that had grown in her throat.

He closed the door behind them.

She stood for a moment, admiring the beautiful room. As in the great room, the old Tahoe lodge design mixed with sleek, modern décor. Ivory couches were set before a streamlined gray slate fireplace. The natural gold and caramel colors of the wood floors and beamed pine ceilings made a warm contrast to the distant bed and the crisp, luxurious ivory and gray bed dressing. The bed itself was beneath an alcove of windows that Harper realized during the day would offer views of Lake Tahoe's cerulean waters from three directions.

"What a lovely room," she murmured, turning toward him. Excitement and trepidation bubbled in her at the vision of him standing so still, soberly regarding her. He was so desirable to her. She might as well face it. Nevertheless, anxiety flickered into her awareness. "All those security people you have working here," she began slowly, "they can't . . . *see* in here, can they?"

"No. These quarters are completely private," he said, walking toward her with that panther-like grace she admired. He reached and took both her hands in his, never breaking their stare. "I wouldn't expose you. What happens in this bedroom is between us, and us alone. Do you believe me?"

She nodded, completely entranced by his eyes and deep, fluid voice.

"I'd like the same assurance from you," he said.

A puff of air popped out of her throat. She wondered if she should be offended by his request, but then realized it was only fair.

"I don't kiss and tell," she murmured, amusement tilting her mouth.

"I'd like your assurance that everything that happens to you while you're with me, everything you observe or experience, is kept in absolute confidence."

"I've promised you that before," she said, her brow crinkling in consternation. "I told you I would never write anything about you, or offer information to anyone at my paper—or any news source—unless we agreed upon it beforehand. I won't even mention it to a friend, if that's the reassurance you need." She glanced sideways in the direction of the great, luxurious bed. "And I'd hardly be gabbing about anything that happens here. I'm a very private person, too, you know."

He squeezed her hands gently in his.

"I know."

"Do you?" she asked, arching her brows. "I don't understand how you could."

"I know that you had an affair with Louis Richton, the owner of the *San Francisco Chronicle*'s largest rival newspaper." Harper gasped, but he continued, ignoring her stunned reaction. "I know you carried out that affair in complete secrecy. To this day, your boss at the *Chronicle* and your coworkers have no idea you were sleeping in the enemy's bed."

"How did you find—"

"Knowledge is my key weapon in everyday business. I can't afford ignorance."

She broke his hold on her hands, turning toward the circular bank of windows.

"I've offended you again," he said.

"I'm not a part of your business," she bit out angrily over her shoulder.

"I'm just trying to be honest, Harper. It might seem to you that an affair is strictly a personal experience. I wish I could say otherwise in my case, but matters of business factor into every aspect of my life. I'm telling you this because I want you to know one of the reasons that I'm inclined to trust you. You have a track record. Try to understand my point of view." She looked back at him. "It's not par for the course for me, to become involved with a reporter."

"I'm not a reporter, at present. I'm an editor. And what have you got to hide?"

"My sexual preference in the bedroom, for one thing," he replied without pause. "That's no one's business but my own."

"And your lovers', I assume."

He nodded once. She was struck by his solemn earnestness. Maybe what he was saying to her at that moment wasn't flattering, but it was honest. She'd give him that.

"I don't appreciate you digging into my private life," she told him stiffly.

"I'm sorry. It was a necessity. I needed to be sure of you."

She rounded on him. "And what about my certainty about the wisdom of getting involved with you? Where's *my* security?"

"I give you my word I'd never expose you in any way. I'll keep you safe, Harper."

She blinked. Again, a strong sense of inexplicable déjà vu came over her. Dazedly, she realized he'd said the same thing last night. *That* must be why it sounded so familiar. But that wasn't even the strangest part about his proclamation.

The oddest part was that she completely believed him.

"What have I got to be kept safe from?" she asked numbly. "What are these sexual preferences that you feel you need to guard so closely?"

Instead of answering her, he reached for her hand. She followed him across the long distance of the room, her heart starting to pound in her ears when she saw where he led her. He urged her to sit at the edge of the bed and came down next to her.

"I would like to bind you at times. During sex."

"You mean . . . like you held me last night while we . . ." Heat rushed through her cheeks at the graphic memory. "You mean bind me with your hands? Hold me down?"

"Yes," he replied. "But more than that. I want to restrain you with other things, so that I can use my hands to touch you." He leaned closer, his agate eyes mesmerizing her. "Control you. Pleasure you."

She licked her lower lip in nervous excitement. "What *other* things?"

"Any number of things: cuffs, harnesses that help me position you any way I like . . . ropes."

"Ropes?" she asked, taken aback. He saw her anxious reaction and cupped her jaw gently, leaning closer. She caught his scent, and her heart fluttered with agitated arousal.

"Soft rope," he murmured. "Rope I have specially made of the softest, strongest black silk. It would look so beautiful against your white skin. Don't worry, though. I won't do that tonight."

Her lungs froze. His lips brushed against hers seductively. A whimper escaped her throat. His head moved back.

"I'm not going to harm you," he said gruffly. "And I don't want you to be afraid. You'll have the power, because anytime you tell me to stop and unbind you, I will. *Any* time. Even if I'm deep inside you and about to see heaven," he added, his mouth shaping into a small snarl.

I don't think you'll have to worry about that happening.

She scowled slightly in response to her enthusiastic mental voice. His gaze ran over her face. She became highly aware of her pulse throbbing at her throat. "Never mind," he said suddenly, standing. He thought he'd read fear on her face, when in fact, she'd been feeling stunned arousal. He turned away, swiping the back of his hand across his upper lip. Had he gotten turned on, talking about binding her with soft rope and being deep inside her?

It'd certainly gotten to Harper. Still . . . she was uncertain.

"I shouldn't have brought it up," he said gruffly, his back to her. "It's just that . . . as much as I might want to, I don't think I *can* be with you partly. I don't want fifty, or seventy or ninety percent. With you, it's going to have to be all or nothing."

"Why do you want to?" she asked.

He twisted around and met her stare. "Why do I want to restrain you?"

She nodded.

"Because I want you at my mercy. I want to know that every ounce of pleasure that you get, every rush of sensation, every orgasm, was due completely to me. I want to *own* it."

She blinked, set off balance by his grim intensity.

"Isn't that kind of narcissistic?" she asked warily.

His brows arched and she sensed his dark amusement. "Narcissistic like some of your past lovers? I don't know. Is it?" he asked, his tone misleadingly mild. "Is that how it felt to you on the yacht? When we were on that chaise lounge together? When I was touching you?"

She blinked. *No. If anything, your entire focus on me felt like the exact* opposite *of self-involvement.*

"I like control in the bedroom," he stated simply.

"Just like you do in the boardroom?" she asked with a half smile. "You can't own everything, Jacob. You can't control everything."

Even to her own ears, she sounded unconvinced. She was under his influence now. She could never forget what it was like to be made love to by him. He'd controlled her mind and body like a maestro, and now all she could think about was submitting to him again.

"Maybe not. But many things, I *can*," he said with quiet confidence.

"I don't want to be beaten or bruised or abused in any way."

"I would never leave you marked. Never. The idea makes me sick."

She was taken aback by his bitterness. His mouth twisted, and again, she sensed that frustration she couldn't understand in him.

"I won't lie. I'll demand a lot of you. I'll want to fuck you hard. Frequently, and in whatever way I want. But only if you're completely with me in the moment, Harper."

She inhaled shakily, aroused by his words and finding the fierceness of his eyes overwhelming.

"This isn't about making you suffer. Never. It's about the opposite. I want you excited. I want you to surrender to everything but the moment. I want you to give in to the pleasure. To me."

It was like he was on fire in those moments, and it hurt a little to stare directly at the flame.

"Does it turn you off?" he asked quietly, his gaze on her rapier sharp. "The idea of giving control to me during sex? I'm going to position you any way I choose. Then I'm going to pleasure you any way that strikes me before I have you any way that I please. It's going to feel so damn good."

Heat rushed through her cheeks and chest.

"It doesn't turn me off," she admitted. "If it's anything like last night, I think . . . I think I'd like giving you control. In the *bedroom*," she emphasized.

He spun around slowly. "You're sure? You're not afraid?"

"I don't think so, no."

He stalked toward her. She couldn't help but notice he was erect. She could clearly see the thick shaft of his cock pressing against his cargo shorts. A thrill raced through her. She could make out the shape of the plump cockhead. He *had* been turned on, just by speaking the words out loud of what he wanted to do to her. He halted less than a foot away from where she sat on the bed.

Without thinking, she reached for him, running her hand along the rigid staff of his cock through his clothing. He muttered a curse, his hand going behind her head. She didn't need his urging, though. She pressed her face against his crotch, running her lips against the hard ridge of his erection. When she felt that ridge beneath the large, mushroom-shaped cockhead that excited her so much, she caressed it with the edge of her front teeth. A fever rose in her.

The next thing she knew, his hands were at her elbows. He pulled her up roughly into a standing position. Harper opened her lips to protest the deprivation, but then he was kissing her forcefully. Angrily? A hot wave of excitement swept through her, taking all rational thought with it. His kiss scorched her. When he sealed it abruptly a moment later, she was panting softly.

"You see why I have to control you," he said, his mouth slanted in a hard line. His fingers went to the small of her back, finding the button of her skirt. "You'd have me coming within a matter of minutes every time, just like you did the other night on the terrace."

"Maybe that's what I want," she breathed, staring up at him. He jerked down her zipper and slid his hand down over her ass, taking her skirt along the way. He shoved his hand into her underwear and caressed her bare bottom as her skirt fell down to her thighs.

"Is it? I thought you wanted me to have control in the bedroom." He pulled her panties down over her ass.

"I do," she whispered, enthralled by his face . . . and his touch on her naked, tingling skin. "But I also liked watching you come that night. A lot. I liked that you came on me."

His small snarl made her blood rush furiously in her veins. She pressed tighter to him, excited by his erection. He pushed her back slightly at the same moment that he took a step back. Harper felt her skirt and panties slither past her thighs.

"You're going to be such a challenge," he said, his mouth setting into a grim line as his gaze dropped down over her naked hips and legs. "Now . . . let's get you out of the rest of these clothes."

He knelt in front of her, making a sweeping motion with his hand between her legs to capture both her skirt and panties. He paused with the edge of his hand against the panel of her underwear. The next thing Harper knew, he was looking up at her with blazing eyes.

"You're very wet."

"I . . . guess I was turned on . . . ," she said lamely.

She was glad when he didn't belabor the topic. Instead, he quickly and efficiently removed the garments and then took off her sandals.

She began to raise her shirt, thinking to help him with the process, but he stood abruptly, towering over her. His hands grasped her wrists, stopping her.

"No. I'll want to undress you for sex."

"Every time?" she asked stupidly.

"Every time."

He held her stare and reached for the hem of her shirt. He swept it over her head. There had been something in his eyes when he'd said those two words: *every time*. Whatever it was had locked her lungs.

He unfastened her bra and drew it off her arms.

"Lie back on the bed." Despite the hypnotic smoothness of his voice, she sensed the coiled tension in him.

The luxurious duvet felt exquisitely soft and cool beneath her naked, heated skin. She reclined, propping herself up on her elbows and peering at him with a mixture of suspicion and arousal.

"What are you going to do?" she asked when he just stood entirely still, watching her. If it weren't for the glint of lust in his eyes—not to mention his cock pressing against the front of his shorts—she might have thought he was entirely impassive.

"I'm going to use a device to position you," he said calmly. He walked toward a closed door.

"Why can't you just ask me to take whatever position you want?" she wondered out loud.

"I could," he said, opening the door. She sat up slightly when he walked behind it and she could no longer see him. A moment later, the door tipped wider and he spoke as he came out of the unseen room. "And that could be gratifying, too, if you took those positions and held them of your own free will. But this"—he emerged carrying an indefinable handful of black leather straps and hooks—"will assure that you stay comfortable while holding the positions I want. Remember, Harper. All you have to do is tell me to release you, and I will."

His stern, steady voice jerked her gaze off the contraption he carried. He'd seen her anxiety while she stared at the device.

"How do I know I can trust you?"

"I don't know," he said, taking several steps toward her. "You either do or you don't."

Her nipples had drawn very tight, from the air-conditioned air, anxiety, or arousal, she couldn't say. In the end, she said the only thing that seemed evident to her at that moment.

"I do," she whispered. "I *can*. On this, anyway."

He walked toward her, the device grasped in his hands.

fourteen

"It's not as intimidating as it looks," he told her, setting the bunch of black padded straps on the edge of the bed and bending to remove his shoes.

"Maybe to you it's not."

"You've never been bound during sex?" he asked, removing his socks without taking his gaze off her. He looked very . . . hungry, Harper realized.

"Just my wrists with some cheap handcuffs once."

"Metal ones?"

"Yes," she breathed out, her eyes going wide because he was lifting his shirt over his head, exposing his cut, muscular torso. She found everything about him delicious, but his round, steely biceps made her mouth water. They were power defined. She ate him up with her stare as he dropped the shirt carelessly to the floor. His smooth, golden brown skin gloved his muscles so tautly. She could bounce a quarter off his abdomen. He possessed the perfect amount of hair on his chest—not a pelt, but just enough to come off as one hundred percent virile male. Not that a thousand other things about him weren't proclaiming that fact, loud and clear. She recalled seeing and touching his cock for the first time in the pale moonlight. He shaved his balls. Just the memory of how round and firm his testicles were, the sensation of the long, heavy shaft in her hand, and that succulent cockhead made her shift her hips restlessly on the bed . . .

"You okay?" he asked, his voice a little hoarse.

She blinked and realized she'd been staring openly at the ridge of his cock pressing against his shorts. He held that black device again. His stare was locked between her thighs.

"Yeah," she replied in a hushed tone.

She held her breath when he came onto the bed. He moved toward her on his knees. A shiver of raw excitement tore through her when she saw that his face had gone rigid as his gaze seemingly caressed every inch of her naked body.

"You're very, very beautiful," he murmured, pausing with one knee next to her hip and looking down at her. "Your skin is much too delicate for metal cuffs. I'd never allow anything so harsh to touch your body."

He reached out, caressing her collarbone with a gesture that was beyond tender. It was cherishing. He slid his hand along the side of one breast. He lifted the globe slightly and examined her through narrowed eyelids.

"I still can't get over the color of your nipples. Such a pretty pink," he muttered thickly, as if to himself. "So fat. So sweet," he added with a small smile as he gently pinched a nipple. She whimpered. She hadn't known her nipples were so sensitive until the first time he'd touched her. His gaze leapt to her face. "You're not afraid, are you?"

She rolled her head *no* on the mattress.

"Good. Let me just put the positioner on you, and you'll see. I only want to make you feel good. You don't need to move," he said when she started to rise to a sitting position in order to assist him. "I'll get it on you."

He spoke truly. The contraption looked pretty confusing to her, but he manipulated it with an easy, sure mastery that amazed. It made her wary, too, to witness his expert handling of the positioner. He clearly had a lot of experience with it.

He clearly had a lot of experience with other women.

But his expertise also excited her, and that was the emotion that trumped her doubt above all else.

First, he secured a thick, padded primary strap around her back and ribs, just above her waist. Various other straps—and she realized, cuffs—came off this main strap.

"Spread your legs, bend your knees, and lift your feet into the air," he instructed. He moved between her open legs, still on his knees. He palmed the back of one of her thighs, his warm touch making her skin pebble. "Wider, Harper. Let your legs fall open wide to the side." His gaze dipped between her thighs. "Let me see that gorgeous pussy. All of it. That's right," he murmured thickly when she had done as he requested.

He attached a pair of thick, padded cuffs midthigh with a grim sense of purpose.

"Oh," she murmured in dawning wonder when he'd finished. The thigh cuffs were attached to the primary restraint that circled her torso. When her legs were in them, it kept her bent, spread thighs open, her feet suspended in the air, with no effort on her part.

"Comfortable?"

"Yes," she replied, giving her weight experimentally to the leg restraints. It held secure.

Next, he took her hands and slid them through a pair of thick shoulder straps. These were also attached to the primary restraint around her middle. He placed the straps around the outer curves of her breasts. When he snugly tightened both clasps on the strap, they plumped her breasts between them. A low, rough growl resounded from his throat, and Harper saw that his gaze was fixed on her straining breasts. He ripped his stare off her to continue with his task. She thought she understood his reaction. Even *she* thought her breasts looked like a sexy decadence, plumped as they were by the shoulder straps, the pink nipples poking upward, the pale delicacy of the globes highlighted by the stark black restraints. His rigid stare had made her recall all too vividly how excited he'd gotten on the yacht as he played with her breasts, how he'd teased and pleasured her until she wanted to scream. How much more focused would he be, given the positioner and the freedom of his skilled hands, not to mention her helplessness to move?

She was finding this almost ridiculously exciting.

"Now we just need to restrain your wrists," he said, interrupting her unfurling fantasies.

He lifted another cuff that was attached, again, to the primary torso restraint. She lifted her head, watching him. He slid the padded cuff around her wrist, tightening it snugly. When he was finished, her elbows were bent, her arms resting comfortably on the mattress. Her wrists were restrained on each side of her body just above her waist. She tugged at them experimentally and shifted her body, her breasts heaving between the shoulder straps. Heat swept through her chest and cheeks at the graphic realization that she was trussed up . . . and good.

He caught her stare.

"You okay?" he asked quietly. He knelt between her suspended, spread legs.

"I think so."

His gaze coasted over her.

"You look stunning. More amazing than I'd imagined."

His stare between her spread thighs was like a physical touch. She couldn't hide her arousal. Her wetness. It was almost unbearable, her vulnerability to him. Her mounting excitement.

"What now?" she asked shakily.

"You tell me that you're comfortable. And promise me that if at any point, your position grows uncomfortable, you'll let me know."

"I'm comfortable," she assured. "And I will. I promise."

His smile made her sex tighten.

"Then let's work on showing you the benefits of the positioner," he said quietly. He reached into his pocket and withdrew something before he reclined on his side next to her, his elbow bent and hand supporting his head, his manner that of a man who was getting comfortable himself for an interlude of leisurely pleasure. He touched her belly with his pinkie and third finger, caressing her while still holding the object he'd taken from his pocket. Her muscles jumped at the charged contact of his skin against hers. Her head came up off the mattress, trying to keep his stroking hand on her naked body in her sight.

"You'd like to watch?" he asked.

She met his stare and nodded.

He reached behind her and lifted her head gently, placing it on a soft pillow.

"There. How's that?"

"Good," she managed.

"You're wondering what I have in my hand?"

"Yes."

He moved his hand in front of her vision as if he were doing a magician reveal. She blinked, recognizing he held a small, sleek silver vibrator. It was maybe three inches long, slender, and came to a tip.

"Normally, I'd use lube," he said, touching the point of the silver vibrator to the skin of her belly. She suppressed a gasp when he hit a button on the thick end, and the tip began to vibrate against her skin. "But considering how wet you are, I don't think anything artificial will be required."

Without any further buildup, he calmly inserted the little vibrator into her vagina and clicked the control button, amplifying the power. Harper's thighs tensed at the sensation, her eyes springing wide, feet flexing in midair. But she couldn't move; she was a prisoner to the pleasure. He pushed the sex toy in and out of her pussy twice, his manner intent, before he slid it out of her and up between her labia, directly onto her clit. Her abdominal muscles jerked as sensation flooded her.

"It's pretty intense, isn't it?" he murmured.

"God, *yes*." A film of perspiration had almost immediately broken out on her upper lip, a product of the flash fire that tore through her body. What he was doing to her was exciting enough, but watching his rigid focus as he did those things was even more thrilling.

He suddenly lifted the vibrator, and she choked off a moan.

"Don't worry. I'll be back. I was just trying to get some of your juices on it." He lifted the vibrator over her chest. Harper saw that it was, indeed, now slick with her arousal. She held her breath as she watched him lower the glistening tip over one of her nipples, pausing a half inch away from the prickling crest. He smiled. "Look at that. Look how hard it gets, and I haven't even touched it yet," he said thickly.

"Jacob," she muttered, tension and anticipation coiling in her. It broke slightly when he pressed the vibrating tip against her nipple. She gasped and rolled her head on the pillow, pleasure snaking through her. He might have been doing brain surgery, as intent as he was on his task. He leaned over her, watching closely as he stimulated her nipple until it was hard and almost painfully sensitive.

Then he moved aside the vibrator and lowered his head, sucking the nipple into his mouth. He'd moved so quickly, a ragged shout erupted from her throat. His tongue lashed and laved at the erect crest before he drew on her with firm force, seemingly intent on sucking every last nuance of her essence into his mouth. Harper forgot all sense of propriety and restraint, moaning helplessly, her head thrashing on the pillow.

By the time he lifted his head, the nipple had grown rosy and distended, and his mouth was slanted and hard from arousal. His gaze fixed on her breast, he dipped his hand between her thighs. He slipped the bullet back into her pussy, pulsing in and out of her liquid channel for a moment.

"I'd like to know what got you this wet, Harper," he said gruffly.

"What?" she gasped, because the vibrator was distracting her.

"What got you so wet?" he demanded, pulling the bullet out of her slit. "Even before we got started."

He watched her narrowly through heavy eyelids as he lifted the relubricated bullet toward her other nipple. She bit her lip to prevent moaning like a crazed woman.

"I don't know," she mumbled, keeping the vibrating silver tip in her sight. "You did."

"Did the idea of me restraining you like this excite you?"

The bullet came nearer, the tip a fraction of an inch from her beading nipple.

"Harper?"

"Yes," she choked. She instinctively arched her back, desperate for the little vibrator's wicked touch on her breast. He'd guessed what she'd do, apparently, because he moved the tip just out of reach of her thrusting breast.

"I'm glad," he said, and despite her intense arousal and focus on the vibrator, her gaze leapt to his face. His expression appeared genuinely gratified. Relieved, even? Surely it was an illusion, that he seemed to care so much that her sexual turn-ons coincided so well with his.

"Were you masturbating? Before I knocked on your door tonight?"

"*What?*" she asked disbelievingly.

"Just answer me. And be honest."

Her gaze skittered anxiously between the bullet hovering so close to her puckered nipple and his face.

"Yes," she gasped unevenly.

He looked hard and satisfied at once. "And what did you think of while you touched yourself?"

Heat rushed into her cheeks. Her head fell back on the pillow. "Don't do this to me. Don't make me say it."

"Say it. But only if it's true."

"You know I thought about you," she blurted out in frustration. "You know I thought of what you did to me last night on the boat. I haven't been able to think of hardly anything else since then. Oh God," she shouted, because suddenly his lips covered her nipple and he was sucking her into his mouth. She writhed in agony, but the positioner held firm. Her nipple popped out of his suctioning mouth a moment later. He looked up, still tonguing her erect, reddened nipple lasciviously. She groaned at the intensely erotic sight. He lunged forward, quick as a flash, and pierced her open lips with his tongue. He kissed her with the savage urgency she was coming to expect of him, yet she knew she'd never get used to it. Never stop craving.

"Your eyes and your hair, your beautiful body," he grated out next to her well-kissed, puffy lips a moment later while she panted, "all of those things turn me on. But your honesty . . ." Her eyes sprang wide and she jumped, because he'd just worked the tip of the vibrator between her labia and was directly stimulating her clit. Her nerves sizzled. Oh God, she couldn't breathe—

"I think I want your honesty most of all. Now give it to me."

She ignited. It felt strange and unbelievably good climaxing while restrained in the positioner, Jacob's hungry stare on her face while she shuddered in pleasure. She felt both controlled and yet utterly in control, like she was in a free fall with a safety net always just inches beneath her. She fell for what felt like an eternity before she nestled down into the security of the restraint, coming to herself at the sensation of Jacob nuzzling her breasts and then running his lips across her ribs. He'd removed the vibrator from her clit, which must explain why she was drawing full—if erratic—breaths into her lungs. His lips brushed across her heaving belly. He hovered just above her mons and inhaled.

"I love your scent," she heard him say gruffly.

She could smell it, too, the fragrance of her pleasure perfuming the air. Biting her lip, she watched as his head lowered. He kissed her labia just above her clitoris, the gesture solemn. Then he was kissing her again, worshiping the tender skin inside her knee and sweeping his lips along the inside of her thigh. This, too, struck her as sweet. Arousing. That such a strong, demanding man could also make her feel precious was a revelation. Because of the restraint, she couldn't duck and hide, or try to reciprocate the pleasure to alleviate the poignancy of the moment. All she could do was lie there and submit to the experience of being prized.

He ran his tongue along the top, inner portion of her thigh, that strip of skin directly next to her sex. She knew she was probably wet there from her arousal. He gathered her juices with his tongue.

He looked up when she turned her head on the pillow and whimpered.

"Is it too much?" he asked her, his deep voice seeming to caress her prickly, sensitive skin.

"Yes. No. I don't know," she whispered miserably. How could she speak aloud what she was feeling in that moment, put words to the heavy, sweet ache in her chest?

He reclined on the bed again on his side, his groin pressing against her naked hip. She shut her eyes at the exciting sensation. He came up on one elbow, his face hovering over her, and cupped her jaw.

"Then we'll use the vibrator again if it feels too intimate. But I'll warn you, I'm not going to wait much longer before I taste you."

She opened her lips to tell him *no*, that wasn't what she'd been thinking. It'd been the intimacy of the unfolded moment that had crowded her consciousness, not anxiety about the shocking closeness of oral sex. But then he was kissing her, more gently this time, but forceful and demanding nevertheless. He pushed the tip of the vibrator again, sliding it between her labia. The friction built so quickly. She didn't want the mechanical caress, though. It was his touch she wanted. His fingers. His lips. His tongue. But the vibrator was nothing if not precise, and his kiss drugged her. Soon, she felt herself rising to the crest again.

He broke their increasingly wild kiss and studied her face with a narrowed stare. His gaze transferred to her flushed breasts and tight nipples.

"I can't take it anymore. I want to be inside you when you come this time."

"Yes," she muttered, spinning from arousal.

He flipped onto his back and fleetly unfastened his shorts. Before he lowered them, he removed a condom from the back pocket. She lifted her head off the pillow, watching him as he jerked both the shorts and a pair of snug boxer briefs over his straining cock. His heavy erection sprung free and thumped onto his belly. Was it the restraint that redoubled her craving for him, the knowledge that she couldn't just reach out and touch that straight, thick shaft or that plump, defined cockhead anytime she chose? It drove her crazy.

A moment of disappointment went through her when he knelt between her spread thighs and rolled on the condom. She wanted him in her naked. She wanted to see her own juices slicking the shaft and gathering beneath the thick rim of that cockhead. God, he really had transformed her into a needy slut, to be thinking such things.

She held her breath as he edged closer between her suspended, restrained thighs, his sheathed cock protruding from his body. He planted one hand in the mattress next to her waist. With the hand that was bound to the primary restraint above her waist, she reached with her fingers, touching his wrist, caressing his skin. It was the tiniest of caresses, but electricity tingled through her at the contact. His gaze shot up to meet hers. Had he felt it, too?

She felt something hard and firm next to her sex. He rubbed the head of his cock between her labia.

"Oh," she mumbled shakily. He glided smoothly against her lubricated flesh, but the pressure was firm. It made her burn. She heard it: the wet, sucking sound of his hard cock moving in her soft, wet flesh. She grabbed at his wrist, her eyes fluttering closed as pleasure swamped her.

"Jacob," she moaned.

"Was it the first time you masturbated, thinking of us? This evening?"

She opened her eyes, bringing him into focus with effort. The vision of him hovering over her, one hand between his strong thighs as he manipulated his cock, so beautiful and powerful, and yet so focused on her: It left her tongue-tied. He stopped stimulating her clit for a moment. Her lungs unfroze and she gasped.

"No," she said hoarsely. "I . . ." She bit her lip, embarrassment penetrating her thick arousal.

"You found me jerking off, Harper. You owe me this."

It was his small, wry smile in the midst of the unbearably intimate moment that did it.

"I brought myself off in the bathroom at work. I've never done that before."

Every muscle in his body looked ready to break from strain. One of them flickered in his tense cheek. He moved his cockhead, rubbing her again. She grew desperate. If he didn't give that cock to her hard and deep soon, she was going to explode. Implode. She didn't know which . . .

"Tell me, Harper," she heard him say.

She lifted her head off the pillow. "*Fuck* me," she wailed. "God, if you don't fuck me now, I'm going to—"

She screamed. He'd given her clit one last, hard flick with the cockhead and then drove into her pussy. It didn't hurt precisely, but the pressure was overwhelming. For a few seconds, her brain overloaded with sensation. His loud, harsh groan brought everything back into focus. He was crouched between her thighs now, both of his hands planted in the mattress. She watched through heavy eyelids as he thrust again, and his cock pierced her to the hilt. A snarl shaped his lips. He pumped her hard for several long, ruthless strokes. Harper screamed again, pausing only when his movements did.

She watched him through narrow eyelids, teetering on the edge of orgasm. He lifted one hand and spread it on her lower belly. He was so big, she felt like he was palming her entire being. His thumb dipped between her labia, rubbing her clit.

There it was. His touch. She came against it thunderously.

Her fingers clutched at his wrist. It was the only contact she had with him, other than his cock throbbing deep inside her. She clung onto that wrist desperately as she shuddered in bliss.

He started to fuck her again as she came, resituating himself slightly, but still allowing her to hold him. Distantly, she heard him praising her. What he said was graphic and lewd, but somehow it sounded beautiful to her, solemn . . . sweet, even. He rocked her without mercy, his possession causing the bed to shake and her body to jerk and tremble beneath him.

"Look at me," he demanded.

He withdrew almost completely, and then re-pierced her from tip to balls in one stroke. Her eyelids sprung open. Their groans entwined, hers incredulous, Jacob's harsh. Savage. He repeated the stroke, but this time, he withdrew completely. The sound of his cockhead popping out of her wet channel emphasized the movement. His turgid cock flicked upward in the air slightly, freed from the restraint of her body. But no sooner had it happened than he dipped his hips and drove back into her pussy. She screamed at the jolt of hard, relentless pressure.

"I'm never going to get enough of your pussy." Somehow, he sounded both amazed and bitter at his declaration.

He continued like that for a breathless moment, using the defined rim of his cockhead to create a suction in her liquid pussy, withdrawing and driving back into her until she was mindless with excitement. She writhed and panted, but she couldn't move, thanks to the positioner. He'd made her his fixed target. She couldn't escape his pounding cock.

The last thing she wanted to do was try.

She saw that he watched himself penetrate her as he took her with those ruthless strokes. His ass and abdomen muscles flexed tight, he drove into her again and again, grunting in undisguised pleasure.

"Never. I'll never get enough," he seethed after a boiling moment.

He drew out of her again, dipping his hips, and sinking his cock into her to the hilt. This time, he didn't withdraw. He pumped her in short, staccato strokes that jolted Harper's body on the mattress. His eyes seemed to blaze as he watched her bobbing breasts for a charged moment, and then he transferred his gaze to her face.

"I'm going to make you pay for this, Harper."

"Pay for what?" she panted as her world shook and her body tensed against his onslaught. The friction was so good. She watched him through a haze of lust, but the sensations he created in her body felt sharp and lancing, almost cruelly precise.

"I'm going to make you pay for making me want you this much."

He plunged, her breasts bouncing as they crashed together. She cried out at the sensation of him swelling huge inside her. He grimaced and lunged slightly, applying pressure on her clit. He unlocked the tension that he'd built in her so surely with a hard, subtle circle of his hips.

She ignited yet again at the feeling of him coming. She shuddered, the sound of his low, savage growl echoing in her ears.

She panted in the aftermath. The tension left his rigid body on one ragged exhale of his breath. He slumped over her, still supporting his weight on his hands, his head bowed. Perspiration darkened the hair at his short sideburns and his nape. Harper experienced an overwhelming urge to touch him, to tangle her fingers in his hair, to slick her tongue along his hairline and taste his sweat, to feel his naked skin pressed against hers and their hearts racing in tandem.

She opened her mouth to voice her request, but something else came out of her mouth.

"What do you mean exactly, you'll make me pay for wanting me so much?"

He looked up slowly. Perspiration glazed his handsome face, chest, and bulging, muscular arms. She was reminded of his physical strength and endurance during lovemaking . . . the power he exerted over himself in restraint. His expression seemed to close off as she watched him. He hitched his hips and withdrew from her. A cry caught in her throat at the ensuing sting in her flesh . . . at the sudden deprivation of him.

"That," he said, sounding a little regretful. He leaned down and touched his lips to hers. She inhaled shakily, craning up to brush her lips against his. He straightened his arms and looked down at her solemnly, perhaps reading the question in her eyes. "I'm being very hard on you."

"I can take it," she whispered.

"Maybe so," he said, rolling over on his side. He unfastened the restraint of her right hand and reached across her to do the same for the left. "I'm not sure I can, though."

What does that mean?

She opened her mouth to ask the urgent question, but she realized her hands were unbound. Suddenly, she wasn't sure she wanted to hear his answer. Besides, she was free now to touch him. Instead of clarifying his enigmatic statement, she reached for him, delving her fingers into his thick hair. His gaze darted to hers. Was he about to emotionally withdraw like he had on the yacht?

Was he thinking of that other woman, the one she reminded him of?

"Come here, Jacob," she dared softly, urging him with her hands.

Her heart charged in the silent pause that followed. At first, he remained unmoving beneath her pressing fingertips. His hesitation cut at her.

Finally, he came. Did he seem resigned? If so, even his resignation came with a flash of his singular fire.

He fused his mouth to hers, and his taste eclipsed her concern. She urged further, coaxing him by caressing and pushing on his muscular, smooth back, and then on his round, dense buttocks. *God help me.* He felt so good. She couldn't get enough. Their kiss deepened. Pleasure suffused her when he pressed his entire weight against hers and she sunk into the mattress, a pleasure that was different but no less potent than the bliss he brought her while she'd lay there helpless, and he made love to her like a firestorm.

She lost herself for minutes, indulging in the dark, sweet addiction of his kiss. Why did she feel like he lost himself, too, and that perhaps this was a novel experience for him, as well . . . as much of a mysterious awakening for him as it was for her?

Abruptly, he parted from her and rose off the bed.

She'd been wrong in her idyllic fantasizing. He hadn't been feeling what she had at all. She grew bereft watching him walk away. The evolving intimacy had been too much for him. She shouldn't have pushed him. Maybe it was for the best.

It'd felt overwhelming for her, as well. She'd told him she thought she could handle a purely physical affair, and already, she was crossing the boundary.

He returned, pausing next to the bed. She watched him roll a fresh condom onto his re-stiffened cock, her heart jumping into overdrive.

She wasn't sure what to make of his serious expression as he climbed back onto the bed and moved between her suspended legs.

He unclasped the clips that were attached to her thigh cuffs. Her legs dropped down to the soft duvet. He fell over her. He caught her mouth with his as the head of his cock nudged at her entry.

She cried out into his mouth as he slowly, but firmly, entered her again.

They came together differently that time, more tenderly, but with every bit of the former intensity and fire. He let her touch him while they made love. And she did: everywhere, each touch, each stroke, bringing her higher into thrilling, dangerous realms.

Afterward, neither of them spoke. Jacob held her fast. Harper lay with her cheek against his chest, wondering if it was only her that sensed the words that surrounded them like too-soft whispers, or shouts that were too far in the distance to fully hear.

fifteen

Jacob awoke in the dead of night at the sound of a woman crying out in distress.

"It's all right, you're okay, Harper."

The room was almost pitch-black. He knew from experience with insomnia that his suite only grew this dark just before dawn. Swiftly, he lunged and hit a button on the bed's built-in console. A lamp illuminated. He twisted around to look at the woman in his bed.

"Harper," he said forcefully.

There'd never been any doubt in his mind whose shout it was. A lot of women had slept in his bed, yet he'd recognized her frightened voice in an instant. There was a hint of the girl she'd once been in that cry.

She lay on her back, her chin twisted in his direction. Her vibrant hair was spread out on the pillow. The expression of tight fear on her face made something sharp twist deep inside him. He slid closer to her, planting his elbow next to her ear. He curled his arm around her head, stroking her hair back from her temple, while he caressed her neck with his other hand. She was damp from sweat, a result of her nightmare. She moved her lips silently, fear still tightening her face.

"Harper, honey. Wake up."

"He's got a knife!"

He started when she jerked in his hold at the same time she shrieked. Suddenly, her aquamarine eyes were wide-open, and she was staring straight at him. It only took Jacob a split second to realize she wasn't *seeing* him, though.

"Harper, it's me. Jacob Latimer. You're safe. No one is going to hurt you." He cupped her jaw. "Do you hear me?" he demanded loudly, intent on penetrating the fog of her nightmare.

Too slowly for his comfort, the fear and desperation faded from her expression. He caressed her cheek and leaned down to brush his lips over her temple and then her eyebrow.

"It's all right. You were having a nightmare."

"Jacob?" she muttered thickly.

He lifted his head to peer at her face. "You okay?" he murmured, smoothing the tendrils of her hair away from her ear and damp neck.

She glanced around the room, seeming to gain her bearings.

"I'm sorry. Did I yell?"

He nodded, studying her face closely. She seemed okay now, but confused. "What were you dreaming about?"

"I . . ." She looked up at him, her blue-green eyes reminding him of pure, untainted pools, when only moments before, primal fear had swum in their depths. "I don't remember."

How could the terror he'd witnessed have vanished so quickly? His stroking fingers paused. "Are you sure?"

She nodded, looking embarrassed. "I'm sorry I woke you. I probably should get up, anyway. It'll be dawn soon, won't it?" she asked, rolling her head on the pillow and squinting to see the time on a nearby clock. He used his hold on her jaw to tilt her face back in his direction.

"You said something about a knife."

She stared at him blankly. "A *knife*?"

He nodded, searching her expression.

"That's weird. I can't remember what I was dreaming. But—"

"What?" he asked, when she cut herself off.

She shook her head. Her cheeks flushed a light pink.

"I guess it makes sense. I used to have a fear. About knives."

"A fear?"

"Yeah, a phobia actually," she muttered, her discomfort clear now.

"You mean you got anxious around knives?"

"More than anxious," she mumbled, avoiding eye contact with

him. "I couldn't be around them. I'd panic. It was one of many phobias I had when I was a teenager. I was a mess, if you want to know the truth."

"I do."

She blinked and looked at him, probably startled by his firm, quick reply.

"No. You *don't*, actually," she assured thickly. She started to sit up, clutching the sheet over her breasts. He moved back reluctantly to give her room. "Don't worry," she said, leaning up on one bent elbow and finger-combing her long hair back behind her shoulders. "I don't have any phobias anymore . . . or panic attacks."

"How come?"

"My dad."

"He treated you?" Jacob asked slowly, recalling that her father was a psychiatrist.

She nodded.

"Isn't that a little . . ." *unethical*, he thought. "Unusual? For a father to treat his daughter?" he asked, repulsed by the idea, for some reason. She stiffened.

"My father was one of the most respected psychiatrists in the country, not to mention arguably *the* most renowned expert in the world in the field of hypnotism. He was the ideal candidate to address my issues."

"Hypnotism," he repeated, stunned.

"Yes," she said, eyeing him warily. "You don't have to look like that. It's not witchcraft, you know. What's more, he was completely successful."

"He cured you."

Her gaze skated away from his. "That's right. Don't worry, I'm not contagious, Jacob."

She flipped the comforter back in preparation to get up. He caught her forearm as she started to slide out of bed.

"You're glad?" he demanded. "That your father was the one to treat you?"

"Of course I am! You have no idea how anxious I was, how shut off from my friends and a normal teenage existence. I was afraid constantly. I'm a different person today, because of my father's help."

Her face was pale and tense. It came to him in a rush, how his abrupt, tactless questions must have struck her. Yet his curiosity still prodded at him. Did her father's treatment have anything to do with why she never mentioned her kidnapping or their flight from Emmitt Tharp? Is that why she didn't recognize him? No, that couldn't be the only reason. She didn't recognize him primarily because he didn't remotely resemble that skinny, helpless thirteen-year-old kid. Jacob had made sure of that.

Maybe Dr. McFadden had merely done what any father would have longed to do when presented with a traumatized daughter. Had his treatment psychologically distanced Harper from the frightening memory of her kidnapping and her assault at the hands of Emmitt Tharp? Or had he tried to totally erase that handful of days and nights from Harper's childhood? Speculation and questions flooded his brain.

Until he focused on Harper's anxious face again, anyway. He couldn't badger her about it. Not now.

Besides, if she had forgotten, she was safe from the memories.

He was safe from her remembering.

He nodded once, his hold on her loosening. "I'm sorry. I think a little of your nightmare rubbed off on me. You looked really scared. I shouldn't have asked so many questions."

He saw the tension melt from her sloping shoulders and graceful back. "It's okay. I'm sorry for freaking you out. I guess we all have nightmares, right?" she asked him uneasily.

He nodded, reaching to stroke her silky shoulder, reassuring her even as he reassured himself.

Yeah. Everyone had their nightmares. The truth was, Jacob had some that involved a knife, too. Not just any knife, either.

The *exact* same knife that apparently still haunted Harper's dreams.

Twenty Years Ago

After they'd locked the sedated dogs in the barn, he'd furtively led Harper over a freshly mown lawn to the edge of the forest. He removed his backpack.

"Climb up onto my back," he whispered.

"*What?*"

"Your walk leaves a trail. I'll wipe it when I go back. Just *do* it, Harper. Get on my back."

Even though she looked exasperated, she put her hands on his shoulders when he turned around. He draped his pack in the crook of his arm and hoisted her onto his back. Willfully ignoring the sensation of her hands fastened on his skinny muscles and her breasts pressing against his shoulder blades, he entered the forest. Fifty feet in, he set her down next to an ancient, branchy oak.

"The angle on the house is good here, see?" Jake said, pointing toward a clearing in the trees. "I'm going back for a few minutes to do something. You stay here. If you see my uncle come out, or any other man come onto the property, hide up there," he said, pointing at the intersection of the trunk and seven gnarly, thick branches. "There's a hole in the trunk up there. Just slide right in it. You're little enough to fit. I hide there sometimes from Emmitt, so I know he doesn't know about it. If I don't come back to get you soon, wait until you're *sure* the coast is clear, and head in that direction." He pointed to the west. He noticed her alarmed expression. "I'll be back in less than five minutes. I'm telling you this . . . just in case."

She caught his arm, halting him as he started back toward Emmitt's property.

"You're crazy. Let's go. What do you have to go back for?" she hissed.

"There's something I have to do," he repeated, holding her stare as he calmly removed her grasping hand from his arm. "It'll only take a minute."

She looked mutinous. "I'm coming, then," she stated, stepping toward him.

He caught her at her shoulders.

"You're *not*. I'm sorry. I told you that you had to do what I said, and you agreed. This is something I gotta do alone. Don't pitch a fit about it."

The anger slowly drained from her face. Maybe she sensed his grim, sad sense of purpose.

"Okay. But . . . hurry," she whispered tensely as he turned.

He merely nodded once. He turned and slunk back onto Emmitt's property.

She had lead feet, Jake thought numbly several hours later. He hadn't hesitated to tell her, either, as they hastened through the woods earlier. Now he heard her stomping on the cave's dusty stone floor a good fifteen seconds before she appeared by where he knelt next to a tiny trickling waterfall.

He knew from years of solitary exploring that the waterfall filtered down through stone from the top of the bluff. It was pure for drinking. Caves like this one pervaded the Appalachian Mountains, but this particular one was different. It was unique to Jake for the sole reason that Emmitt didn't know of its existence. Jake knew this from the simple logic that Emmitt had never successfully discovered Jake there, despite the fact that he'd combed the woods and hills looking for him on dozens of occasions in the past.

He'd brought them there because he was uncertain about the tranquilizer and how long his uncle would be knocked out. Here, he could keep Harper temporarily safe while he determined if Emmitt had picked up their trail.

Harper noisily plopped down on the earth next to him. At least her lack of grace wasn't as important now that they'd reached the cave. Either Emmitt would fall for Jake's false trail in the direction of Poplar Gorge, or he wouldn't. If he picked up their trail to the cave, Harper could be as silent as a flea, and Emmitt would still find them.

During their flight through the woods, Harper hadn't seemed to have any idea what Jake meant about moving through the woods like a ghost. How could Jake ask her not to make the grass rustle or bend, or twigs break beneath her feet?

She had no idea of what it meant to be prey.

Given the racket she'd made approaching him just now, there'd been time to duck behind the rocks and avoid her. Was it what he'd done back at Emmitt's, his fear of being caught . . . or his fascination with Harper McFadden that kept him fixed in place? He was too weary to figure it out. He continued to wash his hands in the cool waterfall when she came and sat beside him.

They'd washed and dressed her cut wrists earlier. The white of the bandages flickered in the light of the small camp lantern. He was highly distracted by the feeling of her knee brushing against his lower leg. Half in dread and half in anticipation, he waited for her to speak.

But she didn't.

Instead, her small, warm hands surrounded his wrists. He stiffened at her touch, but didn't resist when she gently pulled his hands out of the streaming water. When she released him, he sat back on his haunches, his wet hands leaking onto his jean-covered thighs.

"Your hands aren't going to get any cleaner," she stated dryly.

He raised his hands to his face, palms facing him, and peered at them closely. His fingertips were as wrinkled as prunes from being underwater so long.

"What'd you do, Jake?" He heard her whisper from the darkness. "What did you do when you went back to your uncle's?"

He lowered his hands and braced them on his thighs, rocking back and forth slightly.

"I killed Mrs. Roundabout."

"Who's Mrs. Roundabout?"

He was surprised and relieved that she didn't gasp in horror at his confession. She'd asked the question quickly and calmly.

"My dog," Jake answered dully. "Emmitt didn't think she was my dog. But she was. Not that I owned her. Not like that. She was just . . ." *My friend.* He didn't say the thought out loud. Harper probably already thought he was a stupid hillbilly. "My dog, that's all," he repeated lamely. He lowered his head and studied his knees. "All the dogs on Emmitt's property are bought for the fights, so Emmitt thought Mrs. Roundabout was his. She wasn't, though."

"Fights?"

"Yeah. Dogfights. Men bet on a dog to win in the ring."

"How do they win?" Harper asked, sounding puzzled.

"By taking down the other dog with its teeth and claws, injuring it until it can't get up and fight anymore. Sometimes by killing it."

"And . . . and people bet on it? *Watch* it?" she asked, her bewilderment and dawning distaste obvious.

"Yeah. They root on their dog. The one they bet on."

She didn't say anything for several seconds while Jake steeped in his foulness. His dirtiness. She had no knowledge of the things he'd seen, of the brutality he'd witnessed and taken part in, even if unwillingly.

"Why'd you kill her?" He winced at the word "kill" coming out of her mouth.

"Because my uncle made her fight, and she got hurt real bad. I was trying to doctor her, but she wasn't getting better. She was in a lot of pain. Suffering. Since I was leaving with you, I didn't have any choice."

"How'd you do it?" she whispered.

"I gave her a lethal dose of the sedative. She'll just have gone to sleep." He sniffed and swiped at his cheeks. They were wet. He hated that she witnessed how weak he was. He clamped his eyes shut and took a deep, uneven breath. "It's done, now. I guess she's not suffering anymore."

"You did the right thing. You *absolutely* did the right thing. I'm just sorry you had to do it. And I'm sorry that you lost your dog." He looked around, startled at how fierce she'd sounded. She put her arm around his shoulders. Her face was close. Her kindness—and her touch—had almost crowded his grief and fear clear out of his brain.

"Do you think he'll find us?" she asked quietly after a moment. Jake blinked, jerking his awareness off the sensation of her rubbing her fingers soothingly over his upper arm. He wasn't used to being touched kindly. Grandma Rose used to hug him sometimes before she'd gotten sick and taken to her bed. That'd been nice and comforting, he recalled. But Harper's half hug wasn't the same . . . in fact, it was a world of difference.

"He doesn't know where this cave is," he repeated. He'd told her of the whole plan once they'd reached the safety of his cave. By leaving a false trail in the direction of the nearest town, Poplar Gorge, Jake hoped Emmitt would draw the conclusion he'd taken Harper south. In truth, they'd hole up in the cave until it was likely that Emmitt was hot on the false trail, then cross the river and head in the direction of Barterton.

Barterton was farther away than Poplar Gorge, and for all Emmitt knew, Jake had never been there. Jake had traveled there twice now, however, on his own and in secret. He liked the hot dog stand downtown—soft-serve ice cream for a quarter. Once, he'd camped out on the outskirts of town and snuck into the back of the local drive-in and watched a comedy on the big screen. Both trips had been undertaken while Emmitt was in Charleston for extended weekends, supposedly for "business," but probably mostly just for whoring and drinking. Jake had bargained with a kid who lived down the river, Stevie Long, to come over and feed the dogs while he made his little trips in Emmitt's absence. In return, Jake had promised to do Stevie's math homework for six months. Looking back on it, Jake thought he'd struck a good deal with Stevie. His knowledge of the landscape in the direction of Barterton would help their escape.

"Emmitt won't imagine I'd take you to Barterton," Jake told her.

"Why not?"

He stilled his shrug with his shoulders elevated, suddenly aware he might throw off Harper's embrace. Her touch had sent him into a trance. His gaze shot sideways, but he didn't dare to move his head. As if she'd sensed his sudden tension and awkwardness, her hand slid down his back and off of him. He tried to contain his sharp disappointment.

"Emmitt doesn't think much of me, one way or another. He wouldn't think I'd come up with a plan that wasn't the obvious."

"He doesn't get how smart you are," she stated rather than asked. "That's an advantage to us."

He looked at her, his mouth hanging open. It was the best compliment he'd ever gotten.

"You didn't kill Mrs. Roundabout."

"What?" he asked, amazed not only by her firm proclamation, but her blazing stare. She might be a menace in the woods, and a city girl to boot, but Harper McFadden was no weakling.

"You didn't kill Mrs. Roundabout. You set her free, just as surely as you freed me. *He* killed her."

Jake swallowed thickly and nodded, pulling his gaze off her mouth. He still saw it in his head as he stared unseeingly at the trickling water. He shouldn't be thinking about Harper's lips, given the circumstances they were in.

Maybe she was right about Emmitt being responsible for Mrs. Roundabout's death. Something else *was* a certainty. Emmitt'd kill Jake the second he found them.

He didn't want to think about what his uncle might do to Harper afterward.

4

make me
DESPERATE

sixteen

Present Day

Three days after she'd awakened in Jacob's bed from a nightmare, Harper glanced up from her computer when she heard a tap on her office door.

"I'm almost finished, Burt," she mumbled distractedly, paging down to the last paragraph of the story she was editing. Burt Chavis was dressed in board shorts, a Swell T-shirt, and flip-flops. His sunbleached dreadlocks were pulled back in a thick ponytail. He was twenty-eight years old and wore a perennial grin. He was a crappy dresser, but he possessed a surprisingly incising brain for a summertime beach bum and wintertime snowboarder. Harper had decided early on he was the best of the two reporters she had working for her. His easygoing, friendly manner made people open up to him during interviews. Sangar had told her in private that Burt had some issues with backing up his claims for stories with credible sources, but Harper was keeping an open mind. She wasn't that much older than Burt, and they'd been comfortable with each other from their first meeting.

Besides, it was her job as Burt's editor to make sure his stories *were* credible.

"What's this I hear from Ruth about you being invited to the Latimer compound the other night?" Burt asked.

"It was nothing. A cocktail party," Harper said without removing her gaze from Burt's story.

"Ruth said it had something to do with Cyril Atwater wanting to make a movie out of a story you wrote," Burt said, his lazy stance as he leaned against the wall just inside the door belying the sharp intelligence in his pale blue eyes.

"That's right."

"Ruth thinks it'd make a good feature for her column. But what about me?"

Harper looked at him blandly. "What about you?"

"I have the crime beat. I want a story."

Harper blinked at his boldness. All traces of the easygoing beach bum had vanished.

"Going to a cocktail party warrants a crime story?"

"Latimer warrants it. Something new and revealing could be my ticket to a big San Francisco paper."

Harper turned back to her computer. "You don't really want that, do you, Burt?" she asked mildly. "They'll make you put on a tie and wear shoes with laces on them to work every day."

"I want it," Burt said simply. "Any chance you're going to be invited to the Latimer compound again in association with this movie thing?"

Harper sighed, recognizing she wasn't going to shake him easily. "Ellie, the girl I wrote the story about, has agreed to allow film production to go forward, as long as I'm involved. I spoke to Atwater yesterday and he's having a lawyer work up contracts for us. Latimer hasn't been involved, though. Not in the slightest," she said, hiding a frown as she stared at her computer screen.

"He will be, eventually. He produces Atwater's films. The next time you're invited to the Latimer compound, maybe I could go as your assistant."

Harper hit save and print on Burt's story before she turned to face him. "That's not going to happen. Find some other career-making story." Her printer came to a stop and she pointed at the printed papers it'd just chugged out. "*That's* not the one, by the way. I made some notes on it. Get it back to me in twenty minutes?"

Burt picked up his copy from the printer. "Latimer is a big fish. A story we worked up together would be key for your career, too."

She gave him a sharp, assessing look. "If you want to do a story on Latimer, what's your angle?"

He shrugged. "I'm looking for one. That's why I'm asking for your help."

"I'm not stopping you from being a reporter. I'm not quashing anything newsworthy, if it's credible and you have solid sources to back it up. *Do* you have something substantial that you're working on?"

"Nothing but a shitload of rumors."

"Then forget it. And leave me out of the whole thing," Harper said. "I've already had my share of career-makers."

Burt laughed and shook his head. "That's shit, and you know it. I can't get to Latimer. No one can . . . except maybe you. You're really going to sit on your awards and your movie deals and keep Latimer from the rest of us?"

She met his gaze squarely and leaned forward, hands on her desk. "I've got nothing for you when it comes to Jacob Latimer. Nothing. That's because I don't know any more than you do. Do you understand?" She waited until Burt nodded resentfully. "Twenty minutes," she repeated with a smile, nodding at the story he clutched in his hand before she turned away.

She hadn't been lying. She'd given her word to Jacob that she had no plans to use any information she learned from their affair for the purpose of an article or exposé on him or his business activities. But more importantly, she truly didn't possess anything newsworthy when it came to Jacob.

That's a lie.

She grimaced at the snide inner voice in her head, busying herself with her layouts. He was a fascinating, complex . . . and very secretive man.

Her brain flashed back to their parting on that early morning three days ago, to the last time she'd been in his arms. He'd halted her before she reached for his bedroom door and drew her back into his embrace. She'd stared up at him, enraptured, when he cradled her jaw in his hands and lifted her mouth. Then he'd kissed her, and it'd been like the first time, as if he were claiming her all over again. She was leaving him after a night of challenge and passion. She should have been sated, her brain already ticking off the goals and details of her workday. Instead, he'd shrouded her in his spell all over again.

He lifted his head a hazy, delicious moment later, and Harper's toes slowly started to uncurl.

"Have dinner with me tonight?" he'd asked, his low, fluid voice washing over her.

"Yes," she'd replied without thought.

Later that afternoon, she'd received an unexpected call from Elizabeth. The call had come when she was packing up at the end of her workday, flushed with excitement and anticipation at the idea of dinner with Jacob . . . at the prospect of returning to his bedroom and whatever new decadent sexual challenge he'd propose.

"I'm glad I caught you," Elizabeth said. "Jacob asked me to reach you. He sends his apologies, but he's been called away unexpectedly. He won't be able to have dinner tonight."

"Oh . . . I see. I hope everything is all right?" She'd thought she'd heard a slight edge of anxiety to Elizabeth's tone.

"Of course. Something required his direct attention, a minor emergency at his estate in Napa. It happens sometimes. Often, in truth. That he's called away. He has so many different business concerns. So many interests."

Harper blinked. Was it her imagination, or was Elizabeth trying to coyly pass on a message: *You might have his attention for a short span of time, but don't kid yourself into thinking it's anything permanent. You're one of a million things Jacob Latimer has to deal with every day. He has his concerns . . .*

. . . and his interests.

Harper was one of his current interests. So might be any number of other women.

She cleared her throat. "I'm glad to hear it isn't anything dire. Thank you for calling and delivering the message."

Thank you for calling and breaking his date for him, Harper thought irritably three days later.

Forget it. Forget him.

He'd never called after Elizabeth had, so she had no idea when—or if—she was going to see him again. It pissed her off, that she cared one way or another. He'd set something alight inside her, awakened her body and her brain, until she was having trouble sleeping and concentrating. She kept reliving those moments on the yacht. She kept experiencing those minutes that she was held at his mercy by the positioner, when she'd been at the center of his fierce focus and demanding hunger. He'd set her on fire, and then left her to burn out of control.

Bastard.

Her phone rang, cutting off her bitter, frustrated train of thought.

"Harper McFadden," she said into the receiver distractedly, lunging to grab a folder that was about to spill off her desk.

"Go to the ladies' room."

She froze in the action of leaning across the desk, the folder clutched in her hand.

"Jacob?" Her voice vibrated with shock.

"Yes."

"*What* did you say?"

"Go to the ladies' room. The one in the south hallway. Now."

"But—"

"You told me you masturbated in here."

Harper's mouth fell open. Her skin roughened. Did that he mean *he* was in there? In the *Gazette*'s bathroom? Right at this very moment? It wasn't just him saying something so illicit so unexpectedly in that fluid, hypnotizing voice of his that left her speechless. It was the way his bald statement immediately clicked her brain out of the mundane, everyday concerns of life and into a dizzying, dark, sexual reality. His voice—just his voice—took her to a different world.

"If you masturbated in here, that must mean you're confident of relative privacy and that there's no surveillance," his voice continued quietly through the receiver.

"Jacob . . . are you *here*? In the newsroom?"

"Yes."

"You should go. What if someone sees you?" *Like Ruth, or Burt, or Sangar . . . or* anyone *who might recognize their local celebrity billionaire lurking around the newsroom.* How was she going to continue to insist to others that Jacob Latimer meant nothing to her if he pulled stunts like this?

"No one's going to see me, and I'm not leaving. I couldn't stop thinking about you. I haven't been able to stop thinking about you masturbating in here. Sweet, good girl Harper McFadden, bringing herself off at work." He said it softly, but there was an edge to his tone. She pictured him snarling slightly as he spoke. Excitement prickled through her.

"Come here, Harper."

The line went dead.

She hung up her phone, staring blankly into space. Of course she wouldn't go. Out on the main floor of the newsroom, a young female reporter laughed shrilly at something their ad exec said. In the distance, she saw Sangar talking heatedly on his phone through his open office door.

Jacob was out of his mind—not to mention ridiculously cocky— to suggest she go and meet him for a sexual tryst in a bathroom at her workplace.

Nevertheless, she found herself walking out of her office, her feet feeling numb in her pumps and her heart starting a sluggish roll in her ears. *I haven't been able to stop thinking about you.* Was he lying just to get what he wanted?

Did she care, when she craved the same thing?

The south hallway was deserted, still, and dim. The bathrooms down here were private ones, unlike the larger bathroom in the north wing. That was good, but also risky. The private bathrooms were more popular than the common ones.

She came to a halt outside a wood door, her heart now a rapid drumbeat in her ears. She held her breath and reached for the knob. Before she could grab it, it twisted and the door opened several inches. She heard running water, and had a brief impression of Jacob's towering form. He was wearing a dark blue suit, white shirt, and silver tie, and his face looked set and grim. That was all she saw of him, because he grasped her wrist and pulled her into the bathroom. The next thing she knew, her hands were behind her back and he was pressing her against the hard wood of the closed bathroom door. Her heart knocked against her breastbone. *What the hell?*

She heard the click of the lock.

Air hissed out of her lungs when he flattened the front of his body to the back of hers, sandwiching her against himself and the door.

"Jacob, what are you *doing*?" she asked in a strangled voice.

He lifted her hair from her neck, clutching it in his hand. She gasped at the sensation of his lips moving along her skin. He scraped his teeth gently along a cord of muscle, making her shudder. "I'm going to have you, Harper," he said very quietly next to her ear.

"No," she muttered weakly. His mouth opened over her ear, his kiss causing a suction that made her shiver uncontrollably. She struggled against his solid, hard weight, but that was a mistake. He pressed closer, and she felt his erection. It wasn't a partial one, as if he'd just begun to get aroused when they came into contact. He was fully, flagrantly erect. How long had he been waiting, planning to pounce on her here? His long fingers slid beneath her jaw. "Jacob, you can't just come here and—"

He pushed on her face, forcing her to turn her chin over her shoulder. He tilted his head. His mouth covered hers. *Oh, Jesus.* Sensation rushed through her. She tasted him, that increasingly familiar, addictive flavor. But it was more than that. She tasted his hunger. It was like mainlining an intoxicant straight into her blood. He penetrated her mouth with his tongue, stroking her boldly. Lewdly. Harper felt herself rising like a freed helium balloon, her lust rapidly mounting to match his. He pressed tighter against her from the back, the column of his cock grinding against the top of her buttocks and her lower back. He crushed against her hard. His kiss was harsh. It hurt a little, given the awkward angle and his forcefulness. It also enflamed her.

She tangled her tongue with his, moaning into his aggressive kiss. Maybe he considered that desperate moan a surrender—and maybe it was—because when he released her from his punishing kiss, she didn't protest any further. She just panted, looking over her shoulder, trying to see what he was doing. She couldn't see his face, but she felt it when his hands moved quickly. He was slipping a strap around her wrists. It tightened. She inhaled sharply in anxious excitement. He'd just bound her wrists behind her back.

He actually had brought a wrist restraint into her work bathroom. His daring left her speechless. For a few seconds, her breath stuck painfully in her lungs.

"Don't be afraid," she heard him murmur from behind her. "I'm not going to hurt you. If I did, all you'd have to do is scream. Okay?"

She nodded once.

"Come here."

He backed her across the bathroom, guiding her with his hands on her upper arms. His touch was gentle, despite the outrageousness of what he was doing. He urged her downward. Harper sat, hitting the closed toilet seat with a muted thump.

She looked up at him, her mouth hanging open. He was already intent on another task: unbuttoning her red silk blouse with fleet fingers, a grim sense of determination on his lean, handsome face. He jerked her blouse open and lowered the cups of her bra beneath her nipples in two quick, succinct movements. She saw a snarl shape his lips as he stared down at her exposed breasts. Her nipples tightened before he even reached to run his fingertips over the sensitive globes. He squeezed firmly, his nostrils flaring. He pinched lightly at her hard nipples, and liquid heat rushed through her sex.

"Why are you doing this?" she moaned, because it felt so good. So dirty.

"Because I want to," he responded without hesitation. His gaze rose to fasten on her face. He continued to massage her breasts and pinch at the nipples. "I've wanted to do something like this since the second you walked out the door the other day." Holding her stare, he dropped one hand. Harper watched, slack-jawed, as he ran his hand up and down over his cock. The shape of his erection—the long, thick shaft and the succulent, defined cap—were made clear against the fabric of his dress pants and his stroking hand. Saliva filled her mouth, making her close her lips. As if he'd known what reaction he had on her, he lifted a hand to her mouth and pressed his thumb against her lower lip, applying a firm pressure and running it back and forth.

"Jacob—" she mouthed.

"I told you that you were going to have to pay for making me want you this much. I haven't had a moment's peace since I went away," he said.

"That's not my fault."

"No. But you'll still be the one to pay."

He forced her mouth open with his thumb. Instinctively, Harper slicked her tongue along her lower lip, licking his finger in the process. He gave a muted groan, and then plunged his thumb between her lips, running it over her tongue. She closed around him, sucking him deeper and laving his skin with her tongue.

He pushed his thumb in and out of her mouth several times before he removed it. He held her stare as he began to unfasten his pants. She watched as he freed his cock, shoving his trousers and boxer briefs down to his thighs. A moment later, he held his naked, stiff cock in his hand. She stared, rapt, as he fisted himself and moved his hand up and down, squeezing the shaft hard as he reached the flaring crown. He groaned, rough and deep. A droplet of come beaded at the slit. There was a roar in her ears. It was her blood racing in her veins, but distantly, she realized he'd turned on the tap water to create white noise to muffle their activity.

He let go of his erection and reached, gathering her unbound hair with both of his hands. Harper panted softly, her gaze fixed on his cock. He gathered her hair into a tight ponytail at the back of her head. He held it with one hand and grasped his erection again.

"Spread your lips," he directed quietly.

Harper opened wide without hesitation. She saw his cock jump slightly at her eager display. He was crazy, and she was nuts for agreeing, but this was a delicious madness. She felt raunchy. Slutty.

Cock-starved.

"Spread your knees," he demanded.

When she'd followed his instructions, he stepped closer to her. He reached down and grabbed the hem of the skirt she wore, shoving it up her thighs to make room for him. With no further ado, he pushed his cock between her lips. She moaned softly at the sensation of his stony flesh breaching her, stretching her lips wide. The defined crown of his cock passed her clamping lips, and she closed her eyes in peaking lust. She jerked her head back and then forward again, pulling hard with her mouth, intensely aroused by the sensation of that thick rim. By his taste. Her precise action made a wet, popping noise. A rough sound vibrated his throat, and he urged her with his hand at the back of her head. Harper was already bobbing her head again, however, eager to experience the sensation again.

He slid further into her this time, his rigid flesh gliding across her tongue and crowding against the top of her mouth. For a stretched, tense moment, she worked him deeper. His hand on her head was firm. He demanded a lot of her, but even that aroused her. She found herself wanton. Desperate. His cock—his concise hunger—liberated her, somehow. It shocked her a little, how much she wanted to please him, to mount his lust and see him break in release.

She made a strangled sound of dissatisfaction when he suddenly flexed his hips back, using his hold on her head to move her backward. His cock popped out of her mouth. He almost immediately reinserted it between her lips.

"Suck hard," he ordered thickly.

He repeated the action three more times, pulling his cock from her pursed lips and then plunging it into her again, overfilling her mouth while she pulled on him for all she was worth. She knew he liked it— liked the sensation and watching himself pierce her—when she heard his low feral growl. On his last pass, he flexed his hips forward and held her head firm. Her eyes sprang wide at the sensation of him approaching her throat, but she stilled her gag reflex. She managed to do it by focusing on sucking him.

She managed to do it because her hunger matched his.

He groaned roughly and jerked his cock out of her mouth again. He held himself in his hand and massaged her saliva onto the staff.

"Keep your mouth spread wide," she heard him say above her. "That's right." He plunged his swollen cock between her lips once more with a taut, forceful gesture, and then withdrew. "Such a sweet little mouth. So hot," he muttered. "Is your mouth sore, Harper?"

She lunged forward, eager to have his cock filling her again. He pulled firmly backward on her ponytail, halting her greed. She blinked, her lust pierced. She looked up at him dazedly. His mouth twisted slightly.

"Is your mouth sore?" he repeated.

"No," she lied. Her lips and jaw ached. So did her pussy, but in a different way. He was a mouthful. She was desperate to see him lose control, though, wild to feel him explode in such an intimate place.

"That's a very sweet lie," he said, before he thrust into her mouth again.

seventeen

For a moment, he didn't hold back. He thrust into her forcefully and rapidly. Harper strained toward him with each pass, keeping pace, but barely. She lost herself, bobbing her head back and forth as he pounded into her mouth. Even though she was eager, he controlled the rhythm and pressure with his hips and hold on her hair. He was demanding—to say the least—but he never caused her any acute discomfort.

He pulled the fat, flaring crown of his cock out of her mouth, bouncing tantalizingly just inches from her lips.

"Relax. Close your mouth for a few seconds," he commanded.

She moaned as she followed his instructions, watching fixedly as he fisted and stroked his slick erection.

"Your mouth is so pretty. Better to fuck than I imagined. You're so hungry, aren't you?" He lifted his hand and caressed her jaw with damp, warm fingertips. "But you're very small, too. You *are* sore, aren't you?"

She'd groaned from the pain of intense arousal, not physical discomfort. But her mouth *did* ache dully. So did her lips. Even that turned her on. Her pussy was wet. Hot.

"Yes. Let me suck it more," she said hoarsely.

It was like another woman uttered those words: a woman who craved it tense and rough and lewd. A woman who got off on having her hands tied behind her back and being forced to suck cock hard and deep in the bathroom of her workplace . . .

His caressing fingers paused at her words. "You shouldn't say things like that, Harper." The next thing she knew, he thrust his cock into her mouth again while forcing her head forward.

"Is that what you want?" she heard him rasp darkly from above her as he pumped aggressively. Just when the tip of his cock was a whisper away from tickling the back of her throat, he slid out of her and thrust again. His low, restrained grunts rained down on her, sending her into a frenzy. She ground her hips down on the hard toilet seat as she took him. She could come from this, just from being the recipient of his unchecked, greedy hunger.

"Hold still," he ordered a moment later in a voice that sounded muted, but hard. Angry, even.

He began to fuck her mouth in a manner that would have caused her shame if she wasn't nearly as mindless with lust as he was. He pumped the base of his cock with his hand while he thrust into her mouth. She pressed down with her hips, getting pressure on her sex. God, she was a whore. He was using her for his pleasure, and she loved it. She moaned shakily around his cock. He paused.

"Open your eyes."

Her eyelids blinked open at his tense command. She stared up at him with his cock spreading her lips wide. Helpless. Hungry.

He mumbled a harsh curse. His cock popped out of her mouth. He jerked her up from her seated position.

"What—" she squeaked in confusion when he abruptly turned her in front of his body. He'd been on the verge of coming. She'd sensed it. He wrapped his arm around her waist and hauled her against him. She whimpered.

"Be quiet," he grated out as he dragged her skirt up to her belly. He shoved his hand beneath her panties and pressed against the back of her. "You're soaking wet," he said as he rubbed her outer sex forcefully. She whimpered. "Shhh," he hissed, his mouth just above her right ear. "You don't want anyone to hear you come, do you? Did you cry out when you masturbated here before?"

But Harper was too lost in the clutches of hot, blinding lust to reply. She circled her hips, grinding her ass against his balls, getting more pressure on her pussy. Suddenly, he lifted his pleasure-giving hand and gave the side of her ass a muted slap. A startled cry popped out of her throat.

"Answer me. Were you silent when you brought yourself off in the bathroom before?" he said tensely right next to her ear. His front teeth fastened on the shell of her ear, giving her a rough, arousing caress. She moaned.

"Harper," he growled.

"I . . ." She struggled to think. The only thing she could focus on was her craving for him to put his hand back between her legs. She hadn't realized it was so hard to think when she was this aroused. Maybe she'd never been this turned on before? That must be the reason she was writhing against him like a horny slut in the bathroom of her workplace.

"I don't know," she muttered. "It happened more than once."

"*What?*"

"You're making me crazy too, Jacob," she bit out bitterly in a muted tone. She was so aroused, it was like every nerve in her body burned. "What do you *want* from me?"

There was a tense pause.

"I want you to answer my question. Were you able to keep quiet before? The other times, when you came in here?"

"I kept quiet," she panted, clamping her eyelids shut.

"Can you this time?"

"I don't . . . know," she admitted brokenly. Her body shook in barely restrained arousal. "I don't think so."

His encircling arm rose to her mouth. He pressed his forearm against her lips. His deft fingertips resumed rubbing her lubricated, sizzling clit. "Come," he whispered hoarsely near her ear.

She climaxed thunderously, her cries muffled by his sleeve-covered forearm crushed against her mouth.

"Sit down, Harper. Now."

She blinked in disorientation. She'd lost herself to flooding pleasure and heat there for a moment. Jacob had turned her again, and was urging her back down on the toilet seat. The feeling of hitting the hard seat jolted through her dazed state. She opened her mouth to ask a question. He stepped closer and thrust his cock between her lips.

She made a surprised sound. He began to thrust, his hand at the back of her head.

She immediately came back to herself at the sensation and began bobbing her head, taking him eagerly. He halted her by grasping the hair at her nape.

"Stay still. I'm going to come," he ground out. He fucked her mouth tautly for several seconds, the incipient power in him making her eyes spring wide. He jacked the base of the staff with his hand even as he pierced her mouth forcefully. She felt his cock swell.

He withdrew almost entirely from her suckling mouth and began to come. Did he think she didn't want him to come in her mouth? Harper leaned forward, thirsty for the first thick, white ejaculate that began to shoot from the slit. He suppressed a throat-burning groan. He gripped his fingers tighter in her hair, stilling her. He squeezed the base of his cock.

"All right. Open," he said in a choked voice.

She did what he asked. He angled his cock into her mouth and finished coming on her tongue. She stared up at him, wide-eyed, undone as the taste of his semen entered her awareness. His big body tensed and shuddered several times.

After a moment, he exhaled raggedly and withdrew. He lowered his hand to her cheek and caressed her jaw. "Close, Harper," he said thickly.

He held his glistening cock just inches from her face. She looked up and saw him watching her with that feral focus of his as she closed her lips and swallowed.

It aroused him unbearably, even in his sated state, to see the convulsion of her throat, to witness her taking him into her body while she looked up at him, her beautiful eyes glazed with lust . . . and trust.

Discomfort trickled into his awareness. Her lips were reddened and puffy. He'd been hard on her. As usual. He gently stroked her bee-stung lower lip with the pad of his thumb. Her lips parted. She continued to stare up at him, something in her expression amplifying his guilt.

His need swelled yet again, unexpected and harsh, despite the fact that he'd just come explosively. Made even more uncomfortable by the realization, he took a step back and jerked up his briefs before he reached around her, unfastening the wrist restraint he'd brought with him. He shoved the thin, padded cuff into his pants pocket.

"Are you going to make a habit of this?" he heard her ask quietly.

He glanced up from zipping his pants. Was he behaving coldly again, in the aftermath? His gaze flickered downward to her breasts. They were still exposed, poking out from the lowered cups of her bra. Regret sliced through him. Selfish regret. He wanted to haul her out of the *Gazette*'s office and take her home. He wanted to lay her on his bed and put his mouth on every inch of her.

"Coming to this bathroom, you mean?" he asked warily.

She nodded. Relief swept through him. She wasn't referring to him being distant. "Given this time, I just might," he said, holding her stare as he tucked in his shirt.

Her lush mouth tightened, and he sensed her volatile state. Well, what could he expect, given what he'd just done to her?

Out in the hallway, he heard heels clicking briskly on the tile floor. From the sudden frozen expression on Harper's face, she'd noticed, too. The footsteps paused outside the door. He leaned and turned up the water pressure on the tap, making a louder white noise. There was a slight pause, and then he heard the steps going down the hall again.

"Maybe you'd like to see me fired from my job?" Harper asked.

"Why would I want that?" he wondered, stepping toward her again. He took her hands and lifted her to a standing position, drawing her against his body.

"So you wouldn't have to worry about me being a reporter anymore," she said soberly, looking up at him.

"The only motive I had in coming here," he said softly, brushing his fingertips over her cheek. "Was seeing you."

"Wouldn't it have been easier to call me and ask me to dinner?"

A smile pulled at his lips at her droll tone. Again, he caressed her slightly swollen lower lip.

"You're right. I didn't come here to see you. I came here because I *had* to."

"Like a compulsion?" she murmured, moving her lips beneath his stroking finger.

"Maybe," he said, dipping his head. He brushed his mouth over her lips, all too aware of how he'd been so forceful with her earlier. Regretting it.

Wanting to do it all over again.

"Yes," he amended. "A compulsion."

"When did you return to Tahoe Shores?" she whispered next to his lips.

"Just now," he murmured. He plucked at her mouth and drew her closer with his hands at the top of her buttocks. Despite his desire to bring her nearer, she started back and met his stare.

"Just now?"

Undeterred, he leaned down and nipped at her lips again. He didn't reply until she reciprocated.

"Yes. My driver is in the parking lot, waiting. We came directly here."

Again, she pulled her head back. He saw the question in her eyes.

"I'm sorry about having to cancel our dinner the other night," he said, guessing what was behind her unease—or part of it, anyway. "I wouldn't have done it, unless it was completely necessary."

She nodded, and pulled out of his embrace. With her back turned to him, she straightened her bunched bra and buttoned her blouse. She smoothed her hands down her hips and thighs, straightening the narrow skirt she wore. "I understand that things come up, Jacob. Honestly. I do." She turned and faced him. "But you might have called yourself, instead of having Elizabeth do it. It felt very impersonal."

He blinked at her bluntness. For a few seconds, irritation flared in him. He'd grown unused to having someone call him out.

"I thought it'd be easier to have Elizabeth do it."

"Easier for whom?"

His mouth slanted. They just looked at each other for a strained few seconds.

"I should get back to work," she said.

"Harper, don't be mad at me."

He grated his teeth together in irritation at himself. He didn't *say* things like that to women. Jesus. It was something he would have said to her when he was thirteen years old—he *had* said it to her years ago.

"You come into my workplace, pull . . ." She waved impatiently at the toilet, where he'd just fallen on her like a hungry wolf. "*Whatever* that just was, and then tell me not to be mad?" She stepped toward him aggressively.

"Are you mad because I did it? Or because you liked it?"

She gave him a fulminating glance. He shut his eyes in mounting frustration.

"I'm sorry," he said stiffly after a moment, meaning it. He didn't know where he stood with her. He didn't know where he stood with *himself* in regard to her. The need to touch her, to possess her, was overriding everything else, including his doubts about her. He reached up and cradled her jaw with both his hands, lowering his head until it hovered over her upturned face.

"Just . . . just tell me this obsession . . . this compulsion you're referring to, doesn't have anything to do with that woman from your past, the one I remind you of," she said softly.

He blinked and lifted his head, taken off guard. Is this what was bothering her?

"It has to do with you, Harper. Only you. I meant what I said before. I couldn't stop thinking about you. You're the first thing I thought of seeing when I got back."

"I'm the first thing you thought of *doing*," she murmured, and he was glad to see the hint of a smile on her lips.

"Is that so bad?"

Her gaze skittered off him.

"I can't believe I let you do it."

His finger traced the trail of her blush.

"I'm glad you did. It was amazing."

She looked up at him warily. His heart went out to her. He knew how bewildered she was. Who better?

"I'm being an idiot, letting you into my life," she stated bluntly.

He went very still to contain the sharp pain that went through him, hearing her say that.

"You're being unwise, maybe. So am I. Not everything in life is logical. Have dinner with me tonight. I'll have someone pick you up at six at your place?"

He sensed her hesitation. She'd told him that she had a history of getting involved with narcissistic jerks, and he'd responded by ordering her into the newsroom's bathroom, cuffing her hands behind her back, and shoving his cock in her mouth.

No wonder she hesitated.

Fuck it. He couldn't help who he was. He was always dominant with women. *Your need to have her is a bit beyond the ordinary, though, wouldn't you say?*

He ignored the sarcastic voice in his head.

"If I have to cancel any of our meetings in the future, I'll call myself," he found himself saying before she could deny him.

Her pretty, reddened lips—the ones he'd just debauched mercilessly—parted.

"Say yes, Harper."

"I can say 'yes' on my own," she told him with a flash of irritation, but her fixed stare on his mouth was an invitation.

He kissed her gently, coaxing away her impatience with him. *Harper's mouth.* It had driven him to distraction when he'd been a boy. Clearly, it had the power to make him crazy as a man.

"Are you, then? Saying yes," he asked against her mouth.

"*Yes,*" she whispered. She swallowed thickly. "I . . . can't seem to help myself."

"I know the feeling."

He lowered his head again, drawn by her scent. Her taste. A moment later, he released his hold on her reluctantly.

"I should go," she repeated.

"You go first. I'll wait here for a bit, and then leave when the coast is clear."

She took a moment to splash some water on her face and wash her hands. He noticed her anxious expression in the mirror as she smoothed her tousled hair.

"You look beautiful," he said sincerely.

Her startled gaze flew to his. Their stare held in the mirror for a few seconds before she ducked her head, turned, and left the bathroom.

Why had he done it? Why had he wanted her to risk something big, like her job, in order to be with him? It was wrong, clearly, but he couldn't seem to stop himself.

His expression looked grim and cold in the mirror.

It was his childhood longing—it was Jake Tharp—that was controlling him again, Jacob acknowledged as he washed his hands and splashed some water on his face. After that day at the courthouse, Harper had gone with her parents—the perfect, beautiful reunited little family—and left him alone.

Of course he'd known it was the only logical thing a twelve-year-old girl could do. She couldn't do whatever she wanted. She was subject to the will and whim of her parents.

But had she at least *wanted* to keep their connection, like she'd claimed she had?

During Regina's latest crisis in Napa, he'd spent some time with Dr. Fielding, her psychiatrist. Jacob had asked Fielding in a casual manner about hypnosis.

"Could a hypnotist make a patient completely forget their trauma?"

Dr. Fielding's answer had been that a skilled hypnotist could distance a patient from memories of the trauma, make them feel less distinct and emotionally overwhelming, thereby lessening the symptoms of post-traumatic stress disorder.

"Could a hypnotist make someone completely forget a positive relation-ship? A friend, for instance?"

Dr. Fielding's answer: *"Very unlikely. A hypnotist can't make a pa-tient do something that the patient isn't otherwise inclined to do."*

Jacob wiped off his face with a towel and faced the door, mentally donning the cold strength of his public armor.

Something that the patient isn't otherwise inclined to do.

There stood the crux of the issue. If Harper had forgotten him un-der the influence of treatment from her father, then she'd done so be-cause part of her wanted to.

Maybe she'd *needed* to, to free herself from memories of Emmitt Tharp, she had to forget Jake Tharp, as well. It pained him, thinking of *all* the memories being swept away, the ugly ones along with the sweet.

eighteen

Twenty Years Ago

t was pitch-black in the cave that night. He couldn't see or feel her, but all Jake could think about was Harper McFadden's body lying a few inches from his on the hard earth. He wanted to say something to her, but his mind kept going blank as to *what*.

"It's cold," she whispered.

He sat up slightly. "Are you catching something? Your nose sounds stopped up."

"Probably from stress. My dad says you're more likely to get sick if you're under stress. And it's freezing in here. Can't we start the fire up again?"

Jake had insisted they dampen their campfire after they'd eaten their dinner of soup and Pop-Tarts. They'd shared the soup out of the can. He'd only brought one spoon. He'd been glad to learn that Harper didn't seem to think it was gross to share it with him.

He eased back down onto his back. "We shouldn't have a fire, unless we really need it for cooking. It's risky. You can see a match glowing for hundreds of feet on a night as dark as this one."

"Your uncle would have to be in the entrance of the cave to see the light, wouldn't he?"

"Yeah. I'm not saying it's likely anyone would see. Just better to be sure."

The idea of Emmitt standing silently at the entrance of the cave, listening to their hushed voices, creeped him out. She didn't reply, but he sensed her shudder. Maybe she'd thought of the same thing. Or maybe she was just freezing. It *was* chilly out for August. The temperature had fallen into the sixties with nightfall, and would probably go lower. Plus the dirt-covered limestone floor and the air in the cave were naturally cooler than outdoors.

He'd brought a total of four camp blankets, two in each backpack. They'd put down one each for them to lie on, and each of them had one to cover them. He wanted to suggest they could share the same blankets, but he was too nervous to say it out loud.

"How come you live with your uncle?" she whispered.

"My mom's dead."

"What from?"

"Cancer. I don't hardly remember her. She died when I was four. We lived with Grandma Rose 'til then. My mom and Grandma Rose got along, even though Mom wasn't her real daughter, only her daughter-in-law. Then Mom died, and Grandma Rose got too sick to take care of me. She's got a bad heart. Damaged valves. She gets real weak. There was nowhere to put me but with child services or with Emmitt."

He heard her shift in the darkness, and knew she faced him. The cheek nearest to her tingled, like his skin knew she was watching him in the darkness.

"What about your dad?" she whispered.

"Gone. He's got bad blood."

"You mean he was sick?"

"No. Just bad. Like Emmitt. Evil," Jake replied darkly. "Grandma Rose says she doesn't know where her boys got it from."

"You shouldn't worry that you'll be like them."

He twisted his head. "I'm not worried about that! I ain't nothing like them."

"I know. Glad *you* know, too," she shot back, and he sensed her rustling again, trying to get comfortable on the hard ground. "My father says that both your genes and your life experiences go into making you who you are, but there's always the X factor."

Jake came up on his elbow, interested. "The X factor?"

"Yeah. An unknown factor. I don't know why they call it the X factor," she whispered.

"I do. I mean . . . maybe I do. Because *X* is the unknown. Like in math. When you solve equations, you solve for *X*."

"That's algebra, isn't it? We don't start it until next year. What grade are you going into?"

"Eighth."

"Oh, I thought you were younger."

He grimaced. "I'm going into eighth, but they let me take eighth-grade math last year. This year, I'll take ninth-grade algebra. Advanced class," he said, trying to bandage his wounded pride. Had she thought he was younger than her?

"I hate math," she said.

"I love it. I mean . . . I don't *love* it," he amended, embarrassed. "But it's okay. And I'm good at it. What do you like at school?"

"English," she replied eagerly. "Do you like to read?"

"Yeah. I just read *Dune*. Did you read that?" he asked, heartened at how easy it was starting to feel, talking to her.

"Yeah. I love sci-fi. Fantasy, too. Did you read *Lord of the Rings*?"

"No. I will if you think it's good. I have a library card. Well, I *did*," he added under his breath. He'd had to give an address to get a library card. When Emmitt discovered the card in his bedroom, he'd gone stark-raving mad at the idea of Jake putting down the location of his secret mountain property on a legal document. It hadn't mattered that Jake had insisted he'd put down Grandma Rose's address, like he always did for school registration. Jake didn't even know if Emmitt *had* a postal address. Emmitt had been too far gone in his rage at that point, however, to listen to reason.

"I have *The Lord of the Rings*, *The Hobbit,* and most of the *Dune* books in my bookcase in my room," Harper said. "My mom says I'll have enough books to start my own library soon."

Jake tried to imagine Harper's room. He bet it was nice, filled with photos and things she liked. But he really couldn't imagine the details of a girl's room, let alone a rich, city girl's room. He just thought it'd make him feel warm to be in it, just like it made him feel nice to be with her.

"Harper?"

"Yeah?"

"What did your dad mean? About the X factor?"

"Oh . . . I think it's just that nature is tricky . . . hard to predict. Just when you think that you'd understand how someone was going to turn out, nature turns things upside down. Like when a person is born to these great parents and has a nice upbringing and *bam*: They turn out to be a total jerk. Or when someone has really rotten parents or a horrible childhood, but turns out smart and nice. Dad says it happens more than psychiatric journals admit."

"Really? I mean . . . nature does that?"

"Something does. That's why Dad calls it the X factor."

He experienced an overwhelming, inexplicable need to hug Harper McFadden. Embarrassed by his rush of feelings, he remained very still and silent.

"Jake?" she asked after a pause.

"Yeah?" he said, rolling his head on his backpack. He sensed her hesitation.

"What do you think your uncle was planning on doing to me?" she asked in a very small voice.

"I don't know exactly," he evaded.

"Yes you do."

"I think he wanted to hurt you." He swallowed a lump in his throat. "Did he? Already? After he snatched you, and brought you to his place?"

"He hit my head really hard. When I woke up, there was a sack over my head and he was ripping off my clothes." Her voice had gotten so quiet, he almost couldn't hear her. "His hands . . . the way he was touching me, it was like he didn't even think I was a human being. Like I was a piece of meat or—"

"Garbage," Jake finished dully. "Did he force himself on you?" he asked at last, dreading her answer.

"Rape me, you mean?" she whispered. "No."

He exhaled in relief.

"But he took all my clothes. He . . . he saw me naked and treated me so rough, bruising me up with his hands." Something about her voice made him think she was close to tears.

"He's horrible."

"He's going to go to prison, for what he did," she said, sounding fierce and miserable at once.

"Yeah," Jake agreed, even though he seriously doubted anything could stop Emmitt from doing exactly what he wanted, let alone a local police presence that Emmitt regularly paid off or ran circles around.

"So . . . do you think that's why he did it? Because he planned to . . . rape me later? You said he was going to give me to someone else. Were *they* going to rape me?"

"I don't want to say, Harper."

"Tell me. I deserve to know, even if it is horrible. I'm not a little kid. Don't treat me like one."

"It happened before."

"You mean . . . he brought another girl there?"

"Yeah," he replied, his voice just above a whisper.

"What happened? Did you help her get away, like you did me?"

"Damn it, will you go to sleep, Harper?"

"*Jake*, I just wondered—"

"Just shut up! Give me a break, okay? I was a little kid. I was eleven years old, and when I did try to talk to that other girl, Emmitt caught me at it, and he—"

He broke off, horrified to realize the truth had almost all come spilling out of him, that he'd almost just revealed something so deeply shameful to *her*, of all people. One second, they'd been talking calmly, and the next, his weakness had been in the spotlight. He swiped his hands over his cheeks angrily, thankful for the darkness so that Harper wouldn't see him crying like a baby. Neither of them spoke for a moment as he got ahold of himself, and his breathing evened.

"It must have been awful. I'm sorry for asking you so many questions," she said finally.

"It's okay," he mumbled, deeply ashamed of his outburst.

"Do you really think he'll kill you if he finds us?" she whispered, and he heard the tremor of fear in her voice.

"Maybe not. Maybe he'll just beat me. It'll be okay. I'm used to that."

"That sucks."

"I can take it."

"Not the beating. That you're used to it."

Another silence descended, one in which Jake became even more hyperaware of her than he had been before. It was like some kind of invisible cord joined him to her.

"Jake?"

"Yeah?" he replied tentatively.

"Do you want to share the blankets? We could put two of them under us that way, and two on top. We could get close together. Share body heat. That's a thing, right?"

"Yeah," he whispered. It was most definitely a *thing*. "Okay."

He rose from the hard floor, the prospect of Harper's body pressed next to his making him weak.

nineteen

The young, capable-looking young man that had parked Harper's car on the night of the cocktail party was the one to come and collect her that night from her town house. Harper opened her front door before he had a chance to knock.

"Hello," Harper said, stepping over the threshold and closing her door behind her. "It's Jim, isn't it?"

"That's right," the chauffer said, seeming pleased that she'd recalled his name.

He seated her in the backseat of a dark blue Mercedes sedan a moment later.

"Quite a hot spell we've been having, isn't it?" Jim asked her politely from the front seat of the sedan as he pulled out of her complex a moment later.

"Yeah. Tahoe Shores will be packed for Labor Day, I imagine, with weather like this."

She saw Jim nod as he drove. "Yeah, people will be arriving in droves tomorrow. The barge came today. Always a big deal this time of year."

"Barge?" Harper asked curiously.

Jim met her gaze briefly in the rearview mirror. "The barge that will set off Mr. Latimer's fireworks?"

She shook her head, smiling. "I'm new to Tahoe Shores. I'm not sure I know what—"

"Mr. Latimer puts off an awesome fireworks display, both on the Fourth of July and Labor Day. Everybody thinks it's better than anything any of the local towns put on, even Reno or San Francisco. People flock to the beaches around here to see it."

"Oh . . . that's nice of him."

"Yeah," Jim chuckled at her understatement. "He's a really generous guy. Despite it all."

"Despite it all?" Harper asked, interested in what a young employee would actually think of Latimer. Was he referring to Jacob's supposed shadowy past, and the potential need for him to do a lot of positive public relations and philanthropy, in order to make up for it?

"Despite all his money and everything, he's a good guy," Jim explained. "I didn't know what to expect when I first drove him—Ms. Shields was the one to hire me, so I hadn't met him until then. But he's never been anything but nice to me. He really knows a lot about cars and engines and stuff, too, for someone so . . . you know . . ."

Jim faded off, and Harper didn't press him to elaborate. She had the impression his youthful enthusiasm had gotten away from him, and that he'd been given strict orders never to be loose-lipped—especially about Latimer himself—with anyone he drove. Had Jacob learned about car engines as well as the workings of boats from the man he'd mentioned the other night on the yacht, the one he'd worked for when he was a teenager?

Like on the night she'd attended the cocktail party, Elizabeth Shields greeted her on the front steps of the Latimer mansion. She was dressed more casually tonight, but every bit as professionally, in a feminine white blouse and dark blue skirt that emphasized her trim figure. They greeted each other with polite friendliness.

"Jacob is still in a meeting, but will be with you shortly," Elizabeth said briskly as she opened one of the heavy pine doors for Harper. She led Harper into the enormous, windowed great room. "He asked me to put you in the den until—" She broke off suddenly, and Harper realized why. Jacob and another man had just walked through the terrace doors on the far side of the great room. Harper saw Jacob's gaze land on her. Everyone froze for a few seconds. The tall, gray-haired man noticed them, too, but no one said anything for a tense moment.

"Just follow me, then," Elizabeth said in a muted tone to Harper after the awkward pause. A little bewildered, Harper jerked her gaze off Jacob and began to follow Elizabeth in the direction of the staircase and the corridor behind it.

"Harper."

Harper stopped and turned. Jacob was stalking across the long stretch of the great room. He looked *good*, wearing a silver-gray suit, white shirt, and black tie. The coolness of the colors of his apparel seemed to set off the vibrant, warm tones of his bronzed skin and hazel eyes. From the corner of her vision, Harper noticed that Elizabeth had halted, as well.

"I was just finishing up," Jacob said as he neared her.

"Don't let me bother you," Harper assured. "I'm happy to wait." She smiled politely at the older gentleman when he trailed behind Jacob, approaching them. She recognized him as the United States secretary of defense, Stewart Overton. *Well, here's confirmation of Ruth's speculations about Jacob and Lattice still being involved with the Department of Defense.* Jacob glanced back at Overton.

"Harper McFadden, this is Stewart," he said.

"Stewart Overton," the man said, stepping toward Harper with his hand extended.

Jacob's shoulder twitched in a *whatever works for you* gesture. Clearly, Jacob hadn't expected the secretary of defense to reveal his full name.

"It's a pleasure to meet you," Harper said, shaking hands. "Jacob has a lovely view here, doesn't he?"

"Magnificent. We were just enjoying it. Best view of the lake I've ever seen."

"Harper works for our local paper, but she used to be a reporter for the *San Francisco Chronicle*," Elizabeth said tensely.

A silence settled. *Awkward.* Jacob gave Elizabeth a repressive glance, scowling, while Overton assessed Harper with a sharpened gaze.

"Well, Jacob knows how to keep his own house," Overton said with an air of a man who had just made a decision. "I know he wouldn't invite anyone into it who didn't know the rules. Jacob? We'll be in touch?" Overton boomed, briskly shaking Jacob's hand. "No, Elizabeth, I can see myself up to the helipad. My pilot is waiting," he said when Elizabeth began to hurry in his direction.

For a few seconds after Overton left the room, the three of them didn't speak. Harper glanced uneasily from Elizabeth—who looked worried—to Jacob, who was still scowling slightly at his assistant. For a few seconds, she wondered if he was about to call out Elizabeth in front of her—Harper—but then—

"How about a swim before dinner?" he asked Harper suddenly.

"I didn't bring a suit."

"We have suits. In the pool house, right, Elizabeth?"

"Uh, yes."

Jacob didn't notice, because he was looking at Harper, but Elizabeth's brow was knitted in consternation along with something else: disapproval. Elizabeth didn't think Jacob should have allowed Harper and Stewart Overton to come into contact in his home. She disapproved of Jacob for allowing it. Apparently, she believed Harper shouldn't be trusted, and that Jacob was being indiscreet—even foolish?—in allowing her to see too much of the secret inner workings of Jacob's "house" as Overton had stealthily put it.

"Then we're all set," Jacob said, reaching for Harper's hand. His jaw looked tense, and he was obviously irritated at what had occurred during the brief, charged exchange, but he clearly didn't plan to address it with Elizabeth presently.

"Jacob, what should I tell Lisa about your dinner?" Elizabeth called.

"Nothing," he replied without turning around. "I've told her to go home. So should you. We'll fend for ourselves for dinner."

Harper walked with him through the glass doors and out onto the magnificent terrace, going over in her head what had just occurred. The distinctive whistling, harsh chopping noise of a helicopter reached her ears. She paused on the second level of the terrace and looked back up at the mansion.

"I didn't know you had a helipad up there."

"Yeah." He tightened his hold on her hand and urged her down the next flight of steps. "It comes in handy."

"Jacob . . . I'm sorry, if I interrupted something—"

"You didn't interrupt anything. He was leaving. I invited you here," Jacob said firmly without turning around.

"Elizabeth wasn't pleased that I came into contact with the secretary of defense in your home."

Jacob paused slightly and glanced over his shoulder. "So. You recognized him," he said with an air of resigned inevitability. He resumed leading her down the steps.

"I told you I wouldn't leak anything I learned about you," she said, coming up next to him as they reached the pool level and walked toward the pool house.

He frowned. "I wouldn't be asking you here if I wasn't confident of that at this point," he said. "And it's not a big deal, anyway. I just do some consulting work with him sometimes."

Harper thought she shouldn't mention that most people would consider him giving advice to a high-level cabinet member a pretty major deal.

"Maybe you should assure Elizabeth, then. That I'm not here in the capacity of reporter."

They paused outside a glass door. In the distance, she heard the rough chopping sound of the helicopter rising in the air. Wind from the blades ruffled the bangs of Jacob's burnished hair. Despite the novelty of a helicopter taking off just yards away, Harper couldn't take her eyes off him.

"No," he murmured, his rich, deep voice running over her skin and making it tingle. His agate eyes were heavy-lidded and a seduction all on their own. "That's not why you're here, is it?"

She swayed closer to him. Wind swirled around them, and the chopper noise grew fainter by the second. Why did he have to smell so good all the time? Just a nose full of his scent, and graphic memories bombarded her brain about their raunchy tryst in the *Gazette*'s bathroom hours ago.

She cleared her throat and lowered her head, bullying her brain into focusing. "You *should* say something to her. Elizabeth, I mean. She seems concerned about me. And you."

"Don't worry about Elizabeth. I'm not."

He lifted her chin, and their mouths fused in a taut, hot kiss. By the time she opened her eyes a moment later, the helicopter sound was a distant hum.

"Hi," he breathed against her upturned lips a moment later. "I didn't get a chance to greet you properly."

She smiled. "That's because you were meeting with the United States secretary of defense. I'll forgive you. This time."

He smiled and kissed her once more before stepping back.

"This is the women's side," he said, nodding at the pool house entrance behind them. "Suits are kept in the cupboard next to the showers. There are usually several brand-new ones in there for guests. I'll meet you out here in a minute?"

"Okay," she said, feeling a little light-headed and euphoric from his kiss. The idyllic surroundings. The prospect of spending the evening with him . . .

All of it.

She felt a little self-conscious when she exited the pool house a few minutes later. Jacob had been right: there were several suits available. There were bikinis and maillots in a range of sizes. Harper had been determined to choose one that still had tags on it, however; one that was clearly unworn. She didn't at all like the idea of wearing one of Jacob's former lover's swimsuits.

The only one with tags that was in her size was a cute dark blue bikini, but it was brief. *Very* brief. She felt like her breasts were exploding out of the top of it, and the bottoms were tiny. Thank God she'd shaved this evening. To make matters worse, she couldn't find any cover-ups. She grabbed a thick white towel from a cupboard and held it in front of her midriff self-consciously as she exited.

Jacob was waiting for her, wearing nothing but a pair of black trunks that rode low on his trim hips, leaving the entire breathtaking landscape of his bronzed, cut torso exposed. He stood in the bright sun with his arms crossed below his chest, his stance lazy. Her gaze dropped down longingly over the thin strip of fine, light brown hair that went from his taut belly button and disappeared below the trunks.

"All set," she said with fake cheeriness as she approached him. In a second flat, he ripped away her attempt at modesty by whisking the towel out of her hands.

"Jac—"

"Wow," he said, checking her out appreciatively. "You look *amazingly* good in that," he said, his stare now on her overflowing cleavage.

"Down boy," she muttered, embarrassed but flattered, too. He laughed, white teeth flashing. She started in the direction of the pool, but he caught her hand.

"Let's go to the lake," he said, laughter still lingering on his lips, a sparkle in his eyes. Her heart gave a little jump. He was the most attractive man she'd ever imagined, let alone met . . . or allowed outrageous liberties sexually.

"Okay," she agreed.

He led her down to a sandy beach that was enclosed on two sides by massive, stacked granite boulders. The water in the natural enclosure was calmer than it was further out. It shone in Harper's eyes like a shimmering liquid sapphire.

"Do you want to take some boards out?" Jacob asked her.

"Boards?"

He pointed to several surfboards stored on a rack, along with a kayak.

"I don't surf."

"They aren't surfboards," he said. "They're paddleboards." She followed him over to the rack, watching as he lifted down one of the boards, his back muscles flexing and his gleaming golden brown skin snagging her attention "You can't surf on Lake Tahoe. Not enough waves. But it's perfect for paddleboards," he said, standing the board up in front of her and waiting until she reached to hold it. "You've never done it?"

"No," Harper admitted, checking out the board with interest while he turned to pull down another one. It was larger than a surfboard, she realized. "I've seen people doing it, though. Is it hard?"

"The hardest part is standing on it. It's tricky, until you get used to it. Takes a lot of balance. You up for trying it?"

She glanced down at the brief little bikini top she wore and breasts that threatened to break free of their confinement at any moment. When she met his stare, she saw humor glittering in his eyes. "You know very well what's going to happen if I try to stand up on one of these things wearing this bikini," she said condemningly.

"I have faith," he said, grinning.

Something rushed through her. For a few seconds, Harper just stood in place, even when he headed toward the shore, a paddleboard tucked under one arm and a paddle in the opposite hand. He'd looked so young there for a moment, so uninhibited.

So beautiful.

It took her a moment to regain her wits after witnessing that unguarded, boyish smile. It had been in such stark contrast to the sober, contained, utterly in control man she'd grown used to.

And so bizarrely . . .

. . . Familiar.

She blinked, realizing he held out a board for her. He handed her a paddle and they both went to the shore. They shoved their boards out into the water.

After they'd waded in, Jacob instructed her to come up on her knees as a first step. After Harper had balanced herself on the board with effort, they began to paddle around in the cool, calm water. It was very peaceful. Because of Tahoe's pristine waters, she could look all the way down to the bottom of the bright blue lake, seeing smooth, round stones and schools of silvery fish.

She looked over at Jacob and saw he was watching her as he paddled. She smiled.

"It's so beautiful," she said.

"Yeah. You ready for the hard part?"

"Standing?" she asked doubtfully. The board had wobbled quite a bit, even when she'd gone to her knees on it.

"Yeah. You can do it," he said. He put his hands flat down on the board and pushed himself up in one movement, his grace singular to witness given his tall, muscular body.

"You can't expect me to do that!" she called to him when he began to paddle in the stand-up position.

"You can do it," he repeated, his steadfastness amazing her a little.

Maybe he knew she was self-conscious, because he kept his back to her as he paddled. She envied his smooth glide across the water. She eyed the board speculatively. *If he can do it, I can.*

Grinning like a kid, she placed her hands on the board. Her eyes went wide when she tried to shift her feet under her, and the board dipped and rocked alarmingly in the water. Crap. Jacob had made it look so easy. She tried to hoist herself up again, but the board teetered, and then heaved. The next thing she knew, she was going face-first into the cold water.

When she surfaced, sputtering and grasping for her board, she saw him standing above her in godlike supremacy, balancing effortlessly even with all the rough chop she'd made in the water. Again, she saw that small, boyish smile on his lips.

"Show-off," she muttered, casting him a condemning glare before she hauled her upper body onto the board.

"Everybody falls off the first time," he said, using his paddle backward in the water to come to a standstill next to her.

"You could have told me that," she accused, wiping her wet hair out of her eyes. She hauled a leg up onto the board, pausing to gasp for air. Her breasts had nearly busted loose at that point, but she couldn't have cared less. She'd seen that sparkle of humor in Jacob's eyes . . . the glitter of a dare.

"There it is," he said very softly.

"There's *what*?"

"The look," he said, but she was too busy concentrating on proving she could get up on that damn board to pay much attention to his remarks. A minute later, she succeeded, coming to a very shaky standing position on the quivering board.

"There you go. Bend your knees some. Now use the paddle. It'll help you find your balance."

Half a minute later, she gave a victorious laugh as she glided next to him across the calm water. It was a lovely rush.

"See, I told you that you could do it," he said once they'd turned and headed back toward shore.

"I love it," she said, grinning. A lake breeze whipped past them. She shivered. Lake Tahoe was very deep, and its water remained chilly year-round. Jacob maneuvered his board up next to hers. He reached and touched her shoulder, joining them, his hand feeling warm on her cool skin. They bobbed next to each other and came to a relative standstill.

"You're cold?" he murmured.

"A little."

"Throw your paddle in the water," he directed calmly.

"What? Why?"

"It'll float to shore. Just do it," he said, his expression serious as he kept them steady.

What the hell? She did what he said, despite her doubt, tossing her paddle into the sun-dappled water.

Jacob's hand lowered to her elbow. "Now . . . transfer over onto my board."

"Are you *nuts?*" she exclaimed, because he was applying pressure on her elbow, urging her to move her feet onto his board, and her board was starting to shake beneath her. There was no way they could keep their balance. "We're going to fall."

"No we won't. I hate going in when I don't intend to, so believe me when I say it'll work. Do it quickly," he insisted. "I can keep my board steady, but you can't hesitate. One foot on my board, find your balance, then shift your weight all at once. You can do it," he said very quietly.

Like in all things, she found herself responding wholesale to the sound of his voice. She put her right foot on his board cautiously, finding a very precarious balance.

"Now," he said.

He pulled on her arm and she shifted her weight onto his board. Her heart jumped into her throat. The board heaved, and she thought for a split second they'd spill over for sure. Then Jacob shifted back slightly on the surface, and she sensed the subtle, sure force of him balancing the board with his strong body. She felt herself aligning with his power.

"I can't believe we did that," she muttered in anxious pleasure a few seconds later.

His chuckle behind her was delicious. So was his touch on her pebbled skin when he spread his hand on her left hip. His other hand came in front of her, holding the paddle.

"Take it. We need the momentum," he said.

Cautiously, she took the paddle and began to dip it into the water. They zoomed forward. She laughed, ebullient at the sensation at their smooth glide. Until Jacob put his other hand on her hip and shifted forward slightly on the board, that is.

"Jac . . . Jacob, *don't*," she squealed, snorting with laughter as they jiggled around in the water.

"Keep paddling. It's okay. Trust me," he murmured from just behind her.

And indeed, his exquisite balance and strength had steadied them again within seconds. He'd drawn her against him. She felt his thighs pressing against her buttocks and his full groin resting at the small of her back. His hands tightened on her hips, bringing her even closer against him. She paddled, her heart fluttering. She leaned back cautiously, a feeling of wonder going through her at the exquisite sensation of his solid, warm body behind her. For a few amazing seconds, they glided across the serene blue water, their bodies joined. But more than just their bodies, it seemed to her. It was like an ephemeral thread joined them. Every movement she made with the paddle was somehow counterbalanced by him, so that they glided in a still, subtle dance of invisible give-and-take.

She guided them around the still little cove for several minutes.

She'd never been more mentally or sexually attuned to another human being as she was with Jacob in those sweet, sun-drenched moments. His hands moved on her skin as they skimmed over the surface of the crystal clear water. He caressed her hips and belly until her goose bumps disappeared and her skin smoothed beneath his fingertips. His big, sun-warmed hands radiated heat, chasing away her chill. She was intensely focused on the sensation of his cock growing heavier and longer where it pressed at the top of her ass cheeks and lower back. He brought her back against him tighter, sandwiching his erection even more snugly between them. She was so distracted by the sensation, she made the board wobble.

"Shhh," he soothed very quietly, as though he were speaking to both her and the board itself. They smoothed in the serene water. A powerful longing rose up in her. She threw the paddle in the water.

"Hey, what the—"

"Trust me," she interrupted. Using his solid weight to brace her from behind, she slowly, very cautiously shifted her feet on the board. She turned around in his arms. The board vibrated alarmingly beneath them, but soon she faced him as he held her elbows and forearms. She gave him a wide grin. He returned it. He urged her with his hands, and soon her front was pressed tight against his. She hugged him around the waist. She felt a tremor go through him when she crushed her breasts against his ribs. His skin rough against hers.

"That was risky," he said, his gaze stuck on the tops of her damp breasts. "But well worth it."

"What's life without a little risk sometimes?" she murmured, her chin tilted up toward him. His arousal was obvious. Wonderful. Their smiles lingered on their lips as they both bobbed and balanced at the top of the water and their bodies pressed tight. The flutters in her stomach amplified when he slowly began to dip his head to kiss her.

Her heart jumped.

She heaved mightily toward the right. He gave a yell of surprise and they both crashed into the lake. When Harper surfaced, she was already grinning widely. Then she saw his expression as he surfaced.

She immediately dove for the shore, snorting with laughter. He caught her ankle ten feet from shore in shallow water and jerked her backward. He hauled her against him, his sliding, poking fingertips on her ribs making her laugh even more hysterically.

"You should have seen the look on your face," she panted between jags of laughter as they stood.

"I told you I don't like it when I go in without meaning to," he said with fake sternness, his smile breaking free as she squirmed and tried to get away from his tickling fingers.

"Apparently not even—oh, *stop* it—Jacob Latimer can control *everything.*"

He lifted her entire body suddenly against him and captured her mouth with his. His tongue pierced her. His mouth was hot. At first taste of him, she stopped her struggling, craning toward him, sliding her arms around his neck. Within seconds, she was melting against him.

When he broke their kiss a minute later and slowly lowered her back to her feet, he didn't say anything. He didn't *have* to. His kiss had said it all. He controlled a lot of things all too easily, her response to him being one of them.

The paddles and boards had washed to shore. They retrieved them and stacked the boards on the rack without speaking. Harper wondered if he was as attuned to her as she was to him at that moment. She thought he was, but one thing was for certain. He was aroused. His erection didn't dissipate after they'd left the water. The clingy material of his swim trunks made that fact excitingly obvious.

He took her hand and they started up the first flight of terrace stairs. Harper's assumption was that he'd lead her to his bedroom, which was fine by her. More than fine. Something about their fragile togetherness, and then their playfulness out there on the calm, blue water had moved her. Aroused her. She experienced a strange feeling of exhilaration, a swelling happiness that she'd been given the opportunity to be with such an attractive, exciting man.

Nothing and no one could stand in the way of them being together, if it's what the two of them chose. Why did that fact feel so liberating and precious?

She was surprised when instead of taking the next flight of steps, he led her over to one of the many circular, partially covered couch enclosures that faced the lake. He lifted the hand that held hers, urging her to enter the snug little haven of cushions. Harper crawled into the shadowed divan, turning so that she was propped up on some colorful pillows. The cupped couch offered her shade on her upper body, but her legs remained in the warm sun. Jacob crawled swiftly in after her. She smiled up at him when he relaxed next to her on the pillows, his arm going around her. She shivered as she cuddled up closer to his warmth. The view of the sun-drenched lake was stunning.

"This is nice," she murmured, turning her face into his chest. She loved the feeling of his crinkly hair and his smooth, wet skin. He smelled good, like clean water and lingering spice. She pressed a kiss against a solid pectoral. His hand cupped the back of her head. Her lips moved, charting his chest, seeking new, delightful sensations. His hand ran down her shoulder and arm, and she shivered.

"Here," he murmured. She lifted her head when he shifted slightly. He reached for an afghan that had been folded in the enclosure. He opened it and drew it around her shoulders.

"Only I'd get cold when it's seventy-five degrees out," she muttered when he relaxed back on the pillows and put his arm around her.

"The water is cold and there's a breeze." His hand went between the opening of the afghan and slid to her back. She felt him pull on the tie of the bikini top. A moment later, he lifted the piece of fabric over her head and tossed it to the far side of the cushioned enclosure. His hand snaked again beneath the blanket.

"Jacob, no," she murmured when he calmly started to remove the bikini briefs.

His brows went up. "Why?"

"I'm not going to lie here naked. It's broad daylight. Your staff will see me."

He glanced behind them in the direction of the house. The wicker back of the circular couch enclosed them. It was the shape of a cupped hand that had been tilted back slightly. The edge of the back came down several inches above their heads. "No one can see from that direction," he reasoned.

"What about the view from the lake from a boat?"

He looked vaguely exasperated. "Fine. But I'm still going to do what I set out to do."

"What'd you set out to do?" she asked, watching him in amazement as he slid his long body further down the cushion, lowering his head to her chest.

"Warm you up a little," he said, before he nuzzled the bare skin at the opening of the blanket. She watched him as he ran his nose and lips over the skin between her breasts. He twisted his head, his mouth trailing across a pale globe. She tingled beneath his warm lips.

"*That* was your intent in bringing me here?" she asked amusedly.

He glanced up at her briefly, his eyes smoldering. "Actually, my primary intent was to accept the invitation of these"—he glanced down at her breasts—"after all that flaunting you were doing out there."

She gave a bark of laughter and slapped his damp back playfully. "I wasn't flaunting anything. It's the only swimsuit that fit me. Is it my fault you made me crawl around on that damn board and make a fool of myself?"

"This swimsuit *doesn't* fit you," he replied deadpan. "It's a size too small, fortunately for me." He dipped his head and ran the short, silky hair of his goatee across the pale globe of her breast. Her smile evaporated. Her nipple was still covered by the blanket, but it would fall away at the lightest touch. She licked her lower lip, watching him like a hawk.

"You stopped shivering," he said, still running his chin over her sensitive skin. "See, I wasn't entirely selfish. I knew if I played with you for a while, you'd warm up. Just relax, Harper. Enjoy the view." He lifted his hand and deliberately moved the blanket off her breast, exposing a pink nipple. He gave a small growl of appreciation, and then dipped his head, sucking her between his lips. Her skin was chilled.

His mouth was hot.

Harper stared blindly out onto the shimmering water as he laved her nipple with his tongue and drew on her with the sweetest precision. Her hand went instinctively to his head. She delved her fingers into his thick, damp hair and sighed in pleasure. After a moment, however, he lifted his head and spoke to her tersely.

"Put your hands on the cushions behind your head." He watched her take the position, his face shadowed and his eyelids heavy. She stared back at him, her arms stretched above her head, her hands close together, palms outward. For a few seconds, he remained motionless.

Then he reached between his thighs and fisted his cock, giving it a firm tug. He grimaced and let go. A small snarl shaped his mouth before he leaned down, and sucked her nipple into his mouth again.

She lay there for several minutes, awash in pleasure, while he sucked and fondled her. Her breasts grew flushed, the nipples hard and achy.

He lifted his head, both of her breasts in his hands, and licked the valley between them. "Sweet. *Sweat.* Mission accomplished," he said, a triumphant, sexy-as-hell smile curving his mouth.

She shook her head at his cockiness, but she was smiling, too, unable to disguise the truth. He'd not only warmed her. He'd turned her into a hot, sticky mush of arousal.

She glanced aside when he reached to the side of her. He grabbed the discarded bikini top and looped the top strings over her head.

"Time to go," he said, and she saw his playful smile had faded.

"Where?" she asked, even though she knew the answer by reading the rigid tension in his face.

"My bedroom terrace. You can keep enjoying the view from there. But this time, I'm going to have you while you're doing it."

The drapes had been partially drawn in his bedroom suite, making the air feel cool and pleasant against Harper's flushed, tingling skin. Her feet slowed when they neared his big, luxurious bed, but he didn't pause.

He tugged on her hand, and she followed him to the circular bank of floor-to-ceiling windows. One of the doors to the terrace was open. An evening breeze was causing the white curtain to billow inward. They went through the door. The sweeping terrace led up to a waist-high, wrought-iron-constructed fence that blocked little of the fantastic view of the lake and the surrounding mountains. There were several comfortable seating areas and potted plants arranged on the balcony.

Jacob turned toward her. He brushed back her damp hair and planted a kiss on her temple.

"I'm going to restrain you," he said, brushing his lips across her hairline and ear. She shivered in unfurling excitement. "Is that all right?"

"Out here?" she asked shakily, lifting her chin and whisking her mouth across his jawline.

"Yes."

"But . . . how is this an improvement on fooling around on the downstairs terrace?"

"I told you that my personal quarters are completely private."

"But a boat from the lake . . ."

He met her stare, and she saw he wore a hint of that smile that always undid her. "No one is going to see anything. No one but me," he added pointedly. "When are you going to start trusting me?"

"I trust you far too much as it is."

"Are you going to let me show you what I have in mind? You can always say no."

"Can I at least have a drink first?"

A rough bark of laughter scraped his throat. She smiled at the unexpectedness of his flash of humor.

"You've called me out. I'm a shit host. Wait here."

She walked over to the wrought iron fence while she waited, breathing in the fresh scent of the surrounding pines and trying to dampen her mounting anticipation. She blinked, startled, when he was suddenly standing next to her, a glass of champagne in his hand. He was as silent as a ghost. She took the champagne gratefully.

"I'll be right back," he said. His gaze dipped from her face to the champagne flute. "Drink up while you can."

Her brows went up at that. She watched him as he went back inside, admiring his broad shoulders and the shape of his ass in the swim trunks. Excitement bubbled up in her. Wasn't this exactly what she'd bargained for with him? A thrilling sexual affair, a wholesale distraction from the gray grief that had swallowed up her life recently? She glanced around her, seeing a world of luxury, beauty, and brilliant, blinding color. Her breasts and sex ached pleasantly with the knowledge of the pleasure and challenge to come.

He was delivering, in spades. The least she could do was try to return the favor. She swallowed half the contents of the flute, the clean, crisp taste and effervescence only amplifying her anxious arousal.

She was glad for the rush conferred by the delicious champagne when he backed out of the door a moment later and turned, and she saw what he carried. It looked a little like a sitting massage chair, but there were more hinges and movable parts, and some of the cushions on it weren't in typical places.

Definitely in different places, Harper thought when she saw that the place where a person would prop their legs had been split so that their thighs could be kept open. There were other variations from a sitting massage chair. There were straps hanging from the leg portion and below the cushion where a person would rest their forearms and hands. Instead of the donut cushion where one usually placed their face during a massage, there was a narrow chin pad that curved upward, like a thin crescent.

He set down the contraption in front of the fence ten feet away from her. He turned in her direction. Harper downed the rest of her champagne, set the flute on a nearby table, and walked toward him.

"That looks like something from a torture chamber," she said, attempting levity to hide her nerves.

"It's not. It's meant for pleasure."

"Yours or mine?"

"Ideally, both. But its intention is to give me complete control."

Her heart starting to thrum in her ears, she glanced warily at the black metal movable parts and cushions.

"You don't have to do it," he said.

"I know," she replied.

"I set it up here, because the design is thicker on the fence here," he said, pointing to the wrought iron design of intertwining branches. "It'll be enough to hide you, should anyone pass in a boat and happen to be staring, but it's open enough that you'll still be able to enjoy the view."

"Like I'll be paying attention to the view," she scoffed under her breath.

She looked up when he stepped closer and his long finger brushed against the skin below her chin. His eyes shone, looking especially golden in the evening light. She stared up at him, spellbound.

"It'll excite me to have you in this chair. I think it'll excite you, too. But it's your call."

She nodded, swallowing thickly. She turned toward the chair.

"How . . . how do I get on it?"

"First, let's get this off you," he murmured, and she felt his fingers slip beneath the ties of her bikini at her back. Remembering what he'd told her about always wanting to undress her, she stood without moving as he drew the bikini top off her. He knelt and pulled the snug briefs down over her ass and thighs. She paused in the process of stepping out of the bikini bottoms when she felt his hand spread just above her knee. He swept it up, over her outer thigh, hip, and the side of her ass in a warm, greedy caress.

"You're so pretty, Harper."

Her mouth fell open. He'd said something similar to her several times before. It wasn't the compliment a sophisticated, worldly playboy gave a woman. She realized that for the first time. It was the kind of compliment that came from an awestruck boy.

"What?" he asked, and he was towering over her again, a big, powerful figure, his outline blocking the setting sun. He'd noticed the look of wonder and puzzlement on her face.

"We . . . we haven't met before, *have* we? I mean . . . before Tahoe?" she asked.

His eyelids narrowed.

"Why? Do you think we have?"

She blinked, and the moment of déjà vu faded. She laughed at her stupidity. What she'd told him the other night was true. If she'd *ever* met Jacob Latimer, she'd remember it. In spades.

"No," she admitted.

How could she possibly imagine that Jacob Latimer was remotely similar to a boy? Why did his presence keep calling up that sweet, poignant sadness of her early teenage years . . . the regret? Was it the loss of her parents and memories of her childhood inspiring it?

He stepped closer. "Harper, what's wrong?"

"Nothing," she whispered, shaking off the spell. She didn't want to think about her losses. Not now. "I'm ready."

She saw him nod once, but thought a vague expression of suspicion or curiosity lingered on his face. He took one of her hands and guided her to the chair.

"Straddle the seat first, then slide one leg into position while you keep standing on the other foot."

He braced her while she did what he instructed, her heartbeat starting a steady drumroll in her ears.

"Now sit."

It wasn't like sitting, in any normal sense of the word. The center cushions supported her both from below and from the front. When she came to rest, she was tilted forward at a forty-five degree angle. Her lower belly and hips pressed against the abdomen cushion, but the lower pelvic cushion took most of her weight. Her sex pressed at the juncture of both. Once in place, it was only natural to place her elbows on the forward cushion and rest her forearms. Her shoulders were supported by two small cushions. She hesitated, but then slid her chin into the upward-curving crescent.

It was almost scandalous, how comfortable the contraption was.

She felt Jacob's hand on her free lower leg and he lifted it onto the apparatus. A moment later, she felt the padded straps go around each ankle and tighten. Then he came around to the front. She stared at his crotch as he quickly restrained her wrists. Heat rushed through her cheeks and sex. The height of the apparatus had clearly been matched to his—Jacob's—body.

He stepped closer, his crotch coming within inches of her face. Her eyes widened. He placed both of his hands at her temples and smoothed back her damp hair, gathering it at her nape. He swept the tresses over her shoulder, getting it off her back.

"You're comfortable?" he murmured, sliding his warm hands along her bare back.

"Yes," she managed in a choked voice. She shivered at the feeling of his skin gliding against hers.

"You're still cold."

"No—"

"I think I've got something that can help with that."

Her brain whirred in nonstop anxiety and excitement while he was out of her vision, but he probably had only left her side for a few seconds. He came up next to her—again, silently. The snap of a container opening alerted her to his presence. Because of the chin crescent, she couldn't turn her head and alleviate her anxiety. She *could* have lifted her chin out of it, of course, and turned her head. But it excited her to imagine that even her head was restrained.

She felt movement on the skin just above her ass. The cloth of his swim trunks? Yes. He'd straddled the entire bench with long legs, and her body along with it.

"Jacob?" she asked uncertainly.

"Shhh," he murmured. He placed both of his big hands on either side of her spine. Warmth emanated from his hands and soaked into her muscles. He began to massage her back, spreading oil on her skin. It felt divine.

"Oh . . . it's *warm*. It feels so good," she said.

"Then it's doing what it's supposed to do, on both counts."

His hands were so big. He shaped her muscles to his palms, squeezing out the tension she experienced from accepting the challenge of being restrained to the apparatus. She moaned softly when his hands shifted, and he massaged along her shoulder blades.

"You could do this for a living," she muttered after a stretched moment, her eyelids fluttering closed.

"You think?" he asked quietly. She sensed him step forward slightly as his hands smoothed and shaped the muscles beneath her shoulder blades. "It might be considered kind of unethical if I did something like this, though." His hands slid down below her armpits, and he was massaging her suspended bare breasts in his warm, lubricated hands. Her eyelids sprang open, and she was staring at the blue lake through the leaf design of the wrought iron fence. She wasn't really seeing, though. Just feeling. His palms continued to massage her while his thumb and forefinger pinched her nipples lightly. The oil amplified her pleasure. A heavy, achy feeling suffused her sex.

He lowered his hands, cradling her rib cage, and then swept them up over her breasts again, lifting and massaging them. It aroused her, as always, his show of controlled, yet blatant, greed.

"Jacob," she panted. He slid his hands lower again, holding her rib cage so surely, her very heart in his hands. Was that why he did it? she wondered. To exhibit his complete mastery over her mind and body? She was glad when he cupped her heaving breasts again.

"Are you getting warmer?" He ran his fingertips over her beading nipples, rubbing the warming lubricant into them until they tingled and grew diamond-hard.

"Hotter," she admitted throatily.

He tapped her erect nipples lightly with his palm, the taut sensation making her whimper. "God you're responsive. Your nipples get so hard," she heard him mutter thickly as he pinched the crests again with his fingertips. Harper squirmed against the seat cushions. Suddenly, he grasped both of her breasts firmly in his hands.

"Hold still."

Holding her breasts, he bent his knees and flexed his hips. He pushed the rigid column of his cock up her spine, then down, then back up it again. He ground his balls against her. Through the fabric of his swim trunks, he felt heavy and swollen and delicious. Then he was gone.

"Pussy-tease," she mumbled in a beleaguered fashion.

He laughed, the smooth, rich sound washing over her sensitized skin. Where had he gone? She couldn't feel him anymore, straddling her, but she sensed he was still behind her. Then he spoke.

"I'm going to move the apparatus some. You'll still be very secure."

There was a metallic sound. He was turning a rotor of some kind, causing the apparatus to spread her legs even wider. She could feel her sex and even her buttocks parting, the air tickling at her wet, aroused tissues. A moment later, the entire apparatus began to tilt downward. Her head dipped and her bottom rose. Soon, she was staring wide-eyed not at the sunset waters of Lake Tahoe, but the bottom of the wrought iron fence and the edge of the tigerwood flooring. She held her breath. It was a little humiliating, being mechanically manipulated in order to expose her most private areas. It was also embarrassingly arousing.

The metallic whirring stopped. She was suspended in midair on her belly at a downward slant, her ass higher than her head, her legs spread wide. Her clit twanged in sharp arousal, despite her vulnerability. She felt movement at her pelvis. The seat where her pelvis had rested, which had been weight bearing before he'd tilted her downward, jiggled slightly. It slipped away, leaving her entire sex exposed.

"Jacob?" she asked shakily.

He placed his hand on the back of her thigh. "I'm here."

With no further warning, he plunged a finger in her sheath and cupped her outer sex, grinding the hard edge of his palm against her clit. Keeping his finger inserted, he circled his hand.

"Oh . . . oh *God*, Jacob," popped out of her throat.

"If there's one thing I'm not, it's a tease. I'll always come through, Harper."

She bit her lip, too swept up in hot lust to respond. Through a haze of pleasure, she faintly heard the click of a bottle opening, and then the sensation of warm liquid streaming onto her ass. She lay there, gasping and moaning in pleasure, as he rubbed the oil into her ass with one squeezing, shaping hand and continued to grind his other hand against her sex in the most demanding, eye-crossing manner.

"No need for any of the oil in your pussy," she heard him say gruffly. "You're so creamy." He withdrew his finger and plunged it back into her, demonstrating his point with a fluid glide. He circled his hand demandingly, the pressure on her clit divine. Heat rushed into her cheeks. Her feet began to burn in sympathy with her clit. He squeezed an ass cheek tautly, lifting it, and slid his finger out of her channel. He pressed the ridge of his forefinger between her labia, rubbing her clit hard. She cried out raggedly.

"You look gorgeous right now," she heard him say gruffly through the roar in her ears. "Your skin is gleaming, and your hair is like shining copper in the sun. You can't escape, can you Harper?"

"No," she mumbled, nearly mindless with arousal. "I don't want to, Jacob."

"You want to come, don't you? You want to lie there and come, and then have my cock in you. You want to be fucked hard. Say it."

"*Yes.* Oh God, I want your cock in me."

"I brought out a towel," he said, his voice sounding very grim. "I'm going to have you and then come on your beautiful body. If I can't leave myself in you, then I'll leave myself *on* you. It's all going to be for me, Harper."

His tense proclamation sent her hurtling over the edge. She choked as she broke in climax. Her entire body shuddered.

His cockhead was suddenly pushing at her entrance. He drove into her to the balls. Her brain seemed to overload at the sensation. Her climax racked her. It hurt a little, coming so hard against his big, pounding cock. It also felt sinfully hot. So good. She came back to herself at the sound of screaming. It took her a moment to realize it was *her* making the frantic sound. She cut herself off, only to inhale choppily, and let out another groan.

His hands were on her hips, his thumbs digging into her buttocks. He was fucking her hard and fast from tip to balls, his pelvis smacking against her wet, open sex. Slowly, her vision cleared. He continued without pause and with thorough, ruthless precision, rattling her body. Her world. This was *his* show, all right. He rocked her in a harsh, taut rhythm and she made a chuffing sound every time he pounded his cock into her. He was fucking her for his pleasure, and his alone.

The thought aroused her. She stopped struggling to return a counterstroke to his thrusts. The restraining apparatus made it nearly impossible, anyway. Her sex tightened instinctively around him, craving every stroke. She longed to see him as he dominated her, losing himself as he took full possession.

"That's right," she heard him say darkly from behind her. "Just give in to it. There's nothing for you to do but take me, is there?"

"No," she admitted. There was nothing else she *wanted* to do, but even so . . . the blatant knowledge of her helplessness aroused. She was too wound up in the intense eroticism of the moment to decode why that was.

A moment later, he groaned and drew his cock out of her. She whimpered shakily at the unpleasant feeling of aching emptiness. She lay there panting, her eyes wide-open, strung tight on a rack of anticipation.

A low growl reached her ears.

"Jacob," she mouthed, unbearably excited.

Then she felt it, the sensation of his warm semen dripping on her lower back. She bit off a sharp cry, her sex clenching tight. She pictured him in her mind, pumping his cock as fiercely and ruthlessly as he had that night in the pool shower, his beautiful body coiled tight, his expression hard and determined.

More warm liquid pooled at her lower back, the amount of it exciting her, like everything else. Then she felt the firm, succulent head of his dripping cock press against her left buttock, and more of his semen wetted her.

He gave one last throat-tearing groan.

His cock slipped off her ass. She moaned shakily, arousal cutting at her. Her cheeks were scalding and tension coiled tight in her sex. She'd loved having him use her for his pleasure. Why, she couldn't put into words exactly. Strangely, despite his opulent wealth and power and sex appeal, she felt deep inside that he *deserved* this indulgence. She *wanted* to give it to him. She might as well start to accept that fact.

He didn't speak as he dried her skin with the towel. Nor did he say a word when he reached between her thighs again. He must have known that his seemingly selfish taking of her had aroused her unbearably.

He brought her off twice more while she was restrained to the apparatus.

One thing about Jacob. He demanded a lot of her.

But he always returned exponentially.

twenty

He led her into his bedroom suite after he'd removed her from the apparatus, his arm taking most of her weight. She'd grown light-headed, her legs wobbly, after lying there suspended in the air and experiencing multiple, intense climaxes.

He guided her to a luxurious bathroom. The glass shower enclosure was enormous, and included a teak bench. At Jacob's urging, Harper sat down on it heavily, her head bowed. She felt exhausted . . . completely wrung out by the sharp lash of sexual bliss.

A moment later, she felt warm water running over her skin, and even better, Jacob's soap-covered hand. He was cleaning her with a handheld showerhead. It felt divine. Decadent. She wanted to look at him, but her head felt so heavy. He put one hand on her knee, opening her thighs. Warm water rushed over her sex. She whimpered. It soothed the slight sting in her tissues. For whatever reason, his gentle, patient bathing of her, his implicit understanding of what she was experiencing following his demanding possession, struck her as one of the most intimate, beautiful moments of her life.

He was eclipsing her grief and her existential crisis . . . but he was confusing her, too. She couldn't comprehend why she was so trusting of him when she knew with a man like him, hurt was an inevitability.

When he'd finished, Harper found the wherewithal to lift her head and watch in silent wonder as he quickly cleaned his own body. No sane woman would want to miss that, she told herself wryly. He seemed completely unaware of her admiration as he quickly ran his soapy hand over broad expanses of ridged, taut muscle, glistening bronzed skin . . . cock and balls. He was growing erect again. Harper realized with a dazed sense of longing. He fisted and pumped the length of his wet cock, then massaged his balls briskly. Her grew harder and longer in front of her eyes.

Maybe he wasn't as unaware of her watching him as he seemed.

A moment later, he reattached the showerhead. She stared fixedly at the image of him turned in profile, his glistening cock protruding between powerful thighs. It took her a moment to realize he was looking at her with a question in his eyes.

"I'm okay," she said, reading his concern for her wrung-out state. "I didn't know there was such an extreme difference between good sex and mind-blowing sex," she managed through numb lips. "It really saps you."

He smiled that smile. He walked over to her and reached for her hand. Fortunately, her legs held her when he pulled her up. His hand went to the back of her head, where he tugged gently at her damp hair. Her head fell back.

"You come hard, Harper McFadden," he said next to her lips.

"With you I do."

His kiss melted her even more, if that was possible. After he sealed it, he looked down at her searchingly.

"I know what you need," he said with the air of someone who had just made a decision.

"A bed?"

"No. Food," he said, taking her hand and opening the shower door.

She had nothing to wear since she'd left her clothing down at the pool house, so Jacob supplied her with a dark blue microfiber robe that was decadently soft and enormous on her. Jacob himself dressed in a pair of gray workout shorts and a plain black T-shirt. They stole through the now-darkened house, hand in hand, to Jacob's enormous kitchens.

He opened the fridge, and she examined the well-stocked shelves hungrily. She lifted a damp cloth on a large container.

"*Oysters*," she groaned longingly. Her stomach growled loudly. Jacob gave her an amused glance.

"Oysters it is, apparently." He pulled the container of oysters out along with a fresh loaf of French bread and a bottle of champagne.

He'd been right about what she needed, as usual. Harper reanimated during the kitchen raid. They sat on two stools next to the cook's wood-block prep table and proceeded to devour their simple meal. The oysters had a clean, briny flavor. The champagne was dry, crisp, and divine. Jacob entertained her by telling a story about the first time he tried a raw oyster at age sixteen while at a fancy cocktail party, where he'd been a fish out of water. He'd nearly thrown up on the immaculate party hostess and had to make a hasty retreat for the bathroom. The party hostess, who was the wife of the man he was working for, saved him further disgrace by halting him when he initially mistook the cloak closet for the powder room.

"I came this close"—he signified a fraction of an inch with his thumb and forefinger—"to losing my job along with the contents of my stomach all over dozens of rich people's coats and furs."

Harper laughed, shaking her head, holding a half shell in hand. "It's amazing how they grow on you, isn't it?" she said, nodding at the oyster. "My father first introduced them to me on a trip to Baltimore when I was fifteen." She tipped an oyster into her mouth, savoring the flavor fully before swallowing. "I thought they were disgusting at first, too, but now . . ." She closed her eyes at the sublime taste. "I crave them. And these are *especially* delicious. What are you smiling at?" she wondered, grinning.

"Your carnality," he replied levelly, ripping off a hunk of bread with those deft, powerful hands she loved. "You're very sensual. I like it. A lot."

She blinked and straightened on the stool at the heavy-lidded look he gave her before he bit into the bread with even white teeth and chewed. Recognizing her temporary enthrallment, she cleared her throat. He cast a spell effortlessly.

"So, did the infamous oyster incident happen at the house of the man who hired you to take care of his boats? The nice neighbor?"

He paused in the action of lifting his champagne flute to his mouth. "When did I ever say he was *nice*?"

Harper blinked at his sudden coolness. "I guess you didn't," she replied lightly. She regretting saying something that had dampened one of the most carefree moments she'd ever shared with him. But her curiosity was nudged by his sudden change of mood at the mention of the "nice neighbor," as well. "*I* said it when you told me how he let you and his friends take out his boats. Was it Clint Jefferies? The neighbor?" she asked with a sudden burst of intuition, recalling what Ruth had told her about his former mentor and a big financial scandal.

He set down his crystal goblet on the table with a brisk thud, and she had her answer. She damned her curiosity, but merely looked at him calmly, refusing to back down.

"Where the hell did you learn about Clint Jefferies?" he demanded.

"I'm a reporter. I overhear a lot of things, even if I'm not directly involved in a story."

His mouth went hard. He picked up a napkin and wiped off his hands. "So this is your reporter's curiosity rearing its head again."

He didn't say *ugly* head, but she had the impression that's what he was thinking, given his frown.

"I'm interested as a human being. I'm making conversation, Jacob."

"I don't talk about my past. Is that a problem for you?" he asked quietly. "For this?" he gestured between them.

He was asking her if it was necessary for him to share himself on a deeper level, given the temporary nature of their sexual relationship. She set down her champagne flute and wiped off her mouth.

"Is it because it's painful? Talking about your past?" she asked.

"No. It's because it's not important to me anymore. I don't want to emphasize it. I *refuse* to."

Her gaze swung to his. His mouth slanted in anger. He scared her a little bit, in that moment.

"I told you once that I remake myself every day." He waved down at himself with his bunched napkin and tossed it heedlessly on the butcher-block table. "This is it. This is who I am. This is what I can offer."

"The moment," she whispered.

"The moment," he agreed.

Harper got up from the stool slowly. Their former lightheartedness might never have existed. The oppressive silence in the big, sleek kitchen seemed to press down on her.

"I think I should be going," she said.

"Wait." He grabbed her hand and stood, stepping into her. She glanced up at him, seeing his sharp frustration. For a few seconds, she wasn't sure what he'd say. It struck her that *he* didn't know, either, whether he wanted her to go or to stay.

"I'll make the moments special, Harper." He touched her jaw. There was a fire in his eyes, but she saw irritation and . . . concern there, too. "You agreed that you needed something to make you forget your grief, for a while, anyway. I told you I can do that. This is our time now. Don't walk away when it's just begun."

"I don't understand you."

"I know. I don't understand me, either, half the time. It's just that my past . . . Clint Jefferies . . . the work I do. None of it is relevant to *this*."

She nodded, recognizing he was right. Why had it hurt so much when he'd refused to open up to her about his past? His past wasn't what counted. She touched his hard midriff through the T-shirt he wore. The moment felt very fragile. Then he dipped his head, and their mouths met, and she felt the frayed threads of their connection touch. Reweave.

Coil tight.

A minute later, he led her back to his bedroom suite and secured the door. She didn't say anything when he guided her to his bed and removed her robe.

There was something tenuous and temporary about their association with each other. But when they touched, something ignited. It was a chemistry so powerful, it obliterated all common sense. It reconnected them, even after an awkward, severing exchange.

Maybe the moment was enough . . . as long as the minutes and hours continued, anyway. Because he took her places in those moments, places that temporarily obliterated the realization of how alone she felt in the world.

"Stay the night," he rasped near her ear after they'd made love again, and she lay awash with warmth and satiation in the circle of his arms. "I'll have a surprise for you in the morning."

"I have to work in the morning," she whispered at the same time she ran her lips over his whiskered jaw.

"I'll get you up early. One of my drivers will get you home in plenty of time to get ready for work." He leaned over her, taking her deeper into his embrace, pressing his lips to her hairline. She shivered in pleasure. "Trust me?"

"Yes," she whispered.

And there it was again. It didn't feel like his words were smoke and shadows. It didn't feel like her agreement to them was.

She really did trust him, no matter how guarded and elusive he was.

When he wakened her, it was still dark. She squinted when he turned on a bedside lamp. He was sitting at the edge of the bed, dressed in workout clothes—different ones than he'd worn last night. His hair was mussed and he looked a little sweaty . . . not to mention extremely sexy. She glanced around, disoriented.

"Is it still nighttime? Did you just *work out*?" she asked in sleepy confusion.

"Yeah. It's my routine, five days a week." *Well, that certainly explains the rock-hard body.* He brushed her hair back from her face, and she shivered. "So is this next part. You're coming with me for that. Here's your robe."

She rose groggily and scurried into her robe. "Where are we going?"

"You'll see. It's nice."

That's all he'd say as she followed him down the grand staircase and through the great room. They walked out onto the cool terrace, and Harper saw the pink glow of sunrise over the mountains to the left.

"Good morning, Mr. Latimer," a woman said.

"Hi, Gabby. Shelly, thanks for coming on short notice," Jacob said.

"Not a problem at all. Happy to do it," Shelly said.

They approached two women who were standing near a lit outdoor fireplace. They wore white smocks and pants and were smiling. Harper noticed the massage tables that had been arranged near the fire. Shelly and Gabby both peeled back the linens and blanket on them invitingly.

"You get a massage every time after you work out?" she breathed out quietly, for Jacob's ears alone. "An outdoor massage at sunrise?" she added, glancing out to the spectacular panoramic view of the blazing sun peeking over the top of the mountains and sending rays of fire into the glittering jewel of the lake. She noticed Jacob's wry expression and laughed softly. "Of *course* you do."

The masseuses turned away while they undressed and got under the blanket. Harper was faster than Jacob, since she wore only a robe. She watched him with her cheek turned on the soft sheet as he shucked off his clothing and tennis shoes and came facedown on the table, the gold and red of the sunrise gleaming on his bronzed skin and body. He caught her staring as he drew the sheet up over his ass, but she didn't look away. Maybe it was the novelty of the situation, or the warmth on her skin from the nearby fire, but she didn't hide the admiration in her eyes, either. He noticed. Their gazes held and stuck, even as the masseuses approached their tables.

Harper had the flickering thought that she was glad Jacob got Gabby, who was middle-aged and stocky, but strong-looking, while Shelly was younger and attractive. As soon as Shelly began her massage, though, Harper couldn't have cared less if it was a supermodel that occasionally massaged Jacob's gorgeous body in the romantic setting. The woman was talented. Jacob clearly hired her for her skills, not her looks.

The massage in combination with the warmth from the fire had Harper as limp as a cooked noodle by the time Shelly finished.

"That was *fantastic*, thank you," Harper told Shelly through lips that had gone slack and tingly.

"I'm glad you enjoyed it. Please get up slowly. You're very relaxed," Shelly said quietly before she and Gabby exited the terrace, giving them privacy.

She looked over at Jacob. He was coming to a sitting position on the table, the white sheet draped low over his taut abdomen. His blondish-brown hair was mussed and strands fell onto his forehead. He looked good enough to eat.

"Did you like?" he asked.

"So much that I can't move. My muscles have never been so spoiled," she mumbled, throwing back the sheet and reaching for her robe.

"Then we'll do it tomorrow, as well." She glanced up at him as she tossed the robe around her shoulders. "I mean, if you'd like? Dinner tonight, too? I promise I'll do better than raiding the fridge this time."

She laughed. "Don't promise on my account. That was the best meal I've had in years."

"Is that a yes?"

She glanced over at him. His gaze was on her bare breasts.

"You know it is," she said softly. He looked up and met her stare. She felt that increasingly familiar unfurling in her lower belly.

"Jacob?"

Harper looked around at the woman's voice, startled. Her eyes widened when she saw Elizabeth Shields walking briskly across the terrace in her pumps. Harper scrambled hastily into her robe, drawing it closed over her naked body. Unfortunately, she wasn't fast enough. Elizabeth halted in her tracks, her stare on Harper. Then she looked abruptly downward at the stone floor.

"I'm so sorry. I didn't realize you weren't alone," Elizabeth said.

"What is it?" Jacob asked her in a clipped tone.

Elizabeth glanced up cautiously. When she noticed that Harper was covered, she stepped forward. She had a cell phone in her hand, and was covering the receiver.

"It's Alex calling about the ResourceSoft acquisition. I'm afraid there's been a snag," she glanced over at Harper, clearly still uncomfortable airing Jacob's private affairs in front of her.

"It's okay, Elizabeth," Jacob said. "What's the problem?"

"There's a liability issue. A man has come forward and claimed a prior copyright on the software."

Jacob cursed under his breath. He held out his hand, frowning forbiddingly. Harper sensed the shift in his focus, along with his irritation. Elizabeth gave him the phone.

Harper turned away, tightening her robe and smoothing her hair while Jacob talked to whoever was on the phone in terse, brisk language. He didn't take long, but even so, she caught a glimpse of his diamond-hard focus. It intimidated her a little, seeing that brilliant, glacial side of his personality. He signed off as she turned around. His gaze flickered across her, and she sensed his methodical mind working through a myriad of scenarios.

"I'm sorry. I'm going to have to leave for San Francisco this afternoon," he said distractedly.

"Oh." She was expecting him to say something like that, given what she'd just overheard on the phone. Still, she was disappointed. They'd gone from the warmth of the moment and the promise of more excitement and intimacy tonight to having it all ripped away in a second. "Well, I'm sure it can't be helped . . ." She faded off, made uncomfortable with Elizabeth standing there, listening to the whole exchange.

"It sure as hell can't," Jacob muttered angrily, hopping onto the terrace, still holding the white sheet against his lower body, insouciant in his mostly nude state, even in front of Elizabeth. He handed the phone to his assistant.

"Call Jenny and Marianne and let them know I'll be there this evening." He rattled off a few other instructions to Elizabeth, and Elizabeth made a few suggestions. Harper started to feel like a third wheel, they were both so intent on their plans. Finally, Elizabeth nodded and started to walk away.

"No. Wait," Jacob called tersely to Elizabeth. He turned to Harper. "Come with me? To San Francisco."

She blinked in amazement. She'd thought he'd forgotten she was there.

"I have work."

"It's Friday of Labor Day weekend. I'll wait until you're off. We'll fly out of the Truckee-Tahoe Airport and be in San Francisco in forty-five minutes. I'll get you back on Sunday. Cyril is in San Francisco right now. Maybe you two could get together while I'm in meetings, discuss the film contract or screenplay ideas."

She glanced anxiously at Elizabeth, who was watching her closely.

"Okay. I mean . . . I guess that could work," she said impulsively, finding it impossible to resist.

Finding *him* impossible to resist.

For a second, his irritation and preoccupation with the snag in his acquisition might never have been. He flashed a smile. Harper thought he looked relieved. For a few seconds, she was positive she'd made the right decision in agreeing. How could it be a bad choice, when it made him smile that way?

"Make the arrangements please?" he said to Elizabeth, his gaze remaining on Harper.

"Of course," Elizabeth said, giving Harper one last uneasy glance before she walked into the house.

"I'm sorry about your deal complications," Harper told him when they were alone again.

"I'll get it straightened out," he said grimly. His expression lightened a little. "And at least you'll be there."

She forced a smile and walked toward him. "For the weekend. For the moment."

He reached out to palm her jaw and ducked his head, seizing her mouth in one swift, unexpected movement. His kiss was hard. Hot. Greedy. Harper felt her toes curling into the stone terrace. Her brain went blank for several heated seconds.

He tore his mouth from hers and pressed their foreheads together, fisting her hair. She looked up slightly, seeing the gleam in his eyes.

"I'm going to make them moments you're never going to forget. Trust me?" he asked quietly against her open mouth.

"Yes," she whispered.

Because as usual, her doubts couldn't exist simultaneously with his touch. That's what had her breathless at the idea of spending the entire weekend with him.

Not to mention scared half out of her mind.

5

make me
RISK IT

twenty~one

Living up to his easygoing management style, Sangar had no problem whatsoever telling Harper to go home once she'd turned in her work that Friday. Harper called Jacob and let him know she could leave for San Francisco whenever he was ready. His driver and he were there in the parking lot when she walked out of the newsroom ten minutes later.

The glamour and novelty of Lattice's sleek private jet awaiting them at the Truckee-Tahoe Airport that afternoon only added to her sense of general euphoria at the prospect of a weekend with Jacob. He was on the phone a lot during their chauffeured ride to the airport and after boarding the plane. He'd immediately apologized for his preoccupation with business when she got into the limo with him. Harper assured him she understood. He'd already put off leaving for San Francisco because he was waiting for her to finish work, after all. She relaxed in the luxurious seat, listening to him talk and experiencing his concise, drilling intelligence firsthand. Unlike this morning on the terrace, when she'd found him intimidating, she found herself relaxing, however. Wasn't it natural, that he could apply that intense focus of his wherever he chose?

Once the pilot informed them that they'd be taking off soon, he hung up his cell phone and dropped it on the table in front of them with a clunking sound.

He took her hand.

"Hi," he said.

"Hi," Harper returned, smiling over at him.

"Sorry again about all that," he said, nodding at his phone.

"No problem. Does it look like a problem you'll be able to solve?" she asked. She knew by listening to him he'd been conferring with others on the copyright claim on the software for the business he wanted to buy.

"It'll get solved. It's just a matter of how much time and money we have to throw at this thing to get it there."

"Does the prior copyright claim on the software seem legitimate?" she asked.

His stare was on her face. As usual, she felt uniquely aware of herself and her body when his focused attention was on her. "Legitimate enough to bring it to court. It's my job to convince the claimant that it's not worth *his* time and money to take it there." He abruptly planted a kiss on her mouth, making Harper blink in surprised pleasure. "Forget about work. Are you comfortable? Do you want anything to drink?"

"No, I'm fine."

"I've told Cyril we were coming. He invited himself over to my house tomorrow. He has some ideas about the film he wants to run by you."

"That'd be great." She laughed when Jacob made a face. "You act like Cyril is a pain, but you actually like his company, don't you?"

He merely shrugged, but something about his small smile told her that what she'd said was true.

"Maybe it'll be for the best if he comes over. I'll be in meetings tomorrow afternoon. Cyril can keep you company. I promise you a nice dinner tomorrow night, though, and we have tickets to the opera tonight."

"It sounds great."

"Good. You don't want to sit next to the window?" he asked, nodding toward the seat across from him.

"No, I'd rather sit next to you."

The plane began to move on the runway. He seemed tense. Distracted.

"What?" she asked him, sensing he had something on his tongue.

"Is flying . . . or heights, one of the fears you had when you were a kid?"

"No," she replied without hesitation.

"Do you mind if I ask what you were afraid of when you were young? Besides . . . you know. Knives?"

"Why? I don't have those phobias anymore," she said, honestly curious about why he would want to know.

He shrugged, bringing her attention down to his broad shoulders. He was wearing a white shirt and a tweed blazer. She had to restrain herself from putting her hands all over him, he looked so appealing. "I was just interested. It's amazing, the way your father was able to get rid of your phobias so completely."

"Dogs," she admitted after a pause, sighing. "That's why I got a little freaked out when Charger *charged* me on the beach."

His eyebrows went up. "So the fears weren't completely eradicated."

"You saw me with all your dogs. Lots of people would jump if a large animal ran at them, but I keep it under control. I can manage my anxiety."

"Right," he murmured. The plane turned onto the runway. He was looking at her intently, stroking her hand with his thumb, seemingly unaware when the plane began to speed up for takeoff. "Was there anything else?"

"Crowds. Being out in public."

"You were agoraphobic?"

"Yes. School phobic, too, because of it," she said, looking away from his incising stare . . . feeling a little stupid. Embarrassed. She cleared her throat, reminding herself she was a grown woman now and was no longer that frightened girl. "I was never really afraid of people, per se, it was being *out* that got to me. I felt vulnerable. Exposed. I missed a good part of the seventh grade, because of it. Between doing the schoolwork at home, tutoring, and summer school, I was able to enter the eighth grade with my original class. Although, even in the eighth grade, my attendance was still a little problematic.

By my sophomore year or so, the worst of my anxieties were past. I joined the school newspaper and the creative writing club." She shrugged. "Writing kind of brought me out of my shell."

"That's a lot of time lost. Do you regret it?"

"Sure. A whole chunk of my childhood was taken from me." The plane lifted from the ground and began hurtling through empty space. The engines hummed loudly in her ears.

"Why?" he asked.

"Why what?"

"Isn't there usually a precipitating event to phobias like you had? Some kind of trauma?" he probed.

She focused on him, slightly incredulous that he expected her to spill her vulnerabilities. "Sometimes, but not necessarily. Why are you so curious about my teenage neuroses? *Are* you worried they're going to make a reappearance?"

"No. I'm just interested. I want to know you better."

She gave him a *seriously?* glance. His expression flattened, and she knew he'd just recalled their conversation from last night, the one where he'd told her firmly he didn't discuss his past.

"I get it," he said, his mouth pressed into a hard line. "I'm not allowed to question you about your past if—"

"You won't let me do the same about yours? I'm actually okay with you asking, Jacob. It'd be nice if you at least recognized the double standard, though."

He looked out the window, his face turned in profile. In the distance, she saw the Sierra Nevada mountains falling away from them.

"But not of heights," she heard him say very quietly.

"Excuse me?"

"You weren't afraid of heights," he clarified. At first, she was puzzled by his statement, but after a moment, she considered it seriously.

"I used to be pretty nervous about heights, when I was really little," she replied thoughtfully, examining their clasped hands where they rested on his long, solid thigh.

"But not anymore?" Jacob asked. She realized she'd sounded a little wistful, and that he'd turned and was peering at her.

"No," she replied softly. "Not anymore."

"Your father cured you of that fear, too?"

"Not my father. Someone else."

From the periphery of her vision, she saw him open his mouth. He closed it without speaking. She stared out the window as they soared through the air, only feeling a sense of calm power as he held her hand tightly in his.

Twenty Years Ago

When Jake opened his eyes the next morning at dawn, it was like waking up in a different body. A different world. His nose was buried in Harper's soft hair. It smelled of hay from the loft, and peaches. They were on their sides, her back pressed against his front. He held her against him with one arm encircling her waist.

Combining their heat had worked. He was warm.

And he ached . . .

The realization made him scoot away from her as fast as if he'd realized he hugged a tarantula to him. His hasty scuttling in the blankets made her stir. He regretted awakening her. But it was mortifying, the uncontrollable reaction of his body. It was as embarrassing as it would have been if he'd peed his pants in the middle of the night, and a girl was about to discover it. And not one of the giggling, swarming girls from Poplar Gorge Junior High, either.

This wasn't just *any* girl. It was Harper McFadden.

"Jake?" she asked sleepily.

"Yeah. It's okay. Go back to sleep," he ordered gruffly, reaching for a discarded sock.

"'S okay. I'll get up, if you are."

Both of them went to the waterfall and washed their hands and faces, then drank mouthfuls of the cool water. Slowly, Jake started to ache a little less, and his self-consciousness faded. They put on their tennis shoes silently. Harper sat cross-legged on the blankets when she was done. Her nose wrinkled.

"What's wrong?" Jake asked her warily.

"I smell," she said.

"Like peaches," he mumbled under his breath, tying his shoe off extra hard. He froze. His eyes widened at the recognition of his misstep.

"Huh?"

"Nothing," he muttered.

"I wish I could take a bath," she said longingly, staring at the opening to the cave in the distance. Pale morning light was starting to shine through the small hole in the rocks.

"I brought some soap. I could give you some privacy and you could wash in the waterfall. Water's ice cold, though."

"I don't care," she said, sniffing in the direction of her armpit and scowling.

"I have another idea," he said, standing. "It should be safe. One thing I know for sure, Emmitt don't get up until way after dawn, even when he's tracking. It's like his brain doesn't function in the early morning. We probably have an hour or more to do it, and then to get back here under cover."

"Do what?"

He nodded toward the back of the cave. "If Emmitt ever did track us here, we'd have to make a fast escape. There's a small opening onto a river cliff, back there in the second cave."

"There's a second cave?"

"Yeah. The entrance to the second cave is even smaller than that one." He nodded toward the sunlit hole. "Emmitt couldn't get through it, but we could."

Harper smiled. "There are advantages to being small."

He turned his head, afraid she'd notice his cheeks color. She was grinning gamely, and clearly hadn't realized how her offhand comment about his size pained him.

"Are you afraid of heights?" he asked her.

Her smile faded. "A little. Why?"

"Because the only way off the cliff is through the cave, or over the edge. But the New River is nice and deep below. It's safe. I've jumped the cliff six, maybe seven times," he assured when he saw her eyes widen with anxiety.

"How far is the jump?"

"Thirty, thirty-five feet at *most*." Was it his imagination, or did she go pale? "See, the thing is, if we practice it early this morning, we'll know we can do it," he explained in a rush, feeling like he was losing her cooperation by the second. "That way, our escape plan will be in place. We'll know that even if Emmitt walked right up to this cave, we could get away from him. Plus . . . you'd get your bath. We could bring some soap." He added the last lamely.

"I don't know. It sounds scary. Besides, you said that you don't think your uncle could ever find us here."

"I don't think he will. But we have to be ready for the small chance that he does."

She bit at her lower lip anxiously. Her lips reminded him of the color of ripe strawberries. They looked so pretty next to her copper-colored hair.

"Can't I just jump if Emmitt ever comes?" she asked, her voice sounding squeaky.

"How's this? We'll just go out onto the cliff, and you can see what it's like," he said. He was worried—now more so, seeing her nervousness about heights—that she'd freeze if Emmitt actually did show up. Her anxiety could cost them precious seconds, and those seconds, their lives. If she practiced and was confident she could do the cliff jump, it'd make a big difference.

When she didn't respond immediately, he planted a confident, *it'll be all right, you're making it into a bigger deal than it is* expression on his face.

"Okay, but I've got to pee first." He nodded as if it were no big deal for a pretty girl to talk to him about peeing. With Harper, he realized it actually wasn't.

. . .

After they'd both relieved themselves in different parts of the cave, Jake led her farther back to what he called the "second" cave. He kept a flashlight stashed behind a rock at the entrance. He used it now, so as not to waste any of the batteries from the two flashlights he'd put in their backpacks.

"Oh, look!" Harper exclaimed in a hushed tone of admiration when the beam of light lit up the cavern surprisingly well. "Stalactites and stalagmites."

Jake smiled at her excitement, remembering the first time he'd discovered the inner portion of the cave. Compared to the boring and bare outer cave, it'd been like entering a beautiful, alien world. "You know the difference between them?" he challenged her.

"'Course," she sniffed. She pointed up. "Those are stalactites and those"—she pointed down—"are stalagmites." She glanced over at him. He just arched his brows. "Wait. At least I *think* so. Isn't that right?" she trailed off uncertainly when she saw his doubtful expression.

"Do you want me to tell you the right answer?"

"Yeah. I mean *no*," she corrected when he grinned broadly. She shoved him in the shoulder. "I knew I was right," she accused.

"Then what were you so worried about?"

He started to turn off the flashlight—the small opening to the cliff was twenty feet above them now, and light streamed into the darkness. Something caught his eye next to the rock fall of stones and dirt leading to the cliff. He moved away from Harper, shining the flashlight into a dim corner.

"What's wrong?" Harper whispered behind him.

"Nothing," Jake said, hiding his concern at the sight of a large animal's scat. He didn't want Harper worrying about yet another thing. The cliff jump was going to be challenge enough for now. That, and getting her up there to begin with.

He turned off the flashlight and moved next to her. The small opening was twenty feet above them. He climbed up several feet onto the rock pile, extending his hand to Harper.

"You made me doubt myself about the stalactites and stalagmites," she accused, taking his hand and following him up the craggy limestone rock and dirt spill without hesitation. "All that talk yesterday about me being a city girl and everything. *Lead feet*," she grumbled under her breath as they climbed.

"If the lead shoe fits . . . ," he said, hauling on her weight with his hand. She came to a halt, three-quarters up the rock pile. She looked stunned.

"You've got a sense of humor." Her smile made his stomach do a little flip-flop. He frowned to hide that fact.

"What, you think a hillbilly can't make a joke?" he grumbled, climbing up the remaining rocks.

"That's got nothing to do with it," she defended, following him, clearly determined to make her point. "You're so smart about being on your own, and surviving in the woods. My dad would say you're right-brained. That means you know how to work things mechanically."

"And that I don't get jokes?" He hauled her up on the long, narrow rock next to where he crouched. The small opening was just a few feet above them.

"No. Stop twisting my words around."

"Do you want to go first?"

"What?" she asked, blinking. She glanced around them, blanching when she noticed how far they'd climbed up the jagged rock spill. "Oh, crap." She reached, clutching desperately at the edge of the opening above them for balance.

"If it bothers you, stop looking," Jake said firmly. "Look where you're going, not where you've been." He pointed up at the sunny opening and put his hand on her back. "Go on."

"But . . ."

"Just do it," he said, pushing on her back. "It's not hard to pull yourself out. I'm coming right after you." When she wavered in the hole, he firmed his resolve. He pushed on her butt hard. She disappeared with a surprised squawk.

He followed her fleetly through the opening. She was on her hands and knees on the sunny cliff, her head turned, her aquamarine eyes flashing fire.

"It got you up here," he stated simply, coming to his feet. He reached for her hand as a form of apology. Her expression of outrage melted to one tinged with wonder. Slowly, she fell back onto her haunches and took his hand. He hauled her up.

"You were messing with me so that I wouldn't notice how high we were on those rocks, weren't you? You really *do* know more than just how to take care of yourself and math. I think my dad would want to meet you," she said once they stood facing each other, their hands remaining clasped.

He rolled his eyes to diminish the warmth that rushed through him at her compliment. She smiled at his flash of embarrassment, all her fury forgotten. She glanced to the side.

"Oh, *shit.*"

She lurched toward the cliff, jerking him with her. She'd seen the drop-off to the gorge. Her face had gone pale as paper, making the light freckles on her nose appear even more pronounced. She pressed her back to the cliff wall.

"Harper—"

"I'm *not* jumping off that ledge," she declared hotly. "That's *not* thirty feet!"

"Yeah, it is," he reasoned, sensing he was losing her. "The hills and the canyon make a kind of . . . of . . . an optical illusion." *Yeah, that's it.* "It fools the brain into thinking the river is farther down than it is."

"Really?" She cast a wary glance over his shoulder in the direction of the gorge. He'd guessed she'd be convinced by anything that had to do with the brain and psychology, given the way she seemed to hold her dad up on such a tall pedestal. Jake wasn't above using that knowledge to convince her.

"Yeah," he insisted, tugging on her hand. She straightened, leaving the wall but refusing to move her feet and get closer to the ledge. Unfortunately—or fortunately, depending upon Jake's frantic, bewildering feelings about her—that meant that she stood very close to him.

"I can't jump off that cliff, Jake," she said solemnly, holding his stare.

"*You* don't have to. We're going to do it together." He put his hands on her hips. They felt round beneath his hands . . . such an incredible, mesmerizing swell of flesh. How could a girl be so *different* than a boy?

"Like this?" she asked shakily, putting her hands below his waist, mirroring his hold on her. She stepped closer.

He nodded, unable to speak for a few seconds.

"Except tighter. I won't let go of you, Harper."

She glanced soberly to the right. The ledge of the cliff was three feet away.

"I *promise*," he added.

He felt her fear bubbling just beneath the surface.

"Okay," she finally said reluctantly.

He let out a sigh of relief.

"*Wait,*" he said when she started to shuffle cautiously over the ledge, her face pale.

"What?"

"We . . . we have to . . . we have to take our clothes off first—or at least some of them," he said in a desperate burst. "I only had room in the packs to bring us one extra shirt, some socks, and some extra underwear for me, but I didn't have any for—"

"For me. I know," she said, her cheeks coloring. She looked down at his chest. "It's weird, wearing jeans without underwear. *Your* jeans," she mumbled under her breath.

"Sorry."

She looked up at him. "It's not your fault. I know you just want to do this because you don't want me to freak out if—" She blew deliberately out of her mouth. "*Right.* So we'll take off our jeans, since they're the only bottoms we've got."

"And our socks and shoes," he said. "They pop off in the water. Trust me."

"We'll go in with everything else on. The clothes will get a wash that way, just like us," she said, attempting to sound firm and practical, but still coming off shaky. Jake got the impression it helped her, to make some of the decisions on her own.

"Yeah, okay," he agreed. For a few seconds, they both hesitated self-consciously, still embracing each other. Then they stepped back at once. Jake kicked off his tennis shoes and pulled off his socks, keeping his head lowered. After he'd removed his jeans, he dared to look up cautiously. She was standing there looking as serious as a judge, clutching the edge of his Mountaineers T-shirt against pale thighs. His gaze dropped over her naked legs without him telling it to. He'd never thought about legs being *pretty* until Harper.

"Ready?" he asked gruffly, stepping toward her. He'd never been more self-conscious in his life, but he knew he couldn't come off that way. He knew that jumping off the cliff was a relatively easy maneuver. At all costs, he needed to make Harper feel some of his confidence.

She just nodded and stepped toward him. He'd heard the phrase *heart in your throat* before. He saw Harper's neck convulse thickly, and thought that's what she must be experiencing. He determinedly put his hands on her waist, again feeling that amazing swell of her hips.

"We have to get next to the ledge," he said, holding her stare.

She nodded, but looked unwilling.

He edged them over carefully. Her head turned. She whimpered softly as they neared the drop-off.

"Don't look at that. Look at me," he said sharply.

Her gaze darted to his face. He saw her wild anxiety.

"It's gonna be fine. I've told you how many times I've done this before. You know how to swim, don't you?" *Why didn't you ask her that before, idiot?*

"Yes. I'm a good swimmer. I'm on swim team."

"Okay. Then there's no problem. Keep looking at me. Over just a few more inches . . ." He scooted them closer to the cliff. Her stare on him now was focused, like it was a lifeline she was clinging onto. Her face looked pale and rigid with fear.

"Put your hands on me," he said when they'd come to a halt.

She grasped onto his waist tightly.

"Come closer," he said.

She hugged him. Their fronts sealed tight. Her breath tickled his nose and lips. Her small, round breasts pressed against his chest, the tips pointed and hard. He opened his mouth to instruct her—

"Your eyes are so pretty."

"What?" he asked hoarsely, startled.

"Your eyes."

He grimaced in disbelief. "They're like that river down there. Muddy brown-green."

"Maybe your mirror at home is dirty. There's gold in them, and flecks of green and brown. And they're as clear as a clean stream."

He felt his body hardening, which horrified him. If they didn't do this now, she was going to notice.

"We're going to jump out from the cliff as far as we can and fall with our feet straight down. Do you understand? *Harper?*" he asked when she didn't respond for a moment, still staring fixedly at him. She blinked. "Don't hesitate on your jump, or we might fall too close to the cliff. That's dangerous. You gotta jump, all or nothing. Fall feet-first, straight into the water. Got it?"

"Jump as far as out from the cliff as I can. Feet straight in the water," she repeated.

"Okay. On the count of three," he said loudly.

She pressed even closer to him, so that he swore he could feel her heart frantically beating into his chest. His own started to hammer in tandem with it.

"One, two—

"Don't let me go."

"I won't let go," he vowed, clutching her to him for all he was worth. "*Three.*"

They leapt in together. The earth fell away. His stomach dropped seemingly faster than his body. Harper gave a muted squeal. He kept his eyes open as they free-fell, gauging how far they were from the cliff face. He had a fleeting impression of her copper-colored, streaming hair, clamped eyelids, and pale face. Just before they hit the surface of the water, she opened her eyes.

The image seemed to burn into his brain. He saw it even as they plunged into the New River and his eyelids sealed shut as water jetted around them.

He saw it still, twenty years later: Harper's gaze glued to him with a fierce, desperate trust.

twenty~two

Being more familiar with San Francisco in comparison to Tahoe, she thought she knew what to expect as far as a Sea Cliff mansion. She'd dated a ridiculously narcissistic hedge fund investor for a short period—a *very* short time—whom had lived in Sea Cliff. Over the years, she'd also attended a handful of cocktail and dinner parties in the affluent San Francisco neighborhood.

Of course, none of that actually prepared her for Jacob's home. It was located on the farthest point of a promontory where it sat in solitary grandeur, commanding a breathtaking view of the Pacific Ocean. It was entirely made of white limestone, its stark silhouette creating a striking contrast to the dark cliffs and the periwinkle blue of the Pacific Ocean. While his Tahoe compound was warm, rustic sophistication, the Sea Cliff home was cool, sleek grandeur. They were greeted at the front door by a short, stocky woman in her forties who seemed to brim over with a sense of enthusiastic purpose, and an older, attractive woman who struck Harper as elegant, cautious, and sedate.

"Harper McFadden, I'd like you to meet Jenny Caravallo, my admin here in San Francisco, and Marianne Holstein, my house manager," Jacob introduced briskly as they entered a white dome-ceilinged entry hall and the chauffer bustled around them with their luggage.

Both women greeted them warmly. Jenny's energy couldn't be contained in polite greetings for long, though. She almost immediately launched into the latest happenings with the ResourceSoft acquisition difficulties. Jacob put up a hand, and she halted midsentence.

"Excuse me. Marianne? Would you show Harper to my suite? We have a dinner reservation in . . ." He looked at his watch and scowled. "A little over an hour."

"Of course. Follow me," Marianne said to Harper with a smile.

Harper glanced back at Jacob. He was listening to Jenny, but he looked up and met her stare, a trace of annoyance and apology in his eyes. Harper smiled her assurance. She'd been expecting him to be bombarded with work once he crossed the threshold. He'd asked her to San Francisco because of a work complication, after all.

Marianne led her to stunning quarters decorated almost exclusively in whites, grays, and cool blues that matched the jaw-dropping view of the sky and the ocean outside the floor-to-ceiling windows. The housekeeper gave her a tour of the enormous suite.

"That's Mr. Latimer's bathroom over there, and the guest facilities are right in here," Marianne was saying. Harper yanked her gaze off the spectacular view and followed the house manager into a luxurious bathroom. So, Jacob bathed separately from his "guests" here at Sea Cliff.

"Yes, it looks as if Charles has set your bags in here already," Marianne said pleasantly, pointing at an open door that led to what appeared to be an attached dressing room and closet with mirrors. Harper saw her suitcase and carryall near the door.

"It looks as if I'm all set, then," she said warmly to Marianne.

Marianne left with an insistence that Harper call on one of the house phones if she should need anything. Harper sighed when the older woman closed the double doors behind her. She glanced uneasily at the guest facilities, acknowledging to herself that the existence of that bathroom was the reason for her sudden disquietude. For some reason, that room—a stupid *room*—underlined Jacob's typical aloofness with women . . . his determination to keep his personal life ultimately separate from his sexual one.

"Only in the bedroom shall we meet," Harper mumbled under her breath sarcastically as she headed toward her assigned bathroom.

Most of her irritation melted away a few minutes later as she stood in the luxurious steam shower. Was she really going to get pissy over the way Jacob had arranged his home? He wasn't the only person in existence who wanted privacy in the bathroom. She herself preferred it.

She heard the bathroom door clicking shut and jumped in surprise. Jacob walked around the shower enclosure. He was naked.

Gloriously so.

He opened the shower door and stepped in. Her gaze dropped over him as steam curled around his long, muscular body. Her heart began to race in excitement.

So much for craving privacy in the bathroom.

"You weren't getting started without me, were you?" he asked, a lazy smile tilting his mouth. He stepped beneath the shower spray, taking her into his arms. She stifled a groan of pleasure at the sensation of his wet naked body pressing against her own.

"I only washed my hair so far," she replied, looking up at him.

"I wasn't talking about hygiene," he murmured, before his mouth covered hers. His kiss was even more sultry and hot than the shower enclosure.

"Jacob, if I don't get out now and dry my hair, I won't make it for dinner," she said a breathless moment later. Despite her words, she dipped her knees slightly, running her wet body up and down against his. He was so hard. It felt divine, his ribs pressing against her breasts, the column of his stiffening cock sliding across her belly.

He stopped her abruptly by cupping one of her ass cheeks in a large hand.

"So you'll go to the opera with wet hair," he replied, his smoldering gaze on her mouth and his squeezing hand on her ass making focusing difficult. She managed a sarcastic look up at him.

"Okay, no wet hair," he granted. "We'll just have to make good use of our time, then." He put both hands on her ass and guided her over to the shower bench seat. He urged her to sit. She watched him, taking in the wonders of his powerful back, bulging biceps, and glistening ass as he turned his back to her. When he returned, he held one of the shower attachments, a Waterpik massager. There was something about the way he grasped the golden handle of the instrument so . . . *purposefully* that made her eyes go wide.

"I've been thinking about it ever since I washed you last night," he rasped, coming down on his knees in front of her. Harper graphically recalled his intimate, tender washing of her sex after multiple orgasms had left her limp and exhausted. She watched as he used his thumb to flip on the spray. Water jetted on the seat next to her, the pressure good and strong . . .

"I thought it'd be too selfish to bring you off again last night, as wrung out as you were." Water droplets clung to his long lashes. He opened his hand on her thigh, spreading her knees. "But you're not tired now, are you?"

She merely shook her head, made mute by his heavy-lidded stare and the sound of the Waterpik shooting onto the seat beside her. He lifted the massager. Warm water shot onto her thigh, massaging the muscle. He moved it up, just inches away from her sex.

"Do you like a shower massager?" he asked languidly. He stared fixedly between her thighs.

"Yes," she whispered.

His gaze darted up to her face. "I'm asking if you ever masturbate with one."

Her mouth fell open. She'd heard of women doing it, of course. But she'd never had the proper equipment in her house to do it herself.

"No," she mouthed, because he'd aimed the showerhead on her mons. Water ran in rivulets over her outer sex. His head was bowed. His attention on her appeared to be absolute. The vibrations reached her clit. She whimpered softly.

"You've got the prettiest pussy in existence," he muttered, moving aside the Waterpik. He ducked his head over her lap and ran his tongue between her labia, laving her clit hard. She made a choked sound and grabbed at his head, her fingers sinking into his wet hair. His tongue was firm. Deft.

He knew exactly what he was doing.

He lifted his head and lowered the shower massager onto her outer sex. She groaned, her eyes springing wide. The pressure was hard, a little *too* intense, in fact. It eased a mere second after she'd thought it. He'd been watching the expression on her face, and let up on the pressure valve on the nozzle. Now it was ideal. She fell back mindlessly on the narrow seat, the shower wall bracing her back.

"I didn't think I'd like it with you," he said evenly, studying her reaction as he moved the showerhead subtly, stimulating her. His thumb slipped between her sex lips for a moment, giving her clit a good rub. She gasped. "I don't want anything washing away your taste. But there was something about washing you last night . . . I knew I wouldn't rest until I saw you coming from it."

He placed the nozzle directly on her labia, pressing tight. Water jetted onto her clit, but he applied force with the nozzle, as well. He circled subtly.

"Ah, Jesus, Jacob." Her free hand dropped to the edge of the marble seat, where she clutched tight. Her fingers on his head formed a claw in his hair. He moved the gold handle subtly. Her body jerked in pleasure. She vibrated in mounting bliss.

"That's right."

The thick arousal in his tone made her eyelids open a moment later. His gaze was still glued between her thighs. His hand was between his legs, and one of his arms was moving. Her sex clenched. Her arousal spiked. He was pumping his cock as he watched himself bringing her off with the Waterpik. She moaned in anguished arousal, and suddenly his stare was on her face.

"Touch your beautiful breasts," he demanded.

Her hands slid along her ribs and cupped her breasts from below. His arm moved faster between his thighs and his gaze narrowed. "Squeeze them, Harper. Show me your pretty nipples. That's right," he said through a snarl when she presented her nipples to him between her pinching fingertips.

It felt so good, her hands gliding sensuously against her wet skin. The Waterpik gushed between her thighs, making her tense in cresting pleasure. But the thing that sent her over the edge was Jacob's fixed, feral stare on her breasts as he jerked at his cock, faster and faster.

She bit off a scream as orgasm flooded her, hot and delicious. The moment she began to shudder in release, he pulled away the Water-pik. He shoved one thigh wider and ducked his head, running his tongue between her labia, pressing and pulsing forcefully. She let out an uncontrollable shriek of pure pleasure and hugged his head to her, climaxing furiously against his mouth.

His deep, harsh moan brought her back to herself. She blinked open her eyes, panting. She stared between her thighs. Her mouth fell open in dazed wonder. He continued to eat her hungrily, laving her clit with a stiffened, red tongue. Then he covered her with his mouth and created a sinful suction. His focused hunger amazed her. He seemed intent on claiming what the showerhead had taken from him: her juices . . .

. . . Her complete surrender.

His hand continued to move between his thighs as he jacked his cock strenuously.

She slumped in the shower seat, drowning in sensation and plea-sure as he continued to eat her. His mouth was demanding one second, a sweet decadence the next. Arousal simmered in her again. It rose to a low boil. Mindlessly, she began to cup and stroke her breasts again, amplifying her already peaking bliss.

He buried his head deeper between her thighs, his mouth creating a precise suction. He twisted his head slightly, growling. She cried out, the sensation sending her over the edge yet again.

He continued to nurse her with his mouth through the first waves of orgasm. Then his mouth was abruptly gone, and he was coming to his feet in front of her. She looked up at him desperately. He grabbed her hand and shoved it between her thighs. Instinctively, she began to rub herself. She shuddered in reanimated pleasure. Through the slits of heavy eyelids, she saw rapid, terse movement. She forced open her eyes.

He fisted his cock, pumping himself furiously. She whimpered, waning pleasure and arousal mixing in her at the vision of him. His big body was wound as tight as a spring, every muscle taut and delineated. A ripple of tension went through his rigid face. He growled between clenched teeth. Then he was coming, thick jets of semen erupting from his cock and spilling onto the shower floor. He continued to climax, jerking his cock forcefully.

Watching him, she was reminded all too vividly of that other time in the shower . . . the first time she'd seen the power and beauty of him as he lost himself to pleasure, and how aroused it'd made her. She leaned forward rapidly, pushing her lips against the flaring crown of his cock. His girth spread her mouth wide, and she heard his harsh groan. His semen spilled onto her tongue, his salty, musky flavor striking her as clean, somehow. Delectable. She dipped her head back slightly, running her rigid lips over the defined base of the swollen cockhead, loving the sensation. He grunted in pleasure and clutched at the back of her head. He tensed and growled gutturally as he gave more of himself, and she took it greedily.

She looked up at him a moment later, water and the last drops of his semen rimming her lips. He sagged slightly, panting, his gaze on her blazing. Entreating her. She sunk him several inches into her mouth, using her tongue to clean him completely.

The sound of his harsh panting twined with the beat of the water on the shower floor. He reached and grasped her arms, pulling her up. They scooted beneath the warm spray of the main showerhead. He kissed her forcefully beneath the shooting water.

"What do you think you're doing to me, Harper McFadden?" he said against her mouth a moment later.

"Making you late for the opera?"

His solemn expression broke into a grin, white teeth flashing. She inhaled sharply at the sight.

"You're the one who's going to have to go out with wet hair," he said, stroking her slick hip and ass in a gesture that struck her both as lazy and utterly possessive at once.

. . .

He left her to her privacy to get dressed for the evening, something she wholly appreciated because she doubted her frantic scurrying could remotely be considered elegant or sexy by Jacob. She managed a quick blow-dry to get most of the wetness out of her hair, and then rushed to do her makeup. Unfortunately, there was nothing that would diminish the vibrant color of her sex-flushed cheeks.

By the time she'd donned her heels and the dress she'd brought for the evening—a purple, flowing, chiffon number that tied around her neck and left her shoulders and much of her back bare—her long hair was already beginning its typical unruly curl and wave. Fortunately, she'd brought some smoothing infusion. She used it and then whisked her hair up into a twist at the back of her head. A favorite pair of chandelier gold earrings—a Christmas gift from her parents—were her only jewelry, a vintage beaded cocktail purse her only accessory.

She examined herself critically in the dressing room's full-length mirror before she walked out to meet Jacob.

Damn it.

The color in her cheeks had hardly faded. She looked like she'd just finished a vigorous workout . . . or had phenomenal sex, she admitted to herself wryly as she stepped out of the bathroom.

He was already there, leaning over a dark walnut cabinet and shuffling through the contents of a drawer. She stopped in her tracks, just soaking in the image of him for a moment while he was distracted. His hair was still slightly damp from the shower, but his bangs had begun to dry, revealing strands of dark gold. He was shaved and his goatee had been neatly trimmed, giving him a crisp, clean appearance. He wore black tweed pants and a jacket, along with an ivory shirt that came to a slight V in the front. The ensemble looked effortlessly chic and sexy on his long, lean frame.

He glanced up distractedly—even though she was sure she hadn't made a sound—and did a double take. She smiled.

"That color is amazing on you. You look gorgeous," he said, slamming the drawer shut and stalking toward her, whatever he was searching for apparently forgotten.

"Thank you. So do you."

He slid his hands into his pant pockets and paused, his gaze sliding down the length of her and up again to her face. She wondered if she'd ever stop going warm under his steady, somber . . . outrageously sexy checkouts.

"I know," she muttered, embarrassed. "My cheeks. They're still bright red."

His smile unfurled slowly. He reached with his hand, the back of his fingers brushing across her warm cheeks. "I like them. They make your eyes even brighter."

"I look like I had a heyday with my blush."

"No." His fingers moved on her cheek. "No one could ever replicate that color with makeup. *That's* the real thing."

"That's a really hot shower," she breathed, enthralled by his expression as he touched her.

"That's excellent sex," he corrected before he leaned down and brushed his mouth against hers. Her heart gave a jump in her rib cage.

"If anyone could replicate the way you look right now, they'd own the world."

She opened her mouth, stunned by his compliment, and then he was kissing her, slow and deep and toe-curling.

"We're going to be late," he said quietly a moment later.

"Then stop kissing me."

"Stop *making* me," he replied dryly, grabbing her hand.

twenty~three

She was sure they'd be late, both for dinner and the opera, but Jacob's driver worked some kind of miracle in weekend traffic, getting them to Jardinière in record time. It was a favorite restaurant of Harper's, but even so, she'd never gotten so much attention—either from the staff or curious patrons—than she did while accompanying Jacob that night. She had the distinct impression most people didn't know specifically who he was. It was his air of absolute, quiet confidence and epic good looks that had them tittering. Perhaps aware of the intrusive stares, the maître d' seated them at a secluded table to enjoy their pre-opera meal.

"You enjoy the opera, then?" Jacob asked her after they'd been served their wine and salads.

"In San Francisco I do," she said wryly, pulling her gaze off the vision of his strong hands cutting an heirloom tomato with a silver knife and fork. It made her think of him holding that gold Waterpik. . . what he'd done to her in that shower. Her already flushed cheeks heated.

"Why only in San Francisco?" he asked, puzzled.

"They put up the English translation above the stage," she said, smiling. "I never learned Italian. I went to the opera when I was in Paris once, and had no idea what was going on. I was bored out of my mind."

He grinned and took a swift bite. Something about his silence pricked her interest.

"You *do*, don't you?" she asked slowly. His brows went up in a query. "Speak Italian?"

"Only a little," he said with what struck her as modesty. "It doesn't take me much to pick up languages. I've seen a few Italian women over the years, and it somehow sunk in a little."

She laughed and his eyebrows arched in a query. "There you have it, then. I forgot you were good at math. I suck at it. They say people who are gifted in math often are also good at picking up languages. Plus . . . I've never had a 'few' Italian lovers," she added playfully. She blinked when she saw his rigid expression. Had he been offended by her comment about his previous lovers?

He blinked and set down his fork. "What do you mean, you *forgot* I was good at math?"

She leaned back at his intensity, bewildered. "I just meant . . . you're a computer programmer, right? Apparently, a particularly talented one, a savant by most accounts—" She broke off when his stare continued to bore into her. "*Aren't* you good at math?" she asked weakly.

He took a draw on his wine.

"Yes," he said, picked up his fork again. "Where have you learned things like that? About me, I mean," he asked, his tone milder now. Still, she sensed his ruffled mood beneath his calm demeanor.

"Isn't what I just said public knowledge? I know you like to keep a low profile, but it's inevitable that some details about your history are going to be known."

"That doesn't really answer my question though, does it?"

For a few seconds, they just stared at each other from across the table. Finally, she shrugged and gave a bark of laughter, cast at sea by the turn of his mood. "I didn't know that much about you before I was invited to the cocktail party, although I have heard of Lattice, of course, and I've heard your name in passing. Ruth Dannen, our society and entertainment editor, filled me in on some of the details about you."

"Like what?" he asked quietly, pushing back his unfinished salad.

"Like that you were a gifted programmer and that military intelligence recruited you after college to work on anti-hacker software, and you used that knowledge after you left the army to create Lattice."

"And?"

"And *what?*"

"Did she insinuate that my success was suspect? She mentioned the insider trading scandal, didn't she?"

"Yes," Harper replied honestly.

"Did she ask you to dig for a story about me?"

She set down her fork with a clinking sound. "In fact, she did." His face turned to stone. "Is that really relevant? Did you *see* a story on you at the *Gazette* about anything I've learned about you since we've been together—which, trust me—*isn't much,*" she added succinctly with a glare. "Why are you so edgy all of a sudden?"

"Am I?"

"You know you are," she muttered, taking a bite of salad and then pushing back her plate in mounting frustration.

For a few seconds, he didn't speak.

"I'm sorry," he said after a moment. Her gaze jumped to his face. He still looked tense, but also irritated. At himself, she thought. His apology had been genuine. "It's not pleasant for me. To consider you hearing speculation and gossip about my past."

She exhaled slowly, some of her frustration going with her breath.

"You are very secretive, Jacob. You're very closed off. I'm not telling you anything you don't know already. People are bound to gossip, given all that. Nature abhors a vacuum, isn't that what they say?" she asked quietly. "That doesn't equate to being dishonest or a criminal."

"You believe that I'm above reproach?"

"Maybe I just want to believe it," she replied sincerely. She couldn't decode what she read in his eyes at that moment. "I *do* believe that the fact that you are so shut off and suspicious of people's intentions only amplifies the rumors about you. Your aloofness only fans the flames."

"Maybe I should hire you for public relations. You could clean up my murky public image," he said, a mirthless smile tickling his handsome mouth.

"Would you actually want that?" she asked archly, taking a sip of wine, thankful the tense moment had passed. "Why does it matter if people backbite about you? Why do you care?"

"I don't, usually," he said very quietly. He seemed to hesitate. "In your case, it matters."

Her mouth fell open. It was a strange compliment. He'd just told her he cared about what she thought of him. What confused her was the hard slant of his mouth when he'd said it.

He may care, but he wasn't pleased about it.

Jacob seemed intent on making sure she had a nice evening following that tense, bewildering exchange at dinner, as if he was determined to make up for his flash of irritation and edginess. His attentiveness and warmth were very much appreciated by Harper, but they weren't necessary to improve her mood. Instead of ruining the evening, their exchange at dinner had somehow made her feel closer to him. She'd learned they had something elemental in common.

So . . . he was ambivalent about caring about her? She couldn't fault him for that. She was just as prickly and unsure about her strong feelings for him.

The opera was *La Bohème*, which she enjoyed very much from their prime seats in the first row of the lowest balcony. She was highly aware of the man beside her: his thigh brushing lightly against her own, his handsome, stark profile as he stared at the stage, the subtle hint of his woodsy, spicy cologne. His presence and his nearness seemed to amplify her sensual appreciation of the production. During the touching second aria between Mimì and Rodolfo, she glanced over at him, only to find his gaze already on her face. There was something in his eyes . . .

She felt something expand in her chest. More powerfully than she ever had before, she sensed his sharp hunger. She couldn't understand it, but there it was in front of her, impossible to ignore, difficult to deny, even given his doubts. His hand enclosed hers. The tension in her chest broke. She gasped softly and stared at the stage and the romance unfolding there . . . a love story that was destined to end in tragedy.

In the past, she'd occasionally had strong emotional reactions to music, but she'd never experienced this level of feeling during a performance. Of course . . . she'd never sat next to the likes of Jacob Latimer during a production, either.

Embarrassed by her strange uprising of sharp emotion, she immediately made an excuse to go to the bathroom when they reached the lobby during intermission. Jacob touched her shoulder when she turned away.

"Is anything wrong?" he asked her, his brows slanted in concern.

"No, I'm fine," she assured with a bright smile. "I should have warned you. Music makes me a little emotional sometimes. Sorry. It's embarrassing, to get swept up into the drama so easily," she said, rolling her eyes.

His hand tightened on her shoulder and she reluctantly met his gaze, despite her burning eyes.

"It's not embarrassing, to feel deeply."

She nodded, ducking her head, mortified by her bewildering show of vulnerability.

"I'll get us some drinks and wait for you," he said.

"That'd be great, thank you," she murmured, turning away.

By the time she emerged from the ladies' room a few minutes later, she'd collected herself completely. Hopefully, Jacob hadn't thought her display *too* odd. Eager to find him now that she'd calmed herself, she searched the crowd for his head. As tall and distinguished as he was, he was sure to stand out. She didn't see him, however. Maybe he'd decided to use the facilities, as well. No sooner had she stationed herself near a column in order to wait, she caught a quick glimpse of him in the distance. He jogged up a flight of red-carpeted stairs.

That was strange, Harper thought, moving away from the column in his direction. His manner had seemed rushed and tense. Was he looking for her? She walked through the milling crowd of people in his direction. She reached the stairs where he'd disappeared, craning her head to see. There was a bend in the stairs, obscuring her vision. The men's lavatory wasn't in this direction, she knew from prior experience. Maybe Jacob knew some roundabout way to get there?

She rose up the first three steps, getting a better view of the entire lobby. This would be a good pace to wait . . .

". . . you promised me, Regina."

Harper started. It'd been Jacob's tense, low voice she heard resounding from the upper part of the stairs.

"I didn't promise you that I'd never come back to San Francisco," a woman exclaimed.

"You know that's not what I meant," Jacob seethed. "*That's* what I meant."

"It's just champagne!"

"How did you know I'd be here tonight?"

"Elizabeth told me she'd gotten two opera tickets for you tonight. Don't be mad at her. I kind of tricked her into telling me."

"You agreed to stay in Napa until you're more stable," he continued quietly, but Harper heard the anger in his tone, as if he felt the situation spinning out of control.

"*You're* here," the woman replied bitterly. "You told me that you were *so* busy in Tahoe, and yet you have time for the opera? And I saw that woman you're with."

"I'm not making excuses to you. I'm not the one who broke a promise."

"Oh, that's right," the woman said sarcastically. "Jacob Latimer, always above reproach. Always so cold." Her harsh laugh segued into a sob. Harper's heart lurched uncomfortably.

"Why don't you love me the way I do you, Jacob?"

"Jesus," Harper thought she heard him mutter before she became aware of rapid movement beside her. A dark-haired man flew up the stairs next to her and paused on the landing, looking upward.

"Regina?" he called. "What's going on? Are you all right?"

"Is this your escort?" Jacob asked.

"Yes. It's okay, David," Regina sniffed.

Harper started back guiltily when she saw movement and a flash of red. The woman—Regina—put her hand on the dark-haired man's lapel.

"What did you do to her?" David demanded accusatorily, looking up the stairs.

"I didn't do anything to her. *You* did. She's drunk," Jacob snapped. "Are you drunk as well?"

"*What?* I'm not going to—"

"It's okay, David. Jacob and I are old friends," Regina said.

"*Friends?*" David asked scathingly.

Regina turned.

Harper was suddenly face-to-face with the most beautiful woman she'd ever seen. Even with reddened eyes and wet cheeks, she was stunning. Long, shining dark brown hair stood in dramatic contrast to her form-fitting red dress and smooth, golden skin. Dark eyes fastened on Harper. Harper stepped down and clutched at the bannister.

It'd all happened so quickly. She'd been caught red-handed and flustered in the act of eavesdropping. Jacob suddenly appeared on the landing. He tapped David hard on the chest.

"She has a history of substance abuse, you idiot. And she's on medication. Don't give her any more alcohol."

"Listen, you son of a bitch—"

"Stop it, David. You don't know what you're talking about, and neither does Mr. Holier Than Thou here. Just take me back to the hotel," Regina said, her speech slurred. She grabbed David's hand and proceeded very unsteadily down the stairs. It was only then that Jacob noticed Harper standing there. His eyes seemed to blaze in his rigid face.

Regina paused next to her.

"So you're the new flavor of the night? Is this some new kink you've dreamed up, screwing the girl next door?" she called back to Jacob.

"Damn it, Regina." Jacob jogged down the steps and grabbed David's elbow aggressively. He was so large and intimidating, such an oncoming storm, Harper stepped back instinctively.

"Get a cab and take her back to the hotel," Jacob demanded. "I don't want you or her driving—"

"*I'm* not drunk. And I've had about enough of you," David blazed, throwing off Jacob's hold. Harper wondered if what Jacob had insinuated about David being drunk was true. David was clearly the smaller of the two men, but seemed strangely cocky in the face of Jacob's pointed anger, concern, and much more intimidating size.

"Oh shut up, both of you," Regina hissed disgustedly. She shoved David in the opposite direction of a dangerous-looking Jacob. Harper saw her look back once at Jacob in a kind of desperate longing before they disappeared into the crowd.

Jacob turned to her with a jerky movement. His volatility seemed to roll off him in waves. Harper didn't know what to say. It'd all happened so quickly. So unexpectedly . . . and it all seemed so out of character for Jacob.

"I'm sorry," he said thickly. He raked his fingers through his hair in a gesture of sharp frustration. His gaze focused on her. "Regina is . . . an old friend."

She didn't reply. She'd never seen him so frayed. Harper wasn't sure what she was feeling at that moment, beyond confused. It was clear that despite his anger at the woman, he cared about her a great deal.

The chimes calling the audience back to the performance rung. Jacob blinked at the sound dazedly. Suddenly, a handsome, gray-haired man of medium build who was dressed to the nines separated himself from the crowd. He came toward them. Jacob glanced around and froze.

"Clint," he said, his voice hollow with disbelief.

"I saw her. The girl. Gina," he pointed in the direction where Regina and David had disappeared. "You still have contact with her?" the man asked incredulously, his mouth slanting into a frown.

Jacob straightened, all vestiges of his strained state vanishing. Here was the glacial, utterly in control, intimidating man Harper recognized. "I saw her just now. What's it to you?" A strange expression suddenly slid over Jacob's face. He glanced uneasily at the doors where Regina had just exited with her date. "Did *she* see you? Regina?"

Jefferies scoffed.

Jacob lunged toward him. Jefferies's smug, disdainful expression vanished and he took a half step back, clearly alarmed.

"Did Regina see you, damn it?" Jacob seethed.

"No, not that I'm aware of," Jefferies said with bravado, although it was clear he was intimidated by Jacob's pointed fury. He glanced around, seeming to take heart in the fact that they were in the middle of a public forum, despite the diminishing crowd. "Honestly, Jacob. I can't believe you're still letting her get to you. I swear, I've stopped trying to understand you."

Jefferies's gaze landed on Harper and moved over her speculatively, as if suddenly aware that there was a close audience to their charged conversation.

"Clint Jefferies," he said, stepping toward Harper and putting out his hand, all smooth urbanity. He struck Harper as oily and manipulative in that moment. Jacob moved so fast, Harper was stunned. He came between her and the other man and grabbed her hand.

"Don't you even *look* at her."

She walked next to Jacob back toward the theater, his furious snarl echoing in her ears.

twenty~four

During the performance, Harper couldn't help but be aware of Jacob's continued tense state. Although he looked at the stage, he seemed to silently simmer, and she felt sure his mind was on what had just occurred during intermission—on Regina and Clint Jefferies—and not the opera. At one point, she glanced to the left and saw *him* in the audience: Clint Jefferies. His gaze was trained directly on Jacob and her.

She knew from Ruth Dannen's pre-cocktail-party coaching that Jefferies owned the multibillion-dollar Markham Pharmaceuticals and had once been a kind of older brother–father figure to Jacob.

Jacob had made a great deal of money from a windfall sale of Markham Pharmaceutical stock at a very young age. He'd allegedly bought the stock just days before a breakthrough Markham medication for diabetes was given FDA approval. After approval went through, Jacob's investment skyrocketed. Later, Clint Jefferies had become the target of an insider trading investigation because of that very deal in which Jacob had prospered so richly. Harper knew that the SEC usually went after the bigwig suspected of insider trading, not the little guy, like Jacob had been at the time. Was it true what Ruth had insinuated? That even though Jacob had made his first fortune from the Markham stock sale, he'd afterward washed his hands of the taint of Clint Jefferies, sacrificing the man who had supported him in his early career?

And why had Jefferies been so incredulous and disdainful about seeing Regina and Jacob together? More importantly, why did Jacob seem to hate his former mentor with a white-hot passion?

All those questions and many more besides circled around her head, mixing with her already potent anxieties about getting involved with a man as secretive and powerful as Jacob.

After the performance was finished, he took her hand and led her from the balcony even before the first curtain call. His driver was waiting.

The back of the limo was dark and painfully silent. His brooding mood oppressed her. He didn't speak until they were only a few miles from his home.

"I'm sorry about all that," he said quietly after a while, and she knew he referred to the Regina–Clint Jefferies spectacle.

"Is that all you're going to say?"

He blinked and glanced over at her, his face enigmatic in the cloaking shadows.

"I'm just checking," Harper continued. "Because if it is, you needn't bother. I know you didn't plan any of that."

"Do you really want more than an apology?"

"Do you mean do I really want to know about yours and that woman's relationship?"

He nodded once. She saw his eyes glitter through the shadows. His attention was fully on her now.

"I know she must be one of your old lovers," Harper said, turning and staring blankly out the window. "I'm not that naïve, Jacob. I know there must be lots of them. So you ran into one of them tonight? It's not that shocking. And this one"—she looked over at him—"you care more about than most."

He remained completely still.

"You do care about her a lot, don't you?"

"Yes."

Her heart gave a little lurch and she stared back out the window.

"*Is* she an old lover? Or is she still one?" she asked, surprised at how calm she sounded.

"No. Not anymore. Harper, look at me."

She turned her head.

"You're the only woman I'm sleeping with."

"How fortunate for me."

A muscle jumped in his cheek. "Don't."

She inhaled shakily, ashamed of her flash of jealousy.

"You never promised me fidelity," she breathed out. "You never promised me anything except a good time. An opportunity to forget my troubles."

"That's true. But I'm telling you that I have no immediate plans or interest in being with someone else. Doesn't that mean anything?"

She took a moment to absorb what he was saying.

"Yes," she admitted. "It does." She tried to tease out his expression in the darkness, but the shadows prevailed. As always, he was a mystery to her. "You're worried about her still, aren't you?"

"Yes."

She nodded. "Do you want to go to her hotel, and make sure she's all right?" she asked through a tight throat.

He glanced away. "I'd like to call, at the very least. She recently left substance abuse rehab, and it's a vulnerable time for her. I was shocked to see her here in San Francisco. And she's relapsed. Again. Elizabeth is going to hear it from me, for letting it slip I was in San Francisco tonight. I can't imagine what she was thinking," he said grimly.

"Do you love her?" Harper blinked, shocked that the words had spilled out of her throat. "It's just . . . I've never seen you so undone, so clearly upset," she rushed to explain.

"No. I'm not in love with her."

Harper nodded slowly. "And what was all that with that man . . . Clint Jefferies? Why was he so shocked to see you with Regina?"

The car came to a halt.

"That," Jacob replied somberly, sliding over on the seat and reaching for the door, "was just a very unfortunate chance meeting."

Harper awoke in the middle of the night, disoriented. She found a bedside lamp and switched it on.

She looked around Jacob's enormous suite, her heart sinking when she realized she was alone. Jacob's side of the bed hadn't been touched. She rubbed at her blurry eyes and focused on a nearby clock. It was twenty minutes past three in the morning.

Earlier, Jacob had escorted her up to his suite and caught her hand.

"Why don't you get ready for bed? I'm just going to make that phone call to Regina, to make sure she's all right."

Harper nodded and turned to go, but he halted her, squeezing on her hand. He pulled her against him, one hand cupping her hip, the other her jaw. He tilted her face up. His mouth brushed hers. Harper felt her pulse leap at her throat, her reaction to him unchanged despite the weird, bewildering evening.

"I *am* sorry, Harper. You have no idea."

"I know. I hope she's okay," she whispered sincerely.

He'd swept down then, seizing her mouth. It was like he was telling her something with that forceful, quick kiss, but Harper didn't know what. A moment later, he released her abruptly and headed toward a closed wooden door without a backward glance. She knew from Marianne's brief tour of his quarters that the door led to a private office. She watched him open and shut the door behind him, then went to the guest bathroom to change.

Feeling self-conscious and highly unsure, she pulled out the short, black silk nightgown she'd brought. Knowing what she knew about Jacob, she'd guessed she wouldn't require pajamas over the weekend. She'd assumed they'd be sleeping naked. Fortunately, she had brought the nightgown, but now regretted its sexiness, given how the evening was turning out.

Now it was hours later, and she still wore the nightgown and slept alone. She rose from the luxurious bed, listening for any sound of movement or noise that might give her an indication of Jacob's whereabouts. A terrace door was opened. The only thing she could hear was the sound of the ocean surf hitting the beach far below the cliff.

She anxiously approached Jacob's closed office door. For several seconds, she stood poised with her fist in the air, hesitating. She grit her teeth, her knuckles finally landing on the wood.

"Jacob?" she called.

Silence.

She rapped again and said his name.

The knob turned smoothly in her hand. She pushed open the door, and it swung inward, revealing his opulent, dimly lit, completely empty office.

He returned to Sea Cliff just past dawn, bone-tired and bleary-eyed. A surge of adrenaline went through him, however, when he walked into his bedroom suite and saw his made, empty bed.

Shit. He'd assumed he'd be back before Harper woke up. He stalked down the hallway in search of Marianne.

You shouldn't have let her believe that Regina was a former lover.

He'd had no choice, though. The conclusion she'd jumped to had been believable and simple, while the truth was far more complicated and disquieting . . .

. . . Not to mention closer to Harper than she'd ever suspect.

He found Marianne helping his cook, Alfred, unpack some groceries in the kitchen.

"Where's Harper?" he demanded without preamble the second he plunged into the room.

Marianne blinked, looking startled.

"At the pool. Or at least she was as of about twenty minutes ago, when I took her there."

He exhaled in relief. At least she hadn't left the house to return to Tahoe.

He found her just where Marianne said she'd be. She wore a pair of shorts and a T-shirt, and her long, copper-colored hair was in a bun on the top of her head. She sat at the edge of the pool, her pretty legs dipped in the water.

"Hi," she said, looking surprised when she saw him stalk up to her. Her large eyes traveled down him. He was still wearing his suit from last night.

"I didn't think you'd be up so early," he said, trying to read the expression on her face, and failing.

"I've been up since three thirty," she said, setting aside the magazine she'd been reading. "I thought I'd look for the pool when it got light. It seemed like a better option than waiting in your bedroom, wondering where you were."

"I'm sorry. Shit. I've been saying that a lot lately, haven't I?" he muttered, clamping his eyes shut briefly.

"What happened?"

He opened his eyes. She *was* irritated with him, but it was concern he read most clearly on her face at the moment.

"I had to take her to the hospital," he said.

She lifted her feet out of the water and stood, facing him.

"Is she all right?"

He nodded. "Her date had left her, and she'd gotten into the hotel room's liquor. She sounded bad off when I finally got ahold of her last night. By the time I got to the hotel, she'd passed out. I took her over to UCSF's emergency room, but there wasn't much they could do except assure me that she was going to be fine and give her an IV to rehydrate her."

"Didn't the doctor recommend that she go back to rehab?"

"Of course he did, and they had a social worker come and talk to her to try to convince her to return. But they can't force her to go, and Regina was flat-out refusing."

"Where is she now?" Harper asked, stepping closer.

"Back at her hotel room, sleeping."

"Do you think she'll be all right? Alone?"

"No. Last night I arranged for Elizabeth to fly in and stay with her. Elizabeth will get her back to Napa later today. Regina has a psychiatrist there that she trusts. I've let him know what happened. Regina agreed to go back last night. Let's hope she remembers the agreement this morning."

She touched his face with cool fingertips. The caress took him by surprise. He hadn't been prepared for tenderness on her part. He would have thought he'd be reassured by it, but instead he was even more worried. Her calmness somehow made him wary . . . like she was pulling away from him. He would have preferred accusations and tears.

"You look exhausted," she said quietly.

He reached up and held her wrist, keeping her fingers in place on his skin . . . always doubtful something would pull her away.

Even now.

"So do you," he replied, his gaze running over her face. The scar near her mouth looked even paler than usual, and there were light purple circles beneath her eyes.

"You did all that for her," she whispered.

He grimaced. "I didn't feel like I had a choice. She's been diagnosed with bipolar disorder, and she has a history of cocaine and heroin abuse. I wasn't sure what else she'd taken, besides alcohol. She couldn't tell me, the state she was in. That's why I took her to the hospital."

"I understand." Her fingers slipped off his face. He saw her swallow thickly. She looked achingly beautiful to him in the pale morning light. *So far out of your reach.*

"It's just all been . . . unsettling. I had no idea you cared about another woman that way, especially one so beautiful. And to wake up and realize you were gone . . ."

"I thought I'd get back before you got up. I didn't want to wake you last night. Damn it, I don't know how else to tell you to make you believe me."

"Tell me what?"

"I'm not sleeping with Regina. It's not like that."

"You don't have to keep saying that. I believe you. What kind of a friend would you be, abandoning her when she was in so much trouble," she said, staring down at the ground. "I guess her date—that guy, David?—wasn't much of one. A friend, I mean. He left her alone?"

"Yeah," Jacob replied, frowning.

"It seems like you're used to it."

"What?"

"Riding to her rescue," she replied quietly, studying his pant legs. "When you were called away the other night, when were supposed to have dinner. Did you go to Napa because of her? I only wondered because Elizabeth told me you were in Napa for an emergency."

He put his fingers beneath her chin and lifted her face. "I can understand that you're curious. But Regina deserves some privacy in all this. I don't think it's fair for me to talk about her problems to someone she doesn't even know. I realize these circumstances aren't ideal. I'm sorry it happened while we were here together. Trust me, I wish like hell it hadn't."

Her blue-green eyes looked moist. She nodded abruptly.

"You're right. I would have liked you less, knowing that you were the type to abandon a friend when they were in need. I'm glad you went to help her."

"Thank you," he said, holding her stare. "Elizabeth will have things in hand. You don't need to worry about it anymore. It's done. Okay?"

She's not going to be this forgiving forever.

He pushed down the sarcastic voice in his head. Harper hadn't left, and she wasn't freezing him out. For the moment, anyway. Still, he felt uncharacteristically doubtful about how to proceed.

She nodded, attempting a smile. "You should get some sleep before you have to get back to work again."

He glanced around the sunlit pool area and over the balcony onto the Pacific Ocean, really taking in his surroundings for the first time since arriving home. The only thing he'd been able to consider since seeing that empty bed was finding Harper. A gust of sea air rushed over him, sweeping away the cobwebs of his sleepless night and anxiety. Or maybe it was Harper's clear, crystalline eyes and gentle touch that had done that.

"How about a swim? It might help us to sleep a few hours."

"I didn't bring a swimsuit. That's why I'm wearing this," she said, nodding down at her shorts and T-shirt.

"You don't need a swimsuit."

She gave him a *give me a break* look. "You're bound and determined to see me shamed in front of your staff at some point, aren't you?"

"If you don't want to, we won't have sex."

It was like she was fading, and he needed to connect with her again. The only way that felt right at the moment wasn't Jacob's way.

It was Jake's.

He didn't like the idea of reverting back to it, but the alternative of watching Harper continue to move away from him was worse. It was stupid on his part, but the compulsion was strong.

"Come on," he coaxed. "It'll feel good. Then we'll go up and take a nap."

He saw the hesitation in her eyes and thought he knew part of the cause of it. He turned and jogged up the flight of stairs to the glass doors. He opened one and reached inside, touching a button. Opaque blinds began to slide down the terrace windows.

"The staff knows not to come outside if they're down," he said when he returned to her.

She rolled her eyes. "You're hardly reassuring me, Jacob."

He exhaled, seeing his misstep. She'd assumed his staff was trained not to come outside when the blinds were down because he was privately engaged with a woman when they were.

She'd assumed correctly.

Fuck. Sometimes, it felt like all the tools that had worked with him in the past with women—even his aloofness—weren't assets with Harper, but liabilities. He reached up and tucked an escaped tendril of hair behind her ear, then brushed her cheek with the back of his knuckles. She was so soft. So beautiful. Something seemed to well up in him. God, he must be exhausted.

"Just swim with me," he murmured, dipping his head and kissing her nose. "I know you like to swim."

"How do you know that?" she asked, a hint of wariness crossing her features.

"You said you like the water when we were out on the yacht. You just seem like a swimmer," he said, deflecting his error. "Come on, I dare you."

She laughed and shook her head, finally shrugging in acquiescence. Relief swept through him. "What the hell? I don't get a chance to take a dip in a place like this often." She waved at the pool and terrace and the view of the Pacific Ocean.

"Okay," he said, stepping away from her. He reached down to untie his shoes. "Whoever hits the water first wins the prize."

She looked startled, and he thought he knew why. She'd expected a seduction, despite what he'd said. He'd told her he'd always undress her for sex. "What kind of a prize?" she asked.

He stood, shrugged, and kicked off his shoes. "The pride of being the fastest stripper, I guess."

Her eyes caught fire. Victory flashed through him. He knew that look all too well.

"I'll win," she told him steadfastly, whipping off her shirt and immediately attacking the buttons on her shorts. "I've got less on."

He laughed full out and turned away, jerking his jacket off. Even before he could start on his shirt, he heard a whoop and a loud splash in the water.

"Too slow, sucka."

He turned, his expression rigid, his belt buckle clutched in his hand. She treaded water in the center of the pool, grinning from ear to ear.

God bless it, girl.

The voice rang out of his past, crystal clear. It was Jake Tharp's overwhelmed voice. Maybe it was *his*.

He dropped his shirt to a lounge chair a few seconds later, a feeling of inevitability hitting him.

No. It was both of them—Jake and Jacob—combined. Only Harper could have brought Jake to life again in him.

Only Harper could have made it feel achingly bittersweet.

Twenty Years Ago

She surfaced a second after he did in the river, gasping and sucking air into her lungs. She stared at him blankly for a second while she treaded water, as if the fall had rattled her brain and she didn't recognize who he was.

"Harper?" Jake asked worriedly. "You okay?"

Her sudden radiant smile floored him.

"Can we do it again?" she asked.

"*What?*"

"That was so *cool!*"

He scoffed doubtfully, swimming closer to her. "Did you hurt your head?" he asked, examining the bruise and abrasion on her forehead that Emmitt had given her. Maybe the cliff jump had made it worse?

"No." She looked offended. "What, a city girl can't get off on an adrenaline rush?"

"Maybe a city girl," he mumbled. Their treading legs brushed together, sending tingling pleasure through him. "Don't know about you, though. You said you hated heights. Now you want to do it again? Are you crazy?"

She laughed and stared up the stark face of the cliff.

"Wow," she said. Her eyes sparkled. It was like she'd said, *I did that.*

"You did it, all right," he acknowledged gruffly. She looked at him, perhaps startled that he'd read her mind. Her smile grew even wider. She slapped at the water.

"That was the most amazing thing I've ever done. I was scared out of mind." She jetted backward on her back and then spun around completely in a circle, only to swoosh backward again. Jake scurried to keep up with her.

"What are you, a damn otter or something?" he grumbled.

"I can't help it. I like to swim. And that was fantastic."

She let out a whoop at having conquered her fear. Maybe it was more than that. She came to a standstill and pushed with her hands, leaping up in the water like a playful dolphin. Jake went wide-eyed at the vision of his Mountaineer's T-shirt plastered against her supple torso and firm, thrusting breasts.

"God bless it, girl, get ahold of yourself. Do you want Emmitt to hear?" he spat. But that's not really what he meant. What he meant was more like, *God bless it, what the hell are you doing to me?*

Her eyes flashed at him and she sunk down to her chin in the water. Regret and embarrassment swept through him at his show of temper . . .

. . . at her wide-eyed hurt and disbelief.

"Where do we get out," she asked coldly after a moment, her brows slanted angrily.

He waved at a landing thirty feet or so downstream. She immediately launched into the water. By the time he caught up to her, she was already standing and walking toward the sandbar, jerkily straightening the soaked, clinging T-shirt off her hips, bottom, and thighs at the same time.

"Harper, I'm sorry. It's just . . . you were being really loud," he said, sloshing behind her in waist-deep water.

"You're mean sometimes," she declared bluntly, pausing to gather her T-shirt at the thighs and wring it out.

"I ain't *mean*."

She glanced around, her gaze narrowing on his face. He knelt lower in the water, trying to shield any evidence of the hurt he'd felt at her proclamation.

"Do you really want to do it again?" he blurted out.

Her gaze strayed to the stark cliff face, and again he saw that flicker of exhilaration on her expression. "I think so. Do we have time to do it now?"

He looked at the position of the early morning sun in the sky and shook his head. "It'll take too long for us to hike back up. We have to be careful not to leave a trail. It'll take time, not only to get up there, but to sweep our tracks. We need to stay low in the cave for the rest of the day. Maybe tomorrow at dawn we can go again. Tomorrow afternoon, I'll scout around a bit. If there's still no sign of Emmitt in the area, he likely took the false trail all the way to Poplar Gorge. It'll be safe to start for Barterton."

He regretted bringing up his uncle when he saw all the color drain from her face. "So you think he *did* take the false trail?" she asked hopefully.

"Maybe for a ways he did. It's hard to tell. Even if he catches on, it'll take him a while to do it. He'll have to backtrack. Then he'll have to hunt out the new trail."

"Do you think he could? Even with as careful as we were?" She blanched, obviously recalling his admonitions for her lead feet yesterday. "*You* were careful, I mean."

"I doubt it," Jake said with false assuredness, disliking the return of her anxiety. He fumbled beneath the waistband of his briefs, his actions hidden by the river. A few seconds later, he triumphantly held up the bar of soap he'd stashed in his underwear.

"It survived the fall."

She smiled. "Do we have time?"

He nodded. She dove toward him eagerly in the shallow water, stopping in front of him and mimicking his position. They both knelt on their knees, facing each other. His heart leapt when she reached for him with both hands, grinning.

"Nice, clean soap," she enthused, feeling for the bar between his clutching fingers. She lifted his hand above the water, cupped it with both her hands, and moved aside his fingers to expose the soap. She began rubbing. Lather began to spread on their skin. He watched, spellbound, pleasure tickling his nerves. It felt so good, he held on to the soap desperately, not wanting her to stop touching him.

She reached suddenly, scrubbing his cheek. He started, and she laughed. He reached, returning the gesture and including her nose.

Her eyes sprang wide in surprise, and then she was reaching with both soapy hands, raking them down his face.

"Hey," he muttered in a put-out fashion, pinching his eyes closed. "You got it in my eyes."

"I'm sorry," she soothed. She heaved water in his face. He blinked water out of his eyes, bringing her into focus incredulously.

"Oh, you're going to pay for that," he promised.

She laughed hysterically and dove into the water, but he was already after her. He caught her foot, and she squealed.

Their "bath" was a squirming, tickling, poking fight for the soap interspersed with Jake reminding them both to hush their splashing and laughter.

He wanted to stay with her in that water forever, hearing her muted snorts and hushed, sparkling laughter, feeling her smooth limbs tangle with his and her hands on him, pinching and poking sometimes, flickering and sliding against his skin at others . . . making him ache.

It was like he stole those delicious moments from another world, as if they existed in some magical in-between space where Emmitt Tharp couldn't enter, or Harper's parents.

No one. No one, but them.

The fourth time he took note of the sun's position, he regretfully spoke, shattering their golden, fragile little private world.

"We gotta get back," he said, his fingers in her long, wet hair, wiping away remaining suds. She splashed water on the side of his head, rinsing away soap from his ear. He sputtered and rolled his eyes when she splashed him again. "I'm serious, Harper."

She sighed, deflated. Regret swooped through him. Suddenly, she brightened.

"Race you to shore," she said in a rush before she heaved face-first into the water.

"Hey, wait. That's not fair," he called, but she was already showing off her smooth, strong crawl, impervious to his excuses. He watched, enthralled at the vision of her pale, kicking thighs and bare lower buttocks flashing just beneath the surface of the water. She was so pretty, yet so easy to be with. So incredible.

So untouchable.

How could he think that, he wondered numbly, when he'd just had his hands all over her? But that had just been them fooling around. Playing.

That wasn't the real thing.

Instead of taking off after her, he treaded water until she stood on the sandbank. He needed the moment to bring his spiraling, uncooperative body under control.

When he stood and slogged toward shore a moment later, she waited at the edge of the water, wringing out her wet hair and wearing a golden smile.

"Too slow, sucka," she teased.

"You got that right," he grumbled, ducking his head to hide his dark look.

He had an uncomfortable thought that he'd always be too slow—too *wrong*—to ever fit into Harper McFadden's world.

twenty-five

Harper thought maybe she swam faster than she had for her varsity swim meet finals to get away from Jacob, but there was no real competition. He caught her ankle almost immediately, yanking her backward in the water. She broke the surface, snorting with laughter and wiping water out of her eyes.

"Too slow, sucka," Jacob murmured. Seeing his smug smile, she splashed water in his face.

"Hey," he said, brows furrowed in an expression of mock offense. He grabbed the arm she'd been planning on using to splash him again. Then he grabbed the other, bringing her closer to him. She squirmed, trying to get away and laughing at her failure.

"Stupid to resist," he said, still grinning even wider now. She loved seeing that smile.

"Cocky bastard." She deliberately bumped her forehead into his, clunking their skulls. She saw his eye go wide in disbelief before she took advantage of his loosened hold and heaved her body away from him. He grabbed her again on the shallow end, and she surfaced, choking with laughter.

"That look on your face," she gasped as he hauled her against him.

"You could have really hurt me."

"Oh, poor baby," she crooned, rubbing his forehead as if to soothe him.

Their faces were only inches apart, their naked bodies sliding and pressing together. She circled his arms around his neck, her legs tightening around his hips. Water droplets clung to his long, dark lashes, highlighting his beautiful eyes.

"Where'd a nice girl like you ever learn how to do a Liverpool Kiss?"

"Liverpool Kiss?" she wondered, panting. "That thing I did with our heads? That's just a basic lesson from Practical Single Woman Living in the Twenty-First Century."

"Tough world," he murmured, sliding his big hands along her hips, back, and waist. His eyes glittered. "Soft girl," he growled, and something swooped in her belly.

"Don't try to sweet-talk your way out of this," she admonished.

"You're the one who head-butted me."

She grinned. The realization of just how ebullient she felt, even after the strange, stressful night, struck her. That he could make it all fade, all from a few minutes of horsing around in the water together. She shook her head dazedly.

"How do you do it?" she wondered quietly.

"Do what?" he asked, his deft fingers running up and down her spine. She shivered in pleasure.

"Make it all go away so easily . . . make me forget," she mused, shifting her bare breasts against his solid chest and leaning back in his hold slightly, trying to get a better perspective on his face.

"Isn't that what I told you I'd do?" he asked.

"Maybe that's how you're able to keep people at arm's length so effortlessly."

"You're hardly at arm's length," he said with a heavy-lidded glance between their naked, pressing bodies.

"I mean your charm. You make us weak-minded, spineless females forget about getting too close," she mused, her tone light, but sarcastic, as well.

His gaze went sharp at that. Her heart seemed to skip a beat as he studied her face for a charged few seconds. His mouth tightened into a hard line.

"I see. It's some kind of tangible evidence that you want. Some kind of proof that I'm willing to get closer to you . . . to take a risk."

"I didn't say that, I just meant—"

"Clint Jefferies *was* the man I talked about that I met when I was fifteen years old. The *nice neighbor*, as you put it. *I* certainly wouldn't."

Her mouth fell open in shock. She'd been longing for him to open up to her, even if just a little. She hadn't actually expected he would, though.

"This was in South Carolina, right?" She saw his questioning frown. "You told me when we first met on that beach that you were from South Carolina," she reminded him. He must have forgotten.

"Oh, yeah. I had foster parents that eventually adopted me. They were good people—kind—but they were already in their mid-to-late sixties when I went to live with them and weren't in the best of health. It's not that I didn't come to love them, but I guess their interests or energy levels didn't match up all that well with a teenage boy's. It was no one's fault.

"Clint had a summer home next to our house," he continued. "He'd bought up five properties on the lake where we lived and built himself a summer playground and retreat. Clint was everything my mom and dad weren't. Youthful. Dynamic. Energetic. My parents were modest and struggled at times for money, while Clint was very wealthy and not afraid to show it.

"Clint was good to me," Jacob said, frowning in memory. "I won't deny that. There were those who were very jealous of the way he took to me. He dazzled me. That's the embarrassing truth. I was a stupid, naïve kid. I fell for his act, hook, line, and sinker. He took me under his wing, seemed invested in my success. I wouldn't have been able to go to college, let alone MIT, if it weren't for his support . . . and the fact that he gave me a job, of course, working around his property, even when he and his wife weren't in residence. I was just a chore and errand boy, but he paid me well. Gave me opportunities and connections I'd never had in my life . . . never even dreamed of."

He paused, a faraway look in his eyes, a slight frown on his mouth. Harper held her breath, worried he wouldn't continue.

"My dad died of a heart attack when I was sixteen; my mom of a stroke just before my eighteenth birthday," he stated flatly.

"I'm so sorry, Jacob," she whispered.

He nodded. "They'd left me their property and a little money, but if it weren't for Clint helping me with the will and the legalities, I don't know what I would have done. I started to rely on him more and more. I stayed at lot at his house instead of at my parents', even on some nights while Mom was still alive. He helped me with things like applying for scholarships and giving me recommendation letters for the type of colleges I hadn't even considered attending, like MIT."

He grimaced, as though he found the experience of talking about his past unpleasant, but he didn't move. He kept her clasped tight against him, his feet planted firmly at the bottom of the pool.

"I know what people say. I know they think I'm ungrateful, when it comes to Clint."

"Did you sever things with him because of the Markham insider trading scandal?" she challenged softly.

He gave a dry bark of laughter. "Did you know that I'd just turned eighteen years old when I bought and sold that stock?" he asked quietly.

"I knew you were young, but not *that* young," she admitted.

"I thought I was so smart. Turns out, I didn't know shit."

"We're all idiots at eighteen," she reminded him. Like last night at the opera, she was catching a glimpse into his inner world. It pained her to see the weight of his turmoil again . . . the weight of his past. No wonder he guarded it so vigilantly. She touched his face gently. He seemed to come out of the hole of his bitterness, making eye contact with her.

"I looked up to Clint back then. Put him up on a pedestal, thought he could do no wrong. The truth is"—he gave a cynical laugh—"I wanted a father figure so bad, I blinded myself to his faults. Until one night, he did something that tore off my blinders forever."

She absorbed his bitterness, sensing what he didn't say. Clint Jefferies had altered him. At least in part, Jefferies had made Jacob the secretive, suspicious, jaded man that he was today.

"He did a lot to help you," she said, hating the self-disgust she saw on his face at the moment. "Jefferies was very accomplished. It's natural that you'd admire him. He singled you out. Treated you like you were special, which you *were*. You're one in a billion, Jacob," she said, moving her fingertips on his clenched jaw, feeling his tension. "He did something really bad to shatter the trust you had in him, didn't he? Did it . . . did it have to do with Regina?"

His eyes flashed at her. For a few seconds, she thought he wasn't going to say any more.

"He hurt her," he said suddenly, a snarl shaping his mouth. "He took advantage of her when anyone could see how vulnerable she was. But Clint isn't the type to take care around a vulnerability. He's the type to take advantage of it. Nurture it, even, because he gets off on it."

Harper swallowed thickly. His southern drawl—the one she only occasionally heard sliding into his voice—had grown thicker as he spoke. His fury seemed to roll off him in waves.

"Jefferies was no better than a lot of dirtbags out there. It shouldn't have surprised me as a kid, to see his true colors. I *should* have known better. That was a lesson learned: a lot of money and a big house and fancy manners . . . and yet he was just the same as—"

He broke off abruptly. Harper's chest ached at what she saw in his eyes at that moment. Betrayal. Pain. Fury. Tears burned behind her eyelids. Had that naïve young man fallen in love with Regina, only to see his mentor, the man he looked up to, hurt her? Scar her? What had Jefferies *done*? Whatever it was had not only ruptured his relationship with Jacob, it had twisted the memory of it into a caustic thorn in Jacob's side.

Harper's mind went to rape. She cringed inwardly at the idea. Maybe she suspected it because she knew that Regina was still alive. If she'd died, the degree of Jacob's fury might be close to what she saw right now on his face. Regina lived, however . . . and was clearly very troubled emotionally. It just seemed to fit, somehow.

"It was . . . it was something sexual, wasn't it? What Clint Jefferies did to Regina?" she asked, dread weighting her voice.

She thought she read the truth in his eyes. A flash of nausea went through her.

"Never mind," she whispered. She let her legs slide down his hips and touched her feet to the bottom of the pool. An image of the sophisticated, polished man she'd seen last night at the opera flashed into her mind's eye. Jefferies was a wolf parading in a civilized man's clothing. *Why do men have to be such animals sometimes?*

"I'm sorry, Jacob. I'm sorry for prying," she said, miserable that she'd forced him to talk about a past that obviously still hurt him.

She started to turn away but he caught her hand.

"Are you all right?" he asked her pointedly.

A sharp pain went through her, that he would ask about her well-being when he'd been the one recounting something that still made him ache.

"I'm fine," she assured. She squeezed his hand. "Let's go up to bed."

She showered quickly in the guest bathroom and came to bed wearing the black nightgown. Jacob probably didn't want to make love, after what had just happened out at the pool, but she didn't have anything else to wear.

Harper, on the other hand, experienced a sharp longing to have his arms around her, to have him deep inside her . . . to have him take her places where only he could. That was just selfishness, though. She felt heartsore, thinking of Regina, thinking of Jacob . . .

Always thinking of Jacob . . .

The drapes had been drawn on the floor-to-ceiling windows. The large suite was dim and hushed. He was already in bed when she came out of the bathroom. He laid back on the pillows, elbows bent, hands behind his head, dense biceps bulging. His torso was bare. The pose highlighted his chiseled upper body, powerful chest, the mouth-watering diagonal from trim waist to broad shoulders, emphasizing his power even in a relaxed moment. He'd been staring up at the ceiling, but when he saw her coming, his gaze flickered down over her without moving his head. Her skin prickled beneath his stare. When she reached the bed, he rolled on his side and flipped back the sheet and duvet, inviting her in.

She slid between the cool sheets next to him.

For a charged moment, they just lay on their sides, facing each other. His face was shadowed, but she could just make out a few amber pinpricks of light in his hazel eyes.

"You're like Regina."

His lips had moved, and she'd heard his quiet, deep voice, but for a moment, she couldn't compute what he'd said.

"What do you mean?" A horrible thought struck her, taking her breath away for a moment. "Do you mean . . . do you mean that *Regina* is the woman I remind you of?" she asked, aghast.

"No. *God*, no," he said, his brows slanting. He reached and cupped the side of her head with his hand. "I mean that you've been hurt before by a man." He stroked her cheek with his thumb. "I could see it out there at the pool when I told you about Regina and Clint. You looked like you were going to be sick."

She swallowed thickly. "It's nothing," she whispered.

"Tell me."

She blinked at his intensity. "It's nothing, Jacob. Nothing like what I'm imagining Regina experienced. I've never been raped, thank God," she whispered fervently. "It's just . . . men can be so . . ." She winced. "*Evil* sometimes to women." She met his stare, guilt swooping through her. "I'm sorry. Not all men—"

"It's okay. You don't have to apologize. What you say is true. I wish it wasn't, but it is too often."

A tense silence settled. He continued to stroke her cheek gently with his thumb. They just stared into each other's eyes as a bedside clock ticked gently, so many unsaid words, so many anxieties, so much longing seeming to swirl around them. That ache in her chest swelled.

His thumb moved, now drying a single fallen tear off her cheek. The conflict inside her grew untenable: her sadness for some of the harsh realities of life clashing with her overpowering desire for him.

"I feel guilty," she said in a shaky burst of honesty.

"Why?"

"For wanting you to make love to me the way you do, for wanting you to restrain me and take me so hard that I can' t think of anything else. I must be sick—" She broke off when he lunged toward her, and suddenly she was crushed against his chest, his arms around her. Her face clenched when she absorbed his familiar scent. His hand delved into her hair, cupping her skull. She shuddered with emotion.

"If you're sick, what am I for wanting to do it to you?" he mumbled gruffly against her forehead. He pressed his lips against her skin, and she sensed his urgency. "It's not the same, though, Harper. Is it?"

"No," she replied emphatically, hating the doubt that tinged his tone. "You never hurt me, you only make me feel . . . so *much*. I don't want to be ashamed of it. I don't want men like Clint Jefferies or . . . *anyone* who's cruel and heartless and evil to make me ashamed of it. You're not those things. You take what you want in bed, but you're *not* selfish. I don't know how you do that. You're just . . . *you*."

He rolled her back against the pillow and came over her, his face hovering above hers. He pressed close, and she could feel that he wore a pair of thin cotton pajama bottoms. His heat emanated into her skin. His groin pressed against her outer thigh. He was growing hard. His features looked shadowed. She was very confused at that moment, and yet she wondered if she'd ever seen him so clearly.

"And you're *you*. Harper McFadden," he mouthed the two words, barely making a sound but saying the two words emphatically, nevertheless. She held her breath at something she sensed in him, some unfurling power. "Do you know why I like to bind you and have you at my mercy?"

"Because you're a sexual dominant?"

"Maybe. Partly." He leaned down until their lips were less than an inch apart. "But mostly because of Harper McFadden."

"What?" she asked, confused.

"Mostly because that's my fantasy," he continued, his voice low but brimming with fierce emotion. He shifted his hips and pressed his cock tighter against her. "To have you. To keep you. To know that at least for a short period of time, no one and nothing will take you from me. To know for a *fact* that you're one hundred percent mine . . . no matter what. *Are* you mine right now, Harper?"

Her lips parted in aroused disbelief at his stark adamancy. She'd thought that his revelation about Regina and Clint Jefferies, and Jacob's and her subsequent admissions of their conflict about their sexual preferences, would dampen their ardor. If anything, it seemed to have amplified their need. She was confused by his intensity, but what he'd just confessed had struck her like a whiplash of honesty, cutting straight through everything else.

"*Yes*. Completely yours, Jacob."

He swept down on her, taking her mouth in unapologetic hunger. The heat that swept through her was familiar, but stronger now, more dangerous than ever before. He abruptly ended their kiss and shifted his weight, straddling her. He straightened his back. Her pulse leapt at her throat when she saw his grim, determined expression. Holding her gaze, he reached for the hem of her nightgown. He drew it up over her belly and above her breasts. He examined what he'd revealed. Her skin prickled beneath his heavy stare. Lifting his pelvis off her slightly, he cradled her hip in his large hand. His thumb reached down to the top of her mons. He rubbed her skin, but he stroked something deep inside her, making her vibrate subtly with mounting emotion. "Mine," he declared thickly, and she felt the storm building in him. He was about to rattle her world. He already was.

"All mine," he repeated as if to himself before he grabbed her wrists and drew her arms above her head. He pressed her hands into the pillows.

She panted softly, looking up at his large, shadowed form. Whatever she experienced at that moment, it was complex, sharp . . . overwhelming. He brushed his fingertips softly against her sides, making her breath hitch and her nipples draw tight.

"I want to tie you up right now. We're the only two who have to decide. Ours is the only opinion that counts, and it only counts for us. *Is* it sick, Harper?"

"I don't think so," she whispered shakily.

"But you're not sure? You're willing to take the risk of being wrong?"

She hesitated. "For you, yes. As long as you're here. With me."

"I promise."

Her face pinched tight as emotion shuddered through her. She felt that sense of déjà vu again, the one that made no sense to her, given what was happening in the present. She'd never experienced anything remotely like what she was feeling with Jacob, there in that moment, so why did she have a feeling of familiarity? As if he sensed her anguish, he cupped her jaw, his thumb feathering the corner of her mouth—her scar. This time, she didn't flinch away.

He stood after a lung-burning moment. "I'll be right back."

He walked toward his private office, and she knew what he was going to get: ropes. It stunned her. She would never have guessed in a million years she would willingly allow this, of all things. And yet . . . she longed for it. Ropes would declare she was his for the taking . . .

Undeniable, flagrant evidence of their bond.

His hand closed around several bundles of rope.

Why did he feel so compelled to do this after he'd exposed part of his past, and they'd acknowledged their mutual uncertainty about their sexual preferences? Maybe it was because he despised anything that kept him from Harper: even doubt.

Nevertheless, that's what he saw on her face when he closed his office door and walked back toward where she lay on the bed, bundles of black rope in one hand, a towel and a pair of blunt-ended, EMT shears ideal for rope cutting in close quarters in the other. He sat on the edge of the bed, seeing the whites of her eyes as she looked at the shears.

"I need to cut the rope at times, and I want to do it safely," he explained. "Besides, I'll always have the shears on hand. If you start to have any pain or numbness from being in the restraint, or if you start to feel uncomfortable and want to stop, just say so. I'll immediately get you out, if not from the planned releases I'll put in the rope, then by using these. I'm pretty good at knowing where and how hard to bind to maintain good blood flow, but everybody is different. I refuse to have you marked or hurting in any way, but I need your input to make that happen. You have to speak up. Say you understand."

"I understand."

He nodded and set the shears on the bedside table. He saw her look down anxiously at the neat bundles of rope resting on his thigh.

"The rope ties me to you as much as it does you to me. Do you understand, Harper?"

She glanced up, her mouth falling open. She nodded. His reassurance had worked, and that gratified him. He, of all people, knew what a challenge this would be for her.

He reached and turned on a bedside lamp.

"I want to see you better. I've fantasized about this. If you knew how much, you'd probably be shocked. Forget the *probably*," he added harshly under his breath.

With the soft glow of the lamp, he could more easily read her expression, but it revealed other things to him, as well. The soft glow of her flawless skin, the telltale pink flush of her cheeks and lips, the hardness of her nipples. His cock tugged at him. He ran his hand over her chest, glorying in the firm swells and tight, rigid nipples. The ache in him swelled.

He slipped the silk nightgown over her head and tossed it aside.

"I'm going to turn up the air-conditioning," he said, standing and setting the coils of rope on the table.

"Why?"

"I know it may feel chilly now. But I'm going to put quite a bit of rope on you. Things will get hot. Fast."

He saw her throat convulse as he turned away. He thought he saw arousal in her large eyes, and prayed he was right in that assumption. When he returned he saw that her head was turned, and she was gazing at the rope. He sat down at the edge of the bed and picked up a bundle.

"Touch it," he said.

Her gaze rose to his face skittishly before she reached. Her fingertips slid over the tightly twisted silk. Arousal stabbed through him. He lowered the bunch of rope, sliding it across her abdomen. She watched. He had the distinct impression she was holding her breath. The vision of the black rope against her pale, taut belly sent another jab of arousal through him. It was every bit as erotic as he'd imagined.

"I'm going to tell you what I'm going to do before we start, and you can tell me if you have any problem with any of it, either now, while I'm binding you, or at any time after," he said gruffly, watching himself stroke her with the rope, knowing her gaze was on the same thing. "I'm going to have you bend your knees toward your chest and spread your thighs. I'm going to bind your shins to your thighs. I'll be careful of your joints. The ropes won't mark you, but there might be some compression spots left on your skin: nothing permanent, just the kind of thing from a pillow after sleeping hard on it. It'll fade quickly once you're free. I've seen how flexible you are. It should work well, but I want you to tell me at any time if you feel uncomfortable. Understood?"

"Yes," she whispered. He slid the rope over her rib cage, and her abdomen muscles leapt. She stared at the black coils as if mesmerized.

"Harper?"

She blinked and looked at his face.

"After I've bound your shins to your thighs, I'm going to bind your wrists just above your knees. Your hands will be free, though. You'll be able to exert some force on your legs. If I tell you to roll your hips back further, I'll expect you to do it unless you're uncomfortable. You'll be completely open to me. I want you to know that." He saw that she was panting softly. Was she aroused, listening to him explain what was about to happen? "I want you to hear this next part. Are you listening?"

"Yes."

"As soon as you're bound, I'm going to fuck you. Hard. And I'm going to do it for my pleasure, not for yours."

She exhaled softly in a burst of surprise.

"I know you'll think that's selfish. But it's just a fact. I've fantasized about this. It's going to be very arousing for me. What are you thinking?"

"I wasn't expecting you to say that. But . . . all right."

"You're sure?"

She nodded.

"After that, I'm going to make sure that you like the ropes, Harper. I'm going to make you come while you're restrained, several times. But I just wanted to be fair, and tell you what will definitely happen first."

Her lips parted. A pink flush had risen in her cheeks.

"I understand," she said softly.

"Okay," he said, standing. He quickly unfastened the twist on one bundle, and a short black length of the silk rope slithered free. "I'm going to bind your wrists temporarily while I do your legs. From this point on, you're going to be mine."

She licked her full lower lip in an anxious gesture.

"Put your hands like this." He showed her what he wanted, demonstrating by putting his wrists together, palms inward and facing each other. She took the position quickly, informing him that while she might be nervous, she was excited, too. He quickly did a triple column tie, binding her wrists together. To increase her arousal—not to mention his own—while he restrained her, he placed her so that her upper arms plumped her pretty breasts, her lower arms lay on her belly, and her fingers were just inches away from her spread sex. After he'd finished with the temporary hand restraint, the anticipation in him had drawn tight, making even breathing difficult for a second. He touched one of her calves.

"Bend your knees. Spread your thighs."

He pushed her knees toward her chest when she followed his instructions.

He began his task soberly, his cock growing heavier and achier with each pass of the rope. By the time he'd finished binding her legs, a sheen of sweat had broken out on his upper lip and abdomen. He always loved the process of roping a woman firmly and artistically, finding it an explicit slow build.

But there was *nothing* slow about tying Harper up, though. It was hot, spiking torture from the get-go.

6

make me
FEEL

Harper had feared the idea of a rope restraint, worried she'd find the experience degrading and scary. But of course Jacob challenged her fears with his low, seductive voice and patient description of what he'd do. Then the process began, and she found the anticipation almost unbearable.

When he'd told her he planned to fuck her hard once she was restrained, forbidden arousal had shot through her. She'd also noticed the towel he brought, and thought she knew what it signified. He planned to come on her again. It excited her beyond belief, the idea of being the helpless target of his lust, the prospect of watching him lose himself to pleasure.

Besides, it took only a minute of watching him methodically binding her legs to make her realize she was witnessing a sexual art. He maneuvered the rope with deft expertise, applying constant surface tension with his hands. His tightening of knots somehow never burned or chafed her skin. He bound her very firmly, but there was never discomfort. She experienced only a slow, delicious surrender as more and more of the black silk rope covered her skin.

Finally, he stood next to the bed and looked down at her, his expression tight and unreadable. But his eyes seemed to burn her as they completed a tour of her naked, bound body.

He'd looped rope from her ankles all the way up her lower leg, each pass also capturing her upper leg, so that her calves were held very snugly against the back of her thighs. Only her knees and feet were free of rope. He'd wound the rope around her forearms and wrists, as well. With the aid of his expert knot tying, her hands had been restrained to rope just above her knees. She was spread wide. Her dark red pubic hair and pale stomach stood in stark contrast to the black of the rope. Jacob could see more than her. *Much* more. As he stared between her thighs right now, he looked directly at her open, aroused sex.

She couldn't help but see the beauty of his work. The black rope against the canvas of her pale skin struck her like some kind of Japanese sex art: clean, sleek . . . and *oh*, so utilitarian.

"Do you want to struggle, Harper?" he asked, his heavy-lidded gaze traveling the length of her body to her face.

The question took her by surprise. She felt strangely secure in the restraint. There was a surprising amount of rope on her. She found the weight of it somehow comforting. Maybe because it was clear there was no escape. Not that she wanted to escape, but . . .

"No," she said. "Do you want me to?"

"No. It's different for everyone. Some like to struggle. It arouses. I'm glad you don't want to. This time. You're ready to submit from the get-go, aren't you?" he asked thickly.

He reached between her thighs and dipped his forefinger into her slit. She gasped as he penetrated her. "You like to be tied up, period. Don't you? You're so damn wet," he grated out. He bent, lowering over her bound form, and slid his finger out of her vagina. He pushed the ridge of it between her labia, rubbing her in a bull's-eye fashion. Her feet twitched upward in the air at the exciting sensation. She saw his heavy erection flick upward behind the thin, insubstantial fabric of his pajama bottoms. He grunted and reached beneath the low waistband, whisking the length of his cock out of the garment. She moaned. His cock was swollen and flushed, the surface tension of it seemingly as taut as the ropes he'd put on her body. For a tense, thrilling moment, he jacked himself firmly from root to tip, twisting his hand slightly just below the fat, delineated head with each pass. All the while, he stimulated her clit. She stared at him, lust-drunk. She felt so much in those moments, and was helpless to do anything but allow it . . . to drown in it.

He straightened after a moment, his mouth shaping into a snarl. He cupped his firm, round testicles on the last pass of his hand, squeezing them tautly, the stalk of his cock rising high in the air. Heat flashed through her. He'd been right to turn up the air-conditioning. He withdrew his finger from between her lubricated labia, and she suppressed a whimper.

"I'm going to have you now."

Her breath hitched at his grim proclamation. He shoved the pajama bottoms the rest of the way down his long, powerful legs. He stood next to the bed. She watched anxiously as his flagrant erection bounced slightly in the air when he stood. He reached for the bedside table drawer. A moment later, he rolled a condom onto his protruding cock.

He was going to fuck her without mercy now.

She thought she'd die from the sharpness of her anxious excitement. He reached into the bedside drawer and withdrew a length of black fabric. He stepped toward her.

"I'm going to blindfold you for this first part." Maybe he noticed her flash of disappointment. She'd been anticipating watching him lose control while he took pleasure in her body. "I told you, this part is just for me. Selfishness has its place, Harper," he added more softly. Her gaze flicked to his face. What he'd said was so strange. He knew she despised selfishness in men. So why was it that his deliberate, planned selfishness sent a shiver of forbidden excitement through her?

No sooner had she nodded in agreement than he was whisking the scarf around her head. He didn't tie it tight. Her eyes opened behind the soft material, but she was well and truly blinded. A frisson of panic splintered her intense arousal. Then she felt the mattress lower as he came onto the bed. He touched her bare knees, letting her know he was between her thighs. She felt his weight shift forward between her widely spread legs. A choked sound escaped her throat. Her body started to vibrate subtly with nervous arousal. The anticipation was killing her. But he didn't make her wait long.

His fingers spread her slit, and she felt the steely pressure of his cockhead at her entrance. He kept one hand on her knee and rolled her hips back slightly to get a good angle. He started to penetrate her.

"Oh God," she moaned, lifting her head off the pillow.

"Hush," he ground out, and he pushed his cock several inches into her. She gave a broken cry. His other hand came up to her knee. Her flesh resisted his swollen member one moment, and then melted around it the next. He sawed his hips firmly, fucking her for a moment with the first half of his cock. A low growl vibrated in his throat.

"Your pussy is hot. And sweet," he growled. She had a vision of him watching himself pierce her, his eyes glittering with lust, his hard, beautiful mouth twisted into a snarl. Heat rushed through her at the imagined image.

"Yeah, that feels good," he rasped.

He thrust harder, and she gasped. She felt his hands come down on the mattress next to her head. For a moment, he didn't move, his pelvis and balls smashed tightly against her outer sex, his cock fully submerged. Harper panted, overwhelmed by the sensation of him throbbing deep inside her.

"Harper," he rasped.

"Yes?" she managed in a quivery voice. It was strange the way he'd said her name. It wasn't really a question. More like a declaration . . .

A satisfied one.

"Press your knees a little further into your chest with your hands," he ordered tensely. Like her feet, her hands were free. She did what he'd demanded, grimacing slightly at the increase of pressure. His cock pressed impossibly higher and harder into her at the new angle. He must have thought the same thing, too, because he grunted in pleasure.

"This is going to feel so damn good," he said.

He drew out of her and immediately plunged back. She cried out, but he didn't pause. His pelvis began to slap against hers in a taut, rapid rhythm. She lay there, helpless in the restraint as he pounded into her. She screamed. It wasn't something she could stop. The pressure building in her was too intense.

"Can you take it, Harper?"

He continued to fuck her as he snarled the question. She heard him say it through the cries of excitement that were popping out of her throat every time he crashed into her.

"Yes. God, *yes*," burst out of her when he drove deep.

"Because you have to take it. You're mine."

Oh God. Her eyes clamped tight behind the blindfold. It was unbearable, but she wouldn't have traded the experience for anything. Her entire world became the friction of his driving cock. It was like he was igniting a fire in her. She felt his feral focus on her, sensed it as if it were as real as an encompassing embrace. His grunts of pleasure and satisfaction only added fuel to her volatility.

He was so swollen and hard in her. She thought his arousal might verge on pain. She knew perfectly that he would explode first. And that, too, was fuel on the flame.

He drove deep. She felt his cock lurch viciously inside her. She gritted her teeth together, stifling an anguished cry. She wasn't ready for him to leave her. Not yet. But he was about to come, and she craved that, as well.

A moment later, he jerked his cock out of her. She felt his elbow against her bare knee, and the subtle sensation of movement at the joint. He'd removed the condom and was jacking his cock. He grunted savagely, and her body tensed tight as a wire.

Her belly leapt at the first splash of his warm semen on her skin. She lay there, panting and undone, listening to the ominous, low growls that rattled his throat as he continued to ejaculate on her stomach, ribs, and lower breasts. It was the climax to a claiming, more than anything, and she suspected Jacob knew that. Her thought was confirmed when she felt him fall forward after a tense moment, both of his hands planted on the mattress next to her head.

"Mine," he repeated between ragged breaths.

Harper didn't reply. In that moment, it seemed ridiculous to comment further on the obvious.

Even though she couldn't see him, his harsh breathing joined them, somehow. So did the feeling of his testicles pressed tightly against her outer sex and the feeling of the warm liquid coating her belly and ribs. Slowly, his breathing evened and his semen began to cool. He pushed himself off the mattress. She waited breathlessly. Then came the sensation of the soft towel pressing against her skin, drying her of his ejaculate.

A moment later, she heard the bedside table drawer open. The blindfold slipped off her head. She blinked dazedly. The mattress gave as he sat next to her. She stared up at him, hungry for the image. Starving for it. He looked down at her, his expression solemn. He held her stare, but she was aware of his hand moving over the rope restraint, tactilely checking that the rope held secure and that his planned releases were intact.

"You're comfortable?" he murmured.

The dull ache between her thighs, the feeling of the cool air tickling her aroused, wet sex nudged at her awareness. "Yes," she whispered, panting shallowly. He'd built a boatload of sexual tension in her. Her nipples were tight and hard, and the soles of her feet simmered.

A smile flickered across his firm mouth. "All except for this?"

Her eyelids fluttered at the sensation of his fingers brushing softly against the pubic hair over her mound. Too softly. Her sex clenched tight. She moaned miserably. God, she was right on the edge.

"Don't worry," he said soothingly. "I'm not trying to torture you. Just tell me what you want, Harper."

"To come," she said shakily. "Please make me come."

His hand covered her entire mound. She cried out at the forceful pressure. He circled his arm subtly. She gasped, her head coming off the pillow as the first harsh shudder of orgasm shook her. After a mindless moment of flooding sensation, she became aware that he watched her fixedly as he worked every last bit of tension and pleasure out of her body.

She exhaled, her head falling back on the pillow. He continued to stimulate her, but slower now, making her shiver in post-orgasmic bliss. She opened her heavy eyelids. Their stares held as his hand continued to move between her thighs.

"You're beautiful," he said quietly.

She smiled. She was too worn out to speak.

He lifted his hand and stood next to the bed. She rolled her head, watching him. He lifted the towel from the bedside table and used the corner of it to wipe off his hand. He tossed down the towel.

"That's how wet you were," he commented dryly, referring to his glistening fingers. He turned his attention to her bound wrists. He quickly loosened the knot that bound her arm to her leg. He released her other arm, as well, then drew both hands over her head.

"Bend your elbows and rest them on the pillow," he instructed gruffly. "Take a comfortable position."

When she'd done what he'd asked, he tied her wrists together, binding her hands above her head. Then he stood next to the bed, gazing down at her, and she couldn't help but wonder with a mixture of rising excitement and anxiety what else he had in store for her.

Her gaze ran the length of him. He looked hard and awesome, both intimidating and calm at once. His cock was long and firm, neither erect nor flaccid, but at some in-between stage. She had a vivid fantasy of sliding him into her mouth in that state, and feeling him harden against her tongue, his girth beginning to stretch her lips wide . . .

"Don't look at me like that, Harper," he said, his tone a silky remonstrance. He reached for something on the bedside table and sat next to her on the bed. She heard the click of a cap and stared at what he held in his hands. It was a bottle of light pink lubricant. He spread some on his fingers and then closed the cap. He set the bottle aside.

"Your nipples," he said thickly, reaching for her. "I've never seen them so hard as they were when I was inside you. It was driving me crazy," he mused. He rubbed the lubricant onto a nipple. Her back arched slightly off the bed at the stimulation. With her hands tied above her head, he had free access to her breasts, which she recognized was what he'd intended. He turned his attention to the other nipple, rubbing it deliberately with the lubricant.

Watching his intent focus—and feeling the result—made her flex her hips downward on the mattress in mounting excitement. He lifted his other hand and pinched and massaged both nipples at once. She moaned, incredulous as need swiped at her again with a sharp claw.

As if her moan was his cue, he suddenly knelt by the bed. He took a breast into his palm and slipped a nipple into his mouth, torturing the flesh with his agile, firm tongue and precise suction. Perspiration shone on the valley between her breasts. He swiped his tongue along it before he sucked the other aching nipple into his hot mouth. She laid there, a captive to her own arousal, her breathing growing rough. He switched again, sucking her other nipple into his hot mouth.

The moment stretched as he awakened her flesh to a state of sharp excitement yet again. She called his name in dazed dissatisfaction when he lifted his head a while later. He calmly reached again into the bedside drawer and withdrew what she recognized as a bullet vibrator. She heard the slight buzz as he turned it on. He reached between her thighs, pressing it against her clit. She cried out sharply as simmering pleasure swamped her.

"You know I love to watch you come." His deep, fluid voice washed over as the bullet vibrated against her clit. "Does it feel good?"

"*So* good," she gasped.

He leaned down and brushed his mouth over her parted lips, as if he was absorbing the minute trembling of her straining body. She saw the hot gleam in his eyes. She knew it then, that she was his captive . . . in more ways than one.

She was falling in love with him, she realized with a mixed sense of euphoria and dread.

"You don't have any choice, do you?" he murmured.

She blinked. Had he read her mind? "I don't have any choice?" she asked in a quivering voice.

"You don't have any choice but to come."

"No," she moaned, her entire body a tight knot of sexual tension. "God, no."

He pulsed the vibrator demandingly. "Then *do* it."

The knot exploded. She shook violently in the rope restraints.

But they held firm.

twenty~seven

When she'd calmed, he came onto the bed again and entered her. With the blindfold removed, she was free to watch him this time, to bear witness to yet another claiming of her. He staked it every bit as forcefully and completely as he had the first time.

Afterward, tears inexplicably welled in her eyes as he tenderly dried her skin of his semen and systematically removed the rope restraint. It was like he was liberating her in more ways than one, freeing her to a huge, intimidating well of emotion. As he removed the last length of the rope from her ankle, and her aching leg straightened, he noticed her damp eyes.

"I . . . don't know why," she admitted with a shaky laugh, seeing his brows slant in concern.

"It's okay," he said. He came down on the bed next to her and pulled her into his arms. Her cheek fell against his chest. He hugged her tight, his embrace divine. Emotion flooded her.

"The ropes bring out a lot of things, before, during, and after," he murmured, kissing her temple. She gasped against his chest and shuddered. He stroked her hair, soothing her roughened state. "But I'm still here, Harper. I'm still right here with you."

She slept after that, with Jacob holding her fast in his arms. Despite her strong surge of emotion after they'd made love—not to mention her startling realization that she was falling for him—she awoke feeling alert, calm, and content. Their sexual exchange had been intense and the most challenging of her life, but strangely, it seemed to have acted like some kind of catharsis on her emotions.

The soft, muffled sound of Jacob's shower penetrated her awareness. She was a little forlorn to realize that he was already up, but did have a vague recollection of him running kisses along her jaw and neck and murmuring in a sexy, sleep-roughened voice that he needed to get up. She'd been too sleepy to do much of anything but mutter an incomprehensible protest when his warm, hard body moved away from her. Afterward, she'd fallen back to sleep.

She knew he had a lot of work to attend to today, and had already gotten a late start. The memory of what had happened at the opera swept through her then. It no longer had the depressing effect on her that it had just hours ago. What had taken place in Jacob's bed early this morning had been so powerful, last night seemed like it'd happened months ago.

She rose and showered on her own in the guest bathroom. It was already almost noon, and Cyril Atwater was coming here at twelve thirty to have lunch and meet with Harper about the proposed film. She was sitting on a stool at the vanity, wearing a light robe and combing her damp hair, when she heard a knock at the bathroom door.

"Come in," she called, turning toward the door.

Jacob walked into the room, looking appealing in a white shirt, black blazer, and jeans, his hair appearing as dark as his goatee because it was still damp from his shower. Her heart gave a little jump when she saw the expression in his golden-green eyes as he glanced over her. He approached, a small smile tilting his mouth.

For some stupid reason, shyness swept through her. He'd done incredibly intimate things to her in his bed, and here he was, looking like he was ready to do a *GQ* cover, seemingly so miles out of her league, so untouchable. The disparity jarred her.

For a few seconds, anyway.

Until he said, "Morning," in a warm, gruff voice, and leaned down to kiss her. His mouth lingered when she reciprocated, his hand going to the back of her head. She bracketed his jaw with her hands. His scent filled her: soap and his familiar spicy cologne. So male. So amazing. He pierced her mouth with his tongue, and their kiss segued from a good-morning peck to a full-fledged heart-pounder. By the time they sealed it a moment later, she panted softly against his hovering mouth.

"Morning," she finally replied. She saw the hot gleam in his eyes and his smile. He straightened in front of her, his fingers brushing back a loose tendril of damp hair and pushing it behind her ear.

"If I didn't absolutely have to be at these meetings, I'd keep you in bed the whole day," he murmured.

She gazed up at him, warmth suffusing her. His saying that meant a lot.

"And I'd let you."

Again, graphic memories of their lovemaking swamped her. The fact that they'd both expressed their uncertainties beforehand—exposed their vulnerabilities—seemed to make the memories even more intense. Heat expanded on her cheeks. He touched her face with light fingertips.

"Are you *blushing*?" he asked, his brows slanting as if he was both amused and fascinated.

She ducked her head and started to turn on the stool. He stopped her by grasping her shoulders with both hands.

"Harper?" he queried when she had difficulty looking up at him.

"I can't believe I let you do those things," she said, looking at her lap because the alternative was to stare straight ahead at Jacob's crotch, and that was even more uncomfortable than meeting his eyes.

His long fingers caressed the underside of her chin, but he didn't force her to look up.

"You should believe it. Because I'm going to do more of those things to you tonight, and I'd hate for you to be shocked."

She laughed. His low chuckle from above her sent another wave of warmth through her that had nothing to do with embarrassment. This time, she looked up when he urged her with his touch under her chin.

"It wasn't just a first for you, Harper." His stare on her was lambent, and struck her as wholly sincere, not to mention sexy as hell.

She gave a shaky laugh. "What, you got that expert with rope by tying up manikins?"

"No," he replied, his solemn reply instantly quashing her uncomfortable attempt at humor. "I meant it was new to me, too. The way it felt."

She found herself staring up at him, searching for the truth. Her mouth trembled as she smiled, because she was beyond assured by what she saw in his eyes. His thumb feathered across the corner of her mouth.

Across her scar.

She shut her eyes and turned her chin into his hand. What was happening to her? Maybe he sensed her swelling emotion, because he leaned down and kissed her forehead.

"You're meeting with Cyril soon, aren't you?" he asked quietly, and she was thankful he'd changed the subject.

"Yes," she said with fake brightness.

"Are you going to write the screenplay with him?"

"I haven't completely decided yet. I need more information to know if I really can do it and if I have the time."

He leaned down and brushed his lips against her temple before he stepped back. "Time is the main factor, then, because I know you could write it."

"Thanks," she said, flattered. Jacob was the type of man whose confidence in you counted.

"Be ready for dinner tonight at seven thirty? I'm taking you to a place that a friend of mine just opened."

She nodded.

"Don't look at me like that, Harper," he said, his eyebrows slanting.

She blinked, realizing she'd been drinking in the vision of him standing before her. How could she do anything *but*, when he was so beautiful to her? He turned away, looking grim. Harper was glad for that, because she was far from happy at the idea of being separated from him, too, even if it was just for an afternoon.

.   .   .

Harper was thrilled when Marianne escorted Cyril into a salon and she saw he was accompanied by Ellie Thorton. Ellie was the young woman she'd mainly focused on for her article on San Francisco's homeless youth. Ellie was smiling broadly at the surprise, and looked to be brimming with newfound good health. She'd put on a much-needed ten or fifteen pounds since Harper and she had first met, when Ellie was barely surviving and her "home" was San Francisco's underground and alleyways. Her dark brown hair was cut in a cute bob that almost entirely hid the burn scar on the side of her face—the product of a sadistic, drug-addicted "friend" of her mother's. Ellie had carried the scar since she was six. Her clothes, although not expensive, looked adorably chic on her slender figure. Harper shouldn't have been surprised. Even when Ellie lived on the street, she'd managed to demonstrate her individuality.

"You look fantastic," Harper said, beaming after Ellie and she hugged tightly. They'd kept in regular touch since they'd met, but recently only by e-mail and the occasional phone call. "How is college?"

"Great. My advisor says I should try to apply to San Francisco State University next fall. She says almost all of my junior college credits will transfer. And guess what she thinks I should study?"

Harper grinned at her enthusiasm. "Fashion? You're a natural for it."

Ellie laughed. "No, journalism."

"That's perfect. You'll be a natural for that, too."

She greeted Cyril and they made their way to a seating area in the luxurious salon of Jacob's home.

"Are you sure you're okay with the idea of the film, Ellie? You said in the last e-mail that you'd called Roger Findlay?" Harper asked after they'd sat and got caught up. Roger was one of Harper's old friends from college who did a good deal of film production contract work.

"Yeah, Roger's been great about walking me through things. That sample contract you sent over might as well have been written in Russian," Ellie told Cyril. Cyril just smirked back at the girl, and Ellie laughed. "Actually, Cyril's been great, too. He's been really patient with me."

Cyril had been surprisingly modest and quiet during the two women's reunion. Harper had a feeling Ellie and Cyril would probably end up getting on famously. They were both scrappers, after all, both fierce individualists. Maybe Ellie herself was one of the reasons Cyril had identified so strongly with Harper's original story.

Does that mean that Jacob identified with the tragedy of Ellie's youth, as well? He'd been the one to originally suggest it to Cyril. Was his gravitation toward Ellie's story a clue as to what his childhood was like?

It would make sense. Harper thought of Ellie's scar, and her own. Jacob and Cyril weren't the only ones to feel a kinship to Ellie Thorton.

A spike of sharp longing went through her unexpectedly as she listened to Cyril talk about potential filming locations, and Ellie chimed in occasionally. She'd been separated from Jacob for a half hour, and already she missed him. Was that because it struck her hard in that moment how little she really knew about him?

Was it because she suspected she'd fallen in love with him?

Harper jumped into the topic of filming locations, determined to get her mind off the confusing topic of Jacob. She heard the salon doors open briskly. She looked around distractedly, half expecting Marianne.

Instead, Jacob stalked into the room, his gaze flickering across Harper.

"Cyril." He nodded at his friend.

"Jacob," Cyril said, clearly as surprised by his unexpected appearance as Harper was. Jacob put out a hand to Ellie. "Jacob Latimer. Welcome."

"Ellie Thorton." They shook, Ellie looking a little starstruck. Harper wasn't surprised. He looked impossibly handsome and compelling. His unexpected entrance seemed to ramp up the energy level of the room a hundredfold.

"You don't seem half as scary as I thought you'd be," Ellie breathed.

Cyril snorted with laughter. Jacob's back was to her so Harper couldn't quite discern his reaction to Ellie's forthrightness.

"I'm glad to hear it," he replied levelly, but Harper thought she heard a thread of humor in his deep voice.

"I didn't think I was going to get a chance to meet you today. I wanted to thank you," Ellie said, looking up at him feelingly.

"You wanted to thank me for letting you three meet here?"

"No," Ellie said, never breaking her rapt stare on his face. "For Randolph House."

Harper blinked in amazement. Randolph House was a women's shelter on Mission Street.

"Harper helped get me in," Ellie continued. "The staff there built me up while I was there, got me ready to go back out on the streets, this time to start a life, not just survive. I know you prefer to remain anonymous, but I overheard one of the supervisors talking to your lawyer once on the phone. I know that you provide the majority of funding for Randolph House. That's why I'm thanking you."

Harper's stunned stare zoomed over to Jacob's back. She wished she could see his expression. He merely straightened, smoothing his tie as he turned in partial profile to her. "Well, it's a good thing Harper guided you there. I'm gratified to hear firsthand that it helped someone."

"Not just helped. Randolph House changed my life. I can't thank you enough."

"You're welcome," he said. He started to back up toward Harper's chair, and she wondered if he was embarrassed at being unexpectedly called out for his charity. His hand came to rest on her shoulder. Her skin tingled beneath his touch. She gazed up at him, perplexed. "I'm so sorry for interrupting your meeting," he told Cyril and Ellie. "This will only take a second. I realized I'd forgotten something important."

He leaned over Harper's chair and kissed her full on the mouth. She started in surprise, but then the heat, flavor, and pressure of his kiss took over. In seconds flat, she was kissing him back hungrily.

When they surfaced for air, she realized dazedly that Ellie and Cyril were holding a determined conversation in the distance, clearly trying to focus their attention elsewhere than on the kissing couple in the room.

"You've always got a secret up your sleeve, don't you?" she murmured very quietly against his lips, referring to Ellie's revelation about Randolph House.

"I wasn't keeping Randolph House a secret. I had no reason to tell you about it, that's all," he murmured dismissively before dipping his head and kissing her again.

"I'm hoping I won't be in trouble for this?" he breathed out a moment later.

"For what?"

"Interrupting because all I could think about was tasting you one more time."

"Why would you be in trouble for that?" she whispered, choking back a laugh.

His mouth twitched. "I don't know. I've never done it before, so I wasn't sure."

He kissed her once more and stood. Ellie and Cyril glanced over at them cautiously.

"It's all right. The coast is clear," Jacob said before he politely bid them a good and fruitful afternoon. Harper noticed that a slight smile lingered on his lips as he walked away, as if he thought his behavior a little funny, but was pleased, anyway.

The doors shut behind him. Harper had only the pleasant pressure remaining on her lips from his kiss and Cyril's comically stunned expression to assure herself that it'd all really happened.

twenty-eight

Ellie had a shift waitressing at her restaurant early that afternoon, so she had to leave soon after their lunch, which they ate poolside. Marianne heard the girl saying she was planning on walking to a bus stop, and insisted that a driver would take her—a proposal that seemed very agreeable to Ellie.

"So. You and Jacob," Cyril stated with a significant glance once they were alone on the terrace. They sipped coffee in the idyllic setting while the Pacific provided them with a cool, pleasant breeze.

Harper raised her brows. "What about Jacob and me?"

"Don't play coy with me. It's beneath you."

Harper laughed. "You don't know me well enough to know if it's beneath me or not."

"I imagine Jacob would think it's beneath you. He hates false modesty and artifice."

"I'm not so sure Jacob knows me all that well, either," Harper murmured. *Or maybe he does, but it's a mystery as to* how *he does.* She noticed Cyril's incredulous look.

"I've never seen him act this way around a woman. Never," he stated flatly. "For a man who is usually so guarded, to become so transparent—"

"I'd hardly call him transparent," Harper scoffed, setting down her coffee cup.

"Compared to what he's usually like, he's positively see-through."

Harper laughed it off. Cyril had only seen Jacob and she together a few brief times, after all. But then, she began to really absorb Cyril's statement and all of its ramifications.

"I wish I *did* know more about him," she mused after a moment. "Do you know much about his childhood?"

"I assume it was crap," Cyril stated bluntly. "I'm not sure what happened to his biological parents, but he was in the foster care system. He didn't get adopted until he was nearly an adult. He hardly ever talks about it, and doesn't respond well to hints and prods for him to do so." He rolled his pale blue eyes. "Trust me on that score."

"I know that he got a scholarship to MIT and served in army intelligence for several years."

"His history is much better known once he got closer to adulthood. It's his origins that are murky. I'm not sure *how* he's managed to keep prying eyes out of his deep past, but then again . . . he *is* Jacob Latimer. He can do almost anything, including sweep his past clean."

"Sweep his past clean," she repeated slowly. "That's an interesting thing to say."

"Interesting, maybe, but not uncommon. That girl who just left us is the exception, from my experience," Cyril said, making a gesture toward the terrace doors where Ellie had just made her exit. He held up a package of clove cigarettes with a questioning look. Harper nodded her agreement for him to smoke.

"What do you mean about Ellie being the exception?"

"Most people want to deny a difficult past. It's unusual, for a person to be as forthcoming and refreshingly honest as Ellie is," Cyril mused as he lifted the cigarette to his mouth. He took a draw, his expression thoughtful. "Most want to transform into someone new. Forget. I do my fair share of intentional forgetting every day."

"You sound like Jacob."

He shrugged, smoke expanding around his mouth. "We couldn't be more different, and yet we're two of a kind, as well."

"Did you know him in South Carolina? Jacob?" she prompted when he gave her a blank look.

"No, I met him at Tahoe Shores when we became neighbors." He flicked some ashes onto a china saucer. "Does it really matter? That you know about his past?"

Harper considered before answering.

"It doesn't in the everyday, practical sense, no."

"It would serve no purpose."

"It would help me to see him better, though . . . to see beneath the legend and the enigma. To understand him better."

To love him better.

She winced. Jacob was the most elusive man she'd probably ever meet in her life. Was she a masochist, or something? There was no surer guarantee of pain than falling for him. Trying to disguise her sudden transparency, she reached for her coffee and took a sip. She had a sneaking suspicion Cyril had somehow divined her mortifying thought.

"I don't think it would help at all. It might just make him feel exposed, even betrayed, if you insisted upon knowing about every detail of his history."

"Yes. There is that risk," she agreed, squinting out at the sun-gilded Pacific Ocean. Her heart felt heavy. There was *definitely* that risk with Jacob, as shut off as he was. The strength of his armor had to be commensurate to the pain from which he guarded himself, didn't it? That was a forbidding thought.

Cyril stubbed out his cigarette.

"Why did you mention South Carolina earlier?"

"Because that's where Jacob was born and grew up. He told me, on the first day we met."

He shook his head. "He didn't grow up in South Carolina."

"What?" Harper asked, startled from her ruminations. "South Carolina, born and bred," she repeated what Jacob had said on that beach.

Cyril shook his head. "No. He mentioned where he grew up a few times in passing, but it wasn't South Carolina."

"Where was it?" Harper asked, leaning forward in her chair, the back of her neck prickling with curiosity. Why would Jacob have said he grew up in South Carolina that first day if he hadn't? Cyril must be mistaken.

Cyril's brow creased as he thought. "That's just it, I can't recall precisely. As I said, he's rarely mentioned it. And I'm British, you know. I get your states mixed up sometimes, especially some of the eastern ones. Virginia, maybe? Maryland? Somewhere in the backwoods. He's joked once or twice about being the country bumpkin, how he never got on a plane until he was eighteen or on an elevator until he was fourteen, things like that. But no, it definitely wasn't South Carolina. I have a friend who moved to South Carolina, and I've visited there, so I would have remembered that," Cyril said firmly.

"Is Latimer his adoptive parents' name?"

"I'm not sure Jacob would approve of me talking about all this with you," Cyril stated.

"I see," Harper said, feeling awkward.

Cyril exhaled. "Look, I don't think you have evil intentions toward Jacob. It's pretty clear you're as taken with him as he is with you. It's just . . . he's mentioned to me before that he *is* concerned about the fact that you're a reporter. He's not overly fond of your tribe. With good reason, if you ask me. They're always poking around him, looking for a story . . . sometimes making them up when they can't find anything worthwhile."

"I'm an editor," Harper corrected. "And I've told Jacob repeatedly that I'm not doing some kind of undercover exposé on him. I would never sleep with someone to get a story. That's despicable."

"And if you got wind of a story when you were already involved with a man? What then?"

"That's not why I'm asking these questions! I'm asking because I want to know him better. Is that so bizarre?"

Cyril threw up his hands and leaned back in his chair. "It all comes to the same thing, though. It doesn't really matter one way or another *why* you're asking me questions about Jacob—"

"I disagree," she interrupted forcefully. "How can it not matter? Are you saying there's no difference between asking because I care, and asking because I plan to use the information against him?"

"That's *exactly* what I'm saying," Cyril said, his pale blue eyes flashing. "Because either way, Jacob wouldn't want it. Don't you see? He doesn't want anyone stirring up his past. I have the feeling at times that it's like he's buried that part of himself. Laid it to rest, just like you would a loved one. Who he was pains him, somehow. To bring it up now, to start digging around and poking at the skeletons in the closet, it's like trying to raise the dead. Besides," he continued in a more subdued tone. "It's not as if plenty of other reporters haven't tried to resuscitate the bones of his past. They can't find much of anything, beyond Clint Jefferies," he said, rolling his eyes. "And all of that is just sensationalism and empty speculation, not facts."

Harper didn't reply. She suddenly felt very hollow. Sad. Surely Cyril was right. Who was she, to question Jacob's past? Jacob clearly didn't want it, so why should she?

Because you don't like seeing his pain. If the past held the origins of his pain, he'd never really heal if he constantly avoided those wounds.

A sharp feeling of loss went through her unexpectedly. Her thought had sounded like something her dad would say. And yes, Harper agreed in theory. But more than that, it was as if in denying his own past, Jacob was denying *her* something. And for whatever crazy reason that *meant* something to her.

It made no sense, of course. She shook her head, trying to clear her thoughts. She was drawing too close to the fire of Jacob Latimer. The allure of him, the mystery, was confusing her.

She looked up when Cyril patted her forearm.

"You look bereft, you're making me feel horribly guilty. I'm just being practical, Harper. Jacob is my friend," Cyril said softly. "I'm glad to see him let down his guard with a woman. He looked *happy* when he walked into that room earlier and kissed you. *Happy*, right there in the moment. Trust me. That's a rarity. That's what counts. The present moment. I'm just being honest when I say that if you insist upon learning more about his past, it's not going to make *either* of you happy."

Harper nodded, taking a deep breath. She understood Cyril's point. She *did*. But something told her it was more complicated than that. *Jacob* was more complex than that. She heard the terrace door open and turned in her chair. Marianne had come to clear their dishes. There was no more talk between Cyril and her about Jacob's carefully buried past.

Sometime during the hours she spent with Cyril that afternoon, he finally managed to get her to officially commit to writing the screenplay with him. Harper found herself not only getting excited about the prospect, but invested in it. She also began to really like her future writing partner. Cyril was a perfectionist by nature and very demanding, but also savvy, energetic, brilliant, compassionate . . . not to mention completely irreverent. It was hard not to be affected by his enthusiasm for the project. By the time he left at six o'clock that evening, Harper was exhausted, but inspired.

She hadn't heard from Jacob all afternoon, but assumed they were still on for diner at seven thirty. There was still no sign of him in his bedroom suite when she went up to get ready. While she was in the shower, she reflected on everything that had transpired over the past month: starting a new job as an editor, upending her entire life and moving to a strange town, agreeing to write a screenplay with a world-renowned director . . .

Meeting Jacob on that beach.

She certainly was coming a long way in emerging from her shell of grief and shaking up her life. Even if Jacob decided to end their relationship tomorrow, he would have had a permanent effect on her.

But she wouldn't think about their relationship ending now. Not when she felt so invigorated about her life. Not when she was anticipating the evening with Jacob so hugely.

She'd saved a new dress for tonight: a stunning green silk that fastened around her neck and left her shoulders and arms bare. She wore her hair down, adding some soft curl to the waves. When she examined herself in the mirror just before seven that evening, she smiled at the result. The color of the dress looked striking against her skin and hair. Her eyes shone with excitement. Her loose hair felt good, spilling down her back and sliding against her bare shoulders and upper arms. She felt sensual . . . sexy. She owed all that to Jacob's influence.

The sound of a door shutting in the distance got her attention. Was it Jacob, returning? A few seconds later, she heard another door shut quietly, and was pretty sure it was the one to his private bathroom. Her heart racing, she chose a pair of long, dangly gold earrings and finished her makeup. When she walked into the suite five minutes later, she thought she'd have to wait for him to finish showering. He was coming out of his bathroom at the same moment as her, however, looking freshly showered and devastating in a black suit and black striped tie. He glanced up and noticed her.

"Hi," she said.

He didn't respond immediately. Instead, he approached, his gaze sliding down over her.

"What? Why are you smiling like that?" she asked. She sounded breathless. His tiny, sexy smile and smoldering gaze had made her that way.

He reached into his breast pocket and pulled out a black leather box.

"I was just thinking it was serendipity. I thought they'd look pretty with your hair, but I didn't guess . . ."

He faded off, shrugging, and handed her the box. Harper's pulse began to throb at her throat as she opened the black Bulgari box.

"Oh my God," she muttered, stunned.

"You don't like them?" he asked. Guilt swept through her when she saw the flash of disappointment and worry on his face.

"Are you kidding? They're gorgeous," she exclaimed. She looked down dazedly at the emerald pendant earrings. The oval drop stones were enormous—almost an inch wide at the base and glittering with inner fires. They looked like they'd come from the royal family's cache or from the treasure chests of some Arabian prince.

"Then put them on," he said. She blinked and looked up. He'd come close, and he was wearing that deadly small smile again.

"Jacob, I can't," she whispered, but he'd taken the box and was removing the earrings from their fastenings.

"Of course you can. I got them specifically for you. They're insured, if that's what you're worried about," he said, fluidly sidestepping the issue by focusing on a topic she hadn't even thought of, as yet. He held the earrings up next to her face and hair. His smile grew slightly in smug satisfaction, but then he sobered.

"What?" she wondered.

His fingers touched her hair. Nerves along her neck danced with pleasure at the light caress. His gaze ran over her face. "You're beautiful."

"Thank you," she said shakily, her heart squeezing tight in her chest at something she read in his expression.

"Put them on? For me?"

Of course she couldn't say *no* then. She came out of the bathroom a moment later wearing the earrings, her heart full in her chest. She beamed at him at the same time she shook her head in remonstrance.

"I shouldn't accept them. They must have cost you a small fortune," she murmured.

He leaned down, brushing his lips against her temple and spoke quietly near her ear.

"It would have been worth a much larger one, to see that smile."

The restaurant he took her to that night was in the Mission District and was called Geb. It served Mediterranean, Egyptian, and Moroccan fare. Because Jacob knew the chef-owner, they were given a prime spot on the terrace next to an outdoor stone fireplace. Thick palms and ferns surrounded their table, making Harper feel like they were the only couple dining in the exotic setting. The chef, a man by the name of Jason Savoy, came out to the table to greet Jacob and describe his favorites on the menu.

The food was decadently good—rich and aromatic—and only added to Harper's sensual mood. She couldn't take her eyes off Jacob, finding him compelling and sinfully handsome in the firelight.

She asked him about the status of his meeting with Lattice lawyers and the copyright claimant to the company he wanted to buy. He talked openly about the man's claim, and ideas his legal team had for dealing with the issue. There wasn't a hint of suspicion toward her in his manner. She recalled how he'd been much less worried about her coming into contact with the secretary of defense in his home than Elizabeth had been. The realization that he *did* trust her with confidences—with certain key things, anyway—heartened her.

He wanted to know all about her meeting with Cyril and Ellie, and the progress on the film project. They were finishing their main course and laughing over one of Cyril's many acerbic comments that afternoon, when a breeze ruffled the surrounding ferns. Harper shivered.

Jacob stood and waved for her to get up from her chair, as well. "We'll move the table toward the fireplace. It's going to get down in the fifties tonight, and that dress doesn't offer a lot of protection, does it?"

She laughed at his heavy-lidded, appreciative stare at her breasts. She couldn't wear a bra with the dress because of its cut, and the breeze had made her nipples tighten. He'd clearly noticed.

She stood and together they scooted the table and their chairs toward the fire.

"It's nice that they have the fire lit. Labor Day weekend is usually pretty warm in San Francisco," she said when they were seated again.

"I called and asked Jason to light it when I saw the forecast," Jacob stated matter-of-factly. He noticed her surprised look. He reached across the table to grasp her hand. "I know how much you like a fire."

"I do, you're right," she said, smiling as she looked into his eyes.

The fire brought out the pinpricks of amber in them. He ran his fingertip across her palm, and she instinctively opened her hand, giving him free rein. They stared at one another for a stretched moment as he stroked her. A bubble of intimacy and security seemed to encapsulate them.

"A fire means warmth," she murmured, "but more importantly, it means safety."

His lambent stare went suddenly hard. His hand tightened on her wrist. "Why did you say that?"

She blinked, his question and taut grasp jerking her out of her sensual trance.

"Why did I say *what*?"

He leaned forward, his manner intent. Angry. *Hungry?*

"About the fire meaning warmth, but also safety?" he demanded.

Her mouth fell open in disbelief. She snatched her hand from his hold.

"What are you *talking* about?" she asked, utterly bewildered.

He didn't reply for a moment. He just studied her with that laser stare, like he was scanning her insides. Harper mentally squirmed under that harsh examination. Almost as quickly as his mood had shifted, he seemed to bring himself under control.

"It was nothing. I'm sorry," he said, leaning back and smoothing his tie, his expression suddenly unreadable.

"It wasn't nothing. *Jacob?*" He looked up and met her stare coolly. An uncomfortable thought swept through her. "Did . . . did what I say remind you of that other woman?"

"*No*. It's not that."

He noticed her openmouthed, stunned state.

"Harper, I'm with you. There *is* no other woman."

There was something about the way he said it, with such bone-deep, forceful confidence. Still . . . she'd seen that flash in his eyes when she'd asked about the other woman, like a window that was opened just for a moment before it was slammed shut again. She couldn't fathom the enigma of him.

"Jacob, what are you thinking right now?" Harper probed softly.

"Tell me what you're thinking first."

She blinked at his quick counter.

"I'm thinking that you're a puzzle I can't work out."

He gave a small, incredulous laugh, his reaction unsettling her even more.

"*What?*" she demanded.

He looked up when the waiter arrived to clear their dinner dishes.

"It just struck me as funny," she heard him say quietly. "I was just thinking the same thing about you."

twenty~nine

They made a careful return to the front entrance of the cave, Jake guiding Harper step by step on where to stand and walk so as not to leave a trail. After they'd returned, he went back into the second cave and the cliff ledge to retrieve the clothing they'd left there before their dive. When he returned, Harper had pulled their extra shirts out of the pack.

Once they'd dressed again in dry clothes, Jake insisted on checking Harper's abraded wrists beneath the plastic bandages she wore. He was pleased to see the signs of Emmitt's cruelty healing. He thought of suggesting that he doctor her again, cleaning the cuts in the waterfall and applying the ointment and bandages that he'd brought. It was a good excuse to touch her. But she stood close as he inspected her wrists, and he could smell her skin and the soap they'd used in the river, and his body was again reacting like it had a mind of his own. Instead, he gave her the ointment and bandages, and told her to go and wash and dress the cuts. When she returned, he'd steeled himself.

"I'm going out for a little bit, just to look around," he said.

"Let me go with you. Please?" she added when she noticed his stern expression at her request.

"I've got to sweep our trail from the river, just to make sure."

"But we were so careful coming back up!"

"I know, but . . . if you come with me, it'll just cause the problem all over again," he stated in a rush of frustrated honesty.

"Oh. You mean because of my lead feet," she sighed, looking hopeless.

"You're getting better," Jake offered, to ease the sting. She was looking around the cavern anxiously. The early morning sun no longer streamed into the opening between the rocks, making the large chamber shadowed and dark. He knew she was probably scared of being alone, but would never want to admit it.

"If you want, I'll build you a little fire. You can find a stick and toast some Pop-Tarts over it for our breakfast. But you've got to be real careful so they don't burn or fall in the fire 'cause we can't waste the food. Want to do it?"

She nodded eagerly. He built a small fire in the stone enclosure he'd fashioned years ago when he first discovered the cave. He left satisfied that she was less anxious with something to occupy her.

He returned after a twenty-minute scout, reporting to Harper that he saw no obvious indication that Emmitt was in the vicinity.

They spent the afternoon holed up in the cave, talking nonstop the whole time. Jacob wouldn't have believed he had so much inside him to say. Even though they came from very different worlds, they had their school life in common. They entertained each other by describing kids from school and who liked whom. They gossiped about their teachers. He listened with fascination to the activities of a city girl: going with her friends to the mall or to the movies, eating Thai or Italian takeout on Sunday afternoons and watching a movie with her parents, traveling around the DC area and suburbs for swim meets and lacrosse matches. He didn't tell her he didn't even know what lacrosse was.

Despite their differences, he was happy to learn that kids in Georgetown weren't all that different from kids in Poplar Gorge. There were nice ones, smart ones, jocks, populars, nerds, and loners. Then there were the crack babies and basket cases, names that mean kids called kids that just couldn't seem to function in the world.

"I know which ones you are," Jake said at one point, standing to gather some sticks for the fire. He kept a stash of fuel in the cavern.

"What do you mean?" Harper asked him from where she sat.

"You're a popular. And a brain. A nice one, too," he added, ducking his head to hide his embarrassment.

She laughed, and he thought her cheeks had turned pink.

When he returned, he carefully laid some dampened twigs on the fire to keep it smoldering versus burning high. He was thinking of the animal scat he'd seen in the second cavern. He needed a good fire ready at a moment's notice. He kept a pretty decent store of fuel in the cavern, but he'd still gather more before nightfall.

"I think I know which one you are, too," Harper told him smugly after several minutes, and he knew she was talking about the kinds of kids at school. His stomach sunk a little.

"A loner?" he mumbled, averting his face as he tended the fire. He hoped she didn't think he was a crack kid, given what she knew about where he lived and Emmitt's many crimes.

"Maybe a *little* of a loner. A little of a geek, too, but in a really good way. But mostly, you're the one to rule them all."

"What's that supposed to mean?" he asked, frowning. He laid the last twig and sat next to her.

She laughed. "It's from *Lord of the Rings*. You're not evil, like the ring is in the book. I don't mean that. I just mean you're in a category all your own. You're different. You'll probably rule over all of us someday: populars, geeks, and jocks combined."

He thought she meant it as a compliment, but wasn't sure. Maybe she was laughing at him.

As the sun started to dip in the sky, Jake left the cave again to do a little reconnaissance and retrieve more wood. Harper looked relieved when he returned and said he hadn't found anything of significance. She helped him stack the armful of wood he brought. For dinner, they shared a can of chicken noodle soup and a sleeve of saltines. Afterward, they drank cool water from a shared cup and continued talking.

As it got darker, their voices gradually grew more hushed and their laughter died. By the time full night settled, they huddled around their tiny fire, and their conversation waned. Jake wondered what she was thinking as she watched the flames so soberly.

"Jake?" she asked after a while.

"Yeah?"

"What's going to happen to you? After we get to Barterton?"

"I'll go wi h you to the police station. Don't worry. I'll tell them the truth about Emmitt," he said, staring at the glowing embers of the fire.

"But . . . what then?" He could tell by the wariness of her hushed voice she hadn't considered the question before.

"I'll go back and live with Grandma Rose."

"But I thought you said she was really sick, and they said you had to go with your uncle or into child services."

"That was when I was younger and couldn't take care of myself," he said dismissively, tamping down his anxiety over the topic. "I'm older now. I can take care of both myself and Grandma Rose." She didn't reply. His sideways glance told him she was worried. "They'll let me stay with Grandma Rose. Don't worry."

"But what if they don't?" she whispered. "You'll have to do whatever the police tell you to do."

He shrugged. "I'll run away, then. I'll come live here, in the cave."

"But what about school and everything?"

"Don't worry about it, Harper," he repeated shortly. Guilt immediately swooped through him for snapping at her, but he didn't know what to say to make her not worry. *He* certainly didn't have any good answers for her.

He stood and went to his pack, returning with an apple. Neither of them spoke as he retrieved his multi-tool from his jean pocket, extricating the sharp, six-inch blade. The tool was a treasured prize he'd found and claimed after a particularly drunken, wild party at Emmitt's after a vicious dogfight. He cut off a slice of apple and handed it to her. He cut a piece for himself, then for her again, trading off until only the core was left.

"I'll tell my parents about everything you did for me," she said after she'd swallowed her last bite. "I'll ask them to talk to the police and stuff, try to convince them to let you go stay with your grandma."

"Thanks," Jake muttered. In truth, he hadn't thought much about what would happen once he got Harper to the police. That had become the period at the end of the mission. He didn't like to think about the fact that he didn't have a home anymore, and that he'd possibly enter a world of strange adults and the courts and confusing, cold government organizations like Child Welfare Services.

Increasingly, he didn't like to think about the fact that once he got Harper to the police, her parents would soon be there to claim her and whisk her far off to Washington, DC, where he'd probably never see her again.

"I'm going to tell them about everything you gave up for me," Harper continued so forcefully that he glanced over at her in surprise. "I'm going to tell them, Jake. Don't worry. My parents are really nice, for adults I mean. I'm going to tell them that we want to stay friends. You could come and visit me in Georgetown."

He nodded, because he sensed her excitement on the topic and that she wanted him to agree. He tried to imagine it for a few seconds, him traveling all by himself—maybe in a train?—to Washington, DC, and finally seeing Harper's big house and her bedroom and the shelves filled with all her books. But no matter how hard he tried, he couldn't quite picture himself in her world. It was like he couldn't squeeze the concept of his mean existence into her shiny, clean one.

"I hate being a kid," he said dully after a moment.

Harper opened her mouth to reply, but that was when they first heard it: the distant, eerie shriek. The hellish sound seemed to echo off the walls and ceiling of the limestone cavern, amplifying it.

Jake leapt up and started feeding the fire, intent on creating a blaze.

"Jake? What *was* that?"

"Go get more wood," he told her, stirring the sparking embers forcefully.

She hurried to follow his direction. Maybe she sensed his urgency, because she didn't say anything else as he added fuel, building a healthy fire.

"What was it?" she repeated breathlessly when he finally straightened and stood next to her. Before he answered, they heard the ominous shriek tear through the dark night again.

"Mountain lion," he replied quietly, his head tilted as he listened intently.

"Will it come in here?" Harper asked in a high-pitched voice.

"Probably not," Jake said, glancing uneasily from the front to the back of the cave. "It's the first time I've seen spoor in here."

"Spoor?"

"Shit," he stated concisely. "It's the cat's. The mountain lion must have just found the cave. It's a new discovery for it, not a permanent den. I was hoping it wouldn't try and come back. I've never seen signs of one anytime that I've been here before."

"What do we do?"

Jake blinked and focused on Harper's face. She looked panicked. He could understand why. A mountain lion's scream was hair-raising. The first time hearing it would shake anyone.

"Nothing. We stay put." He urged her to sit next to him by the fire. "That's another thing you have to learn about the woods. A fire means warmth. But more importantly, it means safety. Mountain lions are afraid of fires. Most animals are."

She just stared at him for a moment, her face looking pale and her eyes huge in the light of the now-leaping flames. Another scream ripped through the silence. Harper jumped against him, her arms flying around his waist. He felt a shiver tear through her. The mountain lion sounded closer this time, but because of the echo factor of the river canyon, he couldn't discern if the wild cat was prowling at the front or the back of the cave, or even above them on the bluff. He couldn't know for sure which entrance the animal had used the first time, or whether it was familiar with both openings. *That's* what had him most worried.

For a few seconds, they waited tensely, listening. They heard only the crackle of the flames and the distant trickle of water.

"You've been keeping the fire going all day," she said tremulously. "You knew this might happen?"

He shook his head. "I was just worried it would. That's not the same thing."

Another terrifying shriek tore through the cave. Harper put her hands to her ears. "It's *horrible.*"

"I know, but it's harmless. And it sounds closer than it is," he assured, desperate to calm her anxiety even while his own mounted. "They come around Emmitt's place a lot, not only because of all the trash Emmitt leaves around, but they smell the dogs and puppies. They try to intimidate you with their screaming and squalling, but mountain lions are big bullies. All talk and no action."

"You mean they won't try to get in here and attack us?"

"Nah," he scoffed.

Slowly, she lowered her hands from her ears. She jumped when the demon cat growled again, but he saw that increasingly familiar resolve on her pale face. She was straining to hide her anxiety.

"Tell me about the swim team," he said impulsively when the mountain lion tore off another screech. It was definitely getting closer, and he was determined to keep Harper occupied. He thought the cat was circling closer toward the entrance at the back of the cave, but he couldn't be entirely certain. The only thing he could do was distract Harper while they waited, and he figured out which entrance the predator stalked. Once he knew that, he'd move them to the opposite side of the fire from where the cat approached. For now, he kept them cautiously at the side of the flames, both entrances to the right and left of him. "What's your stroke?" he prodded her.

"Freestyle and backstroke."

"Did you win many races?"

Their previous talk resumed, and this time they were even more animated, both of them determinedly ignoring the earsplitting screams and growls of the mountain lion as it prowled outside the cave. Jake knew the animal stalked them, so there was no call for being extra hushed. They talked for more than an hour, until a wild shriek resounded so deafeningly through the cavern, even Jake jumped. He crawled over Harper and pulled her along with him, so that their backs were now turned to the front entrance of the cave.

"Jake, what—"

But Jake had stood and grabbed more timber, feeding the fire.

"He's at the cliff entrance," he said tensely. "I wasn't sure if he was at the front or back before."

"Oh my God."

"Shhh, it's going to be okay," Jake said, gathering more wood and moving it closer to the fire, within easy reaching distance. He came down next to her, trying to see in the deep, murky shadows at the back of the first cave. His arms went out without thinking, closing around Harper when she crowded against him. He hugged her close. The mountain lion screamed again, the piercing sound enough to freeze his heart.

"It's in the *stalactite* cave," Harper whimpered the obvious. The mountain lion's shriek had echoed and rolled like thunder across the cave walls this time, the sound terrifyingly close. He could feel her shaking against him. He pulled her closer, and she smashed her face against his chest.

"What'd I tell you about the fire. Harper?" he prompted, and she knew she was listening with dread for the approaching cat.

"That it's not only for warmth, but for safety. And that mountain lions don't like it?" she asked in a tiny voice.

"That's right," he said, resting his chin on the top of her head and peering toward the entrance of the second cave. "He'll lose patience when he sees he can't get to us. He'll go hunt somewhere else when his hunger pains get the better of him."

"Really?" she asked in a quavering voice, her nose still pressed against his chest.

"Really." The bully cat shrieked again, seeming to rattle the whole cave. Harper shuddered.

"Jake—"

He stroked her hair, never taking his eyes off the back entrance.

"It's going to be okay. We've got the fire. Trust me. Tell me about *The Lord of the Rings*."

"What?" She sounded a little incredulous at his request.

"Yeah. Like a campfire story. We've got a fire. Tell me about it."

He sensed some of her terror receding slightly at that. If he was urging her to tell stories around the fire, maybe things couldn't be that bad. She started talking in a muffled, quavering voice about something called hobbits, which sounded to Jake like these easygoing, fat dwarves who lived in the woods. Just as she mentioned someone named Frodo, Jake saw it: the eyes of the mountain lion glowing at him from the cloaking darkness. The cat was about twenty-five feet away from their fire.

"What kind of a name is Frodo?" he muttered, still stroking her hair, subtly urging her to keep her face against his chest.

"It's a hobbit's name," she scolded, sniffing. "Just listen to the story, all right?"

"Sorry," he mumbled. She resumed the shaky telling of her story. He held her against him all the while, never flinching from the demon cat's stare.

thirty

Present Day

S he was bringing everything up to the surface. Jacob was frustrated as hell at her for that.

He was also wary, not to mention so damn curious, he thought he was going to lose it sometime soon.

Did she remember? Or didn't she?

Sometimes, it felt like all he could do to keep himself from grabbing her and demanding she tell him the truth about what she recalled about the August before her seventh-grade year. What did she remember about a sociopath called Emmitt Tharp, about being kidnapped, of escaping with scrawny Jake Tharp? She'd say things sometimes that seemed like echoes from their past: her onetime phobia for dogs and knives, her wistful musings about someone from her past helping her get over her fear of heights, what she'd said tonight about the fire being for security, not just warmth. Those things, and so many other small mentions on her part, made him wild with speculation and curiosity.

And yet . . . he'd searched her expression each time, and there would be no connection he could discern in her eyes between whatever hint she'd dropped and *him*—Jacob—the man present with her there in the moment. It was as if everything he'd told her about him remaking himself new every day was the literal truth, as if Jake Tharp and Jacob Latimer really were two different beings . . . that there was truly no connection for him to *find* in Harper's beautiful eyes. That rattled him nearly as much as the idea that she *did* remember him.

Maybe he really *had* killed off Jake Tharp in his single-minded mission to become Jacob Latimer. That concept used to reassure him. It'd been the only reason he allowed himself to indulge in a relationship with Harper. But increasingly, he searched for that connection not just because he dreaded it. He *wanted* her to remember Jake, to acknowledge that past connection and their shared history . . .

If only a little.

And that alteration in his attitude had him seriously on edge as they left Geb, and he opened the limo door for her. Because there was no *a little* in this scenario. She either remembered, or she didn't. Either he resolved to promote Harper's apparent amnesia, or he prodded her to recall more, tainting and altering his present-day world. Because it wouldn't just be the sweet, poignant moments of their time spent together that would jump out of that Pandora's box of memory. So many ugly, shameful secrets would spring out of the past as well, truths Jacob vigilantly guarded against. He'd figuratively killed off Jake Tharp so that Jacob Latimer could live and thrive.

And he'd been doing it so well, until she'd walked into his life again.

It wasn't just his concern about what Harper would do with those memories in regard to his life, either. He was worried for *her*, and that concern rose every minute he spent in her company. If her father had truly been successful in making her forget a traumatic kidnapping and assault at age twelve, then Jacob should be doing whatever he could to make sure those ugly memories stayed buried. He knew all too well what effect Emmitt's foulness had had on a victim less fortunate than Harper had been.

The conflict raged in him. The push-pull he experienced toward her mounted, the friction of it becoming unbearable.

The atmosphere in the private enclosure of the limo was almost as stifling and charged as it had been last night, after the opera, Jacob realized with a frown. They'd finished dinner soon after Harper's comment about the fire and Jacob's sharp questions and comments. They'd both skipped dessert and coffee, and had been polite enough with each other while Jacob took care of the check. Still, their former intimacy and warmth had vanished, only to be replaced by a growing, taut strain.

They rode in silence for twenty minutes. As Miguel, his driver, maneuvered them through tight Saturday evening traffic, he found himself unable to restrain his volatility any longer, however.

She sat on the seat across from him, staring out the window, the passing lights glimmering in the stones of the earrings he'd bought her. Her pure, striking profile was what drew his gaze, however, not the precious gems. He clenched his teeth.

God, he wanted her.

"There are times that I feel like you know more about me than you're letting on."

His words sounded harsh, cutting through the billowing silence of the dim, hushed limo. He recognized that a portion of his volatility stemmed from her aloofness at that moment . . . her untouchable quality. Because despite all his ambiguity and uncertainty toward her, the need to touch, to assure himself of her reciprocated need, never once waned. If anything, his hunger seemed to be growing exponentially in the face of his doubts.

She turned to him. He saw incredulity written large on her face.

"Why in the world would I know more about you than I'm telling you?" she demanded. He saw understanding slowly dawn on her face. "Do you think I'm putting on a show? To get a story about you? Did you talk to Cyril? Did he tell you I was asking questions about your background this afternoon?"

Cyril hadn't told him anything, but Jacob's expression didn't shift. His heartbeat began to thrum in his hears. "Cyril and I have been friends for years," he replied neutrally. "We don't keep a lot from each other."

She exhaled, shaking her head, the motion causing her long, lush hair to slide across her pale shoulders and arms. Desire and confusion clashed inside him, making his muscles tense hard.

"I told him I wasn't asking questions about you to get fuel for a story, or to use the information in any way that was harmful to you. I *told* him I was just trying to understand you better. Then he ran to tell you everything, apparently. You have him trained well," she stated bitterly, staring again out the window, her jaw tense. She suddenly made a desperate, disgusted sound and whipped her head around. "Why are you so convinced I want to hurt you?"

"Because you can."

She started. He, too, felt a little taken aback by his honest answer. He'd just admitted point-blank that he cared enough for her that she had the power to hurt him. After a stretched moment, she inhaled slowly.

"Because I have access to your homes? To your world? To you? Don't kid yourself. You haven't given *that* much away, Jacob. Besides, you've asked me to take risks for you," she breathed out coldly. "Maybe you're going to have to decide once and for all if you're willing to do the same for me. Oh . . . and once you make your choice, stop getting pissed off at me every time I remind you of someone else, or make you feel in the tiniest bit vulnerable. That's just the way being . . . with someone else works." She scoffed and rolled her eyes. He sensed her disgust at him, but also at herself. "I almost said 'being in a relationship.' Imagine me, saying that to Jacob Latimer."

"Harper—"

He cut himself off when the limo came to a halt. He realized in mounting frustration that he wasn't sure what he would have said to her, anyway. What he *could* say. He felt blocked at every turn.

They didn't speak as they approached the Sea Cliff house, and he keyed in a security code. She walked ahead of him when they entered, and headed directly for the stairs. He followed, his agitation swelling at the vision of her elegant, stiff back and shoulders. She was pissed, and good. But he wasn't exactly pleased at learning she'd been trying to pull answers from Cyril about him, either. They entered his suite and he slammed the door after him. His frothing frustration spilled over when, without pause, she walked briskly toward the guest bathroom.

He lunged toward her, grabbing her upper arm and spinning her to face him.

"You've got me twisted in every direction, Harper."

"I'm *so* sorry," she said, her voice dripping with sarcasm. "But *I'm* not responsible for your pissy moods."

He gripped her upper arm tight. "I haven't spoken to Cyril since I saw him with you this afternoon. I wasn't saying that you could hurt me because you have access to my life. I was saying it because I care about you. Too fucking much."

He saw her eyes widen slightly before he swooped down and kissed her. She stiffened at first, but he was so far gone, he didn't care. He required her taste, her scent, the sensation of her soft, firm lips moving against his. He bit at her lower lip, demanding she join him in this boiling lust. Instead, she bared her teeth, pressed closer to his body, and nipped him back. He saw red. Her hands clutched hard at his shoulders, and her fingers delved into his hair. The feeling of her nails scraping his scalp made savage arousal tear through him. He opened his hands along her sides, encompassing her slender torso, and plunged his tongue into her mouth.

Need assaulted him. He lifted her several inches off the floor and walked with her pressed tight against him. He set her on the edge of his bed, still feeding hungrily from her hot, responsive mouth. Everything seemed to be striking him in sharp, bullet-like flashes of awareness, like his brain was overloading with sensation. Her hands moved anxiously along his shoulders and neck, pulling him to her, urging him onto the bed. Before he came, however, he reached around her neck and unbuttoned the collar of her dress. He broke from their kiss, snarling at the deprivation of her mouth.

He jerked her dress down, baring her breasts. They felt so soft in his hands, so firm and sweet, the tight, coral-colored nipples killing him. They were his to touch—for now—and that knowledge unleashed a desperate excitement in him. He heard Harper's whimper through the blood pounding in his ears. The next thing he knew, he was pushing her back on his bed and coming down over her, clutching a condom in his hand.

Everything was cast in a haze as he fed again from her mouth, and her supple body writhed beneath him, fueling his lust.

Another flash of clarity came to him. He held his throbbing cock in his hand and was shoving her dress roughly up to her waist. There was a ripping sound of cloth, and he stared at the heaven of her pale, parted thighs and pink sex. He dipped a finger into her, growling at the sensation of her tight, lubricated sheath.

His groan ripped at his throat as he entered her a moment later. He thrust, his eyes rolling back in his head at the slicing pleasure of being submerged to the hilt. The haze cleared as he stared down at her tense, flushed face, reddened lips, and eyes that were shiny with lust. She was stunning. So gorgeous.

Harper.

Supporting himself on the mattress, he used his free hand to reach for her wrists. He pressed both her hands to the mattress above her head, his gaze fixed on her bare, vulnerable breasts rising and falling as she panted. He kept his hand there, restraining her and bracing his weight at once.

There was so much feeling inside him, he thought he'd explode from it. He wanted to feast on her breasts and her mouth. He wanted to taste every square inch of her skin. His hands itched to grab fistfuls of her lush, sexy hair. But he *needed* to take her now . . . to be buried deep inside her surrender.

"You make me so crazy," he grated out before he started to move.

His bed shook. She did. He knew he took her hard, and that he was ruthless. But he couldn't seem to stop himself. It was like something else drove him, some savage force that insisted he drown in her submission. He felt only a single-minded goal to possess her utterly.

At some point, he heard her cry out. He'd paused with his cock sunk deep and pressed his testicles and pelvis against her outer sex, circling his hips subtly, demanding that she burn for him. He registered her flushed face, saw it tighten even as her sex convulsed around him. She cried out his name. Heat rushed around his cock, and he was pounding into her again, fucking the core of her unfurling pleasure, slaking himself like a satyr on it.

Then he was kneeling over her, panting, shucking the condom off his pulsing, rigid cock. He jerked viciously. The sweet pain in him swelled and broke, and he was coming on her pale thigh as wave after wave of pleasure shook him.

His harsh breathing entered his awareness. Slowly, the haze began to recede. He looked down at the bed. Harper lay there, panting, her dress shoved down below her breasts and up to her waist. He fisted his cock hard. A stream of ejaculate still clung between the damp head and Harper's thigh. He noticed something black clinging to the top of her leg. It was wet with his come. He realized it was Harper's thong. He hadn't ripped her panties all the way off her, but just tore through the fabric at one hip before shoving it partially down the opposite thigh. Once the heaven of her had been revealed, nothing had mattered but being deep inside her.

His lungs burning, he dared to look at her face. Her eyes were damp, and her cheeks and lips were flushed. She looked thoroughly debauched . . . and incredibly beautiful. She looked like a woman who had just survived a brutal storm.

He inhaled raggedly at the thought. He'd been that storm.

"Are you all right?"

She nodded. She appeared to be holding her breath.

"Jacob . . . what *is* it?" A single tear trickled out of one eye. "What's haunting you? Please tell me."

Her pressured whisper cut straight through him. He felt completely transparent. He came off the bed. His pants and underwear were bunched above his knees. He flinched. He hadn't even taken off his suit jacket or tie, for Christ's sake. What the hell was wrong with him?

"Let me get something to clean you up," he muttered, hitching his pants and underwear up before he walked away.

. . .

Harper had never been so shaken. She watched him walk toward his bathroom. How could he be feeling so much, and yet keep it locked deep inside the impenetrable shell of his everyday persona? It'd been like he was exorcising his demons when he'd made love to her just now. Harper had been only too glad to be the target of his angst. Even in the midst of his anguish, he hadn't failed to excite her. Pleasure her. In fact, her arousal had been sharp and urgent. She'd looked the true Jacob Latimer in the face there for several pleasure-infused minutes, and witnessed the full extent of his power . . . of his pain.

But she'd seen the way the shutters came down over his eyes as he stood by the bed just now.

No. He wasn't going to be making any more revelations anytime soon, she realized with a sinking feeling.

If ever.

But he had told her he cared, hadn't he? Wasn't his volatility a result of him admitting that to her, and to himself?

When he returned to the bed, she saw that he'd changed into dark blue pajama bottoms. Otherwise, he was nude. He didn't speak as he sat on the edge of the bed. He removed her dress over her head and carefully drew the thong he'd torn off her leg. He took off her pumps, his touch on her achingly tender. She watched him as he solemnly washed away his essence from her skin with a warm, damp cloth and then dried her with a towel. Emotion swelled in her chest cavity. *Such a beautiful, haunted man.*

There was nothing she could think of to say. Everything seemed trite and without substance in comparison to what she experienced on the inside. Even her doubts were washed away by an onslaught of raw feeling.

When he'd finished and set aside the towel and cloth, she shifted on the bed, crawling under the covers. She put her arms up to him, and he came on the bed with her. He held her tight against him, stroking her hair. She felt that inexplicable bond between them surge and quiver, almost like it was a living thing.

He smoothed back her hair with his hand and pressed his lips to her temple.

"I hate wearing a condom with you," he said in a hoarse voice next to her skin. "I hate even that coming between us."

She made a sound of anguished longing and pressed closer to him.

"Harper?" He nudged her cheek and she lifted her head to look at him. "Are you on birth control?"

"Yes," she whispered.

"When we get back to Tahoe, let's have a doctor examine us both. If we get clean bills of health, I want to be inside you. No more barriers."

"Okay," she agreed shakily, unable there, in his arms, to say anything different.

He opened his hand along the side of her head, holding her stare.

"And I want you to spend the nights with me when we return, too."

"Every one?" she asked, stunned.

He nodded. "For as many as possible. For as many nights as we need, I want you with me. And I want you to know that *I'm* there. I don't want you wondering—or doubting—because we're separated."

"You mean wondering if you're with another woman?" she asked, the image of the beautiful, troubled Regina leaping into her mind's eye against her will.

"I don't want you doubting or worrying about anything. I don't want to worry about you."

"I worry about the end," she admitted impulsively, her face and throat tightening with emotion. "*Our* end. Especially if I agree to what you're proposing."

Because wasn't that the unspoken part of his proposal? Wasn't he saying that their attraction was so strong, that they may as well play it out at its fullest, give the fire all the fuel it demanded until it banked, and they were finally free of the compulsion of it?

Or at least . . . one of them was. Her fear about getting involved with him surged inside her.

His hand shifted on her head, his fingers stroking her hair. She'd never seen so much compassion in his agate eyes than she did at that moment.

"It's too late, Harper. I care too much, whether I wanted to or not. I think you feel it, too. We can't go back, only forward. No matter what happens. Surely you sense that, too?"

She made a choked sound and pressed her cheek to his chest. Neither the word *yes* or the word *no* would leave her throat. She felt trapped. His mouth pressed against the top of her head.

It would be nice to believe that she had a solid choice in all this, to cling to the idea that she would never willingly steer herself toward catastrophe or heartache. She hugged him tighter and sensed the powerful bond between them tighten until it hurt. Maybe the volatile attraction between them would eventually wane; who knew?

But maybe Jacob was right.

In that full, poignant moment with him, Harper couldn't help but wonder wildly if it were even *possible* for either her fears or Jacob's ghosts to sever their bond.

By the time it came for them to leave San Francisco on Sunday morning, Jacob hadn't pressed Harper any further about his proposal for her to stay with him in his Tahoe mansion as much as was possible. She couldn't decide if she was glad or disappointed about that.

She kept thinking about his unexpected mood shifts. Was he moody like that with everyone? No. Somehow, she didn't think he was.

It's me who has him so edgy.

She detailed in her mind the topics they'd been discussing when he behaved so strangely, trying to make sense of what had touched him off. Her ruminations only made her more confused.

When they returned to Tahoe Shores at around noon, Harper peered out the sedan window onto a gorgeous, crystalline summer day.

Tahoe Shores brimmed with bustling vacationers, everyone seeming intent on squeezing every last bit of fun out of the waning summer. Lakeview Boulevard was lined bumper-to-bumper with beachgoers' cars.

Harper's attention on what was happening outside the window was fractured slightly when Jacob received a call from Elizabeth. He'd told her that Elizabeth had gone with Regina back to Napa. Was his assistant calling because there was more trouble? He barely said more than five words to Elizabeth before he hung up. He opened his briefcase and pulled out a newspaper he'd bought at the airport in San Francisco. He began leafing through it.

"Look at all the cars and people," Harper murmured.

"It is a holiday weekend," Jacob said distractedly, frowning down at the newspaper.

"Is something wrong?" Harper asked him.

"No, not at all," he replied briskly, folding up the paper and shoving it back in his briefcase. Jim had picked them up at the airport. Jacob opened up the window to the driver's area of the car and spoke to him.

"Can you take us to Harper's first? She's going to run in and get some things to take to my place, then come right back out."

Her heart jumped. Again, she had that feeling of being trapped between her desire and caution. She longed to be with him, of course, to indulge in the lush, sensual connection they shared. She wanted it *too* much. The velocity of their growing attachment to one another, the sheer power of it, left her vaguely panicked that they were on a path together that could only end in catastrophe.

And that didn't even take into account that she was increasingly feeling like she wasn't fully getting what was going on with her and Jacob . . . what was going on with *him*.

"Jacob, I really should run some errands and check the mail," she prevaricated when Jim pulled up to her townhome entrance. She leaned forward to hand Jim the clicker that activated the privacy gate.

She looked back at Jacob when he grasped her extended hand, and was abruptly caught in his stare.

He'd dressed casually for their return trip to Tahoe in jeans and a forest green collarless shirt that emphasized his riveting eyes and broad shoulders. He pulled her hand into his lap and pushed a button, and the window between them and Jim silently closed. She didn't say anything when he silently drew her against him, his hand at her lower back. She put her hands palms down on his chest and inhaled his scent, her logic about why she should resist his demands already melting.

He touched her hair. "It's still the weekend. Still the holiday. Surely you can wait to do errands."

She pressed her nose to his chest and inhaled, sacrificing her last remnants of resistance. His fingers moved in her hair, and she shivered. He slid two fingers beneath her chin and lifted it, so that she met his stare.

"Do you really want to go home?"

"No," she whispered.

"Then why are you hesitating?" he asked, his brows slanting.

"It's nothing." She shrugged helplessly. It was hard to put her insecurities into words. "I just have this feeling—"

The sedan came to a halt outside her townhome. Jacob's hold on her didn't flinch.

"What kind of feeling?" he asked.

"That the faster we go, the more intense we are, the quicker it will end," she admitted.

"You can't know that, Harper."

"I know I can't," she admitted, staring at his chest. "I told you. It's just this feeling."

"Of dread?"

She looked up sharply, stunned by his insight. "Yes."

He nodded. "I think I know what you mean."

"You *do*?"

"Yeah. But it's like I said last night. We can't go back. We can't tread water. The only way to go is forward." He caressed her cheek, and she instinctively moved her face toward his touch. "Besides. It's not just dread, what I'm feeling. Far from it, Harper. Is it for you?"

"God, no. I wouldn't be here, if it were. But aren't you even a little worried we're moving too fast?" she asked softly. *That there's some big unnamable thing happening, something either threatening or wondrous.* She couldn't tell which . . .

"I told you before. I don't think I can be with you in any way but all the way. One hundred percent. Look at me." She met his stare reluctantly. "Everything's going to be okay, Harper. Trust me."

She drank in his quiet confidence. How could she be so intimidated by him and everything he represented, and yet feel incredibly secure with him at the same time?

"The only thing you have to agree to is this afternoon. Tonight," he said.

"What about tomorrow night? And the night after that? You said in San Francisco that you wanted us to spend every night together that we could—"

"Then I'll take it back, if it makes you feel better about it. I guess I'll just have to talk you into every night each day at a time." He reached up the back of her head firmly, his gaze on her a smoldering demand. "I want you with me tonight. I want to go out on the boat and spoil you a little, and make love to you a lot. I want to watch the fireworks with you and fall asleep under the stars with you in my arms. Do you think you can manage that?"

She stared at him, her lips parting in bemused arousal. "How do you do that?" she whispered. She felt his little smile like a tickle in her lower belly.

"Is that a yes?" he murmured.

Of course it was. She was beginning to wonder if she'd lost the ability to even say *no* in his presence.

Harper returned to the sedan a few minutes later, having emptied her clothes from San Francisco and replaced them hastily with clean ones and a few more toiletries.

"Did you bring a swimsuit?" he asked her when she returned, and they resumed their journey via limo to his home.

She glanced over at him and saw his nearly imperceptible smile. "Of course I did. You didn't think I was going to wear that itsy-bitsy one from before, did you?"

He shrugged as if he didn't see the problem. "I liked that swimsuit."

She snorted with laughter, her anxiety fracturing, her happiness swelling when he grinned full out and reached for her, bringing her against him.

Even as she drowned in the bliss of the moment, a flickering, dark thought took shape. Jacob hugged her closer, and it faded.

But maybe it burrowed into her unconscious, like a persistent worm.

How had it happened, that she'd fallen to this dangerous depth, when she was so unsure of him? How was it even *possible* that he could disarm her so completely, when she'd only known him for such a short period of time?

Admit it, Harper.

Why was she having so much difficulty acknowledging her growing, unsettling suspicions to herself?

Because what you're considering isn't a remote possibility, that's why. Because to actually *believe you've known Jacob Latimer in some other time or place—in some other life—is to admit that you're losing it.*

It was just her confusion and longing making her consider such bizarre possibilities. Everything was blending together: her grief over her parents' sudden death, her ruminations about her childhood, and Jacob's inexplicable, powerful effect on her.

The present loss was making her relive the past one.

It hit her then, how odd it was that he'd told her she reminded her of someone else, when she'd been making similar connections, *impossible* comparisons. For the most part, her musings seemed totally wrong, nonsensical . . . just plain crazy.

She rubbed her cheek against Jacob's chest and stared out the window, tears filling her eyes. Jacob pulled her closer against him. The pain of what she'd done so long ago had dulled over the years. But at that moment, the memory of that childhood ghost—that beautiful, brave boy—rose and stabbed at her brutally.

He'd vanished from her life. But unlike in the case of her parents, Harper herself had been the one responsible for *that* loss.

7

make me
REMEMBER

thirty~one

Before he could make good on his compelling promises about taking her to his yacht, spoiling her a little, and making love to her a lot for the rest of the holiday weekend, Jacob had planned ahead to see through another promise he'd made, Harper realized.

Elizabeth was apparently off—or was she still in Napa on the mission Jacob had sent her on to watch over Regina Morrow? Harper didn't have time to clarify the uncomfortable question, because Lisa—Jacob's friendly cook—greeted them in the front entryway of his Tahoe mansion instead of Elizabeth.

"Dr. Amorantz is waiting for you in the den," Lisa told Jacob as she reached for Harper's duffel with a smile. Harper relinquished her bag dubiously.

"What's she talking about? Who's Dr. Amorantz?" Harper whispered to Jacob when he took her hand and led her through the great room.

Jacob explained in a hushed, clipped tone that Amorantz was there to give them exams and draw their blood, all for the purpose of allowing them to have unprotected sex.

"It should only take a few minutes," he assured as they entered the hallway behind the stairs. "Then we can go and change and get out on the water."

"I can't believe you planned all this," she told him, stunned. Jacob abruptly came to a halt when she spoke.

"I told you I was going to, didn't I?"

"Yes, but—" A bark of laughter left her throat. "I just meant that I don't know when you had the time. I've been with you all night and all morning."

He shrugged slightly, as if he thought her concern was inconsequential. "It was easy enough to arrange. Amorantz is my private physician. He often makes house calls."

His insouciant manner made her suspicion finally take shape.

"Jacob, have you *done* this before? With other women?"

His relaxed posture vanished. His face went hard and his stare suddenly seemed to bore down into her.

"No," he said.

"It's just . . . you make this all seem so routine."

He grasped her upper arms and pulled her closer.

"There's nothing routine about you. Nothing routine about us. Haven't you figured that out yet?"

Her mouth fell open at his fierceness. "Yes, I just—"

"You can't believe that *I've* figured it out? Is that it? Just how stupid do you think I am?"

"Jacob, that's not fair," she hissed.

"Do you have a specific objection to us having medical tests to make sure we're healthy for sex, other than the fact that you think I do this as a routine with women?"

"*No*. And I didn't mean—"

"Then you have no grounds for concern. I've never done this before. I've used protection without fail in the past. I just have this . . . this . . ." Her eyes widened when he looked a little wild for a few seconds. "*Compulsion* to have you completely."

She absorbed his frown. "You don't look very happy about it." She'd said out loud a thought she'd been having increasingly. Her heart jumped when he leaned down and claimed her mouth in a deep, hot kiss. He squeezed her arms, bringing her closer to him.

"I'm *not* happy about it at times, to be honest . . . usually when I'm not in your presence. Because when I'm with you, all I can think of is having you full throttle, no holds barred. Nothing between us. Nothing," he snarled next to her lips. "Do you want to do this or not, Harper?"

"Yes," she whispered irritably. "Because apparently, I'm every bit as compelled as you."

He sunk his head again, but this time, she was ready for him. Their kiss was hot and wholesale.

And because of that tense, charged interaction between them in that hallway, Dr. Amorantz was forced to wait even longer than he already had.

The exam and blood test weren't the most comfortable things in the world for Harper to do, given the fact that she didn't even know Amorantz. Jacob had chosen well as far as a private physician, however. Amorantz was friendly, professional, and seemed very competent. The process was over relatively quickly and painlessly, at any rate, leaving Jacob and her to focus on the promise of spending the rest of the holiday weekend together.

Harper found her sense of vacation excitement mounting later that afternoon as they walked together onto Jacob's dock, Jacob wearing swim trunks and a T-shirt, Harper a bathing suit, flip-flops, and a beach cover-up. Jim had just been sent ahead of them on a Jet Ski, his instructions to deliver a large picnic basket that Lisa had packed for them along with some other supplies to Jacob's moored yacht. Harper got onto the Jet Ski behind Jacob.

"I've never been on one of these things before," she told him, her voice brimming with excitement as she hugged his waist and pressed tight against his back.

"I'd ask if you wanted to drive it, but it feels too good having you as a passenger," he said with his chin over his shoulder, his mouth tilted in amusement. She just pressed her smile against his sun-warmed T-shirt, all too happy to have him in the driver's seat at that moment, as well.

When they reached his yacht, Jim was just getting on his tied-up Jet Ski, his errand complete.

"The ramp is down," Jim yelled. The two men exchanged a wave, and Jacob circled the Jet Ski to the back of the yacht. He took them out a distance. Looking back over her shoulder, Harper saw what Jim had been referring to, a fiberglass ramp that descended from the bottom deck of the yacht into the water.

"Hang on tight," Jacob said as he circled in the water, turning them back in the direction of the yacht.

"What?" Harper asked in confusion. Her eyes widened when he gunned the engine on the Jet Ski, and suddenly they were racing straight at the yacht. She tightened her arms around him, staring wide-eyed over his broad back. They were about to collide with the yacht any second. What was Jacob *doing*?

They hit the ramp and jumped out of the air suddenly, flying forward. Her stomach leapt into her throat. Her yell of surprise was cut off when they landed and slid to an abrupt, startling halt. Jacob had cut the engine. He stood, clambering off the craft onto his yacht as if jumping out of the water onto a boat was the most mundane of tasks. He noticed her stunned expression.

"You could have warned me," she told him, half-amused, half-beleaguered as she stood on rubbery legs and took his hand.

"It was a lot more fun not to," he said, and even though he wore sunglasses, she knew that behind the opaque lenses, his eyes were warm and gleaming with humor.

There was a lovely breeze coming across the wide expanse of brilliant blue water, but the sun was intense. Harper opted to lounge on the sectional outdoor sofa on the top deck, enjoying the warm sun while Jacob drove. She could see him piloting the yacht from where she reclined, her head propped up on several pillows. She languidly applied some sunscreen to her bikini-clad body, all too satisfied to watch his skillful handling of the craft from a distance.

After she'd finished applying the lotion, she took another sip of the delicious drink Jacob had made her when they came on board. He'd said he didn't know if it had an official name, but he called it rum therapy. She started to get what he meant, lying there in the sun, her muscles growing heavy and warm and her mind going increasingly blank in regard to everyday concerns. . .

And about the increasing anxiety and the strange thoughts she'd been having about Jacob.

After a while, the engine cut and the boat slowed and came to a standstill in the glistening, serene waters.

Jacob approached a moment later, shrugging off his T-shirt. He slouched comfortably near her feet, one arm draped on the back of the sofa. He grabbed her foot and squeezed gently, kneading the muscles. It felt divine. She smiled, soaking up the image of his bronzed, muscular torso and casual posture. Jacob was always magnetically sexy, but she found him the most compelling when he was like this: relaxed, yet still emanating what she could only call potent amounts of sexual magnetism without appearing to even be aware of his power.

"It's nice, isn't it?" she asked contently.

She sensed his stare moving over her body behind his sunglasses. *There* it was, she thought, a thrill going through her. His simmering sexuality and possessive aura were never far off. Having grown used to his checkouts, she didn't need to see his eyes to feel the heat in his gaze.

"You're right. This one *is* better," he said, and she knew he referred to her teal blue bikini. His big hand transferred to her shin, his fingers massaging her calf. Her sex tingled in pleasure at his touch.

"Thanks," she murmured.

"Your skin is warm."

"The sun is hot." His firm lips curved in a small smile. They stared at each other as he continued to slide his hand against her skin and mold the muscle to his palm. His massaging hand transferred to her thigh.

"I can't get over how smooth you are. How soft." His deep, mellow voice rushed over her, a huge factor in her growing sensual trance. So was the hot, drugging sun, the strong drink, the vision of his male beauty against the backdrop of a deep blue sky, not to mention his languorous, delicious rub of her muscles. His long fingers stretched upward on her thigh. He gently raked his blunt fingertips into muscle. She sighed in pleasure, the ache in her mounting at the nearness of his fingers to her sex.

"It really is hot," he said quietly. "Do you want to go for a swim?"

"Okay," she replied weakly.

His arm came off the back of the couch and he twisted slightly in his seat, leaning toward her. At the new angle, he grasped a good portion of her thigh with his large hand, rubbing her deep. She moaned softly.

"Or would you rather come first?" he asked.

Her lips parted and breath rushed out of her lungs. He really said the damnedest things sometimes.

"Harper?"

"Yes," she whispered. "I mean, if you want to."

"Why wouldn't I want to?" He slid his hands beneath both her knees and hauled her toward him. She cried out in surprise at his sudden move, laughing when she came to rest with her thighs lying across his lap. Without any other buildup, he soberly drew her bikini bottoms down several inches and opened his hand on her lower belly. His thumb slid down between her labia, rubbing her clit. She gasped, her laughter forgotten.

"Feel good?" he asked, and Harper realized her eyes had fallen closed as her body tightened with pleasure. She opened her eyelids and saw him peering down at her.

"It feels fantastic," she managed.

"Good. Just relax and enjoy it."

"*Jacob*," she whispered, her face tightening. He'd somehow caught the notes of her languorous, sensual mood, and now he played it. Amplified it. The pressure of his big hand on her belly felt wonderful. His thumb tapped and rubbed her slick clit unerringly. She could feel his arousal on the backs of her thighs, but the sensation of his swollen cock only added to the sweet, unhurried moment. With his free hand, he continued to massage her legs with lazy strength. The sun beat down on her, and somehow she was melting and tensing at once. She gave herself to the heat, simmering beneath his fingertip. And all the while, she was aware of his steady stare on her face. She'd never felt so prized.

So safe.

It didn't take long until she was shaking in orgasm.

"That's right," he soothed even as his finger quickened, working the shudders out of her tensing flesh. "You're so pretty when you come."

A pleasure-infused moment later, he leaned down and kissed the skin just below the juncture of her rib cage.

She lifted her hand and combed her fingers through his short, burnished hair. He ran his lips along a rib, and she sighed in sublime pleasure. He lifted his head and looked down at her face, a small smile on his lips.

"Ready for that swim now?"

She blinked, dumbfounded by his question. She could feel his cock beneath her thighs. The engorged shaft pulsed subtly against her skin. "Don't you want to—"

"Yeah," he interrupted, as though he was saying the obvious. "But this was just for you."

She sat up partially, propping her body up on her elbows. "But—"

"I'll have my moments, Harper. Don't have any concerns about that," he cut her off wryly, scooping her legs up with a forearm beneath her knees and tipping her playfully off his lap. She caught herself with feet on the deck, her body twisting on the sofa. He glanced down at her naked hip and buttock, his stare sticking.

"Come on." He stood abruptly. "Let's get in the water before I change my mind," he said, his mouth going hard as he held out a hand for her.

For the first time, Harper looked over the railing and saw where he'd anchored the yacht. They were in a small, brilliantly blue and emerald cove surrounded by granite boulders and majestic, towering pines.

Instead of leading her down to the second deck to swim, where there was a small pool and deck, or onto the main deck, where they could have accessed the lake for swimming, Jacob led her over to a diving board on the top level.

"What do you think?" he asked her. "Are you up for it?"

She stood at the rail and looked down. Through the clear water, she could see all the way down to the bottom of the lake to the smooth boulders resting there.

"How deep is it here?" she asked Jacob.

"About thirty feet. If we make our way inland, it gets shallow. And there's a sand beach. Good for swimming."

"I haven't taken a high dive in a long, long time."

"Would you rather swim in the pool or off the foredeck?"

She turned and examined his face, searching. There'd been something in his voice just then. Or had it been her imagination? He still wore his sunglasses, though. She couldn't discern any trace of emotion on his face.

"We could jump together," he suggested quietly.

She blinked, the bright sun and his deep voice making her feel disoriented for a moment . . . giving her a profound sense of déjà vu.

"All right," she agreed slowly.

He whipped off his glasses. A moment later, they stood together at the tip of the board suspended over the water, their arms wrapped tight around each other, her heart beating like crazy. She was a little anxious about the jump, but that's not what was making her heart chug like a locomotive. It felt so secure, being wrapped in his arms and pressed against his solid body. It felt so good. He was still erect. His virility and strength seemed to flow into her, fortifying her.

And yet there was that lingering feeling of the unnamed, a feeling that raised the hair on her arms and nape and cast the vivid day and beautiful man with a glow of the surreal . . .

Almost like magic.

"You ready?" he asked, bowing his head down over her upturned face.

"Yes."

"Jump away from the boat," he directed.

She nodded, excitement bubbling in her veins. "On the count of three?"

"Okay. One . . ."

"Two," she counted.

The second seemed to stretch.

Look where you're going, not where you've been. The voice flew into her consciousness. Again, that feeling of incredulous disorientation came over her as she stared up at the amber, green, and brown pin-points of color in his irises.

"*Jake*," she muttered dazedly at the same moment that he shouted, "*Three!*"

And they were flying through the air, hugging each other like they thought their lives depended on it.

Hitting the cold, refreshing water with such force seemed to scatter her strange, dreamlike mood. Or perhaps her thoughts were so confusing, she willingly repressed them to fully glory in the moment.

They swam for over an hour in the serene, sparkling inlet, talking, playing, and holding each other in the shallow water. It was the most carefree and relaxed she'd ever allowed herself to be with him. She thought he seemed just as happy as her, as eager to forget the rest of the world and sink into the warm intimacy of their togetherness. He let her touch him as much as she wanted, and she relished in her free rein, running her hands all over his back and muscular arms, skimming them across his long legs while they were twined together. She wanted to touch him sexually, too. The cold water had dampened his former arousal somewhat, but his cock still felt long and firm as their bodies pressed together. When she started to cup and caress the delicious weight of his arousal in her hand, he halted her.

"Let it wait," he said, drawing her hand away, and pulling her pelvis closer against his cock. They'd been clinging together in about five feet of water, Jacob's feet on the sandy bottom and her legs wrapped around his hips. Despite what he'd said, she felt his cock swell as he pressed her sex against him.

"But you made me feel so good up there," she murmured near his wet, firm lips. "I want to return the favor."

He kissed her softly. "It wasn't a favor. I did it because I wanted to. I like watching you come. I like knowing I made you feel good," he said gruffly. His mouth fastened on hers again.

"Nothing you said is an argument for me not to make you come here and now. Everything you said is true for me, too," she said breathlessly once their mouths parted.

His eyebrows went up in a droll expression at the same time his hands lowered beneath her swimsuit bottoms and cupped the cheeks.

"I wasn't aware we were arguing. I was just stating a fact. I want to let it build." She gasped softly at the feeling of him squeezing her bare ass lasciviously and grinding her pussy against his cock.

"It doesn't really feel like you want to wait," she said dubiously.

His grin broke free. He smacked her bottom as briskly as he could while underwater and she jumped.

"Do you want to learn how to drive the Jet Ski?" he asked her, pulling away.

And despite the fact that she was disappointed to leave his arms, his idea sounded interesting.

"Can I learn how to pop it up out of the water onto the boat like you did?" she asked, swimming after him toward the yacht.

"Maybe next lesson," she heard him say dryly over his shoulder, and she laughed. She was reminded that not only was he a mind-blowing lover and sexy enigma: Jacob was also just really fun to be with.

After they'd played around on the Jet Ski in the bright sunshine for another hour or so, and Harper had become a competent driver of it, she told him she was starving. It was past time for them to head in, anyway, Jacob realized. Harper's cheeks, nose, and chest were pink from the sun, and as they'd gotten off the Jet Ski, he'd noticed that her eyelids looked heavy.

They showered off on the outdoor shower enclosure and made their way to the galley. There, they investigated the contents of the picnic hamper that Lisa had prepared for them. They settled on freshly made salmon and California rolls along with a banana-and-mango salsa. They ate on the foredeck of the boat in the shade. By the time Harper had eaten their early supper and drank a half glass of white wine, she was having difficulty keeping her eyelids open. He was glad she was so relaxed. She looked happy, and that gratified him. He'd wanted that, for her to feel secure and carefree. He knew she was having second thoughts about the wisdom of going deeper with him.

True, he had his *own* doubts about his wisdom in demanding more from her. But he despised seeing Harper anxious about him . . . about them. And despite his concerns, both for himself and for her well-being, he was selfish. He wanted her wholesale.

"Come on," he said presently, standing from the high-top table and reaching for her hand.

"Where are we going?" she asked, blinking and forcing her eyelids open.

"I'm taking you to bed."

"Oh," she said, suddenly looking more alert, the pink, full lips that had been torturing him all day curving into a smile.

"To take a nap. You look wrung out." He gave a bark of laughter at her scowl.

"I didn't know this was here," she said from behind him a moment later when he'd led her downstairs and opened the door to a bedroom suite.

"Bathroom is through there." He pointed at a door. He flipped back the comforter and the sheet on the large bed and waved her toward him. He forced his face into impassivity as he removed the pretty, sexy blue bikini she wore, the one that matched both her eyes and the shimmering alpine lake, and molded her body in a way that had made him fantasize repeatedly all afternoon, primarily about two topics: either burying his face in between the glory of her high, full breasts or the heaven between her thighs.

He jerked his gaze away from her pale, exposed breasts now, urging her toward the bed.

"You're not getting in with me?" she asked as he pulled the sheet up over her naked body, and then the duvet. She'd definitely gotten sun today, and she looked like a sexy, sweet decadence against the dark gray sheets.

"I'm not tired," he said, sitting at the edge of the bed. "I'm going to take the boat up the coast a bit and position us for the fireworks."

"You mean the ones that you sponsor every year?"

"Who told you about that?" Her hair had mostly dried as they'd eaten their meal. He pushed some copper strands off her temple and smoothed them away from her face.

"Jim mentioned it the other night. But it's common knowledge, isn't it? That you sponsor the Labor Day fireworks for Tahoe Shores? I hope it is, because it was mentioned in an article we did for the holiday weekend version of the *Gazette*," she added wryly.

"I guess it is generally known, yeah. The city council couldn't make a secret of it."

"You're nicer than you want people to think you are."

He paused in stroking her.

"I don't care if people think I'm nice or a troll."

"Liar. You're a good person, and it bugs you when people assume otherwise," she mumbled. A poignant feeling of longing went through him. Her utter confidence in him reminded him of the Harper of old. He wanted to believe her like he had when he was a kid, but his innocence was lost. He'd sacrificed it to become Jacob Latimer.

Since he couldn't agree, he just caressed her silently for a moment. He loved to see her reaction to his touch. He always had, even when they were kids. It was fresh, immediate evidence that he meant something to her. Her reaction at the moment was for her eyelids to drift closed. Despite her obvious contentment, he found he couldn't stop himself from setting something straight with her right then and there.

"Harper, honey?"

"Yeah?" she asked, her eyelids rising a fraction of an inch with apparent effort. The sun had really gotten to her. He was going to demand a lot of her later. That's why he wanted to make sure she was rested.

"When we were on the diving board earlier, before we jumped?"

"Mmm-hmm"

"You called me Jake."

Her eyelids snapped open wider.

"I . . . I did?"

He nodded, closely studying her reaction. Unlike on other occasions when he'd cautiously tested her, he thought he'd seen a flash of anxiety in her eyes.

"Why did you call me that?" he asked tensely.

"I don't know," she whispered warily. "Why? Is it a big deal? Jake is short for Jacob—"

"No one calls me that."

She winced at his sharpness, and he cringed inwardly. She nodded in agreement. "Okay, I won't anymore, then."

"No," he bit out. Recognizing how unreasonable he was being, he leaned down and kissed her brow, trying to smooth his uncertainty and confusion. He spoke quietly near her ear, like he was imparting a secret. "*You* can. If you want to, I mean."

He stood and turned away so that she couldn't see his irritation at his abrupt, irrational change of mind.

thirty~two

Twenty Years Ago

She awoke to the feeling of Jake's hand in her hair and the sound of gentle rain falling. She opened her eyes and saw the cave cast in the deep, gray gloom of early dawn. Memories shot through her, horrifying recollections of the mountain lion's screams rolling off the walls of the cave, of how the predator had stalked them all through the night like a living nightmare.

Sweet memories of the boy holding her and containing her fear also crowded her brain.

"Jake?"

"I'm right here," he said, and again, he stroked her hair.

Her eyes clamped shut at the sound of his reassuring drawl. His voice and his embrace had become her touchstone during that terrifying, seemingly never-ending night. Several times, she'd felt her very being fraying and splintering upon hearing the shrieks of the mountain lion resounding so close to them, sensing the animal's feral hunger and imagining its sharp, white teeth. Then Jake would speak to her in that even tone of his, prompting her to tell him more about *Lord of the Rings*, or reassuring her that they didn't have long now.

"Dawn'll be here soon. He'll go then. You can bet on it."

She sat up abruptly, breaking contact with his warm body. A jolt of panic went through her when she saw the dying embers of their fire. Those flames had come to mean safety to her, and life.

The fire had . . . and Jake.

"It's gone?" she asked turning toward him, her eyes wide. She couldn't believe she'd fallen asleep in the middle of so much terror. It was a testament to how much she'd come to trust Jake Tharp.

She made out his outline in the semidarkness: his scraggly, longish dark blond hair and shoulders. She knew from firsthand knowledge that his hair was thick and soft and that his shoulders, though narrow, were stronger than she would ever have imagined.

Just like the rest of him was.

"It gave up about a half hour before dawn," he said. She watched him as he stood. He was slight and young, but she had the impression he was about eighty years old in that moment. Not only because he always came off as being wiser and more patient than anybody she'd ever known, but because he moved like an old man as he stood from the hard cave floor.

"You held me all night," she said regretfully as she rushed to her feet. He hadn't moved positions since they'd first known where the mountain lion was and put the fire between it and themselves. "You must be so stiff."

"No, just—"

She hugged him impulsively, inhaling the smell of soap from his long, unruly hair. He'd told her yesterday while they'd talked all day in the cave that Emmitt grudgingly would give him money for a haircut every year when school started, but that it grew faster than weeds during a wet season. Grandma Rose used to cut it for him when she was better, but lately, he'd taken to cutting it himself. He'd looked a little embarrassed when he'd admitted that. He'd also said that he wasn't any good at it, so this summer, he'd just let it grow wild.

Harper experienced a surge of emotion thinking about the boy she held in her arms at that moment, his courage, and his kindness . . . and everything he'd given up for her. Her eyes burned. She didn't know how to thank him, though. What she felt was too big to squeeze out of the fullness in her chest and through her narrow throat. She delved her fingers into his soft, thick hair instead.

"I'll cut your hair later. You have some scissors on that fancy knife thing you have," she said through a congested throat. His arms closed around her. He'd sensed her ragged state. She clamped her eyelids shut even tighter, a strange mixture of guilt and relief going through her at his unselfish embrace.

"That's okay, Harper." It wasn't *fair* that such a young kid was forced to sound that grown-up . . . so wise, so *tired*, at age thirteen.

"I want to," burst out of her throat. "You saved us. You took care of me all night, and kept me from freaking out and everything. I want to do something for you." *Because both of us know I haven't got much to give you in return.*

She let go of him abruptly, stepping out of the circle of his arms. She quickly swiped at her damp cheeks and attempted a smile. "I'll cut your hair, okay?" she repeated brightly when she'd composed herself.

"Yeah. Okay."

She was eager to get past her rush of gratitude and embarrassing show of emotion. Jake looked really uncomfortable.

"Can we do the cliff jump again?" she asked him, kneeling to help him scoop some dirt and ash onto the fire. There was just enough light entering the cave now that she could make out the shine of his eyes when he met her stare.

"No. We can't take the chance that the mountain lion won't come back tonight. We have to go. Besides, it's raining out right now, and it's a good steady one. The rain will help to cover our tracks. I've got an old camp tarp stored here. We'll wrap what we can in it, keep our stuff protected from the rain. We're leaving for Barterton as soon as we get packed up."

Present Day

Harper's eyes flew open at the sound of footsteps. She turned over in the soft sheets. There was a wide chest of drawers just across from the bed and a long mirror hung above it. In the reflection, she saw her long, mussed hair and sunburned, damp cheeks. She wiped at her face at the realization, amazed to feel tears on her fingertips. Whatever she'd been dreaming about had made her cry, she realized in wonderment. But no matter how hard she tried, she couldn't pull any details of her dream from her brain. Only a sense of poignant sweetness and sadness remained.

She sensed the subtle movement of the boat. They were anchored. Had Jacob moved the boat while she slept, as he'd said he would? She didn't recall a bit of it. The yacht was large enough that waves didn't rock it much, but there was still a subtle bobbing motion that she found soothing. She could tell by the color and slant of the sunlight coming through the window that she'd slept for over an hour, and that evening had fallen. When she pushed back the comforter, she saw Jacob standing in the open doorway, his hands braced at the top of frame.

"Hi," she greeted him, propping herself up on the pillows but never ungluing her gaze from the sight of him. She'd never been happier to see him. He'd changed into a pair of dark blue shorts, but he wasn't wearing anything else. His smooth skin had grown a shade darker in the sunshine today. There was a shadow of stubble on his jaw, and his burnished hair looked windblown. She drank in the sight of him thirstily.

"I was beginning to think you were going to sleep all night," he said, stepping into the bedroom suite. His brows arched as he sat on the edge of the bed next to her. "Why are you smiling like that?"

"You look so relaxed standing there in the doorway. So nice," she replied. She reached out to touch his hard midriff. His taut abdomen muscles jumped slightly at her touch. She ran a fingertip down the silky trail of brown hair that led from below his belly button down below his shorts. "I was just thinking when I woke up . . ."

"What?" he asked when she faded off.

She swallowed, and shook her head slightly. Sleep and her dreams still clung heavily to her. "Have you ever noticed that some of the worst, scariest things that ever happened to you in your life were also the best?"

He caught the wrist of her stroking hand and squeezed gently. She looked up at him.

"What makes you say that?" he asked.

"I don't know," she mumbled, curling up on her side beneath the sheet, all too aware of his sharp gaze on her. "I just woke up thinking that."

He put his hand on her shoulder and rolled her onto her back. Her heart jumped when she saw his tense expression. He leaned down over her.

"Do you really believe that, Harper? That the good things can be mixed up so closely with the bad?"

"Yes. I think so," she whispered, her heartbeat starting to pound in her ears at his intensity.

"Is that what you think it's like, to be with me? Scary?"

"A little, yeah," she whispered, staring into his hypnotic eyes. "But it's wonderful, too. So much so that I would never want to give up the beautiful part, because of the fear."

"That's what I've been trying to tell you about us being together more."

"I know. I know it is," she whispered emphatically, reaching up to touch his mussed hair. She dragged her fingers through it, loving the sensation against her skin.

He straightened and her hand fell away from him.

"I'm not going to let you push me out because you're afraid, Harper."

"No. I don't want you to."

His face looked achingly sober and beautiful when he reached for the edge of the sheet. Slowly and deliberately, he drew it down to below her thighs. He opened his hand along her hip and caressed the side of her naked body, then her ribs and belly. Her breath stuck in her lungs at the expression on his face . . . at a touch that she could only call worshipful. He caressed her thigh and then opened his hand over her outer sex, lightly rubbing her. Warm, achy arousal flooded through her. She felt it again, that sense of being cherished.

Possessed.

"Turn over," he directed huskily. "Stretch your arms over your head."

She did what he asked, pressing her cheek to the pillow, her arms above her head. That increasingly familiar, full feeling had swelled in her chest. He swept her unbound hair over one shoulder, baring her completely. Pleasure unfurled inside her as he began to caress her . . .

As he silently owned her.

He traced the lines of her shoulders and her spine. He touched the back of her knees and her thighs, and cupped her buttocks gently in his palms.

"Spread your thighs," he said, and she did, feeling the cool air tickle at her damp sex. She held her breath. When he did penetrate her with his finger, air flew out of her lungs. She lay there as he stroked her, drowning in sensual pleasure and mounting excitement. Soft moans vibrated her throat as he took her higher. Just when her body began to tense, he withdrew his finger and used both hands to part her buttocks. Her ass clenched tight at the unexpected exposure. She waited, her body subtly vibrating with arousal.

He lightly brushed a fingertip over her anus. She whimpered softly.

"I want you everywhere, Harper," he said gruffly from behind her. "I want to know you'd allow it. I need it. For me. Do you think that's selfish?"

She couldn't draw air. The moment felt almost unbearably intimate. He continued to spread her ass cheeks, making her entire sex, perineum, and anus tingle beneath his stare. Not for the first time with him, she experienced that potent sharp feeling of arousal at the idea of him taking control, of him finding so much pleasure and release in her body. She thought of how he always gave her so much in return . . . of how strangely safe she felt with him.

"Maybe. But then . . . I like when you're selfish sometimes." And your selfishness isn't like any selfishness I've ever known.

He grunted softly and again ran a blunt fingertip between the crack of her ass, caressing her softly. She tensed in excited trepidation.

"Then I'm going to tie up your wrists and put a dildo in you. Get you ready. Then I'm going to use a spreader bar on you. And I'm going to have you."

Her sex clenched tight in arousal. She wasn't entirely sure what he'd meant, except for the certainty that he planned to penetrate her anally. But her excitement was spiked with trepidation.

"Won't it hurt?"

He released the tension in his hold, ceasing spreading her buttocks wide but still keeping his hands on her ass, rubbing the cheeks tautly.

"You've never done it before?"

"No." She'd never been interested before. With him, it would signify a deeper level of surrender, though. Of possession. *That* excited her. She found herself craving it, maybe even as greatly as Jacob seemed to hunger for this deeper level of intimacy and surrender with her.

His thumbs dug deep into the muscles of her ass.

"It will hurt for a moment maybe, especially with my cock. I'm going to get you ready, though. If there is pain, it will be over quickly."

"What's a spreader bar?"

"It's just a metal bar that's about two and a half feet wide. It has four restraints on it. I'm going to have you stand, and then attach the bar to your ankles. It will force you to keep your legs spread open. Then you'll bend over, and I'll restrain your wrists to the bar. You won't be able to move while I have you."

She stared at him openmouthed over her shoulder, shocked by his calm recital of the facts.

"Do you *want* to hurt me, Jacob?" she asked shakily.

"No. How can you ask me that?" he replied harshly. "I want to *have* you. Completely. I've told you before, *that's* what turns me on. Not pain."

"You'll keep me safe?"

"Always," he replied, his gaze growing extra fierce.

"Then, yes."

He immediately released her and stood next to the bed. She almost turned to watch what he was doing, but realized she could see his reflection in the mirror over the chest of drawers as he crossed the bedroom. He opened what she assumed was a closet door and went inside. When he appeared again, she saw what he carried. Her thighs closed and tightened to alleviate the spike of arousal that went through her. In one hand, he carried a long metal rod; in the other was a bundle of black rope.

Her breathing had grown choppy from arousal by the time he stood next to the bed again, blocking her view in the mirror. Not that she needed the mirror to notice the heavy bulge at the front of his shorts as he leaned the spreader bar on the far side of the bedside table. On top of the table, he set down what appeared to be a package of— she strained to see—antiseptic towelettes? He turned toward her with the rope in hand.

"You can stay just like that, but pull your knees up under you, bottom in the air," he directed, staring down at her.

Harper took the position, bending her knees beneath her, her breasts pressed against the mattress, her arms stretched above her head, one cheek turned into a pillow . . . ass in the air.

"That's good," he muttered thickly. "Wrists together, palms inward."

He put a knee on the edge of the mattress and leaned down, binding her wrists and forearms with several loops of the black silk rope. His body was just inches away from her face while he restrained her, his cock right in her field of vision. She felt that familiar, forbidden sense of anticipation building in her. From the size and apparent weight of his erection, she wasn't alone in her sharp arousal.

He lifted his knee off the mattress and stood again, opening a bedside table. She watched him as he withdrew both a bottle of lubricant and a box.

"It's new," he said quietly as he tore his thumb through the plastic and opened the box. He withdrew a black dildo. It was slender, about six inches long with a thick base. Its shape was realistically cock-like.

"Do you ever use one of these?" he asked her. Something about the way he held it up for her inspection made her thighs tighten to alleviate a stab of arousal.

"No. I have a vibrator, but . . . no. Not one of those."

He picked up the lubricant.

It was pure erotic torture, watching him smooth the shiny lube onto the dildo with his fingers while she watched, her arms restrained above her head.

Her ass in the air.

Finally he set down the bottle of lubricant and came onto the mattress behind her. He positioned himself on his knees next to her bottom. His body was on the opposite side of hers—and the mirror. Heat scorched her cheeks when she realized she could see everything clearly in the reflection. He held the lubricated dildo in his left hand and stared down at her, his expression grim.

"Raise your ass some, Harper."

She bit her lower lip and rose on her haunches, lifting her ass higher in the air. He reached with his right hand, and she realized his fingers were still glossy from the lubricant. With no buildup, he buried his fingers in the crack of her ass and rubbed a fingertip against her asshole.

She jumped.

"I know it probably feels strange, but try not to resist it. It'll make things harder on you, if you do." He pressed his fingertip tighter against her. "Push back against me. It'll go in easier that way."

She bit her lower lip and applied a firm pressure against his finger. He slid into her ass. She moaned.

"That's right," he murmured.

He began to fuck her with his finger. At first, Harper was overwhelmed with a strange combination of shame and arousal. She could see him in the mirror, watching himself as he penetrated her ass firmly with his forefinger, his face rigid. She clenched her eyelids shut. No sooner had she done it, however, than she craved the image of him again. Even in this, she found him compelling. Maybe *especially* in this. He pumped his hand faster, a snarl shaping his mouth. His opened his hand and gently slapped her curving buttocks every time he penetrated her with his finger.

She groaned. His gaze flickered up. For an electric moment, their gazes met in the mirror. Holding her stare, he opened his hand and pressed it against her ass cheeks, his finger sunk deep inside her.

"I'm glad you're a virgin," he said quietly. "Not only because it's going to feel so fucking good inside you. I'm glad because *I'm* the one." He squeezed her buttocks in his hand and pressed again, sending his finger higher inside her. A small smile flickered over his hard mouth. "Does *that* make me selfish?"

"No," she gasped. A subtle trembling had started in her body. "Because I'm glad, too."

He groaned roughly, pressing tighter with his finger, plumping her cheeks in his palm. Then he withdrew, and this time he pressed two fingers against her.

"Press back."

A soughing sigh left her lungs when he entered her. She lay there, watching him penetrate her slowly. Then he slowly, firmly began to fuck her with them. Increasingly, her arousal trumped any anxiety or embarrassment. *He* did. But her shame and uncertainty added a surprisingly potent erotic jolt to the moment, as well. As did having full view of him while he did something so shockingly intimate. Her clit began to simmer at the anal stimulation . . . at the vision of him dominating her. He plunged his fingers deep and grimaced.

"Your ass is hot. You're starting to like it, aren't you?" he rasped. "Harper?" he asked sharply, meeting her stare in the mirror when she didn't answer.

"Yes," she whispered.

"Look at you," he said, and there was a harsh edge to his tone as he examined her in the mirror through a narrowed gaze. She thought she might know what he meant. Her cheeks and lips were flaming pink, and it had little to do with her sunburn. He said something under his breath, and she thought it was a curse. He withdrew his fingers from her ass. He transferred the lubricated dildo to his right hand, and her eyes widened.

"Don't be afraid," he said, obviously sensing her tension. "You're ready for it." He spread back one cheek and pressed the tip of the dildo next to her opening.

He spread his big left hand at the top of her ass, encompassing both cheeks, and gripped her. "Come back on it, honey," he said. He pushed with the dildo at the same time he guided her movement, using his hand on her ass to pull her against the rubber tip.

"Oh," she cried out sharply.

He halted by clutching at her ass and keeping her in place.

"Just give it a few seconds," he said, and indeed, the sharp moment of pain when he'd pierced her with the head of the dildo passed almost instantly. "Better?" he asked, and she nodded her head on the pillow. She was being honest. There was only pressure and mounting excitement at the vision of him pushing the sex toy into her. He looked up and caught her staring at him fixedly in the mirror.

"You like to watch?" he murmured, his voice a deep, sexy growl before he began to pulse the dildo in and out of her, guiding the subtle movement with his grip on her buttocks. She moaned at the mounting pressure. "Answer me, Harper."

"Yes," she replied shakily.

"There's no reason you shouldn't. You look amazing," he said, appearing thoroughly intent on his task. "You *felt* like heaven."

He worked the sex toy into her gently, but firmly, sinking it farther and farther with each pass. Harper lay there panting, increasingly aroused and spellbound by the image of them in the mirror. Her nipples had grown very stiff against the sheet, and her breasts ached. She couldn't believe how much her clit simmered from the anal stimulation. She burned for pressure on her sex.

Finally, he plunged the dildo into her until only the square base remained exposed. He gave a low, rough growl, and his hand tightened on her ass cheeks, making her an immobile target. He flexed his hips forward and pressed his swollen cock against the side of her bottom. At the same moment, he pushed firmly on the base of the sex toy, keeping it deep in her ass. Harper's cry of shaky arousal combined with his guttural groan. She wasn't really aware of doing it, but suddenly, she was bucking her hips slightly, trying to increase the pressure.

"Hold still," Jacob grated out, his finger sinking into her buttocks to control her movement, his biceps bulging to keep her in place. Harper stilled herself with effort, her mouth hanging open as she panted shallowly. Everything burned. Her cheeks, her nipples, her sex, the soles of her feet. The sensation of his heavy erection pressing against the side of her ass felt both intimidating and fiercely arousing.

He kept her in place for the next minute while he fucked her firmly with the dildo. Harper turned her face into the pillow, suppressing a squeal of anguished arousal. He must have known her cry was from excitement, not discomfort, because he fucked her harder with the sex toy.

"You like it?" he rasped.

"Yes," she squeezed out of her throat into the pillow.

"Turn your face back to the mirror," he demanded. "Watch yourself. You're so gorgeous, Harper."

She turned her cheek on the pillow, both because he ordered her to and because she wanted to. He fucked her with the lubricated dildo for another unbearably tense moment, still holding her ass possessively with his left hand, his enormous erection pulsing against her ass and hip.

She groaned roughly. His gaze met hers in the mirror. Her face was tight with agonized excitement. Suddenly, he was holding the base tight against her ass cheeks with his thumb and clambering off the bed to his feet. She whimpered.

"Hold still," he ordered tensely, one arm extended to hold the sex toy inside her, the other stretching to the bedside table. He picked up both the package of towelettes she'd noticed earlier and the bottle of lubricant, and came back onto the bed. Harper watched, panting uncontrollably, as he released his hold on the base of the dildo for long enough to rip open the package of towelettes.

"Jacob?"

"It's okay. Just a second."

While he rapidly cleaned both of his hands, the dildo started to slide out of her ass. He tossed the towelettes aside and pressed the dildo back into her, making her gasp. Then he reached between her legs and stringently rubbed her clit.

She screamed.

Orgasm ripped through her. He continued to stimulate her clit while he penetrated her rapidly with the dildo.

Harper came back to herself a moment later, blinking open her eyelids dazedly, bliss still rippling through her, to see him pulling the black sex toy almost completely out of her ass only to plunge it back in a quick, ruthless rhythm. After a moment, he looked up and saw her watching him in the mirror. A snarl shaped his mouth.

"You're the most beautiful thing I've ever seen," he said, drawing the dildo completely out of her. He reached across her, grasping her far hip, holding her firmly while he ground his heavy cock against her.

"You are," she replied in ragged disbelief, because in that moment, she'd never seen anything as awe inspiring as the savage, blazing desire exposed on his face as he stared down at her.

He was losing his mind, he thought as he hastened off the bed. He was about to be cut wide-open by the sharp, ripping claws of undiluted need. His lust—his longing—was so single-minded that he almost passed on using the spreader bar, the thought of getting back on the bed and just taking her then and there taunting him.

She'd been so incredible, though. So responsive. The idea of having her completely at his mercy, of thoroughly possessing her, battered at his consciousness.

Using every last shred of restraint he had remaining, he unbound her hands from the rope and urged her to stand next to the bed.

"Spread your legs and bend over," he instructed, one hand at the small of her back. He already knew that she was very flexible, but he'd never had her in this particular position before. She bent with supple ease at the waist, her long, copper-colored hair slipping over her shoulders and hanging in the air. He slid his hand down to her ass, spreading her. His cock lurched, making him wince. The vision of her elegant back, round, firm ass, and pink, glossy sex pounded at his consciousness. He felt like one giant, throbbing ache.

Grimly, he turned away from the sight of her, reaching for the spreader bar.

He got the bar on her in record time. When he'd finished, she stood with the bar bound to her ankles, immobilizing her legs so that her thighs were spread wide. There were two cuffs at the center of the bar, where he restrained her wrists. He stood next to her, caressing her ass. He spread her buttocks with both hands and listened to her soft whimper. Liking the sound so much, he reached between her thighs and rubbed her clit. Her sharp cry of surprise segued to a moan.

"God, you're drenched," he grated out.

She was so lovely. And she was his. The strangest mixture of tenderness and cutting, rabid lust coursed through him. Grimacing, he cupped his balls and the root of his cock and backed away from her. He jerked his shorts off and reached into the bedside drawer for a condom. He *hated* that thin barrier, but until they'd both been given the okay medically, he knew he didn't have a choice.

"You okay, Harper?" he asked as he rolled the condom on his turgid cock and walked behind her.

"Yes, but I wish I could see you," he heard her say in a muffled voice. He reached for the bottle of lubricant on the bed.

"I know," he said, flipping open the cap. He poured a liberal amount of lubricant on his cock. He fisted the shaft, spreading the silky fluid. "It's your eyes, though. They always make me lose control, and this is going to be a trial as it is."

"But—"

"I told you this was for me, Harper," he interrupted quietly, peeling back an ass cheek. He pressed the tip of his cock to her. "I need to have you like this. Completely. The next time we do this, not even a damn condom is going to separate us. Do you understand?" he asked with as much patience as he could muster.

"Yes," he heard her say.

He reached around her hip and slid his fingertip between her labia. She moaned. He felt her tense.

"Jac . . . Jacob. Oh God."

She started to shudder in orgasm.

"God *bless* it, girl," he muttered tensely, incredulous at her responsiveness.

He thrust, pushing his cockhead into her ass. She made a squeaking sound, but he rubbed her clit harder. She cried out sharply, her orgasm spiking. He felt her tremors with the tip of his cock. "Christ, you're hot," he groaned, grimacing as he nursed her through her climax. Finally, he couldn't take the torture anymore. "I'm sorry, honey." He gripped her ass in both hands, his thumbs prying back the cheeks slightly. He flexed his hips, sliding his cock into her clamping heat another few inches. "I *have* to do this now."

He saw the fine trembling of her back and heard her sharp cries. He sunk further into the heaven of her, compelled.

As always.

Harper felt like she'd overloaded. She'd been intensely aroused by having the spreader placed between her ankles and then having her wrists cuffed to the bar. Her excitement confused her, as well. Why would she like being bent over and restrained in such a fashion? Jacob had said it was up to them, and them alone, to decide what they wanted sexually and what was sick or shameful. But then he'd said what really made her understand her excitement: *I told you this was for me, Harper.*

She loved the idea of being utterly possessed by him, but she *craved* the knowledge that this powerful, in-control man would lose himself for a blissful moment of time, finding pleasure and release in her body. She wanted to give him that. If she had her way, she'd sacrifice even more of herself.

She clenched her teeth together as he firmly began to saw his cock in and out of her ass. There had been pain at first, when he'd squeezed that succulent cockhead into her, but her orgasm had distracted her. Now there was only intense pressure and a growing sense of wonder. There must be more nerves in her ass than she'd ever realized before. She felt his cock in her body more keenly than she ever had. He was rigid and swollen, the surface tension of the shaft both intimidating and arousing.

He held her ass tightly and sunk into her deeper. "Oh, yeah. God, you feel good." She heard it in his groan, his sharp excitement. His splintering control. And suddenly, something clicked for her, and she understood him better than she ever had before.

"Fuck me, Jacob. Please."

A primal growl rattled his throat, and then he was thrusting.

What followed was both savage and soulful. She gave more of herself than she ever had before, offering it all up. Because somehow, she got what he meant when he said that he needed it this way. Required it. He was like a starved man who needed to drown in decadence in order to assure himself that he *could*. Incredibly, he seemed to sense her total surrender to the moment.

"That's right, just take it. Take me, Harper," he rasped before he drove into her to the hilt, and she gasped loudly.

There was nothing she could do. In the position he'd placed her in, all she could do was feel. Absorb him. After several moments of straining caution, he began to thrust even harder, the sound of their bodies smacking together and his grunts of pleasure raining down on her. His hold on her ass tightened to counterbalance the strength of his strokes into her. She trusted completely that he'd keep her steady. Safe. She imagined him behind her, losing himself to an orgy of pleasure. Was he watching himself fuck her in the mirror, his face rigid, his eyes burning with excitement? It aroused her intensely, as did—strangely—the knowledge that there wouldn't be any release for her in those tense, erotic moments. The spreader bar prohibited her from getting much pressure on her sex, although the indirect friction was mind-blowing.

After several taut moments of rattling her world, she felt his cock swell in her and his thrusts grew faster, his pelvis popping against her ass in a harsh staccato beat. She gritted her teeth. He wasn't hurting her, but the experience was intense. He thrust deep, his fingers digging into her buttocks. A low, primitive-sounding growl vibrated in his throat. She felt his cock jerk in her and bit her lip.

A growl tore out of his throat. Harper felt that groan in the core of her being. She'd never before experienced a lover's orgasm so personally. She wasn't coming at the same time as him, but somehow . . . she was coming *with* him.

thirty~three

E ven before his harsh breathing had begun to ease, he withdrew and bent behind her, releasing her from the spreader bar.

"Slowly," he instructed as he helped her to straighten, his hands on her shoulders. Harper understood what he meant. She felt disoriented and a little dizzy, not only from having blood flow toward her head for a period of time, but from extended arousal. "Stand still a moment," he murmured when she looked over her shoulder at him, and immediately started to go into his arms.

She waited, watching his tense face and the rapid rise and fall of his powerful chest.

"Okay?" he asked after a moment of holding her upright.

She nodded.

"Then come here." He swept down and planted a hard kiss on her mouth, grabbing her hand at the same time.

He led her to the bathroom and opened the glass door to the shower. Harper turned on the water while he disposed of the condom. Then they were standing under the hot water together. He held her tight against him, running his hands up and down the length of her wet body. He didn't say anything, but the fullness of the moment left a tightness in her chest.

"You gave so much of yourself," he said, his mouth moving against her ear and then her neck. "Thank you, Harper."

"You always give so much to me," she replied through a tight throat. She clutched at the dense muscle of his shoulders, emotion flooding her.

"Shhh," he soothed softly, nudging her chin with his nose. How was it he always knew what was happening inside her? She lifted her face, and his mouth fastened on hers.

He washed her after that, his hands on her body a sensual worship. He brought her to climax while he held her, his mouth eating up her sharp cries. And as she recovered from his deep, intoxicating kiss, she finally acknowledged that something had changed. Nothing would ever be the same again.

Not between her and Jacob.

Not ever in her life.

Harper said she was fine after that, but there was a dazed quality to her that made him worry he'd taken too much from her and worn her out yet again. After they'd dressed and left the bedroom, twilight had fallen. He led her up to the galley, where they made a tray laden with Lisa's fried chicken, salad, two small strawberry crème brûlées and a bottle of chardonnay. They took it to the top deck to eat. He demolished the meal, his hunger made sharp by the memory of their lovemaking . . . by the light in Harper's eyes. He'd never felt her smiles so deeply as he did that night, under the light of the setting sun.

After they'd eaten, they took their wineglasses to the rail and gazed out across the rippling water as night slowly descended.

"Is that the fireworks barge there?" Harper asked, pointing toward shore and the dark shape on the water in the distance.

"That's it," he murmured, nuzzling her fragrant neck. She'd thrown on a gold sundress after they'd gotten out of the shower, leaving part of her sun-kissed back and her shoulders bare. He stroked her silky skin as they looked out at the darkening water. He seemed incapable of stopping touching her.

"Why did you start sponsoring the fireworks?" she asked, her relaxed, mellow voice making him think the meal had revived her. He urged her with his hand on her upper arms, and she curled against him, her back to his front, both of them facing the shimmering lake. He wore only a pair of shorts. Her exposed skin felt good against his own.

"I like fireworks."

She twisted her chin and looked up at him, and he sensed her amused exasperation at his enigmatic answer. He smiled.

"I never saw a firework display until I was almost sixteen years old. Every kid should have an opportunity to see fireworks a couple times a year. It should be a summertime childhood guarantee. Fireworks. Ice cream. A barbecue. Maybe I can't supply the ice cream and the barbecue to everyone, but I can provide the show."

She spun in his loose hold and put her hand at the back of his neck, beckoning him. He noticed the blazing quality of her eyes, and then he was sinking into her sweet, generous kiss.

Jacob reclined against some pillows on the sofa, and she lay between his long legs, her head resting in his lap. He'd brought out a blanket. She snuggled beneath it, warm and content beneath it and next to the heat of his body. He'd turned on a stereo earlier, and the sounds of classical music swirled around them in the darkness. She looked up at the brilliant fireworks display in the sky, but her entire awareness was caught up in the sensation of his fingertips lightly skimming her bare shoulder, the feeling of his body beneath her and his long, strong legs bracketing her. She stopped fighting it. For the first time, she accepted the full, sweet feeling in her chest.

She'd fallen in love with him. And there, in that moment shared so completely with him under the stars with colorful fireworks shooting across the sky, she knew that no matter what happened, no matter how short or long their time together, she would do it all again. He was a man who deserved to be loved unselfishly. Wholesale. For all of his many glories. For all of his sadness.

For all of his secrets.

Twenty Years Ago

Jake drove them hard all that day, only allowing them brief respites for food and water. This wasn't hiking like Harper was used to doing with her parents, an easy stroll through pre-blazed trails. This was grueling, sweaty work made even more challenging by the fact that Jake was as fastidious and careful in their movements in the forest as he was ruthless in keeping them traveling at a brisk pace. If they broke a branch during that exhausting ten-hour trudge, Harper would have been shocked. He insisted they move through the territory with utmost caution. She came to admire his agility in the woods, his almost dancerlike avoidance of trees and brittle brush beneath his feet. She came to resent it, too, as the warm summer day wore on and her fatigue mounted. Not just her exhaustion weighed on her. The first several hours of their hike had been undertaken in the rain. The wet, in combination with the fact that Jake's old tennis shoes were a little large on her, had brought out a blister on her right heel. The pain became excruciating.

"Jake, I can't take any more of this. We gotta stop. Please?" she begged him through a parched throat. They'd just approached a clear stream and Jake had bent to refill their canteen. The coolness coming off the water and the soothing sound of the trickling brook had made her long for peace and rest.

He stood and handed her the canteen. She drank from it greedily and then handed it back to him.

"Why are you crying?" he asked her sharply.

"What?" she touched her face dazedly. "It's this blister," she admitted, lifting her foot. "It hurts so bad." She blinked at the sound of his curse and looked down to where he stared. Crimson blood had leaked through the dirt-stained white canvas.

"God damn it, Harper. Come here."

She followed him and sat where he directed, sitting on a large rock beside the stream. He pulled out of his pack the familiar first-aid equipment they'd used for her wrists. He washed her foot in the cold water. She gritted her teeth at the mixed feeling of pain and relief.

Jake noticed.

"You should have said something."

"I didn't want to complain," she grated out miserably. "You've seemed so worried ever since we left the cave."

"We're out in the open now. We're vulnerable," he said irritably as he dried the blister with a corner of a blanket. He smeared on some antibiotic ointment and then bandaged her. For the hundredth time since she'd first met Jake, she wondered at how such a skinny kid could make her feel like she was in the hands of a competent adult. He could make her feel like a stupid little kid like some adults could, too. "Your feet are important, Harper. You should have told me when you first thought you were getting a blister."

"I was trying not to complain," she repeated. Unwanted tears swelled in her eyes, products of her fear and exhaustion . . . and shame at the irritation in his tone. He was scared, and seeing his fear undid her.

He glanced around the forest distractedly as he pulled an extra pair of socks out of their pack.

"Shit. They got a little damp," he said, grimacing at the socks.

"I don't care."

"I do," he snapped. "Don't you know anything? We need to keep your feet dry, damn it."

"Well excuse me! I'm sorry I can't control whether or not I get a blister. You were pushing us like we were on some kind of a death march."

"The *marching* part isn't death," he seethed. "The standing still is. If Emmitt *has* caught our trail, he'll catch up, and it ain't gonna be pretty when he does."

She started back at his harsh statement. After a few seconds, he seemed to focus in on her face. He clenched his eyelids shut. She saw the muscles in his thin neck convulse as he swallowed.

"Do you think you can make it another half hour or so?" he asked her levelly after a moment. "There's a place up ahead that offers a little shelter. We can camp there for the night, and leave at first light."

"You wanted to keep going until night comes. It can't be much more than four or five o'clock, can it?" she asked, miserable at seeing his fraying nerves, hating that she was the one holding them back on their flight to safety.

He shoved her foot into a sock. "It's going to be all right. Just answer me. Do you think you can make it?"

"Yes. I'm sorry, Jake."

He looked every bit as miserable as she felt when he looked up at her, the bloody tennis shoe clasped in his hand.

"It's not your fault," he said. "I'm sorry for . . . you know."

"You don't have to apologize. You have a right to be scared, Jake. We're just kids. You don't always have to be so brave for me."

He ducked his head. She knew, because of that invisible bond they shared, that he was embarrassed.

"We'll be scared together, okay?" she asked, forcing a grin. Somehow, witnessing his flash of fear and watching how he carefully contained it made her want to be there for him. "And we'll be brave together, too. And you're right. Everything will be okay." She reached down and took the tennis shoe from him, hiding her wince as she put it back on.

That night, they camped out on the edge of a bluff that was obscured by trees and a rocky overhang. They put out the slightly damp blankets and clothing to dry. Harper insisted that she hold up to her promise and cut his hair. Afterward, Jake carefully cleaned up the dark blond strands and buried them under a rock.

"I did a good job," Harper told him later, reaching out to comb her fingers through his thick, soft hair. He started slightly at her caress, then stilled like a cautious animal. His hair was a good excuse to touch him, something she increasingly took pleasure in doing. "I can see your eyes better this way. You look handsome."

"Cut it out, Harper," he mumbled, and she knew by his pink

cheeks she'd embarrassed him. He ducked his head and jerkily backed away from her hand.

"You *do*." She studied him curiously as he poked around in his backpack for something, avoiding her stare. "What's wrong? Hasn't anyone every told you you're nice looking before?"

"No. I don't give a damn about what people think of how I look," he said, frowning furiously. "Shit. Where's that cream for your blister?"

"Liar. You care. And stop cussing so much. It doesn't sound good coming out of your mouth."

"Harper—" he began, a dangerous expression on his face.

She cut him off by lunging toward him, grabbing the backpack, and immediately finding the ointment in a side pocket. Scowling furiously, he set about tending to her wounds.

Harper consoled herself with the fact that despite his edgy state, he still seemed to take as much comfort in having an excuse to touch her as she did him.

She didn't need Jake to tell her that they wouldn't be allowed a fire that night. Emmitt might see it if he was stalking them and close on their trail. She'd never camped out in the relative open, like they would tonight. Last night's close run-in with the mountain lion still had her traumatized. She'd *never* sleep tonight, envisioning either a mountain lion pouncing on them and ripping at skin and muscle with sharp teeth, or Emmitt grabbing them from the realms of sleep. She couldn't decide which scary thought was worse, but was leaning toward Emmitt versus the starving mountain lion.

Of course, she couldn't voice any of these fears out loud to Jake. She and her stupid blister were the reason they were exposed tonight, anyway. And while Emmitt Tharp might have something horrible in mind for Harper, he probably would kill Jake . . . possibly right in front of her.

Her fears began to smother her by nightfall.

They wrapped themselves in all of the blankets and huddled on the hard earth, clasping each other tight for warmth. Harper thought of that first night they'd slept together, and how she'd been so shy and uncertain about suggesting they share body heat. Now she couldn't imagine sleeping in that black, oppressive darkness without Jake holding her tight against him. He'd single-handedly kept her terror at bay for the last several days. He's saved her from Emmitt Tharp. She shivered upon saying the name of their stalker again in her head. Homesickness overwhelmed her, a bone-deep longing for the sight of her parents' faces, the safety and confidence her father always instilled . . . her mother's touch.

She squeezed back tears with her clamped eyelids.

"Shhh," Jake soothed, his mouth near her ear. She should have known she couldn't hide her misery from him. Her fear. He pressed his lips to her temple. "It's going to be okay, Harper. I'm going to keep you safe."

"I'll keep you safe, too," she insisted raggedly. "I'm going to tell my parents all about you. They aren't going to let Emmitt see you or hurt you anymore. I know they won't. Jake?" she asked in a small voice when he didn't say anything.

"It's okay, Harper. I can take care of myself."

That feeling of unfairness she'd been having amplified even more. It wasn't *right*, that this amazing, smart, nice boy had to carry so much weight on his narrow shoulders. Surely her parents would see that? They would come to care about him, maybe as much as Harper had.

Maybe she could convince them to take Jake in! Their town house in Georgetown was large. Her mother hardly ever used her den. She preferred to write in the atrium. They could clear the den out for Jake's bedroom.

The idea burned in her, chasing away her boiling fear.

She wouldn't say anything to Jake yet. She didn't want to get his— or her own—hopes up. But her parents trusted in her opinion, much more so than any other parents she knew trusted their child. For now, her plan would have to stay her secret, though.

She exhaled shakily, her head tucked beneath Jake's chin. His fingers flexed on her shoulder.

"You hear that?" he asked softly.

She listened, fear welling up in her.

"What?" she squeaked. "Not . . . not Emmitt?"

"No. That sound, way off in the distance," he whispered. "Listen."

She listened with all her might. Finally, she heard it: the far distant mechanical chuffing sound.

"What is it?" she asked Jake breathlessly.

"I think it's a helicopter."

Excitement zapped through her. She sat up partially. "A helicopter? Maybe we should start a fire to signal them!"

"We can't. It could signal Emmitt, too. Besides, it's too far off. Miles probably, given the way sound travels in these mountains."

He urged her with his fingers, and she came down next to him again, hugging him close.

"Don't be so disappointed," he said quietly after a moment. "We should be in Barterton by nightfall tomorrow."

"Yeah," she whispered. Somehow, hearing that helicopter, that distant evidence of another human being, had made her feel very lonely.

"Tomorrow is going to be another long day," he said bracingly. "I don't want to spend another night out in the open, so we'll have to push hard, even with your sore foot. So try to sleep, okay?"

"I can do it. Don't worry. I won't hold us back," she whispered, going over her secret plan in her head to have Jake come live with them again, taking courage from it like she would the warmth of a fire.

Miraculously, she fell asleep in the vastness of that terrifying night, feeling safe in the enclosure of Jake's arms.

thirty~four

Twenty Years Ago

The following day, their march through the woods went on and on. Harper had numbed herself to the pain of her heel and to her exhaustion, but she couldn't deaden herself to Jake's perceptive gaze as he looked over his shoulder at her. He came to an abrupt halt and spun.

"You're shaking," he said tensely, coming downhill toward her in the rough brush. They'd been on the move now for six hours, Jake moving them rapidly over harsh terrain. He grasped her shoulder. "Harper, why are you shaking?"

Helplessness nearly choked her. She hated disappointing him, being so weak when he was so strong. "My foot. It hurts so bad. I'm sorry," she said miserably, tears pouring down her cheeks.

He launched himself at her. Harper gasped in surprise and the impact of his body bumping into her unexpectedly. He hugged her tightly. She squeezed him back for all she was worth.

"Don't be sorry," he said emphatically near her ear. "*I'm* sorry, for making you think you should be torturing yourself and keeping quiet about it, just because I'm so scared."

He pulled her tighter to him. She felt so *small* there in the middle of the vast woods and intimidating mountains, and in that moment, she knew Jake felt small, too. For a few seconds, Harper couldn't speak, she was so overwhelmed by fear. For the first time, she started to wonder what it'd be like to die.

But then she focused on the boy in her arms.

"You've got nothing to be sorry for," she rallied. "Jake, look at me."

He wouldn't, keeping his face buried in her neck. Harper knew she was experiencing him at his most vulnerable. It broke her heart that it was *she* who had made him this way.

"Jake, I think you should go ahead to Barterton. No, *listen*," she said when he shook his head forcefully against hers. "We only have three or four hours before we get to town, right? I'm just holding you back. I can camp somewhere in a hidden spot. You know the woods so well, you'll remember where I'm at. You can leave me some supplies. You can bring the police back to me!"

She couldn't believe she was saying this. The idea of being alone in the black forest at night terrified her. But the pain of her blistered heel had become her whole world. That and her concern for Jake. He had a chance to make it . . . while she didn't.

"I *ain't* leaving you, Harper."

"But Jake, he wants to *kill* you." She said her unspoken fear out loud, her voice shaking. He didn't move for a moment. She held her breath. The tall trees surrounding them rustled eerily in the wind. Slowly, Jake lifted his head.

"Some people would say what he wants to do to you is worse than death," he said.

"Rape?" she whispered uneasily.

"More than rape. He wants to give you to people who would give you to a lot of men to be raped, Harper. He wants to turn you into prostitute."

"I'd never become a prostitute," she said disbelievingly. "I don't care if I *was* raped."

"They wouldn't give you any choice. They'd keep you a prisoner. They'd probably get you hooked on drugs, so you'd have to depend on them for your next fix. You'd do whatever they say in order to get it," he said miserably.

"I would never—"

"It doesn't *matter* what you would or wouldn't do right this second. You think you can't get hooked on drugs, when someone is shooting you up without your okay? They want to turn you into a slave, a walking shadow of what you are right now, right here at this moment. I'm *not* going to leave you here alone for Emmitt to find!" He shook her for emphasis.

"Well, what will we do, then?" she asked desperately after a stunned moment.

His throat convulsed as he swallowed. Slowly, he began to release her, still holding her loosely. He looked all around them. Harper sensed him bringing himself under control, methodically assessing their situation like the Jake of old.

"We'll set up camp when we get to the top of this rise."

He looked so set and determined, and her whole body seemed to throb in synchrony with the pain in her foot. She didn't have any energy left to argue with him, even when he put his arm around her waist, assisting her in her hobble uphill.

A light rain had started by the time they reached the top. The place Jake chose was a dirt clearing beneath an enormous, towering tree. He insisted that Harper sit with her back against the trunk and rest while he set up camp. He used the tarp, two large tree branches, and some twine to make a low tent that would give them cover from the rain. They were situated about fifteen feet from an overlook.

While Jake went to check the vantage point and scout the area, Harper tenderly tried to remove the tennis shoe from her sore foot. Friction had broken the bandage free. Dried and fresh blood had caked around the wound, but also to her sock and the canvas tennis shoe. Who knew a blister could wreak so much havoc? She pulled the tennis shoe and sock free, wincing. After a dizzying wave of pain passed, she rose from her sitting position, intent on re-dressing the blister despite her exhaustion.

While she was inside the low tent, sitting on a blanket and pulling out first-aid supplies from a pack, she heard a muted thumping sound outside on the ground.

"Jake? I'm in here!" she called, twisting around from her sitting position. "See anything?"

A huge black shadow suddenly blocked the entrance. Harper stared into the face of a bearded, brutal-looking Emmitt Tharp.

All the fear she'd been holding at bay erupted in her like a volcano. She wasn't aware of screaming, but the shrill sound reached her ears as she scurried to the rear of the tarp enclosure and the back entrance. Emmitt caught her ankle with huge hands and jerked her toward him as easily as he might a panicked rabbit. Harper struggled, but the only thing she really managed to do was knock the branch support down, making the tarp fall on top of her.

The next thing she knew, she was on her back and the dark green tarp was whipped off her face. She looked up at Emmitt, who towered over her like a giant, his face nearly covered by coarse, dark brown hair, his eyes glassy. A horrible smile slanted his lips.

"Well look what I found," he said. "Little Red."

"No, *Jake*!" Harper screamed, slapping and punching at Emmitt's arms and face when he reached down. She might as well have been a pesky fly, the effect she had on him. He hauled her up off the ground so abruptly, she lost her breath. He jerked her around in front of him, her back against his front. One hand pressed hard against her neck and jaw, twisting her chin; one forearm dug painfully under her rib cage. Harper tried to twist and escape his grip, but she was like an animal caught in a steel trap. He pushed harder on her jaw. He looked down at her dispassionately.

"It looks like my stupid nephew didn't get the goods damaged too much." His deep, guttural voice barely penetrated the panicked state in which she swam. But then Emmitt twisted her chin roughly in the other direction, and her gaze flew across a pile of something on the ground. She recognized Jake's dark green T-shirt, her heart lurching.

"Jake, *Jake*," she screamed, but his slight form remained unmoving on the ground. *Oh my God, Emmitt's killed him!*

"You son of—"

"Shut up, or I'm going to cut you."

Her eyes sprang wide at the feeling of cold, sharp steel pressing against her throat.

"Do you have any idea how much trouble you caused me, you little bitch? My buyer gave up and went home two days ago. I've been to Poplar Gorge and back twice now and then thought: Why not try Barterton? Jake's stupid enough to take her there. And looky here. I was right," he breathed, pressing the edge of the knife into Harper's skin. Pain pierced her, swelling her terror. He'd cut her throat. She was going to die—

"Let her go, Emmitt."

Her clamped eyelids sprang open. Jake stood just eight or nine feet in front of them, his face chalky beneath his tan, his hands bunched in fists at his sides. Harper thought she saw a rising bruise on his forehead. Did he look a little woozy, as if he was struggling to stand? She felt Emmitt jerk slightly in surprise behind her, but then he noticeably relaxed. His laugh chilled her.

"You gonna take me, stupid? You think you can kick my ass, you worthless little piece of shit? Gonna show off for your little girlfriend here?" He laughed even harder, like he'd just been told a hilarious joke. Jake stepped closer, his face like a mask, his eyes glassy, his stare glued to the man who held her. Emmitt abruptly stopped laughing. Harper made a choked sound of pure terror when he pressed the knife tighter to her neck and she felt the bite of the blade. Jake came to a halt.

"What's a matter, Jake? Worried about Little Red here? Didn't you tell her you like boys?"

"Shut up, Emmitt."

Harper blinked, shock making her rise slightly above her terror for a moment. Jake sounded scared, but also cold.

And hard.

She realized something else. Suddenly Jake was staring at her, not at Emmitt. It was just for a split second, but his eyes compelled her.

"I'm going to cut her right in front of you if you take another step, then I'll make her watch while I gut and skin you. *Get back*, you fucking runt."

Jake held his ground, though. The sharp knife shifted to Harper's cheek. "How would you like a scar on your little girlfriend here?" Emmitt taunted. "Think she'd be so pretty then?"

"Let her *go*."

Emmitt tensed, pressing harder with the knife. Harper clamped her eyelids shut, tears leaking from beneath her eyelids. She was suffocating. She couldn't breathe. Everything went into brutal slow motion.

Something pelted her face—hundreds of little missiles—and time suddenly leapt forward. She felt a sharp stinging sensation at the corner of her mouth, and then her lungs hitched, and she was breathing in dirt. Emmitt's tight hold on her relented. She lunged forward, tripping. Someone caught her—Jake. He righted her forcefully before his hold was gone. She realized she wasn't the only one coughing. Emmitt was, too . . . with hoarse, violent choking sounds.

She spun around, her coughing fit freezing for a moment at the vision of Jake standing next to his uncle. He gripped Emmitt's large knife in his hand. Emmitt was bent at the waist, coughing violently and digging at his eyes with his fists, trying to clear his vision from the dirt and small stones Jake had thrown into his face.

Jake lifted the cruel-looking, long silver blade. Harper's heart stopped. He paused with knife poised in the air and glanced over at Harper. She sensed his terror. His helplessness.

Then something clicked in his eyes as he stared at her.

He brought the knife down, plunging it into his uncle's back and then his side. Emmitt grunted and went down hard to the forest floor on his knees. He fell forward to his hands. Jake made a wild sound in his throat, and the blood-smeared knife fell to the forest floor.

"Grab a pack, Harper," he told her after a few seconds of staring down at Emmitt, who was gagging and writhing around, on his belly now. Jake's voice sounded hollow and funny to Harper's stunned brain, but hearing it unfroze her, too.

She raced over to the fallen tarp, still coughing dust and dirt out of her throat. She tossed aside the tarp frantically and grabbed the two packs. When she turned, she saw Jake picking up the knife, a disgusted, desperate expression tightening his thin face as he stared at Emmitt.

"Jake," she rasped.

He blinked and met her stare. Some message passed between them quick as electricity. He nodded and came over to her, reaching for one of the packs. Hastily, he jerked the tarp completely away from the area, picking up Harper's bloody shoe and the fallen bottle of antiseptic cream from a blanket. He tossed them into his pack along with Emmitt's horrible knife.

"Let's go," he whispered tensely. His hand closed around hers, and as always, Harper followed his lead.

She took one last look over her shoulder at Emmitt gasping and writhing, struggling to push himself up off the ground. Then Jake pulled on her hand, and they were running like mad through the forest.

thirty~five

Harper awoke with a small sob. Again, tears dampened her cheeks. She remembered more details of her dream than she had earlier today, but it was still murky. Mostly, it was the swelling emotion in her chest that lingered.

It took her a moment to find her bearings. She saw the glow from the distant yacht bridge and felt their subtle rocking in the water. The star-strewn sky curved above them, a half-moon lighting the surroundings to a surprising degree. Memory hit her in a rush. They'd fallen asleep after watching the fireworks.

"Jacob?" she murmured. She flipped over onto her belly on the sofa.

"Harper?" He stirred at her movement, his fingers falling out of her hair, his knee bending and rubbing against her shoulder. She rose up over him, planting her hands next to his head and settling her body beneath his spread legs. He felt warm and solid and wonderful. His hand rose again to her head, but his eyes were still closed. "It's okay, Harper. Everything's going to be all right," he said groggily.

A pain went through her at his automatic, unconscious response. Again, that feeling of sharp longing sliced through her. She thought of how Jacob took care of the troubled Regina Morrow, and gave children of his town a moment of carefree summer fun with the fireworks; how he sponsored the women's shelter Harper had gotten Ellie into, and how he protected neglected or abused animals with the local shelter. He did all those things—and probably countless other acts of kindness and generosity that she didn't know about.

And how the first thing he did, even in the midst of sleep, was assure her—Harper—that everything was all right

Even so, people like Ruth Dannen and thousands of others made sly, nasty comments about his character.

A huge, powerful feeling of love and compassion rose in her. She pulled her sundress up to her waist and yanked the blanket up over her shoulder and part of her head, tenting them partially. She leaned down and rained small kisses on his jaw, finally settling on his mouth with a fevered kiss. It took her a moment to awaken him, but knew she had when his firm lips started to move beneath hers and his hands grasped her upper arms.

"Harper?" he mumbled against her mouth even as his lips plucked at her hungry ones. "What are you doing?"

"Making love to you," she whispered, turning her head to get a better angle on his mouth and penetrating his lips with her tongue. He tasted divine. Their kiss turned hot and wet. He tried to shift her off of him onto the wide couch. She instinctively understood he wanted to come down over her, hold her down, make her a fixed target to ensure she received every ounce of pleasure he conferred.

"No," she whispered, gripping his hips with her knees and keeping herself in place. "I'm making love to *you*."

"It's a mutual thing," he replied wryly, tangling his fingers in her long hair.

"It is, but it isn't. *You* give and take. You take from me, and I offer it willingly. But you hardly ever let me *just* give," she murmured, plucking at his lips hungrily. His hips flexed up slightly against his weight, and she felt his arousal. Relief swept through her. Given his preferences in bed, she'd worried he might be turned off by her aggressiveness. "Just relax, Jacob. Let me make you feel good."

"You always make me feel good."

"*I* have something to give. Let me *touch* you, Jacob."

Her plea seemed to hang around them, swirling in the cool night air. Had he sensed that she meant more than touch him physically? She thought maybe he had, given the tension level of his body. He didn't reply or move. Slowly, cautiously, she began to move her hands, sliding them across his muscular shoulders and powerful chest. Tears stung her eyes for some reason. She was reacting purely on feeling in that moment. He was so amazing to her. So miraculous.

She sunk her head, her lips moving feverishly across his skin.

"Harper, honey," he said, and there was an edge to his tone as she delicately licked and then sucked at a small, flat nipple, making it stiffen. His fingers dug in her hair aggressively. By the time she kissed and ran her tongue along the side of his ribs, small bumps had raised along his skin. She flicked her tongue and he growled softly. She closed her eyes. It was sublime, feeling his body react so completely to her touch, feeling his power coil and tighten, starting to strain to break free.

A moment later, she knelt over his thighs and held the base of his cock in one hand, caressing the shaft and fat crown with the other. She stroked him for a while, admiring him in the soft starlight. She flicked the thick rim beneath the head with her fingers, and he made a rough sound. She looked up and saw that he'd come up on his elbows, and was watching her through narrowed eyelids. His face looked hard and shadowed, mysterious and beautiful in the glow of the stars. Holding his stare, she came down over him and squeezed her lips around the flaring head of his cock.

He held his breath, watching her take him into her mouth. Why were her cheeks damp from tears? The moment felt so fragile to him. Harper herself seemed like something from a dream, her graceful limbs and stunning face nuanced by moonlight. Her mouth wasn't made of smoke and shadow, though. She clamped him hard with her lips. She sunk down on him, and he shuddered as pure pleasure rippled through him. Her mouth was hot. Sultry. And her suck . . .

"Harper," he whispered harshly, one hand cupping the back of her head. She took him deep again, her mouth pulling at him. Not just his cock. She drew on something deep inside him. Her head bobbed forcefully for a moment. He winced in pleasure. Christ, it felt good.

And she was so beautiful. He couldn't take his eyes off the vision of her giving . . . and giving. He briefly fantasized about standing and bringing her to a sitting position, holding her head while he pierced her beautiful mouth . . .

. . . But the experience of being the target of her desire held him spellbound, as well. His paradoxical need created a friction in him: the need to dominate fighting with the desire to accept what she was giving him, to accept love rather than take it.

To acknowledge instead of demand.

A sweet, agonizing moment later, she rose over him, lifting her dress to her waist with one hand. She started to come down over his naked cock. He paused her by tightening his hold.

"Do you know what you're doing?" he asked.

"Yes," she breathed. "I want you in me this way. Now. I'm like you, Jacob. I've always been very careful about making sure I was safe. Only for a moment. *Please*."

"You don't have to beg me," he said incredulously. There was an intensity to her tonight that he couldn't quite comprehend. Her cheeks were no longer wet, but her eyes looked mysterious and deep in the moonlight.

He helped her by guiding her hip. She sunk down over him, sheathing him in her sleek body. He saw ecstasy tighten her face, and knew her pleasure matched his. She paused in his lap and whipped the dress above her head.

He held her to him, the pleasure cutting at him. The feeling. She began to rise and fall over him. She looked so beautiful, naked and bathed in the glow of the stars and moon. Need tore at his throat. Desperation. He pulled her to him, clenching his teeth hard at the sensation of her erect nipples pressing against his ribs. He gripped the hair at her nape in his fist.

"What is it?" he hissed tensely against her mouth. "What happened, Harper? Tell me. Why were you crying when you woke me up?"

"I don't know," she said brokenly, and she looked every bit as desperate as he felt. "I had a dream."

"*What* dream?"

"About a boy," burst out of her throat. "A boy I knew a long, long time ago. Why am I dreaming of him now? Why do I keep thinking of him?" she murmured, and it was as if she asked herself. Her face crunched tight.

Wild emotion rushed through him at the vision of her pain. It was like a knife in her side. In his.

"Make me forget, Jacob," she whispered. She began to move her hips, pumping his cock in and out of her body. He gripped her head tighter.

"Come here," he said, his mouth slanting. He'd seen her pain, and it'd driven a stake of urgency into him.

She'd dreamed of Jake. *Surely* she'd meant Jake.

Surely she'd remembered me?

The thought both panicked and excited him. He didn't know on what side of the ledge he existed anymore, only that he felt like he was constantly falling off it, free-falling into Harper's sweetness.

He kissed her voraciously, using one hand to guide her strokes over his body, mounting their frenzy of need. From every direction, he felt pummeled. Maddened. Because even while he gave her what she needed, he couldn't have said for himself what desire was sharper inside him: for her to remember or for her to forget, for her to acknowledge him for who he was, or for her to remain veiled, safe, and protected. Did he want her to recognize the vulnerable boy he'd buried long ago? Or did he want even more to continue drowning in the sweetness of her loving him for whom he'd become, forever ignorant of whom he'd been . . .

Forever blinded to what they'd meant to one another.

The morning dawned crystal clear and luminous out on the vast, blue expanse of Lake Tahoe.

After they'd made love on the top deck last night, Jacob and she had gone down to the bedroom and slept the rest of the night in each other's arms. Harper awoke before Jacob, studying his face in repose for a moment in the light of dawn. Her chest grew tight when she recalled their emotional, charged . . . *bewildering* lovemaking last night beneath the stars.

She wasn't sure what had happened. It all seemed so confusing: the dream, her uncontrollable eruption of feeling, his passionate, soulful response. What really bothered her was how she kept recalling that dream. His face was emerging from the shadows with startling clarity.

Jake.

Jacob had promised her an affair that was about forgetting, about staving off grief and loss. But strangely, she was remembering *more*.

Is this what it meant to really fall in love? she wondered numbly as she stole from his arms a moment later. Did it mean that you felt *everything* more clearly, the sad along with the amazing? Maybe so. She'd considered herself to be in love several times in the past, but that pale feeling had nothing to do with the vibrant, powerful emotions Jacob evoked in her.

She was making them breakfast with the eggs and a freshly baked loaf of bread that Lisa had packed for them in the hamper when he found her. She turned upon hearing his tread on the stairs, her heart in her throat.

He touched her almost immediately after he entered the galley, taking her into his arms and kissing her deeply. She was glad to realize that their newfound closeness and intimacy remained, despite her uncertainties and vague embarrassment about her emotional display last night. Maybe he sensed her uncommon shyness or some shared strain, and was determined to melt it. Knowing him, and his bullheaded determination to have nothing separate them physically, that was probably it. If so, it worked in spades, Harper realized dazedly a moment later when he lifted his head from their kiss, and she very reluctantly left his arms to finish making the eggs.

By some silent pact, neither of them spoke of what had happened last night under the stars. They spent a nice morning on the top deck basking in the bright sun. He read some files from his briefcase and

Harper consumed a book Cyril had given to her about writing screenplays, her feet resting in his lap.

"Is it good?" Jacob asked a while later, nodding at the book she read, setting aside his file and grasping one of her feet instead, massaging the muscles deeply.

She sighed in pleasure and lowered the book. "It is. I'm excited to start writing."

"Excited is good. Very good," he murmured, his deep, mellow voice washing over her and prickling her nerves to life. "I have some of Cyril's movies at the house. Do you want to watch a couple, when we get back?"

She nodded eagerly, warming as she saw that small smile she loved shaping his mouth before he picked up the report again. This time, even with his attention focused on his reading, he continued to massage her until she drifted off into a sun-warmed sleep.

They anchored the yacht at about two that afternoon. Harper was a little sad to leave the water and their temporary escape from the rest of the world. It'd been heaven being out there on the water, just the two of them.

When they returned to the mansion, Elizabeth stood at the top of the terrace, ready to greet them. So . . . Jacob's faithful assistant had come back to his side. Harper wanted to ask Elizabeth about Regina Morrow's well-being, but recognized it wasn't her place. Harper could tell by the urgent, strained look Elizabeth gave Jacob even before they'd exchanged hellos that she wanted to confer with him privately.

"Why don't you go up and shower and I'll meet you upstairs in a minute?" Jacob asked Harper.

"Sure," Harper replied, her smile assuring both Jacob and Elizabeth she was fine with that plan. In truth, she'd held on to a small hope that Jacob would tell Elizabeth that she could speak openly about Regina in front of Harper. That wasn't the case, though, Harper acknowledged grimly as she went through the terrace doors. Apparently, there were still secrets regarding Regina that Jacob wasn't ready for Harper to know.

But in all fairness, what Jacob had said in San Francisco in regard to Regina was true. Regina obviously had a lot of emotional and mental health issues. As a friend, Jacob couldn't in good faith go around blabbing about her problems to someone like Harper, who was a stranger to Regina. But Jacob had also admitted Regina was a former lover, and that he cared for her deeply.

It's only natural that the hush-hush, charged aura surrounding Regina Morrow bothers me a little.

Maybe because of her conflicting thoughts, she was overly sensitive about reading Jacob's mood when he joined her in his suite a while later. If he seemed a little subdued at first, his preoccupation passed quickly enough.

His attention was all for her.

He showed her for the first time how a wood-paneled wall in the sitting area of his bedroom opened to an entertainment center. They agreed to be lazy for the rest of the day, watching two of Cyril's movies, talking . . . making love. They became so involved in the latter that they forgot dinner. When Harper's stomach rumbled loudly at one point while they were entwined in bed, Jacob rose despite Harper's protests. They ordered Thai food and ate it in bed naked. She thought it was the most delicious meal she'd ever eaten in her life.

"Back to work tomorrow," Harper murmured later against Jacob's bare chest. She loved to press her lips against the crisp hair there, feeling the heat of his skin and the density of muscle beneath. The lights in his suite were out, but star shine poured through the open, circular bank of windows. She turned her head slightly, brushing her mouth against him and inhaling his scent. "It seems like a month since I was at the newsroom, not three days."

He didn't reply. She rested her cheek on his chest, sensing his preoccupation.

"Are you thinking about work, too?" she asked him after a pause.

His hand cupped her shoulder. "No. Harper, there's something I didn't tell you about this weekend. I guess I should now."

She came up on one elbow, peering into his shadowed face.

"What's wrong? It sounds serious."

"I wouldn't say it's *serious*." He exhaled and rolled over on the mattress. He switched on a lamp. "Maybe it'd be easier if I just showed you."

He rose from the bed. Harper watched him walk over to the sitting area, the dim lamplight gilding his ass and muscular back. He withdrew a newspaper from his briefcase and walked back over to the bed. Harper recalled him looking at what appeared to be the same paper in the back of the limo yesterday morning, when they'd returned from San Francisco. It was a copy of the *Chronicle*, a minor detail she'd noticed, having worked for that paper for a good part of her professional life.

When she held up her hands to receive the paper, he paused before giving it to her.

"Don't be mad at me for not showing you yesterday. It was selfish on my part, but I was mostly thinking of you. I didn't want anything to come in the way of you enjoying the rest of your holiday. Besides, there was nothing you could have done about it at that point, anyway." He shrugged and gave her the paper. "There's nothing you can do now, either, except to be prepared for any flak when you return to the *Gazette* tomorrow."

Her brows creased in concern at his buildup. She sat up in bed, the sheet tucked around her breasts. He came down next to her.

"Page twenty-three," he said.

Harper whipped through the pages. A moment later she was staring openmouthed at a fairly large photo of Jacob and her leaving Geb on Saturday night in San Francisco. They both looked serious. Jacob's hand was at the small of her back. The caption read, *Lattice owner and CEO, Jacob Latimer, and his escort for the evening, former* Chronicle *reporter and current news editor of the* Sierra Tahoe Gazette, *Harper McFadden.*

"*Escort* for the evening. Charlie Nelson." Her lip curled in bitter disgust when she saw the name of the photographer.

"You know him?"

Harper nodded grimly, skimming the rest of the brief article, which was mostly about Jacob. She rolled her eyes and folded the paper with haphazard forcefulness before tossing it aside irritably.

"I never saw any photographers that night. Makes sense that it was Charlie. That swine makes it a practice to hide behind garbage cans, where he belongs."

"Do you think it'll be a problem for you at work?" Jacob asked.

"It'll certainly make it more difficult to deny that I have any inside track to you or Lattice with Ruth, not to mention Burt, one of my reporters who's been nosing around." She noticed his somber expression. "Don't worry. I'll handle it. Because they know that you and I are seeing each other doesn't change a thing. If anything, it should send a clearer message that what's . . ." She hesitated in describing their relationship, realizing it was a glaring question mark. How exactly did one describe Jacob's and her involvement—especially after their intense, amazing long weekend together? "What's happening between us is private and not a topic for public consumption."

"They're going to be curious. They're going to ask a lot of questions. Do you think your editor in chief is going to give you a hard time?"

"Sangar? No. He's a pussycat compared to Ruth, or even Burt Chavis." Her gaze flickered over his face. Her heart squeezed a little at how sober he looked. "Are you regretting getting involved with a reporter again?" she asked softly. His eyebrows arched a question, and she sighed. "Cyril told me you were still having doubts about seeing me because I was a reporter."

"I'm managing those doubts pretty well. Wouldn't you say? Just like you're managing yours, about being with me?"

She gave a bark of laughter and rubbed her eyes, suddenly feeling tired. "Damn Charlie Nelson. I'm going to call him tomorrow and let him have it."

"It's okay, Harper," he said, coming down in the bed and urging her to recline with him.

"It is?" she asked incredulously as he twisted around to shut off the lamp.

She felt his shrug against her chin as his arms encircled her a moment later.

"At least you won't have to tiptoe around the topic at work anymore."

She rubbed her lips against his skin distractedly. "No more sneaking into the newsroom's bathroom, now that the spotlight has been turned on." She squeaked in surprise when he was suddenly rolling her on her back and coming down over her.

"I'm not promising anything. Being with me is risky business."

She laughed and encircled his neck with her arms. "The reward has far outweighed the risk so far."

"I could say the same about you," he replied huskily before he covered her mouth with his own.

The next morning, Harper got up extra early with Jacob to jog. Much to her amazement, Elizabeth was already at the mansion, waiting for them at the bottom of the stairs. She informed them she wanted to orient Harper to the compound's security measures so that Harper could return there anytime she chose without difficulty. Harper gave Jacob a surprised glance, but could tell by his relaxed expression he'd been the one to give the direction to his assistant in the first place. Knowing that he'd expressed to Elizabeth his trust in her by giving her total access to his home gratified Harper.

After her orientation, she and Jacob jogged on the beach during a glorious sunrise.

"Do you want to take a few of the dogs out for some catch?" Jacob asked her upon their return.

Harper checked her watch and nodded, liking the idea.

He ended up doing most of the ball throwing to three or four of the adult dogs, however, while Harper sat in the sand with her legs spread, watching him and playing with Milo, the puppy that'd had his foot amputated by some sadistic sociopath.

"He likes you," Jacob said as he walked toward her a while later, and the golden sun blazed over the tops of the mountains. Warmth went through her at the magnificent vision he made, wearing running shorts, his dark blond hair damp at the nape from jogging and play, his simple gray T-shirt molding his muscular, fit torso in the most distracting way.

"Do you think so?" she asked hopefully, petting the puppy's ears and scratching his back.

"I know so." He reached for her hand and pulled her into a standing position while Milo nuzzled her ankles. "What's not to like?" He leaned down and brushed her cheeks with his lips, as if he couldn't resist feeling the heat that had risen in her cheeks at his compliment. Then he transferred his mouth to hers, and Harper lost time for a moment.

"I'm going to be late for work," she murmured against his lips.

He grabbed her hand. "If you're late, what difference does it make if you're a little or a lot?" he asked.

He led her to his bedroom.

She wasn't *terribly* late by the time she got out the door. She *was* flustered, happy, and extremely sex-flushed. The chances of her appearing cool and contained in front of her colleagues following the *Chronicle* photo with Jacob were pretty much nil.

She realized she couldn't have cared less.

After Harper left for work, Jacob put in a call to Dr. Larry Fielding in Napa. The psychiatrist immediately began talking about Regina's recent relapse and what he planned to do in regard to her treatment.

"She's very depressed," Dr. Fielding told Jacob. "I've moved up her outpatient therapy to four times a week, so I can better assess if she's suicidal."

"Shouldn't she be in the hospital?" Jacob asked.

"Possibly, but as you know, I can't admit her involuntarily unless she expresses active suicidal ideation or shows signs of being unable to

care for herself. I'm going to add an antidepressant to her mood sta-
bilizer. That's another reason I want to see her several times a week, to
assess how she reacts. She'll also continue with the outpatient group,
so they'll be able to monitor her, as well."

"As long as she goes," Jacob muttered as he paced back and forth
in front of his office windows.

"You've done everything for her that you can," Dr. Fielding said
patiently. "God knows it's light-years more than most people would do."

But it's not enough. It'll never be enough.

"Jacob, you're not her savior. She has to want to save herself," Fielding said as if he'd read Jacob's mind—which he probably had.

He closed his eyes and stopped pacing. "I know. I *know* that."

"With your head, you do. I know you're still working on believing
it in your heart."

Jacob began pacing again, determined not to go down the familiar
path with the psychiatrist again. He'd made a lot of progress in accepting his limits in regard to helping Regina. And in point of fact,
he hadn't called Dr. Fielding primarily to ask about Regina. Elizabeth
had already filled him in on her status yesterday when they returned
to shore. And he hadn't even experienced a *slight* urge to call about
Regina when he'd been spending those idyllic hours with Harper on
the yacht.

"There's something else I want to speak with you about," he told
Dr. Fielding. He'd been increasingly anxious about Harper ever since
she'd awakened him the night before on the yacht with tears on her
cheeks saying she'd dreamed of a boy . . . ever since she'd been so urgent to have him make her forget that dream. "Remember how I
asked you about a person who had a trauma, and then underwent
hypnosis for treatment?"

"Yes, I recall you asking me some questions. You wanted to know
if it was possible for hypnosis to make someone completely forget their
trauma, if I recall."

"And you said that someone could be distanced from a trauma,
but that it was unlikely it would be completely erased from their

mind? Under what conditions would a person like that, a person who had been free of any anxiety about their trauma for years, start to have nightmares again . . . maybe even start to remember the trauma in more detail and think about it more?"

"Jacob, it's hard for me to say without knowing the specifics and the individual in question—"

"I realize that. But just give me an example of *why* a person who's been cured of anxiety and phobias might start to have bad dreams about their original trauma again."

Dr. Fielding sighed at his persistence. "Well, nightmares are associated with rising anxiety, of course."

"That's what I assumed," Jacob said, frowning as he thought about Harper.

"It could be any number of reasons why the person is starting to re-experience memories and anxiety. Perhaps he or she is going through a particularly stressful time, either psychologically or physically. Perhaps a trigger enters their life that wasn't there before."

Jacob halted his pacing and stared out the window unseeingly. "A trigger?"

"Yes. Something that calls to mind the original trauma."

"Like a person, for instance? Another person involved in the original event?"

"Yes, possibly a person."

"But what if this person looked completely different than the one associated with the trauma, and the person I'm asking about didn't even *recognize* him."

The psychiatrist made an exacerbated sound. "You're asking me to make wild speculations based on very vague information."

"Please, Larry."

Fielding groaned. "Okay. So, you want to know if a subject who suffered a trauma might show signs of relapse when they come into contact with a person who had originally been part of the traumatic event, even if they don't *recognize* said person? Am I getting all this straight?"

"That's right."

"I *suppose* it's possible, theoretically speaking. There are qualities to a person beyond their physical appearance that might signal the unconscious mind."

"Like what?" Jacob asked tensely.

"Many things . . . anything that promotes a feeling of familiarity. A mannerism, a tone of voice, background information, ways of relating. A feeling of *knowing* someone is a very subtle phenomenon. It's not just about physical appearance."

"But the person I'm referring to is completely different than he was."

Dr. Fielding gave harsh laugh. "No one can become *completely* different, Jacob. I'm sorry if you think I'm being annoyingly intellectual, but I've based my life's work on that belief. We all carry some kind of trace or some kind of scar of our past. Our histories echo into our future. And if we accept that to be true: then whomever you're referring to might have a response to that trace. The question is, to what degree? And will it be a positive or negative response to that echo?"

thirty~six

The first thing that greeted Harper upon returning to work Tuesday morning wasn't a rabidly curious Ruth Dannen or a persistent Burt Chavis or a bewildered, condemning Sangar. Instead, a huge bouquet of stunning purple hydrangeas and white lilies sat on her desk. Harper set down her briefcase and hurried to find the card.

See? Not all bad. Now nothing can stop me from spoiling you at work, too.

—J

Movement caught her eye. She looked up to see Ruth Dannen standing in her office doorway. Harper realized belatedly she was smiling widely after reading Jacob's card. In a fit of rebellion, she refused to disguise her happiness . . . even when she noticed what Ruth held in her hand: a copy of Sunday's *Chronicle*.

"Morning, Ruth. Have a good holiday?" she asked, putting the card back in the envelope and walking around her desk.

"Not as good as you, it would seem," Ruth replied, flicking the newspaper against her skirt for emphasis. Refusing to rise to the bait, Harper calmly picked up the vase of flowers and placed it carefully on a nearby credenza. She admired them for a moment, only to turn and see Burt crowding behind Ruth. "Move it, Ruth. I work for Harper. I get first dibs on an interview."

"*I'm* the one who told you about Harper and Latimer," Ruth said scathingly, glaring at Burt. "Go to the back of the line, junior."

"Cut it out, both of you," Harper said, going back behind her desk. "There's not going to be any interviews. There's not going to be anything, except for business as usual."

"Business as usual?" Ruth asked, blond eyebrows arching sardonically. She flicked the *Chronicle* in Harper's direction. "Do you mean you sitting on top the biggest story in town—no pun intended—and keeping it all to yourself?"

"There *is* no story," Harper said, exacerbated. "Okay, so I'm seeing Jacob Latimer. That's hardly a story, unless you're in Charlie Nelson's league."

"Nelson is a photographer for the society and entertainment section of the *Chronicle*. I'm the society and entertainment editor for the *Gazette*. Are you putting down my beat?" Ruth demanded.

"No, I just—"

"Give it a rest, Ruth," Burt said disparagingly. He squeezed past the other woman and plunged into Harper's office. "We're not talking about society gossip. We're talking about real news," he said, his pale eyes shining with excitement. "I did what you said, Harper. I dug for a story. I think I found something that might be worth pursuing. Can we talk?"

His obvious eagerness and excitement alarmed Harper. But what could she say, really? If Burt was working on a story, and it was newsworthy, it was her job to hear him out and guide him.

"Okay. Ruth, can you give us some privacy please?"

"I'm not going anywhere. I've been digging around for something on Latimer for years. I at least deserve to—"

"Ruth, please?" Harper interrupted. "Let me do my job?"

"You've been *doing* more than your job, McFadden," Ruth snapped. She looked at Burt. "If I were you, and if I really had a story, I'd take the lead to Sangar. At least you'd know it's not going to be quashed in Latimer's bed tonight."

"Get *out*, Ruth," Harper insisted angrily.

"I want to talk to you when you're finished," Ruth told Burt pointedly before she exited with a dramatic slam of Harper's door.

Harper plunged into her chair with an annoyed sigh. She waved wearily at a chair in front of her desk.

"What have you got, Burt?"

Burt looked a little sheepish once he'd sat. "You're not mad at me, are you? For attacking the Latimer story? I was gobsmacked when Ruth told me about the photo in the *Chronicle* this morning. It'd suck if my timing on this was all wrong."

"Don't worry about that stupid photo or your *timing*. If you have something solid, spill it."

"Well, Ruth is right about one thing. Latimer *does* put Tahoe Shores on the map, just by living here. But I didn't know that you and he were—" He gestured with his hand. Harper rolled her eyes.

"Do you want to go to Sangar with this instead?" she demanded.

"No. Sangar will shut me down."

"You're not boosting my confidence much, if you're saying Sangar wouldn't give you the time of day for whatever you've got."

"No . . . no, I still want you to hear this. Of course I do. You're my editor, right?" He leaned forward eagerly. She experienced a mixed sense of dread and curiosity. As a reporter, she recognized that look on his face. Burt *really* thought he was onto something.

"Simply put, I got lucky. You know how there was that big blow-out with the Clint Jefferies insider trading scandal, and how Latimer made his first millions off it, how the SEC investigated, but found no hard evidence to prosecute Jefferies? And how ever since then, Latimer refuses to associate with Jefferies?"

She thought of the barely contained fury on Jacob's face when he'd seen Jefferies at the opera. "Yes," she said, her curiosity growing despite her discomfort at Burt's excitement . . . at this topic in general.

"Well, part of the problem with investigating Latimer is that he seems to just pop up out of nowhere. The earliest reports of him are when he first went to college at MIT. By the time he went to MIT, his name was Jacob Latimer. That's the name that was used in the official records for the SEC's insider trading investigation against Jefferies—although his previous name *was* listed there, as well. Local legend has

it that Latimer was a sort of protégé to Jefferies, and that Jefferies favored him, treated him like a son, even. But the local records don't
show a Jacob Latimer living or attending grade school or high school
anywhere near Jefferies's vacation property. There are rumors that Latimer was adopted and lived in proximity to Jefferies, but adoption
records are closed. Shut *tight*, actually. That's the brick wall that most
reporters run into when trying to find out more about his past."

"So Latimer *wasn't* his adoptive parents' name?" Harper asked
quietly.

"No. Latimer's former name is listed in the SEC investigation,
even if it is buried pretty deep in the details. It's Sinclair. And there *is*
a Jacob Sinclair listed as attending school at a Charleston High
School. I'm assuming that was his adoptive family's name, even
though like I said . . . the official adoption records are sealed tight."

"So Latimer changed his name from Sinclair to Latimer?" Harper
said, puzzling it out in her head. He'd said he loved his adoptive parents, even if their advanced years and medical issues had prevented
Jacob and them from getting as close as they might have. Why had
he wanted to change his name after they'd passed away? Why was he
so intent upon denying his past . . . upon remaking himself in a new
image?

"Yeah, the name Sinclair isn't breaking news. A select few reporters have mentioned that in stories before and drew the connection
between Jacob Sinclair and Jacob Latimer. It's not a huge secret, just
one of the many snags and barriers in Latimer's history that throws a
lot of reporters off the mark. Who he was *before* he was Jacob Sinclair . . . that remains under wraps."

"Why does it matter what his name was before he was adopted?"

Burt shrugged. "Why does he seem interested in people not putting the microscope on his origins? Maybe he's got something to
hide . . . either about himself or his biological parents?"

"And you think Latimer is responsible for erecting these barriers,
don't you?"

Burt shrugged, giving her a sly look. "Actually, I suspect there might be a government agency or key contact or two who is helping him obscure his history, but yeah . . . if they are helping him in that little magic act, it's under Latimer's direct request."

"You're suggesting that government officials are helping to bury Latimer's history in exchange for . . . what?"

Burt shrugged. "The guy's a computer genius. Word has it he still works for the Department of Defense. He pats their back, the DOD pats his."

"Do have any proof of that?" Harper asked.

"No, but—"

"This is all speculation," she interrupted dismissively. "And by your own account, it's not even fresh news about him going by a different name at one time. So Latimer has a murky history and has been known by at least two, but probably three, different names. So what?"

"Wait a second," Burt said, holding up his hand. "I figured that since most reporters have hit a brick wall by trying to uncover anything about Latimer himself, why not delve into the next best thing? The time period when Jefferies supposedly mentored Latimer? Why not see if I could uncover any unusual incidents involving Jefferies or his property during the time when Jefferies and Latimer were supposedly thick as thieves?"

She gave him a sardonic look when he twitched his eyebrows while saying *thieves*. She may be enduring this, because it was her job, but the very act of talking behind Jacob's back was making her a little nauseous, like she was doing the very activity that he'd been suspicious she'd engage in. Still . . . her curiosity pricked at her.

"Go on," she told Burt.

"I have a good friend that I've known since grade school who ended up moving out east when we were in college. She just became a detective for the Charleston PD. So we got to talking the other night, and I told her about my interest in Latimer and Jefferies. She agreed to do a little digging, just between the two of us."

"And now just between the three of us," Harper added dryly. "Is your friend willing to go on the record about whatever she uncovered?"

"Of course not. She'd probably get fired. You know that. She's an anonymous insider source; what's wrong with that? The information she gave me was solid."

"Go on."

"So I asked Trish to look for any incident reports or arrests associated with Jefferies and his property in the time period of interest before the insider trading investigation was announced . . . say fifteen, sixteen years ago?—in that general vicinity. Well, as it turns out, there *was* something that happened on Jefferies's property in the summer before Jacob Latimer officially showed up for his first semester of college at MIT, flush with cash from a certain recent windfall sale of Markham Pharmaceutical stock."

"What was it?"

Burt opened his notebook and began to read.

"On August second, a 9-1-1 call was made by a Jacob Sinclair, age eighteen, in regard to an emergency involving the drug overdose of a twenty-year-old female by the name of Gina Morrow." Burt glanced up when Harper's hand jerked involuntarily on the desk, but she smoothed her face into impassivity. He continued. "The woman was reportedly found at Clint Jefferies's summer lake house. When EMTs arrived, she was unconscious and was pretty bruised up—the report said it was from a fall while she was intoxicated. A cruiser was sent out to Jefferies's property, as well. Jefferies himself was interviewed in the police report, although notably, Jacob Sinclair *wasn't*. Jefferies claimed Sinclair had gone home, but that Sinclair didn't really know Morrow anyway, so the police weren't missing anything crucial. Sinclair had just found her unconscious and called 9-1-1.

"According to the police report, there was a huge party going on at the Jefferies estate that night. Despite all these people at Jefferies's house, it seems like the police were having trouble getting anyone to give testimony about what had happened to Gina Morrow. Jefferies said that Morrow was a family friend from Charlotte, and that she had a history of drug abuse. But three other women that were interviewed said Morrow was from Charleston."

"Okay," Harper said slowly, her mind buzzing with the information. Gina Morrow and Regina Morrow *had* to be the same person. *"He hurt her. He took advantage of her when anyone could see how vulnerable she was."* She recalled the barely repressed anger in Jacob's voice when he'd said that about Jefferies and Regina. Had Jacob discovered Regina Morrow being abused in some way at this specific party, and rebelled against his mentor because of it? "What's all this got to do with the insider trading scandal?" she prodded Burt.

"You sort of have to read between the lines of the police report," Burt told her. "I don't think this was any ordinary summer party at Jefferies's estate. First of all, the cop noted that a lot of the guests were intoxicated, and a lot of the women were 'young in appearance' and 'barely dressed.' They put in the report that they couldn't identify any concrete evidence of drug use at the scene."

"But just the fact that they mention it in the report indicates they suspected it."

"Right. Also, there's the ages of the three women who did go on the record about this Gina Morrow." He glanced down at his notebook. "Ages eighteen, nineteen, twenty-one . . . and Morrow was twenty." Burt gave her a knowing glance. "Jefferies was forty-two at the time."

"So you think Jefferies was throwing a big party involving drugs and hookers," Harper said.

"Possibly underage ones. No working girl is going to give her age as anything but eighteen or up. But Jefferies has a big influence in that area, so the incident was kept pretty quiet, it sounds like."

"I feel like I'm missing something. Why do you think this relates to Latimer and his purchase and sale of Markham stock?"

"Because this incident report was filed less than two weeks *before* Latimer bought and then sold Markham stock just as it skyrocketed on announcement of FDA approval for Zefcor, a breakthrough Markham drug for diabetes."

Harper just stared at Burt for a moment, listening to her heart beat in her ears.

"When the SEC investigated Jefferies for insider trading, they were doing so under the assumption that Jefferies had passed on information about FDA approval to Latimer because Latimer was Jefferies's favorite and a protégé. It hadn't become clear at the time of the SEC's report that there had been a falling-out between Jefferies and Latimer—or Sinclair, as Latimer was known then. A month after that big, sexy bash at Jefferies's vacation home, Jacob had changed his name from Sinclair to Latimer, had moved to Cambridge to attend MIT, and had millions of dollars in the bank from the Markham sale," Burt finished smugly.

"So you think insider trading between Jefferies and Latimer happened, but not because Jefferies was so fond of Jacob. You think Latimer blackmailed Jefferies into giving him insider information, or Latimer would expose potentially damaging information about something that happened at that sleazy party?"

"It's plausible, isn't it?" Burt asked excitedly.

Harper put her elbow on her desk and rubbed her eyes, thinking furiously.

"It's still very thin, Burt. You don't have anything."

"I know, but there's *something* there. I can smell it. Something that makes it worthwhile to keep digging, right?"

"You never said what happened to Gina Morrow," Harper said.

"She checked out of the hospital two days after the party."

"And what else? There's no other mention of her that you could find?"

"No, but that doesn't mean I can't try to find her, though," Burt said

A feeling of trepidation went through her. "I don't suppose your friend gave you a copy of the official incident report regarding Gina Morrow and the party at Jefferies's house?"

Burt grinned widely and pulled a piece of paper from his notebook. It sailed onto Harper's desk.

"That was risky of your friend," Harper said, staring at the faxed report.

"She's a *very* good friend," Burt said with a knowing smile.

"Not good enough of a friend to go public with her name, though.

Get me another participant that will go on the record that Jefferies was throwing a hooker party, preferably involving underage prostitutes and illegal drugs."

"No one is going to admit to being at a party like that!"

"Get me evidence of some kind of argument and falling-out between Latimer and Jefferies afterward that might indicate bribery as a motive for insider trading versus patronage on Jefferies's part. And those things are just more simple building blocks to a story, Burt. At the moment, you've got absolutely nothing," Harper said, standing.

"There's no way! There was never evidence of a falling-out between Latimer and Jefferies," Burt said, flying out of his chair. "If there'd been evidence of that, it would have come out in the SEC investigation."

"*Exactly.*"

"Come on, Harper. You have access to Latimer. You could just *ask* him why he refuses to associate with Jefferies."

"I'm not asking him anything," Harper fired back. "This isn't a newsworthy story, Burt."

"How can you say that when—"

"I can say it easily. Because the fact of the matter is, unless we get a confession from Clint Jefferies or Jacob Latimer that they were involved in insider training, there is . . . no . . . damn story," she said succinctly, tapping on her desk. "Do you think you can get a confession from Jefferies or Latimer?"

"Of course not, but what about that police report? Doesn't that mean anything?" He pointed angrily at the fax on her desk. Her gaze bounced off the piece of paper, and then zoomed back. She snatched up the report.

"Charleston, *West Virginia*?" she said hollowly, reading part of the printed address of the police department at the top. Shivers tore through her.

"Yeah. What's wrong?" Burt asked, startled. "I *told* you Charleston. That's where my friend finished school and where she works: the Charleston PD. Jefferies had a huge vacation home on a nearby lake there. He's sold it since, but that's where the party in question happened and where Jacob Sinclair worked for him. Why do you sound so surprised?"

She struggled to find her composure.

"I thought you meant Charleston, South Carolina, earlier, that's all."

"Why would you think that?" Burt asked, puzzled.

"Charleston, South Carolina, is a lot bigger town, isn't it? I just assumed," Harper eluded, waving her hand impatiently to distract him. In truth, she'd been put off the mark by the fact that Jacob had told her he'd grown up in South Carolina. Jacob had certainly *never* mentioned West Virginia. That would have stuck in her head, for sure.

"Look, you've got a *long*, long way to go if you want a credible story," she told Burt, clearing her thoughts with effort. "I won't risk you implicating the paper in a lawsuit," she said with a sense of finality, handing Burt back the police report. She knew on the outside that she appeared calm. On the inside, her limbs tingled unpleasantly and a strange ringing had started in her ears.

Burt looked a little surly as he left her office, but at least he went without further argument. When he opened the door, she noticed Ruth leaning against a desk in the main newsroom, waiting for him. Harper had a distant, unpleasant thought that she was going to pounce on Burt in an effort to get him to tell her what he knew about Jacob.

She shut her eyes, trying to still a sudden dizziness.

West Virginia.

No. It couldn't be.

But she'd been having all these weird, out-of-nowhere dreams and feelings of loss associated with her childhood . . . and now *this*?

It's Mom and Dad being gone that's bringing it all up the surface, one loss making me recall another so vividly.

But why now, *when my parents have been dead for a year?*

According to this document, Jacob had spent at least *part* of his youth in West Virginia. She recalled vividly being in the pool with him in San Francisco. She'd mentioned him knowing Clint Jefferies in South Carolina, and he hadn't denied it or corrected her. Yet he'd clearly known Jefferies in West Virginia.

Cyril Atwater had told her that he was sure South Carolina had *not* been the state where Jacob had grown up. He had insisted Jacob had said he was from another state out east. She'd thought Cyril was mistaken at the time, but now . . .

There was no doubt about it. Jacob had deliberately been keeping where he grew up a secret from *her*—Harper.

8

make me
FOREVER

thirty~seven

That afternoon, Jacob received a surprise phone call from an old friend, Miranda Meyer. He'd known Miranda for a long time. She was one of less than a handful of people from his past that he accepted into his present. Miranda had been his caseworker in the Adopt a West Virginia Child program, and they'd managed to maintain a friendship ever since then.

They caught up for a minute or two. Miranda followed some of Lattice's business news and commented on what she'd read, and Jacob filled her in on some of the unreported background details. He congratulated Miranda for being promoted yet again, this time becoming the current cabinet secretary of the West Virginia Department of Health and Human Services.

"That's quite a climb up the ladder, from being a caseworker in the adoption program to the secretary of the whole department," he told her.

"You're not the only one who was destined for greatness," Miranda joked. "Never fear, though. The adoption program is still under my supervision."

"And so we get to the reason you're calling?" Jacob said smoothly, leaning back in his desk chair. A call from Miranda of this kind wasn't a common occurrence, by any means, but it did happen sporadically enough for him to be comfortable with it. Miranda'd had many jobs at the WVDHHS before becoming the department head, and she'd made it her business to look out for Jacob while in each of those jobs . . . Jacob and Jake Tharp, that is.

Jacob had learned early on in his career that information was key to success. He'd cultivated a number of important contacts in both the government and private sector. Miranda was different, though. They'd kept in touch over the years, but he didn't think of Miranda like an informant. He didn't pay or exchange key information for her efforts. She did what she did because she was a friend.

"Yeah, you guessed it. Someone's been calling about the Jacob Sinclair adoption again," she said with a sigh. "A supervisor in the adoption department told me about it over lunch today—she'd gotten the information from one of her caseworkers."

"You usually e-mail when someone is nosing around," Jacob said, staring out the windows onto a sparkling Lake Tahoe. "Any reason this time warranted a phone call?"

"Aside from the fact that we haven't talked since two Christmases ago? Not really, it's just that the reporter calling and asking questions was from a paper right there in town with you. The *Sierra Tahoe Gazette*?" Jacob sat forward abruptly, his chair squeaking loudly. "You've told me Tahoe Shores is a pretty small town. I figured it might be someone you're hobnobbing with there, and if so, that you'd want to know that they were digging for information on you behind your back."

"Did you get the name of the reporter?"

"I did," Miranda said and he heard some paper shuffling. "It was a Harper McFadden. She called this morning. Know her?"

"Yeah. I know her," Jacob replied, his voice sounding even despite the icy sensation that suddenly poured through his veins.

After he'd hung up his phone, memories kept bombarding him. He recalled how sexy and fresh and uncontrived Harper had looked this morning following their hot, heavy, and hasty lovemaking, and her subsequent mad rush to get ready for work. She'd looked that innocent . . . that *loving* . . . just before walking into her office and digging around in a past that he'd told her again and again was dead?

She's remembering.

He felt a little sick at confronting that unavoidable fact. He honestly didn't know if he was supposed to be left angry, panicked, concerned, or grateful at that realization. It was bewildering, to view the world while standing at the still eye of a cyclone.

Dr. Fielding had certainly alluded to the fact that there was a possibility she'd remember. He—Jacob—could be the very trigger that was prompting her memories.

But that's only true if you assume what Dr. Fielding says is true, the logical part of his brain reasserted itself. Did he believe that he'd successfully buried weak, ineffective Jake Tharp and had evolved into an independent, utterly self-reliant man? Yes, he did.

Or at least he *had* . . . until Harper had walked back into his life.

There was no telling what Harper would do with those volatile memories. How much did she remember, and *when*, exactly had she begun to recall?

Or had she remembered all along, and knowingly reinserted herself into his life in order to get an inside position for this story?

Most of him thought that idea was paranoid and ridiculous. The tiny remainder that doubted only added a small, but rich vein of fuel to his unrest.

Something told him everything was about to blow up in face: his carefully buried past, his present, hard-won identity as Jacob Latimer . . . this incredible, dangerous *thing* he'd started with Harper.

He'd been wrong to think he could handle getting involved with her. The only chance he had of keeping them both safe was to convince her that the only future they had together was to leave the past where it belonged. If he couldn't accomplish that . . . he needed to seriously consider the fact that he was a harmful agent to her life.

It was time to seriously consider the bleak possibility that he might have to cut all ties with the only woman he'd ever loved . . .

. . . With the only woman he strongly suspected he'd *ever* be able to love.

. . .

Harper felt like she was watching herself from a distance that evening when she packed up and left the *Gazette*'s offices with the intent of returning to Jacob's home.

Elizabeth had gone through the protocol with her that morning on how to enter and exit the Lattice compound. Clarence, the stocky, friendly security guard who had spoken to Jacob from the woods on the first night she'd come to the mansion, was called in to enter Harper's fingerprints and record her speaking into a voice recognition system.

Upon Jacob's orders, Elizabeth had also instructed Jim to drive Harper to work that morning and pick her up again in the evening. When Jim picked her up after work, he started to take her directly to the mansion, but Harper stopped him.

"Can you take me back to my townhome, please?" she asked.

Jim glanced back uneasily. "But Elizabeth said I was supposed to take you back to Mr. Latimer's."

"I just need to pick up a few things at my place first," Harper told him. "And my car. I don't want to have to bother you about running me around."

"But I'd be happy to take you wherever—"

"I know, Jim," she assured, smiling at him when he looked at her anxiously in the rearview mirror. "But I'd prefer to have my car there, just in case. I'm pretty used to getting around on my own, you know."

She recognized that her insistence upon having her own vehicle at Jacob's compound was her small way of asserting her independence. Her car was a tangible means to come and go as she pleased. Today's meeting with Burt had stunned her. It was *always* hard for her to get a good perspective on Jacob, but after that meeting with Burt, everything had gotten worse. She got downright dizzy every time she tried to focus on what Jacob's guardedness meant . . .

. . . When she tried to puzzle out who Jacob was.

What Burt had uncovered about Regina Morrow was shocking,

but at least it made some sense, given the little Jacob had told her about Clint Jefferies taking advantage of Regina and hurting her. If Burt was correct in his suspicion about the nature of that party at Jefferies's, didn't that mean Regina had been a prostitute? How had Jacob known her? And had he been in love with Regina Morrow at the time he'd found her intoxicated and bruised up at his mentor's party?

It felt disorienting, entering the mansion that evening with no one there to greet her. In fact, a strange, surreal quality had settled on her consciousness ever since she'd seen those typed words on that report this morning.

West Virginia.

She had so many questions to ask Jacob, but knew she couldn't. She felt blocked at every turn. For one, she couldn't reveal that she'd been consulting with one of her reporters today in regard to a story about him. He'd think she'd betrayed him. Two, he'd made it very clear that his past was off-limits in their personal relationship.

She'd spoken with him briefly on the phone earlier at work, and he'd told her where to find him when she returned to the mansion. She traveled through the enormous house like a sleepwalker, passing the familiar entrance to Jacob's bedroom suite and continuing down the hall. She rapped softly on a pinewood door.

"Come in," Elizabeth called.

Harper entered. Elizabeth's portion of the office was large and airy. She had her own spectacular view of the lake and pine-covered mountains. Jacob's assistant sat behind her desk, her demeanor striking Harper as contained, but tense. Harper suspected it was her own presence in Jacob's private offices that made Elizabeth that way. Elizabeth continued to be polite and highly efficient in regard to Harper, but Harper still sensed her caution and a hint of disapproval.

"Hi," Harper greeted her.

"Hello," Elizabeth said, standing and coming around her desk. "He's waiting for you."

She led Harper to a massive door and knocked. Harper heard Jacob's distant, deep voice. Elizabeth held open the door for her.

"Thanks," she told Elizabeth before she walked into Jacob's office.

It was an enormous space. Three of the walls consisted of book-lined shelves, while the fourth was floor-to-ceiling windows and doors with the spectacular view of Lake Tahoe through them. Jacob's large, L-shaped desk was situated to the right of the room, so that he could easily look out at the panoramic view as he worked. He sat behind the desk. Harper was immediately aware of his stare on her as she walked into the room. Elizabeth closed the door behind her.

Harper walked toward him, gazing about the handsome, incredible room.

"You have quite the library here," she said, forcing a smile. "All these beautiful bookshelves and incredible books."

He stood as she approached him, looking very appealing in a pair of dark blue pants and an ivory collarless shirt. His appearance struck her as new and magnificent in that moment . . . freshly amazing, like she'd never seen him before. Yet he was achingly familiar. He was so big and tall. Somehow, his sense of graceful power struck her as miraculous. His expression was impassive, but his eyes shone with feeling as he regarded her.

She swallowed back a lump in her throat. He walked around his desk and rested his butt at the corner of it. When he held out his arms to her, her dazed, strange state fractured for a moment. She stepped between his legs, warmth thawing her when he wrapped his arms around her waist and brought her against him. Without saying a word, his mouth fastened on hers.

His firm, hot kiss further scattered her disorientation. Her arms snaked around his waist. How was it possible to be dazed and confused logically, when her senses grew so sharp and brilliant beneath his touch?

He smoothed back her hair with one hand, cupping the side of her head, and sealed their deep kiss. He continued to nibble hungrily at her lips.

"I missed you," he said.

"I missed you, too," she replied, shivering at the sexy sound of his gruff voice. His sharp gaze moved over her face. He slid his butt a few inches off the desk, his feet planted firmly on the floor, and pulled her more tightly between his legs.

"What's this I hear about you telling Jim you wanted to get your car?" he asked. The bright evening light off the lake made his agate eyes seem to glow. His hands lowered to her ass. "Are you planning on an escape, Harper?"

"Hell, no," she drawled, ducking forward to kiss his mouth again, diverting both him and herself from the fact that his teasing about her car had come a little too close to the truth. He caught her to him and deepened their kiss, pressing her against him tightly in a way that made it clear to her just how much he'd missed her. This time when he sealed their kiss, he straightened and stepped away from her. Harper tried to contain her disappointment as she watched him walk around his desk. Her gaze dropped down over his lean, powerful body. Despite both her reanimated and new doubts, her desire for him was cutting as it'd ever been.

Possibly even sharper.

He lifted an envelope from his desk and handed it to her. Harper took it with a questioning look, but he merely gestured that she should look for herself.

She unfolded several pieces of paper. They were lab reports and a written note from Dr. Amorantz. She looked up, her breath frozen in her lungs. Jacob wore a small, enigmatic smile.

"We're both as healthy as they come. Nothing else between us," he said, and there was something in his tone of voice, a quiet but profound victory.

She swallowed with difficulty and smiled.

"What's wrong?" he asked. "Aren't you glad that he cleared us for sex without protection?"

"Of course I am," she managed thickly.

"Then what is it?" he asked, coming around his desk with that predator's stalk she loved, but which also intimidated. She floundered for something to say. Her gaze flickered anxiously across the bookshelves behind him because she was having difficulty meeting his stare.

She froze with her mouth open, staring at very fine, gilded copies of *The Hobbit* and *The Lord of the Rings* directly behind his desk. Suddenly he turned, following her stare to the bookcase.

"Jacob," she said abruptly, recognizing the break in her composure and rushing to fill the vacuum. He glanced back at her narrowly. "I was wondering about something. You uh . . . you *did* say that you grew up in South Carolina, didn't you?" she asked in a rush. She was desperate, for some reason. It wasn't possible that he could see down into the heart of her, but she still got that impression sometimes that he *could*.

That he was doing it, right at this very moment. She waited for him to reply, her heart starting to throb in her ears.

"That's what I said, yes," he replied, stepping toward her, his face a mask.

"Oh. Did you mean for your entire childhood?" she asked, and despite her efforts at appearing light and calm, her voice broke.

"Why?" he asked, coming to a halt just inches in front of her. She couldn't seem to break his boring stare.

"I just wondered," she said with fake casualness, shrugging. "Someone at work today used the term 'born and bred.' They said they were born and bred in Tahoe Shores, and they meant they'd never left it until they went to college. So I was just wondering if you meant the same thing when you said the same about South Carolina . . ." She faded off lamely. His stare seemed to drain the oxygen from her lungs.

"I've told you that I don't want to talk about my past. I don't want to focus on it. But you can't seem to let it go, can you?"

His quietly uttered words seemed to strike her like bullets. She didn't reply. She couldn't. It was like there was a squeezing hand at her throat.

When it became clear she wasn't going to answer him, he grabbed her wrist.

"Where are we going?" she asked him when he started toward the door and she had to jog to keep up with his long-legged stride.

"To get your head out of the past and into the present, where it belongs," she heard him reply with steely determination.

thirty~eight

A moment later, he slammed the door of his bedroom suite shut behind them and fastened the lock.

"Jacob—"

She cut herself off when he dropped her hand and moved past her, his face rigid. She didn't really know what to say, anyway. What could she do or say to reassure him, when she couldn't reassure herself anymore?

What the hell is happening?

Her heart pounded out an excited, anxious tattoo in her ears. He crossed the suite and opened a door—a door that she'd seen him go into on several occasions in the past. When he walked out a moment later, her gaze dipped to what he held in one hand: several bundles of black rope.

"Don't look at me like that," he said quietly, his eyes flashing as he walked toward her. "You know I'm not going to hurt you." He paused in front of her, his hard mouth slanted. "Do you not want to do this?"

"I . . . I don't know."

"I'm trying to haul you back into the moment, Harper," he bit out.

For a few seconds, her whole world was the vision of his stormy eyes and the throb of her heart in her ears. She wanted him so much . . .

I love him.

She found herself nodding, compelled by his eyes.

As always.

"Come over to the bed," he said.

She followed him to the foot of his bed. He tossed down the bundles of rope and turned to her, immediately beginning to unfasten her blouse.

"Jacob, don't be mad at me."

His gaze shot up to her face.

"I'm not mad at you, Harper. Do you think I should be? Do you think I should be pissed at you for keeping secrets from me, just because you're mad at me for not babbling on about my childhood?"

She blinked, startled by his slicing vehemence. She opened her mouth to respond, but he cut her off.

"I'm not going to make love to you right now because I'm mad." He unfastened the last button and jerked her blouse open, pushing it down her arms. "I'm doing it exactly because of what I said before: to get your head into the moment."

"Because you know I can't think about anything else *but* the present when you tie me up and make me feel?" she accused.

He paused in the action of unfastening her skirt.

"*Make* you? Is that what you think? That I'm *forcing* you?"

"No," she admitted, a little ashamed at how condemning she'd sounded because of her anxiety.

His expression hardened. He methodically stripped her, all except her black pumps.

"Leave them on," he said, referring to her shoes. He turned to pick up the coils of rope. "Lie on your back in the center of the bed. I'm going to restrain your arms and legs to it."

Her heart felt too big for her chest as she climbed onto the bed, but she was feeling something else besides trepidation. His seemingly dispassionate undressing of her and his instructions to lie on the bed so that he could tie her up had created a low burn of arousal at her sex. Who knew why she liked it so much, to be restrained by him? To give complete control to him? She only knew she *did*.

Both her anxiety and arousal elevated in tandem a moment later when he gave her terse instructions to take a spread-eagle position on the bed. She watched him, having trouble catching her breath, as he soberly and expertly began to restrain her. She realized that the four separate bundles of rope were pre-tied for this specific task. All he had to do was slip a thick coil around wrists and ankles, tighten it, and then fasten the free end of the rope to a corner of the bed.

When he finally straightened after tying off her last limb, he looked very forbidding. She studied his face as he walked around the bed, and then his body. His flinty expression wasn't from anger. Her gaze stuck on the fullness of his crotch. No. She thought that *determinedly aroused* might describe his state better.

The spread-eagle position he'd told her to take left her feeling glaringly vulnerable and aroused . . . turned on and unable to hide it. She panted shallowly, her rising and falling breasts betraying her excitement as did her tight, prickling nipples. Cool air tickled at her spread sex, as well, informing her that she'd grown damp watching him methodically restraining her.

He began to undress. His averted gaze hurt her a little. Until he removed his pants and underwear anyway, and she confirmed how thoroughly excited he was, despite his dispassionate expression. He was hurting, somehow. Just like she was.

The recognition only added to her chaotic state.

He reached into the bedside drawer, grabbing something. He crawled onto the bed, coming down on his side next to her, his elbow on the mattress, his hand propping up his head. She swallowed thickly when he met her stare.

"Jacob, what *is* it? What's wrong?" she whispered. Frustration simmered in her, because not only would he not help her clarify his turmoil, he wouldn't even acknowledge it existed.

"*Nothing* is wrong, Harper," he said evenly, opening his hand over her belly. He began to stroke her naked body, holding her stare. He brushed his fingertips over her ribs and her sensitive sides, making her nipples pull so tight that the ache in them swelled to sharp pain. She clamped her eyelids shut, unable to keep meeting his determined, blazing stare. "Why can't you believe me when I say that everything is fine? That there's no reason to go digging around for reasons to doubt me."

His fingertips brushed over her rock hard nipples. She gasped shakily. He leaned over her. "Do you *want* to doubt me, Harper?"

"No," she said with shaky emphasis.

"Do you doubt, right here in the moment?"

"*No.*"

God, no. The only thing she did in that moment was hunger.

Then his mouth was on hers, feeding that hunger . . . mounting it. He massaged her breasts forcefully while he kissed her, pinching lightly at her hard nipples. It felt so good. She grew so desperate, she thought she might explode from the nipple stimulation alone. Then he was lifting his head and kissing her neck, whispering hotly in her ear.

"Just let go. You're mine right now. Completely mine. No one is going to take you from me. Nothing is."

She sobbed raggedly, sinking into the mattress, surrendering to the moment. And his mouth was on her breast, his hand caressing her naked thigh, and she felt herself falling deeper under his spell. His tongue lashed at her nipple, torturing the exquisitely sensitive flesh. He drew on her with electrical precision. She cried out, her eyes going wide. *Could* she climax with just his mouth on her breast?

She never found out, because suddenly his hand was between her legs, and he was pressing a vibrator to her clit. She seized in climax.

When she came back to herself, he was drawing on her other breast just as forcefully as he had the other. He'd lifted the vibrator from her clit, but his hand was still between her legs. As she panted, still in recovery from her climax, he set the bullet vibrator on her mons and thrust a finger into her sheath. She moaned his name, but he seemed impervious to her sweet agony as he continued to suck on the tip of her breast and finger-fuck her as deep as he could. Harper lay there, swimming in sensation, hating her helplessness . . .

Loving it, because she was in his hands.

A while later, he released her nipple and fastened on her mouth, instead. He thrust his tongue between her lips, kissing her demandingly, and lifted the vibrator from her mons. He slipped it between her labia, buzzing her until she burned in agony again.

When she ignited, she screamed into his marauding kiss.

"Jacob, please," she muttered when he finally released her mouth after her shudders of bliss had waned. She didn't know what she begged for, though: more torture or freedom from it? It didn't matter. There was no escape from him. He kissed and licked her everywhere, his appetite shocking her. She grew dizzy at the sensation of him kissing her inner thigh. Then his lips brushed her labia and his head dipped. Harper stared blindly into space, held hostage by his hot, deep, demanding kiss on her sex.

He brought her to climax again with his firm, demanding tongue. Not until she lay panting on the bed, her muscles and nerves spent, completely wrung out by pleasure, did he crawl between her thighs, brace his upper body by pressing his fists into the mattress, and enter her.

She gave a sharp cry, her body tensing. It was the first time he'd been in her raw. He was steely hard and swollen. Because she couldn't tilt her hips to better accommodate him in the taut, spread-eagle position, the pressure was intense at first . . . almost uncomfortable. He paused at her cry, but she saw the fire in his eyes. His patience wouldn't last long.

"Are you all right?" he asked her thickly, waiting for her body to get used to his cock being buried inside her at this angle.

"Yes."

He thrust, wincing in pleasure when his balls pressed tightly against her outer sex. He looked heartrendingly beautiful to her in that moment, his burnished hair mussed, his hard mouth still slick from her juices.

"God, you feel like heaven," he rasped. Harper held her breath, awed by the emotion she heard in his voice.

He began to move, slaking his thirst on her, holding her stare the whole time. He took her hard, his hips and ass moving in a tense, erotic rhythm, his pelvis slapping briskly against her spread thighs with every downstroke. Pleasure finally melted away his impassive mask.

He thrust deep. A muscle in his cheek jumped from tension.

"Mine," he growled. "*Say* it, Harper."

She gasped, staring up at him incredulously. "I'm yours," she said, shaking her head on the pillow. "And you're *mine*, Jake."

He started, his eyes flashing at her words. He began to shudder. He groaned gutturally and began to pour himself into her for the first time—all of his need, all of his longing and pain.

All of his shame.

She panted, held in a grip of shock, unable to believe her senses.

Maybe Jacob hadn't meant to reveal the truth during their emotional lovemaking, but he had, anyway. *Hadn't* he?

He'd stamped himself onto her soul just now. And in doing so, she'd spied a crack in his armor. He met her stare, still panting heavily from his orgasm. She peered disbelievingly into his eyes like they were a window to her past.

"*Jake Tharp?*" she whispered. "It is you, isn't it?"

Twenty Years Ago

Harper and he burst through the front doors of the Barterton Police Station at around dusk, hand in hand and gasping for breath. From the alarmed look on the female receptionist's face, Jake guessed they looked pretty bad after finishing the last leg of their journey fueled solely by adrenaline and fear.

The sheriff of Barterton, Adam Maddington—a thin, serious man in his late thirties—was notified of their arrival. He immediately informed the state police and the FBI via phone.

The small police station had been relatively sleepy when Jake and Harper stumbled into it, but it started to bustle with a sense of emergency and purpose with their arrival. From snatches of distant conversation between employees, Jake started to realize that Harper's kidnapping and the hunt for her was a gigantic deal.

"Guess we know the reason for that helicopter we heard now," Jake mumbled to Harper as they sat side by side, listening to Sheriff Maddington and two deputies talking tersely on separate phones.

"You mean . . ."

He nodded. "Yeah. They were searching for you."

Sheriff Maddington also called for some EMTs to come check their injuries. Afterward, he settled in to patiently listen to their story.

"You mean your uncle, Emmitt Tharp, is still back there in the woods somewhere?" he interrupted Jake's description.

Jake glanced over at a dirt-smudged, bloodied, bruised Harper uneasily and nodded. It made him sick, to think of how he'd plunged that knife into human flesh . . . how Harper had watched him. He'd felt like he didn't have any choice. If he didn't disable Emmitt, his uncle would catch up to them for sure.

Is that what Harper's memory of him would be? Is that how she'd remember him, as a killer?

State troopers and two FBI agents arrived at the station during the sheriff's questioning. They joined in the interrogation. Occasionally the adults talked tensely with each other in a muted tone Jake couldn't make out. The overhead lights in the police station felt very harsh on his dry, burning eyes. He and Harper just sat there on two straight-backed chairs, gripping each other's hands tightly.

There was talk of organizing a search party to find Emmitt. Jake volunteered to go with them to the location where he'd stabbed his uncle. The two agents wouldn't agree to that plan, however. Instead, they got a map and Jake pointed out their path on it as best he could. One of the deputies who was familiar with the area told him that his descriptions of the landscape were top-notch and extremely detailed.

"Jake's an expert in the woods," Harper told the group of men. "He saved my life more than once."

"You were lucky Jake was there. We all were," one of the agents agreed, patting Jake on the shoulder before he walked away with the map in his hand. Jake flushed in mixed embarrassment and pride at that, ducking his head to hide it. Harper just held his hand even tighter.

The EMTs arrived. After examining them both, they proclaimed them essentially healthy. They told Sheriff Maddington that the worst of their combined injuries was the knife cut at the corner of Harper's mouth. She required stitches.

Harper squeezed his hand so tight it brought tears to his eyes while the female EMT put four stitches in the wound. He knew she suffered far worse, though, so he didn't say a word.

"Mr. Maddington, has someone called my parents?" Harper asked after the EMT had finished. Jake noticed she was visibly trembling.

"Do you think she could lie down somewhere, Sheriff?" Jake asked before Maddington could reply to Harper.

Maddington looked over at Jake, and then at Harper, and nodded. "That's a good idea, young man." He called out a request for some cots to his deputy. "And your mom and dad *have* been contacted, Harper. It was one of the first calls I made. I understand they've been staying at a hotel over in Poplar Gorge ever since you went missing. They're coming here to the station, and should be here soon. Those are going to be two relieved parents." Maddington transferred his gaze to Jake. "I put in a call to your grandma too, Jake. I need to check the number you gave me, though. It said that line was out of service."

"It's the right number," he said, embarrassed. "She hasn't had the money to pay her phone bill for a while."

Maddingon nodded. "I'll send up one of my deputies to her place whenever we get a free moment here."

The deputy brought over the cots and set them up in the midst of the large common-area office of the police station.

"Lie down too, Jake," Harper whispered to him when the deputy walked away to get some blankets. He started to lie down on the cot next to her. "No. Here," she whispered, scooting over on her cot to make room for him.

He hadn't realized how numb he was until he lay down next to Harper and she put her arms around him. Her body felt warm and good next to his. It thawed his shock. They huddled together, chasing each other's shivers away. After the deputy came over and covered them with a blanket, Harper whispered to him.

"You did it, Jake. You saved my life."

She pressed her lips to his cheek softly, the bandage at the corner of his mouth tickling his skin. It was the first kiss he'd ever gotten from a girl.

It was the sweetest caress he'd ever received in his life.

"They're going to split us apart soon," he said through a swollen throat. He knew that by some unspoken agreement, they didn't speak of the invisible bond between them, but he couldn't seem to stop himself at that moment.

"No they're not," Harper whispered fiercely, pulling him closer against her. He felt so raw, so turned inside out. "I'm going to talk to my parents about you. It's going to be okay. You'll see. Jake?" she asked softly when he remained stiff and frozen, trying to hold in so much feeling, straining like crazy to do it while holding her in his arms. He felt her warm lips brush against his temple, and he shuddered.

"I'm yours," she whispered. "And you're mine. Not in the ugly way, like your uncle thought he owned the dogs. In a beautiful way, like Mrs. Roundabout was yours, and you were hers, because something tied you to each other. And you just feel the bond, and you know it's true. *No one* can change that, Jake."

He couldn't believe she was saying his thoughts out loud. It was too incredible to believe. He lifted his head slightly, needing to see her face. Without really telling himself to do it—if he'd thought about it, he would have chickened out—he leaned down and touched his lips to hers.

"Go to sleep," he said quietly. In those moments, her insides were his. He knew how exhausted she was.

Her heavy eyelids drooped, but then she fought it, opening them again.

"I can't," she whispered. "I don't want to leave you."

"I'm not going anywhere." *I ain't got nowhere to go.* "Get some rest, Harper."

He watched as her eyelids finally grew too heavy to support anymore, and she succumbed to exhaustion. As much as he wanted to believe the things Harper had said about her parents and the future, he was Jake Tharp.

He hadn't been taught to believe in miracles.

That was how Harper's distraught parents first saw their daughter following the nightmare of her kidnapping: fast asleep, bandaged, pale, and obviously traumatized . . .

. . . And held fast in the arms of the nephew of the monster who had stolen her from them.

thirty~nine

Present Day

"Jake Tharp? It is you, isn't it?"

His rough breathing ceased completely at her whisper. Harper, too, held her breath, the handful of words seemingly hanging suspended in the air between them. Suddenly, he rose from the bed, naked and beautiful.

"Jacob?"

She saw a muscle flinch in his cheek as he went to the corner of the bed. One by one, he released her restraints and loosened the rope from her limbs. By the time he'd gotten to the fourth one, he still hadn't responded to her question. She watched him methodically go about his task, his face and body rigid, his cock still formidable and slick from their combined essences. It was that vision—the very image of a viral, powerful male—that made impossibility crash wholesale into reality.

Harper flew off the bed.

"Harper?"

She ignored him, hurrying into the bathroom and finding the two soft robes they'd used occasionally in the past week alongside each other on hooks. When she returned, he took the proffered robe wordlessly. She hurried into the garment, needing armor, no matter how fragile that protection was. She was relieved that he shrugged into his robe, as well. They faced each other. For a stretched moment, she just stared at his face, absorbing every detail. He looked very hard to her in that moment . . . indescribably miraculous. His agate eyes moved over her face.

"Are you going to be okay?" he asked quietly. "Harper?" he prompted when she didn't immediately respond.

Bitterness sliced through her unexpectedly like a knife at his quiet, cautious tone.

"How could you not have *told* me?"

His mouth pressed into a hard line.

"How could you not have told me?" she repeated wildly.

He flinched slightly at her shout. "I thought maybe it was best for you not to remember. Your father had cured you of your anxiety about what had happened . . . about Emmitt—"

She started forward, stumbled, and started to go down to the floor. Jacob leapt forward, catching her. Her cheek bumped against his solid chest. She gasped for air. It'd been hearing him say that name from her past . . . *Emmitt*. She hadn't realized it until then, but part of her had remained unconvinced until that very moment. But the truth had just slammed into her consciousness with one word, smashing any chance of denial to bits. She *wasn't* deluding herself. She wasn't going mad. He'd just said Emmitt's name.

"Oh my God. Oh my God, I thought you were dead."

"What?" His hands tightened on her upper arms. "*Harper?* What did you say?"

She looked up at his handsome, hovering face incredulously. A man's face. *Jake's* face.

"I thought you were dead."

"Who told you *that*?"

"My parents. After we went back to Georgetown, my parents told me you were dead," she stated numbly.

"Harper, come over here and sit down," Jacob insisted when he took in the paleness of her face and the glazed quality of her blue-green eyes. Was she about to have a reoccurrence of the panic attacks she had as a girl?

He put his hands on her shoulders and drew her over to a couch in the seating area of his suite. He urged her to sit. She had the strangest expression on her face as she stared up at him. He came down next to her on the couch. She never took her eyes off his face.

"You're really Jake Tharp?" she asked weakly.

He frowned. "Harper, are you okay?"

"What? Yes."

"You don't feel like you're going to have a panic attack or faint or anything?" he asked concernedly, brushing some strands of copper-colored hair off her face. She caught his hand with her own, halting him against her cheek.

"*Answer* me. Are you Jake Tharp?"

He studied her closely. She looked distressed and shocked, but not to any degree out of proportion to the situation. Certainly, she didn't appear to be any more shocked than he felt at hearing that she'd believed him to be dead all these years . . . and that it was her parents who had told her that bald-faced lie.

"I *was* Jake Tharp." He felt a shudder go through her. He cupped her face. "I haven't been him for a long, long time, though, Harper."

"And you *knew* it was me, didn't you? From the beginning?" she asked incredulously.

His thumb brushed across her scar. Again, he absorbed her trembling.

"I knew it was you," he said. "I've followed your career. I knew where you lived."

A tear skipped off her cheek and wet his forefinger when she shook her head. "How could you not have *told* me? Why didn't you come and see me, if you . . . if you knew where I was?" she asked brokenly. Her disbelief and hurt sliced through him.

"I thought you wouldn't want to see me. When we did run into each other here in Tahoe Shores, it seemed pretty clear you didn't remember me. There was no recognition on your face. You never mentioned being kidnapped as a kid. You *didn't* recognize me, did you? When we first met?"

"No. How could I? The Jake I knew was barely five foot two and skinnier than I'd been. You're six feet plus and as strong as a giant. Why would I think of Jake after first seeing you?"

A feeling of mixed grim satisfaction and inevitability went through him at her words. "But you were curious, weren't you? You had to keep digging for the truth? You contacted adoption services at the Department of Health and Human Resources in West Virginia today."

"I don't know what you're talking about," she whispered.

He dropped his hand from her face. "I know that you called West Virginia adoption services today and were asking questions in the adoption department about my adoption. I'm friends with the department head. Back then, when I was a kid, she was my adoption caseworker. She told me about you calling soon after she learned about it from one of her managers. Miranda has been pretty protective of my case over the years."

"I never called there."

He opened his mouth to argue, but took in her blank expression of shock.

"Who did, then? Miranda told me that a woman called, and she gave her name as Harper McFadden. That's what brought this whole thing up with you today, right?"

She swallowed thickly. He found himself touching her again, cupping the side of her head, moving his fingertips along the column of her neck. He couldn't stand seeing her so discombobulated and knowing the reason why was him.

"One of my reporters—Burt Chavis—came to me today. He's been wanting to do a story on you, preferably one on the insider trading scandal and Clint Jefferies. He wanted my permission as his editor to pursue it."

He stiffened. "Did you give it to him?"

"Don't look at me like that, Jacob," she said. Despite his prickle of annoyance at being told that a local reporter was indeed intent on re-animating his ghosts, he was glad to see the familiar flash of fire melt Harper's shocked expression. "I told him that what he had was unsubstantiated and weak. I also told him that I'd never use my relationship with you to gather insider information."

He winced. "All right. Fair enough. Who do you think did call the adoption offices in West Virginia, then?"

"That's what I started to say—Burt Chavis came to me with some information that was weakly relevant to a story, and Ruth Dannen, our features editor, overheard him broaching the topic with me. I think they might have teamed up after Burt left my office today. Ruth wasn't very happy when I shut her out of the conversation. She accused me of protecting you because I'm sleeping with you."

"So you think Ruth could have called the adoption offices, asking about my case and pretending to be you?"

"I think there's a pretty good chance, yes. One thing is for certain: It *wasn't* me," Harper said so steadfastly he believed her. Her gaze flickered over his face. "Don't worry. I'll confront Ruth about it. And as long as your adoption records are kept sealed tight, I honestly don't think that story has legs to run on."

"So how did you connect Jake Tharp to me? I thought that with time and your dad's hypnosis, you'd completely forgotten me. And back then—when we were kids—you never answered my letters—"

He started in shock when he felt a violent shudder go through her.

"*Oh my God,*" she exclaimed, her hand covering her mouth. For a second, he thought she was going to be sick.

"Harper, it's going to be okay—" he began, alarmed. She threw herself at him, cutting him off, her arms encircling him. Emotion swelled in him. She hugged him so tight. It was the way she used to hug Jake Tharp.

The sweet, desperate way she used to hug *him*.

"I never got them. I never got any letters, Jake. Never. Oh my God," she repeated, her hands running anxiously over his back and shoulders. She leaned her head back and abruptly shoved at his chest. He gaped in bewilderment at her blazing expression. "I'm so *mad* at you! How can you *think* I wouldn't remember Jake Tharp?"

"I just thought . . . maybe it all didn't mean to you what it did to me. You had a family who adored you, a safe home." She moaned, shaking her head furiously, but he continued to try to make her understand. "And when you told me about your dad treating your phobias and panic attacks with hypnosis, I thought maybe he'd encouraged you to forget the whole trauma . . . and Jake. I thought *I* was forgotten with all the rest of it."

"I would *never* forget you," she nearly shouted, touching his shoulders and then his hair. "After they told me you were dead, your memory haunted me even more. I felt like you were dead because of *me*. It was all my fault. If I hadn't begged you to risk your life and save me, you'd still be alive. The world just felt like this big, horrible, unsafe place when I thought you were dead . . . knowing it was my responsibility that you *were*."

"No, Harper, listen to me," he insisted, grabbing one of her anxiously moving hands. He worried she was about to spiral into a panic. "You didn't cost me my life. You *gave* it to me. Don't you get that? Defying Emmitt and fighting him was the defining moment of my life. I would have never had the courage to do it, if I didn't have you to do it *for*." He hesitated. "You know he's dead, right?"

He could tell by her blank expression she didn't.

"He died in prison two years ago from a heart attack."

She hugged him again, and for a strained moment, neither of them spoke. He clutched her tight to him, feeling the indescribably sweet beat of her heart against his.

"I can't believe this is happening," she gasped after a moment. "You look so different. You *are* so different . . . and yet, you're *not*. I felt so close to you from the beginning, even though I couldn't figure out why. I've been thinking more about Jake—about you—than I have since I was a teenager. I kept dreaming about being with him . . . you. I couldn't figure out what was happening to me—"

He pulled her tighter against him when she shook with emotion. For a wild moment, they were those two ragged kids all over again, so desperate to touch each other, so needy to affirm their bond and to know that they weren't alone in a vast, scary world. He just held her while she cried, trying his best to absorb her grief, her disbelief . . . and yes, her joy. He sensed her stunned happiness in the way she continued to touch him frantically, as though she were trying to reassure herself of the reality of him. It was her anxious touch that tore at him more than anything.

"I don't understand . . . and I want to so badly," she said wetly. "There was never any car accident?"

"Car accident?" he asked, leaning back and peering at her face, puzzled.

"They told me that you'd been killed while you were in a car accident with a friend of your grandma Rose's. That's what they said. They told me when we went back to Georgetown, after Emmitt's sentencing."

He stared at her, stunned. "I was never in a car accident. I was transferred to a temporary foster home in Charleston after Grandma Rose died that October. But I was never in an accident."

He'd seen her glaze-eyed expression before. She was in shock. Maybe he was, too, come to think of it.

"Your parents must have told you I was dead because they were worried about you. It was after you went back with them to Georgetown that you started having those panic attacks, right? Maybe your dad thought that if you got letters from me, or if we insisted on seeing each other, it would remind you of your kidnapping. Maybe he thought you wouldn't be able to heal if I was in your life."

"No," she whispered, shaking her head adamantly. Another tear bounced down her cheek, and he dried it with his thumb. "I didn't start having those panic attacks until after they told me you were dead. I was inconsolable, Jake. *Jacob. That's* why I turned into such a mess."

She squeezed him tight again. He hugged her back, struggling to wrap his head around the fact that Harper McFadden not only had never forgotten him, but that she'd mourned his loss even more than he'd suffered hers.

forty

She couldn't believe her parents had done it. They'd witnessed firsthand how attached she'd grown to Jake Tharp. They knew how she owed him her life, and how close they'd become on their escape from Emmitt. The contrast of her love for them, her grief over their sudden deaths, and her disbelief that they'd intentionally lied to her about Jake left her feeling ripped wide-open.

And increasingly, angry. Not just at her parents. At Jacob.

He must have noticed her inconsolable state, because he abruptly stood and announced that he was going to have Lisa bring them something to eat.

"You're pale. I think we need some fuel if we're going to continue this conversation," he said grimly, picking up the house phone.

"I don't want anything to eat," Harper insisted, thinking the idea of calmly eating a meal in these circumstances was annoyingly bizarre. Jacob ignored her, however, turning his attention to talking to Lisa and requesting that some herbal tea and a light dinner be sent up to his suite. Harper responded to his stubbornness by gathering up her clothes and going into the bathroom to change. She already felt vulnerable enough in front of Jacob. *Jake!* Being dressed would help to ground her. She was relieved to see when she returned from the bathroom that he'd re-dressed, as well.

Did that mean he felt as exposed as she did?

"I'll never forgive my parents for lying to me about it," she said after the dinner tray had been delivered and sat on the coffee table in front of them. She hadn't touched either the poured chamomile tea or the salad and fresh-baked bread. She stood and began to pace in front of the fireplace. Jacob remained seated, watching her soberly as he held a cup of steaming tea in his large hand. "All that grief I felt. All that guilt for feeling like I contributed to your death—"

Jacob set down his cup loudly.

"They did it because they loved you so much. Surely you can understand that they'd want to completely cut away that experience from your life."

"How can you *defend* them?" Harper asked, spinning to face him.

"I'm not saying what they did was right. But I understand why they did it. If I was a parent, and I had your father's particular skills, I might have done the same thing."

His somber defense of her parents' actions only frothed her fury.

"You're defending what they did because you're *like* them." He gave her a startled glance, and she realized she was shouting. She couldn't seem to stop herself, though. The lid had just popped off her emotions. "You tried to cut Jake Tharp out of *your* life, just like my parents tried to slice him out of mine. You killed off that little boy and buried him like he was some kind of shameful secret."

"Harper—"

"No, I'm telling the truth and you know it! You say you didn't tell me that you were Jake Tharp because you worried it'd re-traumatize me, erase all the good work my dad did in treating me," she said sarcastically. "But the truth is, you didn't want me to remember Jake Tharp because you're ashamed of him."

"What if I am?" Jacob bellowed suddenly, flying to his feet. She started back in surprise. "I was helpless and weak. I was Emmitt's whipping boy. Do you think I *want* to remember that? I spent my life trying to be the opposite of Jake Tharp. You have no right to criticize me for wanting that. Not privileged, rich, adored little Harper McFadden."

"You *jerk*. Privileged, adored little Harper McFadden thought Jake Tharp was the bravest, smartest, nicest person she'd ever met in her life," Harper yelled, stepping toward him aggressively. She checked herself when she saw his face stiffen, as if she'd slapped him or something.

She wanted to rage at him, and she wanted to cry, and she wanted to never stop hugging him . . . and she didn't know what she wanted. "Why are you looking at me like you're surprised?" she demanded, clamping her eyelids shut to get ahold of herself. "I loved you, don't you get that? I asked my parents if they'd become foster parents and let you come live with us! I had your room all planned out. I couldn't wait to show you the museums in DC and give you my copy of *The Lord of the Rings* to read and so many other things." Tears gushed out of her eyes as the poignant memories rushed her. "And you have the nerve to stand there and tell me that both you and my parents were right to stage Jake Tharp's death? Well, fuck you, Jacob Latimer."

She started toward the door of his suite but he halted her with his hands on her shoulders. He spun her to face him. He towered over her—so tall and strong, so commanding, so pivotal in her aware-ness . . . so different from Jake Tharp . . .

So *like* him.

"I *was* worried about you, Harper. How can you think that either me or your parents were only being selfish in wishing you could forget Emmitt and the kidnapping?"

"You can't just cut away the bad," she seethed. "You take the good with it. That's what you and my parents tried to do to me. They stole Jake Tharp from me. *You* did." She shoved his hands off her shoulders. Jacob's furious, bewildered expression convinced her that he thought she was babbling nonsense.

Well, too bad.

"Just leave me alone, Jacob."

She turned and walked out of the room.

Three days later, Harper glanced up from her work and saw Ruth Dannen passing her office, purposefully avoiding Harper's stare. She was clearly still pissed at the dressing-down Harper had given her for calling adoption services in West Virginia and pretending she was Harper. Their ensuing argument had been loud enough that Sangar had heard, and demanded they both go to his office. After he'd listened to both of them, he'd called Burt in to give his input.

Afterward, Sangar had fully backed Harper in the idea that there was no story in regard to Burt's lead. He'd forbidden Burt and Ruth to pursue it any further. Harper and Burt had left Sangar's office, while Ruth remained. Whatever Sangar had said to Ruth afterward had silenced Ruth, all right. It'd also turned her into a frigid, silent bitch every time Harper was around.

Harper couldn't find any energy to care one way or another.

She'd been having difficulty concentrating for days. It'd been that way ever since she'd left the Lattice compound last Tuesday. She was a walking zombie. Her chaotic thoughts wouldn't allow her to rest. She couldn't eat. If it weren't for the rote quality of some of her work, she would have been completely dysfunctional in the newsroom, as well.

When she'd stormed out of the compound Tuesday evening, Jacob had immediately tried to contact her. He'd called her cell repeatedly. When she'd refused to answer, he'd even shown up at her town house. Harper had laid huddled in her bed, sleepless and miserable, listening to him pound on her front door and once—horribly—calling her name in a wild, angry, worried tone. At the sound of his voice, Harper had finally sat up and thrown off the covers. She'd raced down the stairs and flung open the front door.

But by that time, he'd gone.

A black mood had descended on her and not left her since then.

She glanced up distractedly when she heard a knock. Burt hovered in her open doorway like he wasn't sure he wanted to cross the threshold.

"Come on in, Burt," she said, pushing back her keyboard. "What can I do for you?"

Things had been a little awkward between them since Sangar intervened in his story idea the other day, but nowhere near as strained as things were with Ruth.

"Look. I know Sangar has quashed the Latimer story, so I'm not trying to say we should do anything with this . . ."

She arched her eyebrows when he reluctantly faded off. "*What*, exactly?" Harper asked.

He inhaled slowly and stared at a piece of paper he was holding. "It might not be too pleasant for you to know, but I thought you'd want to, anyway. I wouldn't have felt right, not telling you."

"Know what?" Harper prodded, growing impatient with his hesitance.

He tossed the piece of paper on the desk. "I'd done some digging before Sangar shut us down, and this just came through. It's about that girl, Gina Morrow. She goes by Regina Morrow now. She lives in Napa. And apparently . . . she lives with Jacob Latimer."

Harper froze before she snatched up the paper. "*Lives* with him?"

"Maybe not lives *with* him," Burt said, shifting on his feet restlessly. "But the address of her residence is right there. She lives on his property in Napa. I just thought you'd want to know."

She glanced up, dazed. Burt looked extremely uncomfortable.

"I do want to know. Thanks, Burt."

forty~one

Jacob stared out the floor-to-ceiling windows onto a brilliant early fall day. An unusually strong wind had made Tahoe choppy today, making the deep blue water sparkle and flash in his eyes.

He'd reached a breaking point.

He'd had enough of Harper avoiding him. Her anger at discovering that he had been Jake Tharp stunned him to the core. He'd expected shock. He'd expected disbelief and anxiety. But her fury had completely taken him off guard. What she'd said before she stormed off had altered him, somehow. Transformed him. He still could hear her voice as clearly as if she stood next to him, three days after the fact.

"Harper McFadden thought Jake Tharp was the bravest, smartest, nicest person she'd ever met in her life." And then, "I loved you, don't you get that?"

His feeling of shock and amazement remained as well, as fresh as the moment she'd uttered those words. He would have questioned her veracity in saying it if he hadn't witnessed firsthand her fierce anger.

He recalled how in awe he'd been when they were kids in that police station, huddled together on that cot, when she'd spoken out loud about their invisible connection. But his amazement on hearing her say three days ago that she'd thought Jake Tharp was the bravest person she'd ever known had been far greater. The simple reason for his shock was that while they shared so much, and felt so much in common . . . Jacob held the opposite opinion of Jake Tharp.

And Harper was pissed off at him for that.

At first, he'd been just as furious at her for her stubbornness. What right did she have to be mad at him for wanting to transform himself into something that was the opposite of what he'd been as a boy? But then as the hours turned into days, and she continued to avoid him, he'd had time to think. Slowly, it began to dawn on him. Her anger at him was the official stamp of truth. Harper *honestly* felt like she'd been robbed of Jake Tharp. Not only by her parents. But by him—Jacob Latimer.

It was a jaw-dropping revelation to him. It was her anger at her loss that made him first start to reconsider that scared, weak little boy that he'd been. If Harper had loved Jake that much . . . didn't that mean Jake had been somehow worthy?

He didn't have all the answers. He only knew he wasn't going to figure any of it out, without Harper at his side. The ability for deep, restful sleep had abandoned him. How could he possibly rest enough to puzzle out his life, with Harper gone? It'd become an acknowledged fact in his mind during the past several days. He loved her. He'd never stopped loving her, even though the type of love he felt as a man was more complex than it'd ever been when he was a kid. It was deeper. Exponentially more compelling.

Another thing he knew? He was worried sick about her. He knew better than most how stubborn she could be.

But so was he.

He knew precisely where she was at that very moment. He knew plenty of people in town who had been willing to report back to him whether or not her car was in the *Gazette* parking lot and if she appeared reasonably healthy over the past few days. Harper was no Regina, of course. She wouldn't fall to bits just because they'd argued. Apparently, she wasn't going to disintegrate even at the discovery that he was Jake Tharp.

Did that mean she wouldn't flee or freak out if she discovered his other shameful secret?

One thing was certain: He was never going to find out standing in his office. He'd go over to the *Gazette*. He'd demand that she talk to him. When they were little, Harper had told him nothing could sever their bond. If that was true, not even her anger at him could cut it.

That was all there was to it.

He jerked around and stalked rapidly toward his office door. Before he could touch the knob, however, there was a knock on it. He opened it impatiently.

Elizabeth stood on the other side.

"Jacob," Elizabeth said. She looked startled.

"What's wrong?" Jacob asked, recognizing his assistant's atypical discomposure.

"It's *Regina*," she said under her breath, nodding subtly behind her to her office. "She's . . . not well."

"Jacob," Regina Morrow called loudly. "Jacob, I have to see you. *Now.*"

Jacob saw Regina striding toward him. She wore a pink trench coat belted at the waist, four-inch brown leather heels, and a matching purse. Her breasts swelled at the opening of the coat. Her lush, long hair was mussed and her lipstick was smeared. He immediately knew she was either intoxicated or in the midst of a manic episode by the shiny brilliance of her eyes, her plastered smile, and the way she put her hands all over his chest and abdomen. She leaned in to kiss him. He caught her wrists and frowned down at her. Her scent entered his nose.

Sex. She smelled like perfume, sex, and semen.

"What the hell are you doing, Regina? You didn't *drive* to Tahoe Shores, did you?" he asked, going cold at the thought.

"Why shouldn't I visit you? You act as if we're not old friends. Haven't we known each other for twenty-two years?" She gave Elizabeth a sly, sideways look. "Did you know Jacob and I have known each other that long? He was the skinniest little thing you ever saw back then, but sweet. *So* sweet," she said, breaking her hands free of Jacob's hold and rubbing his lower abdomen suggestively, her fingers stretching downward. "It's hard to believe that this *big*, gorgeous man ever could have been so tiny, but he was. Little Jake Tharp. Of course he'd started to come into his own by the next time I ran into him," she crooned, staring fixedly at Jacob's face and sliding her hand down onto his crotch.

Jacob snapped up both of her wrists again and pulled her into his office. She staggered after him, laughing outrageously.

She's a loose cannon.

He urged her over to a chair. "Sit, Regina," he ordered.

"But Jacob, I came all this way—"

"I'll be right back," he insisted, pressing on her shoulders to keep her in place in the chair when she tried to stand again. She turned her chin, planting a kiss on his inner wrist.

"Regina," he warned. She smiled up at him innocently. "I know. I'm a bad girl," she whispered. "I mentioned Jake Tharp in front of Elizabeth. I know you hate it when I say that name." She motioned locking her lips and throwing away the key.

"I'll be right back," he said again sternly. When she appeared to be willing to stay put for the moment, he walked over to Elizabeth where she hovered in the doorway.

"Security let her through, but I can't figure out how or why," Elizabeth said in a tensed, hushed voice. "She's on your list for allowed guests, but they have instructions to always call me first in her case."

"Does that new hire, McDougal, have guard duty?" he asked distractedly.

Elizabeth blinked. "Yes, I think he does."

"Regina had him for lunch, and she was his dinner. *That's* how she got through."

Elizabeth looked startled at his blunt assessment of events, but his assistant didn't know Regina like Jacob did. McDougal may have been a decorated army captain and possessed six years of top-notch corporate security experience, but he was relatively young and virile, and would be no match for Regina . . . especially a manic, hypersexual Regina. She'd known how to wind men around her finger since she was a girl.

She'd been *forced* to learn how to get what she could from men.

"Jim was just here," Elizabeth whispered. "He'd gone out to park her car when she pulled up to the house earlier. She just bulldozed past him, but Jim got a look in her car. He came up to tell me that there's several bottles of prescription medication empty in the passenger seat . . . along with a dress and some underclothing."

"Go down and get the bottles, please. Bring them up. I'm going to call 9-1-1, and then Dr. Fielding. I think she's manic . . . and high."

Elizabeth nodded and hurried out of her office. Jacob went over to his desk, moving aside some papers and locating his phone. The phone thumped on his desk when Regina grabbed his arm roughly and jerked it.

"Jesus," he muttered incredulously. She was completely naked, save her heels.

"Surprise," Regina said, her red lips curving. She stepped into him, pressing her breasts against his ribs, her hands making a manic tour of his body.

Apparently neither Jacob nor Elizabeth had altered her security clearance since she'd stormed out of the Lattice compound three days ago. Harper entered Jacob's mansion without incident and jogged up the grand staircase.

What Burt had revealed in her office just minutes ago kept pulsing in her brain. The inflammatory information certainly confirmed the many fears she'd long held about men of Jacob Latimer's caliber.

But now she knew that Jacob was in a class all his own. What's more, Jake Tharp would never be so callous or cold-blooded. And she very much wanted to believe that Jake Tharp hadn't completely been killed off by Jacob.

When she approached Elizabeth's office door, she was surprised to see that it was open. She stepped over the threshold. Elizabeth didn't appear to be anywhere around. Jacob's door was ajar, though.

"Hello?" she called. She looked around the door and froze.

Jacob stood next to his desk in profile to her. Regina Morrow was pressed tightly against him. She was completely naked. Harper stared, her stunned brain absorbing a myriad of details in one stomach-dropping moment: Jacob's hand on Regina's hip, her naked, large breasts smashed against his lower chest, her upturned, pouting lips . . . the fact that her buttock looked reddened, as though it'd been spanked.

Suddenly, Jacob was staring directly at her, his face rigid.

"Harper."

She stood there, speechless, the graphic image of the pair of them pummeling at her unprepared consciousness. It was as if her worst fear had sprung out of her brain and taken shape. Regina turned, her gaze landing on Harper. Her full lips opened. She started to laugh hysterically, pushing on Jacob's chest and stumbling in her high heels. Jacob caught her by grasping at her elbows. Her bare breasts swayed. They looked liked they'd been manhandled. They were reddened. Harper realized numbly she could see the outline of fingerprints on the flesh.

She wasn't aware of turning around, but suddenly she was face-to-face with Elizabeth.

"Harper, I didn't realize you'd—"

"Excuse me, Elizabeth," she said woodenly, gliding swiftly past Jacob's wide-eyed assistant and out the door.

She was so badly shaken that she just left her car where it was at Jacob's and headed toward the terrace. She plunged out the glass doors, jogging down the multiple levels. When she hit the beach, she kicked off her shoes and tossed them in her purse. She didn't look to the left, where she and Jacob had played with the dogs the other morning before he'd taken her up to his bedroom and made love to her with a fierce wildness. She didn't look to the right a moment later, to the spot where he'd first walked up to her on the beach, putting her under his spell from the very first.

Harper just stared straight ahead toward her townhome, using all her energy to block the image of Regina and Jacob from her head.

. . .

She plunged into her townhome, gasping for breath. As disoriented as she was, however, something had altered in her on that sunny flight down the beach. She'd gained a little perspective.

It'd been horribly damning, of course, the nude Regina, the signs of recent, forceful sex on full display on her lush body. It'd looked bad. *Very* bad.

But as she hastened to her kitchen, Harper admitted to herself that her nearly panicked state had as much to do with what had been going on inside her for the past several days as it did the volatile image of Jacob with a naked, beautiful woman in his arms. It related to her grief over losing that special boy, and her parents' intentional lies, and the fact that she'd fallen in love with a man who intimidated and overwhelmed her.

Jacob Latimer had the power to crush her heart to dust. Knowing that he'd once been Jake Tharp only increased his ability to hurt her, and that very thought had been increasingly terrifying her.

He's turning my whole world upside down. What's happening to me?

She took a glass down from her cabinet, panting. After she'd drained a glass of cold water, she stood there, dazed and breathing heavily. Powerful emotion rose in her, bursting through the surface.

She grasped the edge of the counter, shuddering with feeling.

"Get ahold of yourself, Harper. You're your own worst enemy, I swear."

She shook again, but this time, she inhaled with effort and brought her ragged emotional state under control.

It'd been her father's familiar voice in her head. It's been something he'd say to her with patient exasperation sometimes when she was going through that bad period after returning home with them from West Virginia . . . after she'd reluctantly left Jake behind that last time, after Emmitt's sentencing . . .

After she'd been told Jake was dead.

She clamped her eyes closed tightly. She was so confused. She'd never missed her father more. Her dad had guided her steadfastly through the most difficult chapter of her life. She missed *both* of her parents so much. Their absence burned inside her. She struggled to recall what her father used to tell her when she was a child on the occasions when she'd verge on hysteria.

"You know you catastrophize when that anxiety factory in your head starts chugging away. Go back, Harper. Remember what you saw, but see everything this time—not just the things that sets those anxiety red flags to waving around your head, vying for your attention."

Harper took another swallow of cool water, willing her racing brain to slow. Deliberately, she called up the inflammatory image of Regina in Jacob's arms.

True, there were signs of rough sex on the brunette's body . . . but when had Jacob ever left such vivid marks or fingerprints on her—Harper's—body?

Never.

Regina had stumbled, she recalled, and Jacob had reached out to steady her. Had that been why his hands were on her hips when Harper had walked into the room? In order to stabilize her or even push her away? She recalled how Regina had been wobbly on the night of the opera, too.

And Regina's *laugh*: It'd filled Harper with a sense of horror when she'd heard the high-pitched giggle reverberate around Jacob's office. Now, as she stood in her kitchen on bare, sandy feet and her mind began to calm, that laugh suddenly struck Harper as hysterical.

Intoxicated.

Desperate?

Jacob's face suddenly leapt into her mind's eye at the moment when he'd turned and seen her standing in the doorway of his office. He'd looked tense and wild, and not in the out-of-control, delicious way she'd seen in his expression when he was in the grip of lust as they made love. Instead, he'd looked worried.

She pressed her hand to her chest when she felt the uncomfortable jump of her heart.

"Shit," she said out loud.

She tossed her purse on the counter and began to dig for her phone. No sooner had she closed her hand around it than she heard the wail of sirens in the near distance. She froze, staring in the direction of the sirens . . . and of Jacob's house. An unpleasant wave of dread swept down her spine. A strange prescience overcame her.

"Oh *no*," she whispered.

She hastily found the number for the newsroom on her phone.

"Cassie?" she asked, recognizing the voice of one of the newsroom's interns. "It's Harper McFadden. Can you do me a favor and go and turn on the newsroom's police scanner right away?"

Harper jogged into the North Lake Hospital ER, searching the waiting area for Jacob's familiar tall form. She didn't see Jacob, but she saw Elizabeth sitting tensely in the back row of a seating area all by herself.

"Elizabeth?" she asked breathlessly as she approached.

"Harper? How did you know?" Elizabeth asked, standing awkwardly.

"The newsroom police scanner. They didn't give any names, but I guessed . . . it's Regina?" she asked, dread weighing her words.

Elizabeth nodded. Jacob's assistant looked so frayed, Harper grasped her upper arm for reassurance.

"Let's sit, okay?" she prompted.

Elizabeth let her guide her down to the chair. Harper sat down next to her.

"She passed out," Elizabeth said numbly. She blinked and focused on Harper's face. "It was just after I saw you . . . after you left." Harper nodded, recalling seeing Elizabeth in her office before she'd run out of Jacob's house. "We found more pill bottles in her purse. Jacob thought she might have taken them just before she came up to his office. He had me call 9-1-1, but while I was on the phone, Regina stopped—" Elizabeth gasped, her eyes going wide at the memory. "Breathing. Jacob did CPR, and she started to breathe again, but—"

"Is Jacob with her now?" Harper asked, pulling some tissues out of her purse and putting them in the other woman's hand, so that she felt them. Tears spilled onto her cheeks. Elizabeth nodded and removed her glasses. She blotted her eyes with the tissues.

"He was so upset. He cares about Regina so much. All he's done for her—gotten her jobs, paid for her treatments, given her a home to live in . . ." Elizabeth faded off, blowing her nose.

"He obviously cares for her a great deal," Harper said, sitting back in her seat. She felt numb. "And Regina still loves him. I heard her say so, while we were in San Francisco."

"Still?" Elizabeth asked, wringing her hands and crumpling the tissue she held.

"Still . . . even though they're not a couple anymore. Are they?" Harper asked uncomfortably when she saw Elizabeth's bewildered expression.

"Jacob and Regina? A couple?" Elizabeth laughed mirthlessly and shook her head. "You misunderstood, if that's what you thought. They've never been a couple. Jacob *saved* Regina. He saved me, too. He'd never sleep with any of us—not the ones he saves."

"Saves?"

"Regina was a high-priced call girl when he found her ten or fifteen years ago," Elizabeth sniffed. "It was before he hired me, so I'm not exactly sure about all the details. I've helped him out with her over the years; Regina was constantly in crisis. Neither one of them would talk much about how they knew each other. I only know they have a long history. Jacob never gave up on trying to get a better life for her, even though Regina—bless her—gave him plenty of reasons to wash his hands of her. He's probably spent hundreds of thousands of dollars on her and countless hours. Who knows why he does it?" Elizabeth shrugged helplessly. "Who knows why he came to *my* rescue? He's driven by something. Not demons, though . . ." She faded off, a faraway look on her face. "His angels, I think. That's what drives him."

Harper's heart squeezed tight when Elizabeth sobbed quietly. She dug for more tissues and handed them to Jacob's assistant.

"He . . . he came to your rescue?" she asked when Elizabeth had composed herself somewhat.

Elizabeth nodded. "Lattice sponsored a job fair seven years ago, and Jacob insisted that people in San Francisco shelters and halfway houses be invited and given priority. I was living in a battered women's shelter at the time. I was a wreck . . . not even a whole person . . . more like fragments of one. The only thing that glued me together was shame. He must have seen something in me, though. I had secretarial experience, but nothing in comparison to what I do now. He remade me . . . somehow put me back together again, and even added some major parts. He's good at that. I'm not the only one he's saved. But Regina . . . I think she was just so far gone, even when he'd found her." Harper put her arm around Elizabeth's shoulders when she shook again.

After a moment, Elizabeth sniffed and glanced over at her. "I'm sorry," she whispered. "It was just so scary, seeing her like that. It brought back so much. It made me think of what it was like, to be so vulnerable."

"I can imagine," Harper empathized, squeezing the other woman's shoulders more tightly. So many thoughts spun in her head.

If Jacob and Regina had never been involved sexually or romantically, why had he led her to believe that they had? Why would he feel the need to hide amazing acts of kindness and charity?

"He'd never sleep with any of us."

She thought of Jacob's sexual preferences, how exciting and challenging she'd found them. It made sense, though, that he didn't want to expose vulnerable women to his bent for bondage, for fear of traumatizing them.

"Harper?"

She started in surprise at the sound of his familiar, deep voice. She turned and saw Jacob standing in the aisle. His face looked weighted with grief. Her heart squeezed unpleasantly in her chest.

"Jacob?" Harper mouthed, dread settling on her.

"How's Regina?" Elizabeth asked hopefully, but Harper already knew the answer. She'd read it in Jacob's eyes as he'd fixed her with his stare.

"She's gone," he said.

Harper hugged Elizabeth tighter to her side when she heard the other woman's miserable moan. She continued to hold Jacob's stare, though. In that moment, when death hovered around them, she clung onto their invisible bond like she would a life raft in choppy water. Still hugging Elizabeth to her, she reached for Jacob's hand. He grabbed it, and she inhaled shakily in relief. Somehow, she sensed he was accepting her support and taking strength from their bond. For that, she was profoundly grateful.

After Jacob had seen to some necessary arrangements in regard to Regina's funeral, Jim came to get them at North Lake Hospital. Upon Jacob's request, the driver dropped all three of them off at Elizabeth's. His assistant had taken the news of Regina's overdose and death hard.

Elizabeth lived in a cozy little ranch home on a cul-de-sac in Tahoe Shores. Harper cleared the last remnants of the herbal tea she'd made earlier to help calm Elizabeth. It soothed Harper, to do something domestic and ordinary in the midst of a crisis. It helped, to have something mundane to focus on while grief and sadness seemed to cloak Elizabeth's neat home.

Jacob walked out of the hallway into the living room. She looked up and their stares held. Her heart began to throb in her ears. He looked strained and tired. Yet he was freshly amazing to her. She questioned numbly when that feeling of miraculous wonder at his existence would fade.

Or if it ever would.

"Is she resting?" Harper asked him softly.

He nodded. "She'll be okay, I think, after some rest. I didn't realize she felt so close to Regina."

"I think she felt like they were two of a kind," Harper said slowly, setting the mug and sugar bowl on the tray. "She told me in the waiting room that she and Regina had something in common." She noticed his slight puzzled expression and met his stare squarely. "Elizabeth told me you'd saved both her and Regina."

The ensuing silence seemed to press on her ears. Her heart. Jacob looked so solemn to her as he regarded her unblinkingly.

"Is that what you were doing with me?" She asked a question that had been hovering in the back of her mind ever since she'd spoken to Elizabeth in the waiting room. "*Saving* me?"

"No," he said emphatically, taking a step toward her, but then abruptly halting himself. "It's not like that, Harper. Jesus," he muttered, raking his fingers through his short hair in a frustrated gesture. She straightened and walked toward him, feeling guilty for making him more upset when he was clearly already distraught over Regina's death.

"I'm sorry," she said honestly. "I'm sorry for asking you that. And I'm *so* sorry about Regina."

His gaze flickered over her face and caught. Her chest hurt at what she saw in his eyes.

"What you saw in my office with Regina . . . it wasn't what it looked like. She'd just shown up there. She was high and out of control. I thought she was out of it, but I've seen her worse. I think she might have taken more pills while I was talking to Elizabeth. I tried to call 9-1-1, but Regina stopped me before I could even dial one number. Then you walked in—"

Pain shot through her when he shut his eyes reflexively, trying to block the potent memory.

"Jacob, it wasn't your fault. She took you by surprise. It all happened within a matter of minutes. Seconds, even. You did everything you could."

Slowly, he opened his eyes and pinned her with his stare.

"Why didn't you tell me she lived on your property in Napa? Why did you make me believe you two had been lovers? Jacob?" she asked when he just continued to look at her. "*Is* Regina the woman you talked about that reminded you of me?"

"You must know that you're not like anyone else, Harper," he said gruffly after a pause in which the ache in her chest swelled. "When I told you in the beginning that you reminded me of someone else, I was talking about *you* when you were young. Not Regina. I was . . . torn. I felt guilty for wanting you the way that I did, but I couldn't stop myself."

She swallowed thickly, partial understanding dawning. "At least it helps me to understand why you seemed so ambivalent about me at times," she admitted with a mirthless laugh.

"You're different than any other woman I've met. And you know why. You're the one who said it out loud first."

A clock on Elizabeth's mantel seemed to tick abnormally loud in her ears. She knew what he meant. He referred to what she'd said when they huddled together under that blanket in the police station, when she first spoke out loud of their bond.

"I'm yours," she said softly.

"And you're mine."

They stood with several feet separating them, but she'd never felt their bond so deeply.

"While we were in San Francisco," Jacob said, taking one step toward her. "I told you that you and Regina were alike, do you remember?"

She nodded. "You meant because we'd both been hurt by men. Regina by Clint Jefferies and countless others. Me by Emmitt Tharp."

"*Both* by Emmitt Tharp."

"What?"

She saw his throat convulse and he glanced away. "I don't know yet how much you actually remember about details from when we were young . . . those days and nights we spent together, but—"

"Everything. I remember *everything*, Jake," she interrupted, stepping toward him. "What do you mean, Regina and I were both . . ."

Jacob looked over at her when she faded off. "Oh my God," she whispered disbelievingly. "You told me when we were kids that Emmitt had done it before. That he'd taken another girl, and when you'd found her and talked to her, he'd threatened to cut out your tongue before . . ."

"He killed me," Jacob finished.

"That other girl was *Regina*?" she whispered.

He nodded once, his face a mask, his eyes the only windows onto his turmoil. "Back when I first found her tied up in the barn, she'd gone by the name Regina Stellowitz. Even though it was seven years later when I next saw her on Jefferies's property, I recognized her right away."

"*Jake,*" she muttered feelingly.

She rushed into his arms. She felt his lips move in her hair, and then press tight against her skull.

"I never knew what had happened to Regina until I was eighteen," he said hoarsely. "Then I saw her one night, coming out of Clint's bedroom. She'd been beaten. There'd been hints before that Clint was rough with women during sex, but I hadn't really gotten the depth of how twisted he was until that night. I already knew he was regularly unfaithful to his wife and had a penchant for call girls. Young ones," he added bitterly. "*I* was young, still, as well. He tried to keep me at a distance when it came to his more severe proclivities. I didn't really get the extent of his sickness until Regina walked out of his bedroom that night, and I recognized her as being the girl Emmitt had kidnapped years before.

"Emmitt'd sold her into a sex slave ring. They'd hooked her on drugs. Raped her repeatedly. Starved her. Beat her. Eventually, she began to prostitute willingly. Who wouldn't, given the alternative? When I saw her that night, she was twenty years old, but she might as well have been fifty, for all she'd seen and done since Emmitt had first gotten ahold of her when she was thirteen years old."

Harper shook her head against his chest and squeezed him tighter.

"That's what Emmitt would have done to me, if you hadn't saved me. How horrible for Regina," she said shakily. She sent up a silent prayer for the other woman. Regina's life could so easily have been hers, if it weren't for the man she held in her arms.

"It was at a big party at Jefferies's lake house that it happened, wasn't it?" she asked against his chest. "You called 9-1-1 and an ambulance came for Regina?"

He moved back slightly. She looked up to see him peering at her face.

"How did you know that?"

She sniffed. "I've told you I had a reporter, Burt, who was angling for a story on you in addition to Ruth. He has a friend who is a detective at the Charleston PD who looked up any incidents associated with Jefferies or his property during the time period before you showed up at MIT with a different name—"

"Before I bought and sold the Markham stock," Jacob interrupted grimly.

She nodded. "Anyway, his friend sent him an incident report regarding the 9-1-1 call regarding a Gina Morrow. It was called in by a Jacob Sinclair."

"And you realized that Gina Morrow was Regina and that Jacob Sinclair was me. Is that when you started to suspect I was Jake Tharp, as well?"

She tried to read his expression, and couldn't. Was he mad at her for her revelation that a reporter under her watch had been investigating a past he guarded so closely?

"I actually didn't start to suspect that in any solid sense until I realized the police report was from Charleston, West Virginia. Before that, it was just the occasional sense of déjà vu, intense dreams . . . unbelievable suspicions." She swallowed thickly. "You told me you were from South Carolina. You kept West Virginia secret from me, because you were covering any associations between you and Jake Tharp."

His brow quirked. "And you're still mad at me for that, aren't you?"

She opened her mouth to deny it, but found she couldn't.

"I'll never agree to you making that little boy disappear, Jacob," she said softly. "I've fallen in love with you. But I've always loved Jake Tharp. I'll always be loyal to that brave, incredible kid."

He just stared down at her, his eyes alight with emotion.

"You believe you love me?" he asked her thickly.

"I don't believe it. I do."

"Despite what everyone says about me?"

"Yes. And even if some of the lies hold a grain of truth."

"Is that reporter at the *Gazette* going to continue to dig for a story?"

"No. Sangar has quashed it. He's forbidden both Burt and Ruth to pursue a story. It so happens that he agreed with me. There's nothing solid to print. You've buried your secrets well, Jacob. I know your soul," she whispered. "I understand you, I think. Finally. And your secrets are safe with me."

He flinched slightly at that. "Are you sure? I'm no saint. What if I told you that a lot of the rumors are true about how I made my first fortune?" he asked bitterly. "I *am* guilty of colluding for gain when I was eighteen years old. I'd have done almost anything to make myself powerful."

"It's not too surprising, giving how helpless Emmitt and even Jefferies must have made you feel. You blackmailed Jefferies, didn't you? You threatened to expose his violent, illegal sex practices and love of young prostitutes to the press, his wife, or both. He offered you inside information on that breakthrough diabetes drug, and you took the information in exchange for your silence. You did it in one desperate last-ditch effort to climb above all the chaos, evil, dysfunction, and helplessness that you couldn't seem to escape, even when you'd *thought* you had by gaining Jefferies's patronage and friendship. And you succeeded because of your own brilliance and savvy. Afterward, you did everything in your power to wipe the taint of your one sin clean. You washed your hands of Jefferies. Then you sought out Regina Morrow—and any other victims of greed and sadism that you could reach—and you tried to save as many of them as you could."

She noticed his incredulous glance at the evenness and calmness of her tone.

"Did you really think I'd be shocked, Jake?" she asked, shaking her head. She reached up and touched his face, tracing the miracle in every chiseled line. He reached up and covered her hand with his. Her breath hitched. "I told you I know you, in and out. I'm starting to get just why it was so important to you to rise above your past. Like I said before, I don't think you have anything to worry about. Unless you or Clint Jefferies comes forward and confesses about why he gave you insider information, I don't see how a case could ever be re-opened by the SEC. And I'm starting to really get just how hard you've worked to make up for the way you rose to power. All the charities, and the job fairs . . . the way you helped women like Elizabeth and Ellie and Regina. Especially Regina. I *get* it now. I realize how guilty you felt as a boy, for not being able to save her from Emmitt, like you saved me."

His expression turned stony at that, but his eyes shone with emotion. She touched his jaw and then his brow, pouring so much love in every caress. He was so big, and so strong, and so powerful . . . and he didn't fully get that.

Still.

"Do you remember what I told you about Mrs. Roundabout?" she whispered.

He didn't reply. She saw his throat convulse, and thought maybe he couldn't.

"I told you that you had nothing to do with her death or the cruelty she knew while she was alive. Emmitt was solely responsible for that. Did you believe me when I said that, when we were kids?"

"Yes," he said, his stare on her unflinching.

She stepped closer and encircled his waist with her arms. "This is the same. Emmitt and Jefferies, and so many like them, were responsible for the tragedy of Regina's life. You did what you could to help her. I know she must have had some happy moments, amidst all her suffering. You were the one to help her have those. You took her away from a life of degradation. Those were huge things. But there was nothing else you could do," she whispered, looking up at him, entreating him to understand. "You were brave and kind and so generous. But Regina was hurt too badly, Jake."

She felt the slight give in his solid body. She hugged him tighter to her, absorbing the grief he felt not only for Regina, but for the loss of the boy he'd once been.

A moment later, he lifted his head and spread his hands at the small of her back. She looked up at him, and he solemnly kissed her mouth.

"I'll ask Jim to come back and stay the night here, just to make sure Elizabeth is okay. Let's you and I go home," he said a moment later.

Harper nodded.

As bone-tired as she was upon entering his suite, Harper knew that Jacob was exponentially so. She encouraged him to take a shower and she'd call Lisa to see if food could be sent up. He insisted he didn't want anything. While he was in the shower, however, Harper did contact Lisa and request that some tea, water, and a light meal be sent up, just in case Jacob changed his mind.

Harper took a quick shower after him, slipping into the soft robe. When she left the bathroom, she paused in the open doorway. Jacob sat on the sofa in the seating area of his suite. He wore a pair of black pajama bottoms. The soft lamplight gilded the tanned skin of his ridged abdomen and muscular arms. She saw a red and white shoebox in his lap. The lid lay on the cushion next to him. As she neared him, she saw that the shoebox was old: a Converse All Stars. He stared fixedly at a piece of folded notebook paper.

"Jacob?" she asked softly.

He looked up at her, his gaze unfocused, like he'd been miles away. Slowly, his stare sharpened on her.

"Come here," he said, scooting aside the lid of the shoebox and patting the cushion.

She came down next to him.

"Better late than never?"

She blinked at his wry question, confused. She looked down at the box and saw several dozen envelopes, each with *Return to Sender* marked on the front in a bold hand.

A tremor went through her. *Oh God*. Was that her father's writing?

She picked up the piece of paper he'd been reading, squinting to read the handwritten note penned in blue ink.

Harper,

It's almost Christmas, and I'm worried. Two of my letters to you have come back to me. Others might have been returned, too, but I've moved twice in the past couple of months, and I might have missed them. I'm starting to think I copied down your address wrong, but you were right next to me in the courthouse that day. (Remember, your dad looked mad because we were sitting so close?) Anyway, since you were right there, I think you would have noticed if I got the address wrong. I want to try and call, but the Stevensons—my new foster family—don't have a lot of money, and I think I'd get in trouble if I tried to call long-distance. I'll try to save up my lunch money and call on Christmas Eve.

I'm living in Charleston now, so I'm including my new address. I'm not sure if you've been getting my letters or not, but just in case you haven't . . . Grandma Rose died last October. I told you it in another letter, so I won't go on about it again here.

The family I'm with has three other foster kids, one older than me and two younger. The littlest one is four. Her name is Abbi, and she likes me for some reason. She doesn't really talk, just cries and grunts a lot. I think she had it really rough before she came here.

*She said "Jake" the other day while we were playing with her ball
in the driveway, though. Judy, my foster mom, was all excited. She
told me Abbi had never said a full word before, but I think she
just said that to make me feel good. Judy is pretty nice, but my
placement here is just temporary so I'm trying not to get too close.
I think Judy and Bob (that's her husband's name) might adopt
Abbi, though, so that's good.*

*My caseworker told me that there might be a couple that lives
nearby that might take me in permanently. Adoption services calls
me a "special" kid—ha—because I'm so old, and no one really
wants older kids, let alone a thirteen-almost-fourteen-year-old.
But Miranda says this couple is "special" as well, because they're
old, too, like grandparents instead of parents.*

*Charleston is okay. The library is tons bigger than the one in
Poplar Gorge. They've got computers I can use, and I've been
spending a lot of time on them after school. Oh yeah, I checked
out* The Lord of the Rings *yesterday. I'm already to the part where
Frodo, Sam, Merry, and Pippin get to Bree. You were right, it's
really good. I still like your version better, though.*

*I hope you and your family have a good Christmas in
Georgetown. Do you get a big Christmas tree? Remember how
big some of the evergreens were in the woods? Well, maybe you
don't want to remember that . . .*

I hope you aren't forgetting me.

*Merry Christmas, anyway. Write soon. I want to hear about
your tree and lacrosse and what you've been reading and stuff.*

Your friend,
Jake

The folded piece of notebook paper fell from Harper's numb fingertips. Grief tore through her, choking off everything for a pain-
filled moment. She'd read loneliness and longing between every
blue-inked word.

And there had been no one to hear him. No one for twenty years.

She realized that his arms were around her, and his lips were on her ear. "I'm sorry," he said hoarsely. "I didn't mean to upset you. I never thought I'd show them to another person. I've been going back and forth since I first saw you here in Tahoe Shores about whether or not to show you."

"Don't be sorry. I want to read them all," she said emphatically in a rush. "They were meant to be read. They were meant to be read by *me*."

Another wave of sadness washed over her at the realization, and then he was silently urging her to stand. He lifted her into his arms and carried her over to the bed, where he put her down gently. He slid onto the mattress with her and took her into his arms.

"Don't cry," he entreated quietly as he held her, as she sensed his misery. "Please don't cry for me, Harper."

She hugged him tight to her, unable to stop the torrent of grief. "I'm crying for Jake," she said.

He didn't try to halt her grieving then. He just held her until the storm had passed, and she slept.

When she awoke the next morning, she immediately thought of the box of letters, and knew that she'd rise from bed in a moment and read every last one of them, finally hearing that lost boy's thoughts, finally acknowledging his dreams.

For the moment, though, she lifted her head and studied the man who had held her fast throughout the night. Something told her he always would hold her so securely, always would keep her safe, even when he himself suffered.

Jake had always been like that.

Again, she visually traced the miracle of his handsome face as he lay sleeping.

He'd been the one to pull out that old Converse box. He hadn't meant to upset her, of course. Her grief had been inevitable. But surely in revealing those letters, he was unburying a part of his past . . . revealing a vulnerable part of himself.

Exposing Jake Tharp to her loving eyes.

He looked strained, even as he slept, and Harper wondered if he'd just recently fallen asleep. She touched his face softly, willing some of his tension to fade. Maybe in time, it would. Something told her that perhaps she hadn't been the only one grieving the loss of Jake Tharp last night.

And that was just as it should be.

forty-two

Two Weeks Later

Harper looked up at the sound of the door opening. She sat cross-legged on the floor near the fireplace of Jacob's suite. Actually, they'd both started to call it *their* suite or *their* bedroom in the past few weeks. Harper had even caught Elizabeth saying *your* suite a few times recently. It was a natural consequence of the fact that she'd spent every hour there at the mansion with Jacob when she wasn't working, ever since Regina's death.

"Are you reading those things again?" Jacob asked her, a small, incredulous smile on his mouth as he walked toward her. He looked especially tall and incredible to her from her position on the floor. He'd come from his office, she knew, even though it was Sunday. She scanned his face, looking for signs of fatigue or grief, but no . . . He looked good. *Very* good . . . all powerful, virile male. He wore a pair of jeans that looked fantastic on his tall, fit body and a dark blue T-shirt that showed off his muscular arms and chest ideally. They'd been out on the yacht yesterday afternoon, and the sun had given his skin a healthy glow. His gaze on her was warm, as always.

Even though he spent a lot of time with her in the evenings, he'd worked every day since Regina's funeral, often returning to his office once Harper fell asleep. Harper tried not to complain. She thought focusing on work was helping him through the difficult period. But increasingly, she was growing worried. Often she was aware of him returning to bed at night, and holding her against him. When that happened, she sometimes sensed his arousal. But they didn't make love. They *hadn't*, ever since Regina had died.

There was a chained quality to him she couldn't comprehend.

Although he was attentive and loving to her when they were together, he seemed strained. Although he touched her frequently, and they'd never been more intimate in their communication, they never came together in the fierce, no-holds-barred manner in which she'd grown used to . . . which she loved. Harper was starting to suspect that Regina's death, and the guilt he'd carried since he was a child, had scarred him more deeply than she'd first suspected.

Even though she was nervous about confronting him about their strained physical distance, she was determined to do it tonight. The longer she waited, the further he might move away from her. And after all they'd been through, distance between them was something she refused to tolerate.

He sat down on the couch near her and she set aside one of the letters. Milo was in her lap. She idly petted the drowsy puppy's ear.

"I like reading the letters," she replied to his question with a smile.

"They don't make you cry anymore," he said quietly, studying her face with that sharp, narrowed gaze that saw so much. "I'm glad."

"It was natural that they made me sad at first. All those years we missed together."

"Are you still mad at your parents?"

She exhaled and looked away, finding the topic a difficult one. "Yes. But I think I'll come to terms with it. Someday. I know they thought they were doing the right thing for me."

"I agree," Jacob said.

She gave him a sharp glance. "They were wrong, though."

He didn't respond. He didn't need to. They both knew her parents were wrong. They hadn't understood Jake's and her connection. They'd considered her connection to that boy to be an adolescent infatuation, a side effect of her trauma . . . something to be erased so that she could get back to her old, safe life. They hadn't realized that their precious daughter had been changed forever in those West Virginia mountains.

"It wasn't the trauma of being kidnapped that made me so dysfunctional and anxiety-ridden for years, Jake," she said quietly. "Believing you were dead was the final straw. My parents were responsible for me thinking that. I was smothered by guilt and sadness. I'd never truly felt like the world was random and meaningless and scary as hell until my parents told me you were dead."

"That's a pretty good description of how I felt," he said after a pause. "When I thought you were forgetting me. And then eventually, when I finally accepted you'd forgotten."

She inhaled for courage.

"Jacob, do you love me?"

He started slightly at the question.

"I only ask because you haven't been . . . you know. Wanting to have sex. Ever since Regina died," she stated bluntly in a rush.

His expression darkened. "You think I don't want to have sex with you?" he asked quietly.

"I assume not, because we haven't. And you've put me off quite a few times."

He made a hissing sound and stood abruptly.

"Jacob?" She gently moved aside a dozing Milo and stood. He abruptly turned to her, his eyes stormy.

"You don't get it, do you?"

She blinked at his terse question. "I guess not," she replied dubiously.

He raked his fingers through his hair in obvious frustration.

"Jacob? Just tell me," she insisted, becoming alarmed at how tense the topic had made him. Had she been wrong to bring it up?

"It hasn't been since Regina died that we haven't had sex," he said. "It's been ever since you understood I was Jake Tharp."

Her mouth hung open. "What difference does that make?"

"It makes all the difference in the world." He exhaled in frustration when she just stared at him in bewilderment. "I want to restrain you, Harper. Tie you up. Have you at my mercy. That hasn't changed. You want to know if I love you?" he asked, stepping toward her. She resisted an urge to step back, he looked so fierce. "I worship the ground you walk on. I love you more than anything on this earth. I'd sacrifice everything for you."

"Then why—"

"Because when you didn't know I was Jake Tharp, when you didn't know that we'd both been abused by the same man, when you didn't know that the man who was tying you up to his bed was the same person who had untied you from that monster's ropes . . . well, it was all a damn different scenario, wasn't it?"

She just stared at him for a moment, shocked, trying desperately to absorb what he was saying . . . what he *meant*. Her heartbeat began to throb in her ears, and it finally hit her.

"You're worried I'll think you're like *Emmitt*?"

His face stiffened. "I'm *not*," he replied succinctly.

Compassion poured through her. "I couldn't agree more," she blazed. She shook her head. "Jacob, you told me in the beginning of our relationship that it was our choice, what we wanted sexually. You never make me feel anything but cherished and prized. And safe. Don't you know that?"

His fierce expression broke slightly. She stepped toward him, placing her hands on his chest.

"From the first day I've known you, I trusted you. I still do," she whispered. "I know you'd never hurt me. I believe you want to do just the opposite. I think you want me safe."

"I do," he said thickly, looking down at her face. His hand rose and encircled her wrist. "I want to keep you safe forever, Harper."

"I want to keep you safe forever, too."

"Do you remember what I told you weeks back, about why I wanted to restrain you?" he asked. "Because I want to know that at least for a short period of time, no one and nothing will take you from me? That was my fantasy as a kid. Not to tie you up and have sex with you. I wanted you, that was a given, but I didn't have a clue when it came to sex back then. But I'm a man now."

She felt his heart beating beneath her hands. "I know that," she whispered. Did she ever.

"But that core of the fantasy remains. Now, in the act of sex, I want—no, I *need* to know that nothing in the world can take you from me. Not the state or some other faceless bureaucracy, not your parents, not Emmitt Tharp or any other evil thing or person . . . not even your doubts. Not mine. None of it can take you from me. I won't let it."

She reached up and cradled his jaw with her hands. She went up on her tiptoes and brushed her mouth against his in a kiss of cherishment. Benediction.

"I understood, Jacob. I do," she whispered. "Nothing will come between us. Show me it's true."

For few breathless seconds, he just looked down at her. Then she felt it: the chains breaking loose, and he was kissing her forcefully, his hands at her back pulling her against him. They groaned in unison, their tongues dueling, desperate for each other's taste, wild to partake of sexual communion. Harper strained toward him. She couldn't seem to get close enough. As if he sensed her struggle—as if he shared in it—he slid his hands to her bottom and lifted her against him. She hung on to his shoulders, her legs encircling his hips. Their kiss continued, hungry, hot, and wild. How could she have thought he didn't want her? He was like a volcano of erupting need.

She recognized they were moving and suddenly, he was spilling her back on the bed and coming down over her, unbuttoning her shirt even as he plucked and bit at her mouth. Somehow, they managed to get their clothes off—something that would seemingly have been impossible since they couldn't keep their mouths and hands off each other.

His tongue plunged between her lips at the same time that he pushed a finger into her sex. She moaned into his mouth, writhing beneath his solid, naked body while he penetrated her forcefully. Then he was pushing her hands above her head and pressing them down into the mattress.

He stared down at her, fearsome and beautiful.

"Tie me up," she whispered.

"I don't need rope at the moment," he replied grimly, rearing up over her. He pressed her hands harder into the mattress. "You're not going anywhere. Are you?"

"No, Jacob."

He pressed the head of his cock against her damp outer sex, finding her slit.

"You're mine, aren't you?"

"Yes. All of me. Forever, if you want me for it."

"Oh, I *want*," he ground out.

He thrust. She cried out at the impact of him. His face tightened in a rictus of pleasure . . . of feeling.

"Harper," he ground out, sounding wild. "I'm gonna have to fuck you so hard . . . hold you down and fuck you . . ."

"Yes, yes. I'm yours to take. Prove to me it's true. Prove to yourself. *Fuck* me," she goaded mindlessly.

Then he was pounding into her, slaking a need that might never be extinguished, only temporarily quenched. Harper knew she'd be there for him, whenever he needed it. Always. He had so much need, and he'd been left hungry so many times.

He rocked her, the bed . . . her whole world. He took her as hard as he'd promised, his sexual hunger rabid at being held in abeyance for a period of time and sharpened by exposed need.

By love.

At one point, he halted his forceful strokes into her and kept his cock plunged deep. He shifted his grip, holding her wrists down with one hand and freeing his other. Rearing over her, he reached between their bodies. He rubbed her clit while she moaned shakily, holding her stare the whole time. He continued to stimulate her while he shifted his hips ever so slightly back and forth, fucking her with the tiniest, most electrical strokes. She gasped and burned beneath his fingertip, the pressure from his swollen, embedded cock making her eyes cross in cresting pleasure. Her eyelids flickered closed as she rose over the edge.

"Open your eyes," he said harshly. "Look at me."

She forced her eyelids open. She watched him as the first shudder of orgasm shook her. A convulsion tightened his big, rigid body. A roar ripped at his throat. She felt his warm semen spill into her while she shook in a seizure of bliss.

He fell down over her, panting. He separated her arms, pressing her wrists down firmly into the mattress with both of his hands. He thrust his cock in and out of her, still ejaculating powerfully.

A final shudder coursed through him. He winced, looking pained.

"I want to fuck you forever," he grated out, and she sensed his frustration that the peak of intimacy had passed, when he still felt so much inside. She shared in that longing. It was a kind of agony, to know she'd never be able to express fully in word or deed how much she felt for this man.

He opened his eyelids and pinned her with his stare. "I'm going to tie you up in a minute and have you again."

"Yes," she replied without hesitation.

Something crossed his face then, something wild and vast and beautiful. He leaned down and pressed his forehead to hers.

"I've waited so long to have you. I'm never going to let you go," he grated out next to her lips.

"I'm counting on that," she said with a smile.

He lifted his head slightly, and she saw the shiny, fiery quality of his eyes.

"I love you. Jake. Jacob. All of you," she whispered.

His nostrils flared slightly.

"If *you* do, I suppose I should try harder to love all of me, too."

"You better."

He gave a small smile. She smiled back, but he quickly became serious again.

"Marry me," he said.

Her grin evaporated. "Are you sure?"

"Of course I am," he said impatiently, his brows slanted. She laughed.

"You're laughing, at a moment like this?" he asked disbelievingly.

"I'm sorry. I've never been proposed to before. It took me off guard," she tried to explain as euphoria dawned inside her, a golden, pure, sweet feeling.

"I've never proposed to anyone before, either."

"Really?" she asked. He shook his head. "I'm speechless."

"Not too speechless to give me an answer, I hope. Do you want me to tell you the right answer?" he asked drolly when she just stared up at him in awe. A smile tickled her lips at hearing the same question he'd asked her twenty years ago when she'd hesitated about stalactites and stalagmites.

"No."

"What?" he asked sharply, frowning.

"That's not my answer. I *meant* that I can answer for myself. And the answer is *yes*."

His slow smile caused something to curl tight deep in her belly. God, she loved him so hard it hurt. He was such a living miracle to her.

He leaned down, kissing her softly on the mouth.

"That was definitely the right answer," he told her, before his kiss deepened, and his heat warmed her whole world.

Turn the page for a special preview of

behind the curtain

Coming soon!

is longtime friend Jimmy Rothschild wore an amused expression as he watched the waitress walk away.

"That look might rock it in Aleppo or Cairo my friend, but you're scaring the locals in the good old US of A," Jimmy joked quietly, nodding at the back of the retreating waitress, and then Asher's face. Asher knew Jimmy referred to his full-out beard and rough appearance. Or possibly he'd been frowning as he ordered from the blonde, thinking more about the meeting with his parents tomorrow morning than being civil and pleasant in front of a pretty woman?

Or maybe everyone really *did* notice how out of place he felt in his the city he'd once called home.

Rudy Fattore, his other friend, snorted. "The waitress wasn't afraid of him," Rudy told Jimmy with a wise air. "She was thinking about where to start in on him. With that beard and tan, Ash reeks of the desert and intrigue. Trust me, women love the smell of danger. He's giving off that 'most-interesting-man-alive' aura. It's concentrated testosterone, I'm telling you." He grazed his fingers across his own clean shaven jaw. "I may not be up for a Pulitzer Prize or the Gazette's new European bureau chief, but I'm still an award-winning photojournalist, aren't I? I think I'll give a beard a spin."

"You'd only be overcompensating for the lack of hair on your head," Jimmy said. He smiled calmly at Rudy's glare.

"You tried to grow a beard in college and it sprouted in patches," Asher reminded Rudy.

"Things are different now," Rudy insisted. "I've got eleven years on that patchy kid."

Asher grinned despite his bad mood. Rudy was always good for a laugh. Well, most of the time, anyway.

He slumped in the uncomfortable, sleek chair, searching the Lincoln Park, upscale French Bistro. It took him a moment to realize he was scanning for a potential threat amongst the loud, carefree crowd of diners. He halted the instinctive reaction with effort. He, along with a lot of other Western reporters, had been banned entry to Syria several few years ago. But working there, out of all his assignments, had especially created a constant hyper-alert state in him. It was weird being back in the States after spending most of the last eight years in various parts of the Middle East.

Not a lot had changed in the old Lincoln Park neighborhood. Even Petite Poulet, the French bistro, looked unchanged. Yet everything looked strangely gray and muted to him, like he was a sleepwalker in a dream world of the past that had remained strangely congealed in time while he—Asher—had transformed into something alien that didn't fit into the scene anymore. Of course he'd been back in the States several times since becoming a foreign correspondent years ago. Maybe it was being in the familiar restaurant with his childhood buddies that made things especially surreal. He hadn't been out with both of them in years. Jimmy still lived and worked here in Chicago, but Rudy had moved to L.A.

In fact, the three of them hadn't been together in eight years. Not since those bittersweet days in Crescent Bay that had been, in many ways, the last, elusive hours of his youth.

"Are you *actually* going to meet Madeline in the morning wearing that beard?"

Asher forced his mind out his nostalgic musings at his friend's question.

Jimmy was right to question his grooming choice, of course. Jimmy Rothschild had known Asher's mother, Madeline Gaites-Granville, almost as long as Asher had. Their mothers had been friends forever, taking turns bragging or complaining about their sons, showing off their latest designer shoes or handbags at the latest high profile charity event, digging up gossip and hobnobbing at the Union or Cliff Dweller's Clubs, or looking down their noses at social climbers at exclusive Winnetka dinner parties. His mom would probably have a stroke, seeing her only son's swarthy skin and thick beard.

Maybe he'd shave before showing up for the dreaded brunch in Winnetka tomorrow. His full beard and one of his mom's silver-and-crystal-gilded brunches definitely wouldn't mix. Asher resented that it mattered, but what else was new?

"If what you told me is true," Asher said to Jimmy as he lifted his glass of Chivas, "Mom's going to have more to worry about than my beard."

"What's that mean?" Rudy demanded. When Asher remained brooding and silent, Rudy turned to Jimmy. "What's going on?"

Jimmy exhaled slowly. "I told Asher earlier that according to my mother, Asher's parents are under the impression that the prodigal son has returned home to Chicago to do his filial duty and *finally* take over the helm of the Gaites-Granville media empire," Jimmy replied with attempted levity. Still, his dark eyes looked worried as he examined Asher. Asher frowned, trying unsuccessfully to tamp down his ever-present mixture of annoyance and guilt when it came to the topic of his parents.

"I didn't have a clue that's why they thought I was coming to Chicago. I have some rare time off between jobs, and I owe them a visit after being away for over two years. That's all. It was purely coincidental, me being here close to my birthday," Asher said.

"It's not surprising that Clark and Madeline jumped to that conclusion, though. You know it's the moment they've waited for now for thirty years," Jimmy pointed out fairly.

Asher slouched his large body further down in the uncomfortable chair. *Of course* his mom and dad thought that was why he'd arrived in Chicago this autumn: to lay claim to the principal of his trust fund. How could he have been so stupid as to blunder blindly into a hornet's nest?

If he accepted their money, he'd have to follow their plan for his life, wouldn't he? Maybe that was never explicitly said, but it'd certainly been the depressing implication Asher had gotten since he was nine years old.

His parents couldn't fathom that Asher rarely thought about his inheritance for the past ten years of his life. He willfully repressed the idea of that money, along with all the invisible strings attached to it. Strings? Try titanium steel chains. Those hundreds of millions of dollars had come to symbolize his parents' hold on him. No, it better represented Asher's refusal . . . *no*, his *inability*, to give them what they wanted. What they *needed*: a suitable, polished, *biddable* Gaites-Granville heir.

That inheritance, along with all the other privileges his parents offered, were the crown Asher cringed from accepting. But according to his parents, that symbolic crown was his privilege. His birthright.

His duty.

Bullshit.

He grimaced at the snarling voice in his head. Asher had ritualistically done whatever he wanted with his life, despite his parents' rampant disapproval. Publicly, his mother and father had regularly made passive-aggressive comments and broadcast their disapproval of him with every glance and gesture. In private, they'd threatened dire circumstances in regard to his choices. When he'd remained steadfast in his plans, they'd stiffened their backbones and pursed their lips against their anger with such silent forcefulness that sometimes, Asher feared they'd shatter into a million pieces solely from concentrated disappointment. Despite all of their disapproval, he knew that his parents also smugly bragged about Asher's career to their business acquaintances and friends as though he was doing *exactly* what they'd planned for him all along. And all the while, Grant and Madeline just *waited* for the day when Asher would return to toe the line.

They believed that day had finally come.

"*Right*, the big day is finally around the corner," Rudy drawled presently, snapping his fingers in remembrance. "I've been waiting for you to turn thirty since we were at Stanford. I mean, you haven't exactly been a pauper up until now, seeing as how your grandfather left you a nice little nest egg, and that's more money than most of us will ever see in a lifetime. But that's all petty cash compared to the big enchilada. It's finally here: your thirtieth birthday and *total* control over your trust fund. *Freedom*, man. What are you going to buy first? Please say a race car. You'll have to get me one, too, to have someone to practice against. Wait, no . . . a yacht. Hey, the three of us should plan a trip to climb Mt. Everest! Or what about a beach house like that one your parents have in Crescent Bay? The chicks love that. Damn you're going to get *laid* morning, noon and night—"

"He's not accepting it," Jimmy interrupted Rudy's fantasizing bluntly.

Rudy blinked. "Not accepting *what*?" He studied first Jimmy's, then Asher's stony faces. His blank expression turned incredulous. "You're not accepting control of your trust fund? Are you *crazy*?"

"How can he accept Madeline and Clark's money when he's planning on leaving the country again? He's going to London to become the New York Gazette's European bureau chief. You know that," Jimmy reminded Rudy.

Rudy set down his highball glass with a loud clunk. He looked floored. Asher was thankful to Jimmy for backing him up. Jimmy knew what it was like better than Rudy, to have that gilded cage hovering over you for most of your life, ready to crash down at any moment. Jimmy had finessed his parents a lot more gracefully than Asher ever had, though. He'd remained in Chicago after getting his law degree. He'd quickly earned a reputation for being a brilliant criminal prosecutor. Rudy and Asher were two of the few people on the planet allowed to call him Jimmy. Most people in his professional and social circles knew him as James Rothschild, Esq. Elite local power-brokers had already tagged him as a promising candidate for the state House of Representatives. But despite all his career success, Jimmy had quietly but steadfastly defied his parents' designs for his life and determinedly carved out his own path. He routinely ignored or denied his parents' little fantasy scenarios amongst their social circle about him being the most desirable stud in Chicago.

"Last I heard, money travels just fine overseas," Rudy insisted heatedly. "There's no stipulation on that trust fund that says Asher has to live in Chicago or Winnetka if he accepts his inheritance."

"There's stipulations, all right," Asher replied grimly.

"But not legal ones," Rudy protested, glancing over at Jimmy for assistance. "Clark can't stop him from taking what's his legally, can he Jimmy? He can't *force* him to become an executive at GGM and become a WASP clone of himself, for Christ's sake. Take the money and run, Ash."

"I don't want the money, Rudy," Asher snarled.

"But they'll probably just give it to that traitor, pretty-boy cousin of yours, *Eric*," Rudy hissed as if he'd just said a venal word. He referred to Eric Gaites-Granville, who hailed from the New York faction of the family. Rudy had disliked Eric ever since they'd met eight years ago, in Crescent Bay. Because of Eric's actions that summer, his dislike had quickly morphed to hate. Asher wasn't in disagreement with Rudy's assessment. Not in the slightest. He'd detested his cousin from the cradle.

"They gave Eric the position you were supposed to have at GGM a couple years ago when you went to Cairo, after the Syrian government kicked all the western reporters out. Your parents thought for sure you'd be returning home to Chicago after that, but you stayed in the Middle East. Why wouldn't they give Eric your trust fund too, if you won't take it now?" Rudy demanded.

Asher shut his eyes and grasped for patience. Jimmy groaned and shifted in his seat.

"Give it a rest, Rudy. It's not up to you. If Ash doesn't want to take his parents' money, it's his choice. Don't you get it? That money may mean freedom to you, but it means the opposite to him."

"But—"

"Can we please change the subject?" Asher bit out. "I asked you guys out tonight for a little R and R before this meeting with my parents tomorrow. You didn't come all the way from L.A. just to lecture me, did you?" he asked Rudy.

Rudy opened his mouth to protest, but then noticed Asher's expression. Air puffed out of his mouth. He shook his head resignedly.

"If only I could have your problems, Ash."

"I'd give them to you in a second if I could."

"Meaning you'd give me your parents?" Rudy asked wryly. "I doubt Clark and Madeline would ever claim *me* as a surrogate son. They've barely put up with me being your wild Italian friend from the East Bronx. They thought I was going to jump 'em the first time we met. The nerve of me, to get a scholarship to Stanford and picked as their precious son's roommate. But no worries, I've charmed my way into their shriveled little blue-blood hearts since then."

Asher laughed gruffly. Yeah, Rudy could be annoying at times, but there was no one truer. He hadn't hesitated to say he'd fly into Chicago immediately when Asher told him he'd be in town, even though they hadn't done anything but converse through email for the last two years.

The waitress returned, serving them their appetizer order of *moules à la bière*. This time, Asher did take notice of her warm smiles and cautious, but engrossed glances at him from beneath heavily mascaraed eyelashes. He tried to work up some returned interest, but failed. Maybe he'd lost the talent for casual flirting. He'd been seeing Claire Moines, a German television correspondent based out of Istanbul, for over three years before their relationship had finally fizzled out due the long distance romance, infrequent visits, and dwindling chemistry. Between a grueling work schedule, and Claire as a place filler girlfriend, he'd grown pitifully backward in the skills of wooing a woman. Rudy took over, smooth-talking the pretty waitress. His charming grin and rapid-fire one-liners were stale as old beer to Jimmy and Asher, but apparently fresh and appealing to the waitress.

"Hey, you know what might get your mind off your doomsday

meeting with Clark and Madeline tomorrow?" Rudy asked. He pulled his gaze off the retreating waitress's swaying ass with apparent effort. "Yesenia."

"What's a Yesenia?" Asher wondered, digging into the mussels they'd just been served.

"Oh, yeah. *Yesenia*," Jimmy said, his usually somber expression growing animated. "The singer. She performs over at the State Room. They converted the old State Theatre into a nightclub, and Yesenia headlines there."

"What's so great about her?" Asher asked.

"She's supposed to be incredibly talented, for one. I read about her in *Inside Chicago* recently. Apparently, she writes her own music: jazz, blues, pop, R&B. She just got a recording contract too, from an indie studio."

"Forget all that. All you need to know is she's supposed to be hotter than Hades," Rudy interrupted. "I read a small article about her in the entertainment section of the Times. She's starting to bust out of the local scene and is getting some national interest. I'm dying to see her perform. You'll get what I'm saying when you see her, Asher. Or more accurately, when you *don't* see her."

Asher paused with is fork paused in midair and gave his friend a half-amused, half-exhausted glance. Rudy grinned slyly.

"See, that's the whole thing that Jimmy failed to mention—"

"I thought her *music* was the most crucial thing," Jimmy interrupted.

"Yesenia performs behind a curtain," Rudy continued as if Jimmy hadn't spoken. "It's a sheer curtain, so you can make out her smoking body and the way she moves and everything. But you can't really see the details of her face. The press has taken to calling her The Veiled Siren."

"Why does she sing behind a curtain?" Asher asked, thinking the whole idea sounded ridiculous.

Rudy waggled his eyebrows. "No one really knows that, do they? That's part of her mystic. Her allure. She makes people wild to tear down the curtain and get a good, *hard* look at her, if you know what I mean." Asher rolled his eyes. Rudy's grin widened. "There are rumors about why she does it. Supposedly, she has some pretty bad scarring. She doesn't want anyone to see her face. *But*—" Rudy nodded down next to his chair where he'd set his camera case. As a talented freelance photographer specializing in celebrity photos, Rudy was rarely without the primary tool of his trade. "The Veiled Siren can't stay under wraps for long, as popular as she's becoming. What do you say we try and get a glimpse behind the curtain tonight?" he said. "She's right on the cusp of becoming famous, it sounds like. I'll probably get a good buck for an unmasked photo of her."

"What's your plan? Have Asher and me jump on the stage and jerk down the curtain while you snap photos?" Jimmy asked sarcastically. "We're thirty, Fattore, not eighteen. You're not putting me at risk of getting arrested. *Again*."

"What are you complaining about? Tiger Woods never prosecuted, did he? Don't *worry* about it. Let's just go to Yesenia's performance and we'll see if any opportunities arise for a photo?" Rudy suggested with fake innocent casualness. He noticed Asher's doubtful look. "I'm not gonna' do anything illegal," he defended. "Come on. Are you guys in?"

Asher shrugged. The woman's performance sounded distracting. It might keep his mind off the dreaded morning meeting. For a few minutes, anyway.

"I'll go for the show, but I'm with Jimmy. You're not roping me in to any of your stupid schemes. I still haven't forgiven you for that extremely *personal* case of poison oak you gave me when you insisted I hide with you in the woods to get that picture of Jennifer Lopez leaving that vacation house in Big Sur. I swear I feel a rash coming on every time I hear her name."

"At least you weren't arrested," Jimmy muttered in a beleaguered fashion under his breath.

"Yeah, and it's not my fault you exposed the little general because you had to pee," Rudy told Asher.

"What was the logical outcome of that scenario? There was nothing else to *do* but drink that Jim Beam you brought while we were sitting there like idiots in the woods. I'm just saying: No. Stupid. Stunts," Asher repeated succinctly.

"You better believe it," Jimmy said sternly.

Asher smirked at Rudy's wounded-puppy-dog expression of the falsely accused.

ABOUT THE AUTHOR

Beth Kery is the *New York Times* and *USA Today* bestselling author of over thirty novels including *Glow, Glimmer, The Affair, Since I Saw You, Because We Belong,* and *When I'm With You.* She lives in Chicago with her family. Visit her online at bethkery.com.